The Rainbow's Daughter

Also by Lynn Rogers:

Fiction:

Born in Berkeley

Where The Flowers Have Gone

A Valley of Ashes

Non-fiction:

Edgar Cayce and the Eternal Feminine

Images of America: Alviso, San Jose

The Rainbow's Daughter

Lynn Rogers

Lynn Rogers

Inkling Press
Menlo Park, California

Published by:
Inkling Press
P.O. Box 2598
Menlo Park, CA 94026
www.inklingpress.com

Illustrations by the author.
Cover design by R B Productions.
Book formatting by Joseph Haddox.
"Afterwards" photographs copyright J.V. Stier (pages 340–357).

Printed and bound in the United States of America.

ISBN: 978-0-9711039-5-5

First Printing, 2007

To Marsha wherever she may be

The Choir at Sunshine Hall
Led by Sam (left) and Stephen (right with guitar). Choir includes
Constance (second from left), Patsy, (third from left), Russell
(above Patsy) Rexford (to his right) and Page, (second from right)
with Acacia and Rebecca's daughter foreground in the audience.

Introduction

Looking back, it's hard to believe I was ever that naïve. Searching for my spiritual path, I became involved with what some might describe as a cult. But it wasn't that way in the beginning. It was more Camelot than cult, a soul family with past life dynamics.

Daisy Anne Buchanon Forrest (Castle)

Chapter One

I was with them seven years and then one day I walked out and never came back. They are all like faint shadows to me now, almost within my grasp. I won't let them go—I can't let them go. On nights like tonight I remember them easily.

It was another January night in 1970 in Northern California and the sprawl of city at the end of the bay was not much different from L.A. twenty or thirty years earlier, awkward but still imbued with a sense of beginning.

I was nineteen when I walked up to the door of that house on North Redwood Street for the first class of a course on how to remember your past lives, my hands pushed down in my pea coat pockets. I'd read about Edgar Cayce and past lives and followed a hunch to come here. Would this class show me more? Flashing lights from the Doggy Diner way across the wide lanes of traffic on Stevens Creek Boulevard spun ribbons of azure blue, gold cream and burgundy gossamer around the circumference of the housetop. The sky wore a new moon as a single accent. A light rain, a little wind, and the whir from the distant lanes of traffic that fled from view at the end of the old tree-lined street, offset the sound of my own nervous heartbeat.

The front door to the little house had been left slightly ajar. I stepped over the threshold into an empty living room, heard muted voices through an open doorway to the right in what looked like a kitchen. Too shy to approach the voices, I stepped timidly across the hardwood floors only as far as the open doorway.

An odd, though pretty picture of a bare breasted woman with an archaic hairdo, was suspended, to the right, perfectly balanced. And a similar painting of a genie hung in the opposite space of wall. I liked to paint, and I noticed right away that the difference between these and other home decorations I'd seen was not only one of content or of showcasing (the paintings weren't even framed) but of a kind of care. They didn't seem to be thrown about just for color or shape or style. I sensed that they meant something to someone in this house. Each had beauty, like a sprig of happiness attached. Someone here could make beauty—I just knew it!

The exotic bare busted blonde smiled cheerfully out at me and the friendly giant of a genie disappeared through the swirl of his lower body into an Aladdin's lamp—a bottle marked by a star. I liked looking into their eyes. Their casual presences lent an exotic, erotic presence to the room. Of the two, though, it was the woman....

Her wide intelligent eyes and proud breasts were both uplifted. She stared at me expectantly. Somehow I just couldn't settle my gaze onto the sensuously painted tips of her breasts when her eyes compelled me to look into them. As I looked, I felt I too was waiting, and watching for something. I turned and a blonde woman in a too-tight colorful dress that shone; casually entered the room chatting with one or two who had followed her from the kitchen.

Brash blonde hair was piled unnaturally high on her head. Her dress—full length and filmy like a nightgown—was gathered beneath plump shoulders and low around her bust to which it clung. She turned to speak to someone who had moved near me and lifted her bright eyes and looked into mine. "Hello, sweetheart," she said, as if she knew me. It didn't seem odd even then that a young woman of maybe twenty-seven or so would call another girl sweetheart.

She walked over to a big green vinyl chair between the front door and the painting and settled into it, still laughing. Did she laugh because of me or about me? I laughed too. She propped a footstool beneath her feet on which she wore hot pink slipper socks, drew a breath, folded her hands tightly in her lap and looked firmly out into the faces of those who had come from somewhere to gather about her.

I took off my jacket and dropped to the floor across from her, nearer the genie and out of her line of vision. The murmur died away. She waited for more people to appear I guessed. She had what I thought up until now was a stiff hairdo; it reminded me of people who were kind of hard, but she was very pretty, though heavy, and had a softness when she spoke, obviously nervous, and in the way she moved her hands.

I was at peace, although I didn't know anyone, and shyly interested in the faces of the people sitting near me, walking from the kitchen to the living room carrying coffee. There was something neat about this house—I strained to phrase my thoughts—something just so, something symbolic, something meaningful.

Then the blonde woman tipped her face and looked into me, lightly, as she began to speak to the group. "Hi. Welcome. My name is Daisy. I want you all to know—tonight is my first class before the public. And I'm a little nervous, aren't you?" She laughed. We all laughed as one. "Let's begin by finding out what has drawn us here to be together at this very moment in time.

"You know, all of our lives we are searching for something more. Sometimes we feel there's something missing. I always thought I was different from other people and that I had a mission, so I waited, I hoped, I listened; but after awhile I set that feeling aside. I kind of lost hope. I spent a lot of years just taking care of my family, not thinking of much of anything else. You know what I mean? A lot of times I thought that love, that being in love, was the answer.

"But guess what? I loved—I mean I loved a little bit, let me tell you, but like most of you I've come to realize that it's not the whole thing. I don't know about you, but I was disappointed. Not in anybody else, but in myself. Do you know the feeling? That feeling of longing, of waiting, of searching, for the answer to so many questions. And I guess, for the first time in my life, in this life"—she giggled cryptically, looking at a slender dark-haired woman and at a younger, short-haired blonde woman to her right—"I can honestly say to you now that I feel there are answers. So let's start. Let's just plunge in right now, putting all our prejudice aside—I was a Roman Catholic, so it gets a little crazy for me, too—but seriously, being here with you at this moment in time is…I feel, I sense that we are drawn here together to fulfill a destiny; that together we will knock and the door shall be opened, together we will ask and it shall be given, together we will seek and we shall find…."

Her voice echoed through me like a muted bell, sounding down a time wave, flooding corridors with light, opening locked doorways.

From the hazy aquamarine eyes now focused out, beyond us in the distance, through the graceful plump arms and hands and stiffly gesturing fingers; from the emerald words that issued from this madam's lips, there emerged a crystalline presence.

When it was done, we were all left staring stupidly at this young woman who was silent—still looking through us. We looked up only when a big, bulky man filled the doorway that led from the kitchen. Dressed in a sort of glorified towel sewn to look like a robe, he winked at each of us with the same warm eyes as the genie in the picture.

"Can I help you with anything? We have coffee, tea—'round here just about anything you could want." Daisy began to reemerge. She smiled absently at the man.

"I want to introduce you to my other half," she said shyly, surfacing from within her pale blue eyes. "This is Arthur Forrest.

"Goodness. Such formality. Art, please." He hung his handsome head, slick hair a relic from the 1950's, and smoothed the chocolate terry folds of his robe with a broad paw like hand.

Later, when I tore myself away to drive north to my dark apartment at the midpoint of the bay, thoughts flushed through my mind, answers that had eluded me in months of therapy groups, in the faces of lovers, seemed promised here. It was a relief to consider: for every question there exists an answer. Did Daisy say it? Did I read it? Maybe God said it, and someone passed it along, at last to me.

And the desolation, the panic, the time of enduring drug flashbacks, the sense of homelessness, the wandering, the backlash from a disturbed childhood; if these were not over, then at least the time of rebuilding was to begin. Had I found, at last, that center, that activity, that place that I had always felt was occurring without me?

I pumped the gas pedal in the fast lane, detached, and rolled open the driver's side window. The new-moonlit air rushed through me, blowing my long fine hair about my face. I drove as if it were a race to catch up to the happy rush of thoughts, the bubbles of insight rising up and breaking on the surface of my mind: The destruction of one thing is the beginning of another; death is rebirth; it's always darkest before the dawn—why, these were true!

I slowed the engine for the turn to Palo Alto, decelerating, tapping the pedal in time to the last sentence lingering in my mind. Now at last it's time to hope; now at last it's time to hope; now at last it's time to hope.

Arthur Edward Forrest

By the next Monday night I was wonderfully excited, and approached the house on North Redwood Street early, pausing halfway up the walkway that led through the moonlit grass. The lamp light emanating from behind the pulled living room drapes emerged with the same degree of brilliance as that of the neighboring houses; but despite visual similarity to the small older suburban homes lining the shadows on this street, the emotional pull to this particular dwelling was such that I halted hard before the door, as though waiting to be transposed and allowed to enter into the realm of magic. The moon splayed tendrils of light from above me down over the porch through the ivy. Bewitched by the light, I was resplendent, wrapped in the beams like an ancient coat. "Tonight we're going to talk about dreams," Daisy intoned when the room was full. "Dreams are the stepping-stones to many other experiences, including past lives, the keynote of this course. I want you to begin to keep a dream notebook. Then next week we'll talk about your dreams together.

"When I decided to look into dream interpretation," Daisy continued, "I found it to be complicated business. I felt that there should be an easier way to begin to interpret your dreams.

"Our subconscious (the deeper part of our mind that we're not aware of) is always trying to reach us and surely it knows that it takes years to become a Jung or a Freud. After plowing my way through several books far over my head, I realized I was more confused than ever. And boy, were my dreams showing it.

"They were using symbols I'd never even heard of. Finally I discarded everything and put all thoughts of interpreting my dreams out of my mind. I let myself rest.

"When I felt I had recuperated enough, I began a series of meditations aimed at discovering how to interpret my dreams myself. It didn't take me long to uncover this easy method.

"When I started reading books on dreams, what had happened? My dreams tried to use those symbols to get through to me. My subconscious used the information I was gathering. How? By using the information I was putting into my conscious mind. See?

"So I decided to try an experiment. I would bring into my mind the symbols I wanted to use in my dreams. In other words I would communicate to my inner self the things which I couldn't understand.

"And so I began a booklet using numbers and simple interpretations of their meaning. We'll get into numerology later—that's Art's specialty, isn't it, sweetheart?" Art nodded from around the doorway where he seemed to abide, at least whenever I glanced up. "Anyway," Daisy added, "later I added some other symbols that had special meaning for me. For instance, a candle to me represented the light of Christ. A dress came to mean the mood of the dream—because I do dress according to my moods—"

Amy, the blonde girl to her left who'd introduced herself earlier tonight as Daisy's sister, giggled loudly at that, as though privy to some special confidence. Suddenly I imagined being Daisy's sister. Did that relate to a past lifetime? I wished I understood more about all of this. Distracted and aware that I might have missed something, I piped, "What did a dress mean, Daisy?" No one else was asking questions now. Amy snickered into her lap demurely. I hung my head. "I—I'm sorry."

"What's your name, chicken?"

"Caroline Ryder, Daisy."

"She doesn't look like a Caroline, does she Amy? Is that your whole name?"

"I have a middle name but I never use it."

"What is that?"

"Page."

"With her hair hanging down, such shiny bangs—she looks like a page boy. Page, I'll call you Page."

"O.K."

I was sick of being Caroline Ryder and wanted to put my former life all behind me. Page I would be from now on. Daisy resumed the dream discussion as if nothing unusual had occurred.

"In regard to your question, Page, it's good to ask," she smiled kindly. "I've asked and asked and asked, otherwise I wouldn't be here now, would I? Just remember that you can ask yourself too. That's what I discovered about dreams—the secret to interpreting them was within me. A dress…a dress became a symbol of the mood of the dream. Do you understand now?"

"I do," I murmured, eager to go on, vindicated somehow by Daisy's special attention.

"O.K. Remember now, I wrote my symbols—letters, numbers or whatever—before I had dreams of them. For example, I read that the letter 'D' referred to concentration and strength of character, and I related to that. Next I reminded myself that I could use these symbols in the dream state. Understand? Then I would go to sleep reminding myself to remember my dreams and that I could use the symbols at hand.

"My first experience in having a dream turned out to be simply a picture of a tree with flowers shaped in the letter 'D' growing from it. The symbol was showing me to have strength of character and concentration in a situation I was going through."

Watching Daisy, I glimpsed that tree, simple and happy leaves raised to the sunlight, growing up from the fresh green grass of Daisy's subconscious. And daisies, there would be daisies laced through the green...

"The tree has always represented to me," she was saying, "for some strange reason, God's answering of prayers or the promise to answer prayers. This answer really did help me to see the situation through.

"Once I learned a symbol it never seemed to change. I did, however, realize that my mind would use the most recent symbols. So when my standard ones began to be replaced by too much of the unknown, I would just sit down and review my booklet. Again the symbols would come back in my dreams.

"After awhile of course, you develop a certain knowing about your dreams and will more easily recognize your new symbols and their meanings." I hoped so, peeking hopefully into her blue eyes to decipher secrets as yet in store.

"Simply by learning to tune into the real me, I've solved physical problems—even money problems, I've received health dreams for the things my body was lacking, as well as some answers in my search for my own past lives—well, that's getting ahead of ourselves isn't it? Speaking of that, two weeks ago I even gave myself a complete astrology reading for the month with only a basic understanding of the signs. It turned out to be quite accurate. Last weekend I even got told through a dream who was coming to dinner on Sunday."

"And he did, huh Daisy?" Amy chorused. "We were really wrecked when Stephen showed up out of nowhere after you'd dreamed about him." Stephen, the only man in the room besides Art, who chuckled from the doorway, turned his comely blond head gently towards our respectful gaze. "I didn't know I was coming either, I, kind of had to, right?"

"Just to make Daisy's dream come true," I joked, gazing evenly at Amy. That drew a laugh.

"Ok, on that note let's quit talking about dreams for now until next week when we all have some dreams in our new notebooks to work with. Ok?" We nodded assent. "Happy dreaming." Daisy rose from her chair, swept the liquid folds of her acetate housedress from behind her and meandered toward the kitchen, stopping to hug Art in the doorway. He grinned down at me over Daisy's shoulder as if in answer to my thoughts. I sighed with relief like a little child brought home after being lost in the dark, secure that everything would be all right.

Inside on a rainy class night, the last one on reincarnation, the room was very full. Most people sat on the floor now except for a woman whose name I've forgotten—Carla, I think—with her teenaged daughter Charon. Charon's eyes were slightly crossed, and one was glazed and blind. When Daisy had first brought up past lives, her mother had remarked, "I've always known that this happened to Charon for a reason." That night they uncovered the lifetime that appeared to account for the partial blindness of the girl today. Carla told Daisy about a vivid wrenching dream that frightened her. "You said we would dream, you told us to, and I have, Daisy," Carla spoke up, after the people who entered late fought for space next to me on the floor. Rainwater from one girl's trench coat dribbled onto the hardwood and beaded up in the space between us. I drew my knees up and leaned over them, looking into Daisy's eyes, bright like twin suns illuminating the dreary February night.

"It was so real I couldn't stand it," Carla said. I've wanted to discover the past life source of Charon's blindness. You all know that. I've really thought all these weeks that someone must have done some terrible thing to her—in the past, you know." I scanned Daisy quickly, hoping that she would see that I, always the quick student, knew that it would have to be something that the girl (or the mother) did herself. I mean that was how it worked, wasn't it? I didn't have to wait long. Carla's eyes brimmed with tears. "But my dream was worse than that, Daisy. The dream was about some time when we all wore robes, like nuns...but darker than any that I've seen. And Charon and I—but somehow she wasn't Charon then; she seemed to be my sister—wore the dark robes too.

"Somehow our robes seemed darker in the dream than all the others'. About our necks we wore huge burnished crosses. I've always avoided the Church in this lifetime because of the fear of the orthodoxy, yet I'm powerfully drawn at times to its pageantry and symbolism too. Just the sight of a nun on TV reminds me of something I can't put into words—and I was not brought up a Catholic, Daisy. Why is this? Anyway, when I saw the crosses in the dream it was the same feeling, and," she faltered, "and it was as though the crosses were emblazoned, somehow; then they were in our hands, and we were using them to put people's eyes out, shouting in another language, 'Repent in the name of the cross!' Then faces rose one by one from the darkness, into the light of fire, the faces of helpless people who seemed to be bound—chained at the hands and feet and neck.

"I pushed my sister—Charon—ahead of me with my fingers prodding into her back, and raised my cross high to light her way as she got near to them and—I just realized that the crosses we held were not the ones about our necks but wooden ones, so they might burn." She shuddered. "I stared straight into the wretched face of each prisoner. 'Repent!' I shouted. Then I murmured to my sister, 'You know what you must do,' and I held my torch higher.

"Then slowly, purposefully, stiffening both of her arms, locking her fingers around the shaft of her flaming wooden cross, Charon would thrust it at the devil. Then came a sweet scent like burnt candle tallow, a sizzle and then a shriek, a howl as an eye was gouged.

"Daisy, we walked away from this horrible scene convinced that we had changed their beliefs in some way. We were happy, no, not happy, but self-righteous I think—that's the way it was—self-righteous that we had converted them or something."

Cassandra Stevens, a social worker and a skeptic, sitting in the far corner of Daisy's living room, muttered, "The Spanish Inquisition." Otherwise there was not another sound uttered. After what seemed to be a long time, Daisy suggested, softly, that we take a break.

We did, and I looked long and hard at the pictures that had drawn my interest the first night. Daisy had told the class she'd painted them impulsively from her soul's memory "These portraits are of Art and me from long, long ago before we were who we are today."

Is life purposeful, I wondered, is there a reason for everything? Is there a reason I came here tonight, and no other night? Do I know these people who are so different from me? I stepped out of the living room and down the hallway toward the bathroom. Above me, thumb tacked to the white plaster walls, were a series of astrological posters; one for each family member. Davy, the youngest of Art and Daisy's three boys, was a Virgo, too, like me. I was reading the description of that sign when Charon emerged from behind the bathroom door and approached. "Hi," we whispered like sisters of long acquaintance—Oh my God, was I in that lifetime too? I stopped, to get out of her way, deciding to use the bathroom some other time.

In the living room, Charon was crying. Daisy bent over her, smiled, consoling. I wondered, could Charon's tears wash her past misdeeds from her eyes? Healing could be a gradual thing, I somehow knew, or happen in an instant. I realized that each soul has a choice: no hereditary, environmental or even astrological influence could take from us the divine prerogative to change, to undo what we had done, start creating at once a better person. If Charon created the karma of blindness in another life, she had the power to change it. We could all start anew, and build a new hope, like Daisy.

"Can I come with you?" I asked.

"Sure."

After class we all piled in cars and drove to the nearby Lyons on Stevens Creek Boulevard. It was a ritual, a custom now for them to do this. Never mind the long drive back to Palo Alto. (Perhaps it was better that I didn't drive away right now, high as I was from the class proceedings. Last week I'd taken my hands off the steering wheel in the fast lane on 101, secure that mind would prevail over matter if I demonstrated perfect faith—only the police officer who stopped me didn't appreciate the experiment.)

Tonight was special. There were twelve of us. Steven stayed with Art and the sleeping children. We took three adjacent tables. I got to sit with Daisy, Rebecca and Amy at a booth that opened out like a maroon upholstered fan. They all ordered coffee, I had buttermilk. They had pie. I did too; my rhubarb was a delight.

Now we were all giggly, high. The night's events were reviewed. I listened, hanging over Amy to hear them discuss Daisy's latest dream about a golden microphone. "Microphone, mike," Daisy ran over the dream aloud (she'd taught us that helps). "I just don't get it. Micro," she tried.

"Michael!" Amy exclaimed.

"You're right, Amy, somebody's going to get a message," Daisy said, looking down at her apple pie plate, pausing, her little finger delicately lifted.

Rebecca, right next to her, looked up, her dark eyes magical and alive at something I hadn't been privy to—oh why had I driven back to Palo Alto on Monday nights and not come here? "I bet it's going to be me," Rebecca hinted, half comically. "I don't know if I can take this again."

"I'm getting rain on that," Amy added, with an elfin smile that suffused outward through her shaved, re-penciled arch-wing eyebrows. Rain? I remembered rain. "Rain," Daisy had explained to us in the second class, was a shiver you feel when you hear the national anthem sometimes, or the cold tingling waves that runs up and down your spine in a movie that really gets to you.

Now she didn't say anything but looked attentive, far away, and serious. "I'm getting rain too, Rebecca," Daisy added. "You'd better be ready when it comes."

"Oh oh. You don't really think it's going to be Michael again?"

Daisy and Amy regarded her significantly.

"I'm getting rain again," Amy whispered between lips pursed like a capital "O".

I felt it too. Sometimes the rain was so intense that you couldn't speak.

"I'm getting rain too, Daisy," I offered.

"Are you, chicken?" she replied, kindly, distracted.

"Who is Michael, Daisy?" When I said "Michael," I felt a shock of rain start as a trickle at the nape of my neck, shimmer down my back in electric rivulets.

"Michael is…" Rebecca began to answer.

"The Archangel—sometimes he comes through Rebecca," Amy whispered to me distractedly. We were both watching Daisy now.

"What is it, Becky?" Daisy looked right at her.

"He's...here.... I can feel him." She held her lips almost shut when she spoke.

"Go ahead, Rebecca, it's all right. You know it's important."

"Here?" she pleaded, embarrassed, and reserved as always, her eyes dancing with pride.

"You might as well or he'll...you know he'll...."

Daisy couldn't finish because Rebecca's mouth opened out and said: "I will be among you as long as there are those that seek. Seek in my name and you will find. Even as I go before you..." Here Rebecca tried to close her mouth and look around but Daisy fixed her in a steadying gaze and Rebecca looked back, barely reassured, and tried to speak: "I didn't know he...."

"Even," returned the powerful, male sounding voice.

"Even," it boomed, as tears began to squeeze down over Rebecca's cheeks. She squinted her eyes to stop them.

"Even as I go before you shall you go before men..." Then Rebecca stopped with a helpless laugh.

All twelve of us had stopped eating pies and hot fudge sundaes and drinking tea and felt the message had been aimed at each one of us and at all of us together. Cassandra, the skeptic, began to laugh, but I could tell it was the kind of laugh used to break a deep silence that is too much for someone. Her eyes too, were brimming.

"And those left among you," Daisy began to murmur, "will go as a remnant...and though you think none will know that you passed; you will be known in me."

Daisy uttered this slowly. Everyone listened. "I heard the rest," she explained, "in here." She touched her temples.

"What does that mean?" she asked aloud. "I understand the first part, I think, but who is the remnant?" Puzzled, she stared into me without looking as though I didn't matter that much and she could be alone with her thoughts. Chills coursed down the back of my neck. Could it be me?

Caroline "Page" Ryder (Mitchel)

Chapter Two

The end of the last class became a beginning. The house on North Redwood Street bustled with activity throughout the early spring, even in the daytime. The members of the original class had swelled. Now there were two classes filling the living room on Tuesday and Thursday evenings and a stream of people in and out to see Daisy for a "reading": her psychic counsel. "It got pretty bad," Art joked later. "Sometimes I wondered if you girls were going to call her up and ask for a reading every time you had to go to the bathroom."

She called us girls her "chickens," including Stephen. "He looks like a girl to me; do you see it, Amy?" Daisy asked her sister once at class—that was no insult because, in a subtle way I think Daisy was biased toward her girls at the beginning. I don't know whether or not she thought of the two or three other men who had begun to hang around as her chickens too, but it was evident that they too were powerfully fascinated by Daisy and the doings on North Redwood Street.

Daisy pointed to the spiritual forces as the source of the magnet that drew us to her; she called to them, in times of trouble and for joy and uplift. She meditated regularly in the afternoons when the house was stilled, hermetically sealed for her by Art, who was out of work from Red Star Laundry now and waiting. When Art had ordered the kids outside on those blithe afternoons, he held court on the porch in his tee shirt. Inside, the late afternoon sun streamed across the hardwood floors Art had swept clean before he left.

On one of these afternoons when I was allowed to visit, Daisy had her last cigarette before meditation; she had on the orange, green and yellow wrapper she'd worn all day after rising late. I sat on the shiny black vinyl ottoman in the now quiet living room, reading a pamphlet based on the Edgar Cayce material, written by Elizabeth C. Barrett, a woman Daisy had vowed I would one day meet. It was a lecture delivered by Barrett for the A.R.E. Los Angeles Lecture Series in 1952. "Your Karma Is Your Opportunity," was the title. On the first page, Barrett quoted from the readings, or discourses Edgar Cayce had given in a sleep state: "When a soul enters a new body in a new environment a door is opened leading to an opportunity for building the soul's destiny. Everything which has previously been built, both good and bad, is contained in that opportunity."

We were interrupted once by voices outside. "Be quiet, Davy." Eight-year-old Davy lurched up in front of the plate glass window. Art grabbed his son back out of view.

"Page, I want you to watch the door for me, and answer the phone if it rings."

"Sure."

Daisy snuffed her cigarette and rose slowly from the orange vinyl kitchen chair. "Page, honey, think, will you, with me. It's time we were directed to the next step." I watched Daisy stand up against the background of the steam-streaked kitchen window; I could hear the washing machine that Art had loaded hum in the background. Suddenly I thought I saw her aura: it was a foggy white blue like a lace shawl caught in the wind and blurred around her. I thought I saw red, just a thread but bright and winding through the shawl—a telltale thread, came the silly thought—red hidden at the back.

Daisy didn't wear red now, ever, and she had given away her black wig. I had heard she'd sent the parcel to Elizabeth Barrett, who lived in Los Angeles, with a cryptic note attached: "I want you to have this, Elizabeth. I can't keep it anymore. When I wear it I become a different person." That was a reliable rumor. (One day recently I'd stood in her bedroom on the polished hardwood floor while she cleared out the closet she shared with Art. That day she'd given me a funny long necked orange bottle covered with glitter. I used to believe dresses and wigs and bottles like hers were sleazy; now I wondered if there might be magic in the bottle—certainly in her because she knew how to imbue things with her past self and give them away.) Of course, there were other rumors, circulated by her detractors—one Vicky in particular, who was the only one of us outside of her family who had known Daisy before.

Vicky told Cassandra that Daisy used to drink too much and that she had to fish her out of motels on Monterey Road before Art got home from his laundry route at 4:30. Vicky was violently jealous of Daisy, I thought, loud and frustrated because she had no "chickens" to follow her. Cassandra, on the other hand, was skeptical about anything and everything she heard, but recounted the rumors in full as if it were untidy to delete any details, and unfair to us not to know what we should be skeptical about.

I suppose it was Cassandra too who revealed that Daisy made a pass at Vicky after a night when Daisy and Art and Vicky and her husband had been out on the town. Vicky said that Daisy had reached around the front seat to slip her hand on her knee. Vicky, apparently appalled and indignant even when drunk, swept Daisy's hand away with characteristic gusto. The story had a slight ring to it at the time, even though Vicky seemed to be given to wild exaggeration, even about herself. (She revealed, for example, that her own mother, a domineering spiritual leader in another state, had "de-possessed" her of a rebellious "entity" that had inhabited her as a teenager, and that she had gained the name Vicky, rather than her birth name of Barbara, in a flash during that night of transformation.)

Now, as I gazed into the spaces above and beyond Daisy's shoulders, I really believed I could see her aura. Red still glinted within the bright opaquery of angel-wing blue that obscured the steamy window. Daisy always said that if you had a plain background it was easier to see the aura.

"Keep this door open just a little, will you, chicken, so I can hear Art if he needs something. Well, let's see what happens if we try to tune in." She walked into the living room slowly, dispelling her aura with her first deep breath. She appeared to be thinking hard about something. Probably about money. "We're coming under the wire with this job bummer," she confided, bleeding into my thoughts, "something has to happen soon."

Art had some of us kids selling Best Line Products door to door, with big positive words about the freedom and potential of that business. Away from Daisy he made wheeler-dealer remarks when we hustled downtown to the place where you picked up the soap. But I didn't sell anything myself, and I didn't think they had much money left.

Daisy lay back into her recliner. I lighted on the couch, screwed up my concentration and felt important, helping Daisy. I took a deep breath, meditating in the new way Daisy had taught me, lying down, instead of the constrained, rigid sitting I'd learned in T. M. in the sixties. In a minute it felt as if the very air of the house hushed and that the fine blue foggy mist from before enveloped the couch and the living room. In the dark sweet interior peace of meditation, crisp thoughts, scarcely audible words, and tiny pictures came into fleeting focus and sparkled like prisms cast by crystal.

I saw the images and heard the words, but I fell into a kind of sleep, and, unusual to me, couldn't remember them. When I sat up a long while later, Daisy commented quietly, "You were helping me out of the body, chicken." If I did, I wondered amid the vinyl couch cushions pushed askew during my "sleep," who must I be to do this and not remember? Who must I really be? Not the victim of parental turmoil and theories of therapy to describe me, not only that, but spirit, rising up through the fog of my life to reach out and help people, to help myself. I can help myself now, I thought suddenly, because I can reach up. The booklet I'd been reading earlier had fallen open on the rug beneath me. I glanced at the rest of the Edgar Cayce reading on the first page: "Changes come, and some people say luck has intervened. But it is not luck. It is the result of what the soul has done about its opportunity."

Daisy and I smiled at each other; bright blue and happy smiles. The sun, pulling back from the day, dropped beneath our view outside and drew about itself shadows of black.

"I'm gonna do you a favor," Daisy pronounced after we'd all gobbled tuna macaroni and wine at the table that night. She sat dressed in bell bottom pants, a lacy shirt and a fake fur vest, reflective, with a cigarette.

"I'm gonna get you out of that place. You're not there anymore anyway. And tonight's the night—we'll move your things." Startled, I quickly decided she might be right. Oh yes, my body had lain in that dank dark apartment by Highway 101 near the university turnoff in Palo Alto every night, but I hated to be there, among my last boyfriend's things all piled up. Lately I'd been spending every bright day swinging hopefully up the freeway north on 17 in the direction of Santa Cruz, and then dreamily, beckoned by the behemoth Bekins Van and Storage sign, I would take the Stevens Creek exit off to Daisy's.

At nighttime too, I drove these routes, awakened vividly with visions of all of my past lives as abandoned houses scooped up by a bulldozer and eerily piled by the side of a freeway transforming itself into a dream road that became increasingly more narrow. And a little volume I'd picked up somewhere, "The Life of the Mystic," promised that the road within was often solitary and fraught with treacherous choices of mysterious outcome.

"So, tonight's the night! We'll jump in your car, drive up and take with us everything we can fit—the rest you don't need anyway, right, chicken?" Daisy dispatched Art to put the kids to bed (which he did anyway) and to handle all calls. With a twinkle he suggested, "I guess you'll be staying with us for awhile?" He looked as if he were happy about the prospect.

"Where will I be staying, Daisy?" Daisy didn't bother herself with bromidic details when guiding others, and was preoccupied; so I shut up on our drive, content to have her at the wheel. I flicked on the radio in the Mustang. "OOOOHHHHH Happy Day," the radio rang out, "Oh Happy Day, when Jesus wash, oh, he wash es—he wash my sins away. Oh, Oh Happy Day…"

The voice held me like a cradle, its dark arms lifting me to spirit. I felt myself rising on the current of the truth: that we are eternal beings, rooted in a time that was before the morning stars sang together, just as it said in that Elizabeth Barrett's book. I was prepared to gather with these friends, deeper than any I had known in this worldly world so far, deeper than my own family.

We were gathering out of a love of a purpose, out of a subconscious commitment to the vow we had taken at the time of the order of Melchisedek, that one Daisy told us about who later became Jesus. In that lifetime, she read to us from Elizabeth's book, "The Past Lives of Jesus and Mary", He had entered as Melchisedek who had neither mother or father, but who had merely walked into embodiment from the other side as he, as many of us had been able to do in Atlantis. Oh happy day: to be healed, to find him again, rather to find the Christ way for which he was the pattern.

We were led to meet Daisy, led to meet self, for as Edgar Cayce gave, "Ye are meeting self. Ye are ever meeting self."

Where were these thoughts coming from? Not from Daisy. She drove my car steadily, eyes fixed as though her mind was gathered into other realms and her body left as the only guardian of its flight. The announcer's voice bled into my awareness: "I've got to share this new cut of Amazing Grace with you." I lay back in the seat and surrendered to the low molten liquid of the singer's voice, not unlike the inner voice that continued even now, from the wellspring of deepest peace. "I once was lost, but now I'm found...."

"Last stop for Palo Alto, chicken. Is this where we get off?"

"I...I think so, Daisy." My eyes began to register surroundings. Now I knew where Daisy was when she stared out at us from those great distances at Tuesday night class.

We pulled into the dark driveway, behind my duplex a few blocks from the Veterans' Hospital. No more wandering old men peering into my bedroom window from their Thorazine nimbus. No more loneliness, no more wending through the streets of Palo Alto toward St. Michael's Alley, no more wanting something— what did Daisy say? No more searching, longing for answers.

The next day after the move, Saturday, was a lazy day. All of us, including Amy, who was spending the weekend with her three kids, and Stephen who'd come by late to discuss a dream that had been bothering him and stayed over, stumbled sleepily toward the kitchen to eat a little of the breakfast that Art had made when he'd gotten up early with his and Amy's kids. I basked in the luxury of being wanted in this warm house. After breakfast, I lay back down on the couch afterwards to invite another dream.

And after he'd eaten, Stephen followed me to the living room, climbed into the recliner across the room and drew a piece of fake fur about his head to snooze. (He loved soft textures on flashy fabrics—Daisy would make this into a vest.) With the spring sunshine pushing at the closed drapes it felt overly warm—wasn't he sweltering? I slipped off the sweater I'd slept in. Today we'd have time to unpack. Stephen, gay, Daisy's male pet, was wry, earnest, thought he'd been in Palestine, believed he'd been somebody special—too special to Daisy, I thought, but I accepted Stephen as I accepted everything special to Daisy, even as I swallowed intellectual truths I couldn't digest at all emotionally.

Like a lawyer arguing my case all alone before no one but myself, I wrestled with the sarcastic darts I wanted to aim at the beloved Stephen. Was he really Jesus' right hand fellow, or did he just have a crush on him now? Disgusted with myself, I leapt out of bed shirtless as we'd done in the hippie days, grabbed my sweater, shoes and socks and ran to the bathroom away from Stephen and all spotted thoughts. This was to be the happiest of days, coming to stay at Daisy's.

Dressed, washing at the sink, I heard Daisy speaking in softest tones. "I will, don't worry." Amy answered her and knocked on the bathroom door, entering without waiting for me to open it.

"I saw you run to the bathroom with no shirt on. We all respect Art and Daisy's marriage, if you know what I mean."

I was ashamed, and didn't try to explain to her how that was accepted behavior among the artistic fringe that hung out in the dives on University Avenue in Palo Alto, and among the people I'd met at life drawing classes and had tried to emulate as an end to loneliness.

"No, of course not. I won't. Not ever again."

I thought I had injured Daisy and that I'd be thrown out by nightfall. But when Daisy emerged for a late breakfast, it was as if nothing at all had happened.

When she finished her dry toast and hard-boiled eggs, I complimented her, eyes averted, on the weight loss that was beginning to show. Cassandra had said Daisy had a beautiful face and an excellent bone structure and that without the extra poundage she'd be gorgeous. "Listen, chicken, it's easier than you think. I just tell my subconscious every night that I will eat whichever food I see in the dream. And last night it was hard-boiled eggs."

I proceeded to give her a helpful lecture to substantiate the dream, deriving facts about protein intake and the resultant decreased craving for sugars, from the empty intellectual wisdom of the university side of the Palo Alto milieu.

She thanked me. "That makes sense, sweetheart." As her cheekbones emerged, she looked remarkably like Jane Fonda as the blonde Barbarella in the movie Daisy had taken us girls to see. A blue collar Jane Fonda was all right with me. As an angry former radical, Fonda's defiant, courageous stands pleased me no end. Feeling utterly forgiven, sipping coffee and watching the blue haze from four cigarettes—even Art left one burning as he loaded the washer in the garage—I found it easy to forgive the fact that Richard Nixon was a favorite in this circle for the upcoming elections. That Daisy worshipped Jack Kennedy was no contradiction. Political allegiances sprang from behind the closed door of the afternoon meditation room. I vote the way I "get told," she'd told us. "If you don't like Nixon, I can't help it. There are deeper reasons for things, that we can't see at the time, deeper purposes served sometimes, even by allowing something destructive to come to a head."

Alert, watching the smoke nimbus, I spoke up. "How did all of this start, Daisy? Did you always know about all of this stuff?"

"Not in this lifetime, Page."

Art, passing by to the washers in the garage with his arms the base of a pyramid of laundry, agreed.

"You couldn't have told Daisy about any of this a few years ago."

"No, and you'd better not have. I was a Roman Catholic as I told you girls at class—although my mother Blanche had some interest in these things. But for me, to reincarnate meant you came back as a cow or something."

"Then what changed you?" I asked, waiting for what came next expectantly like a child starting into a fairy story. I wasn't disappointed.

"Not what…who."

"Who?"

"Miriam. That's what she said her name was."

"Miriam who? We don't have a Miriam in the classes and I haven't heard you mention her before."

Daisy giggled.

"Miriam, sweetheart, isn't physical—if you know what I mean."

"What do you mean, Daisy? Do you mean…."

Daisy interrupted me in a tone suggesting she was thinking better of the way she had begun, and proceeded in a quiet serious manner. She recounted that she had been in a supermarket one day, toying with several books on the rack—she'd always liked to read—and put the book, Many Mansions, by Gina Cerminara, down the minute she read the word "reincarnation" on the dust jacket. Then a voice—"really a voice, Page" said "Buy it."

Daisy had turned around, really freaked out but there was no one else there at all, started to walk away and then felt a tap on her shoulder. So she swung around and grabbed the book and threw it in the shopping cart with the pork chops and celery and bread and stuff, and drove home fast trying not to think about what had just happened.

"I can see why," I leaned closer, waiting for her to go on.

"Well then," she said, "it was about a week later—it was a week, wasn't it, honey?" she called to Art at the washer who apparently couldn't hear her because he didn't answer. So she continued, holding her voice low as if she were trying not to sound fantastic. She finished quickly and in a matter-of-fact tone. "Well, it was just about a week later and we were lying in bed together; Art was already asleep and I was just about to go to sleep when close to the rug, very gradually, I began to see a woman's feet—in sandals—materializing like. At first it was only the feet, but then I could see the bottom of a robe, and then the shape filled in all the way up to this face and then Miriam—well later she said her name was Miriam—then Miriam was there before me, all of her at once."

"Weren't you scared?"

"I was scared shitless, Page." Now Daisy became animated. "But it was so soft all around her, and the room was whispery quiet. She was in a mist, and she said, 'Daisy,' so softly, so sweetly, and then I wasn't really scared at all anymore. 'Yes,' I must have squeaked back so quietly you couldn't hear me— because Art didn't wake up or anything. 'Yes?' I repeated. 'Daisy, you must read the book I brought to you.' Well, that's all she said."

"How did she say it? Loud, like a real voice in a room, or what, Daisy?"

"I don't know. I don't even know if she spoke out loud—that sounds funny, doesn't it, talking about someone like that—well, you know what I mean.

"Yes. Yes, I do. Go on."

"I just knew she told me to read the book. Maybe I thought it, or she spoke to me in my mind, but I knew."

Now I understood what Daisy meant when she said "I got told to do it,"—to vote a certain way or whatever. "What happened, Daisy?"

"Miriam started to dissolve then, from the top down, opposite from before. First her face dissolved and then her shoulders, and then her robe just faded away, until I could see her feet again, just the feet. And lying there in shock, I began to hear music, beautiful, celestial-sounding tones in sequence, even more beautiful than when Stephen played the song he'd written for me on his guitar. Sorry, honey." She squeezed Stephen's knee.

"Go on," I urged.

"Well," Daisy continued, "the tones were like the colors of the rainbow itself. Then I turned to Art, who looked so far away across the bed. 'Please, Art, wake up,' I called to him and shook the bed." Daisy shook the edge of the hexagonal kitchen table when she said this, as if it were happening again right this minute. Stephen patted her hand to reassure her. "'Art,' I begged, 'did you hear it?' And then from the other side of the bed came the strangest whisper. It didn't sound like Art at all. 'You mean…the MUSIC?' 'Yes,' I answered him in a loud whisper, still afraid to talk out loud—'YES, the music. Oh sweetheart,' I shouted, 'you hear it, too.' And I got rain for the first time, in sheets and shivers, and Art was blown away."

At class the first time she'd told us about rain, she'd looked to Art, who'd stood in the doorway. "You know what rain is, Art. Remember Miriam?"

And he'd nodded, smiling without speaking. They know great secrets together, I'd thought at the time, great mysteries. Now I rained too, got the same shiver bath.

"What did you do next, Daisy?"

"I did what anyone would have done. I jumped out of bed and ran to the bookshelf. But I couldn't find the book anywhere, Page. I tore all of the books out of the bookshelf, pulled the bookshelf out from the wall, looked behind it, under it, but it was gone! Art and I tore the house apart that night: chairs, couch, cupboard, everything; and the next morning we asked the kids and then Amy and her kids and Stephen—even Vicky—and everybody else we could think of. But Page, it was gone-gone. That book just disappeared. By this time it was becoming clear to us that something was happening that we couldn't ignore.

"Finally, three days later I lay down on the couch in the afternoon for a nap and fell asleep. I wasn't sleeping as well as I normally do at night by now; this thing was really getting to me."

"I can imagine."

"But all of a sudden I woke up and—I guess my eyes were half open, I don't know—I saw the feet again, bare, in sandals. No one was home, Art was still at work and the boys were at Amy's, and there were those feet again in those sandals. I sat up fast, not at all asleep anymore, jumped up quickly and I didn't see anything in the spot where she'd been a moment before; but there between the couch cushions, quite visible, was the book."

"Maybe you missed it when you looked, Daisy; that could have been it, couldn't it?"

"No it couldn't, chicken, because Art had literally turned the couch upside down when we looked before, and I'd vacuumed down into it since."

Art, back from the garage with folded towels in his arms, dropped them on the table and pulled up a chair.

"No way, Page," he said. "I personally searched all the furniture twice more before Daisy found the book in the couch, because it was really starting to get to me, too; when Daisy tells you it wasn't there, she means it wasn't there."

Daisy, embarrassed I guessed, said "Well that's how we started—you asked." We were made to read Many Mansions, "the" book, about reincarnation and the Edgar Cayce readings. Then Mom invited me to a conference at Asilomar and I met Elizabeth Barrett, who shared her experiences with the Edgar Cayce philosophy. And, at Elizabeth's next conference this May, Gina Cerminara will be speaking about the book. Synchronicity. That's the way things happen sometimes. Daisy stood up to go but smiled at me soft like, as Miriam must have smiled at her, I thought, rain still tumbling off the top of my head down through my spine (that's how it felt).

"Let's go outside and wait on the porch with the boys, Page." Art rose and I followed him outside. I knew of course that he kept everyone away when Daisy meditated in the afternoon. Now I knew better why. I wondered, sitting on the spring cool concrete in the new after-winter sun, watching Art's smoke puff away and into the light breeze like the folds of Miriam's gown about her sandaled feet, whether Miriam would come to me. Somehow I doubted it and felt almost in awe of Daisy and snug as a lightning bug in a gossamer rug, enveloped in the regularity of Art's laid-back, under shirted strength, and in Daisy's magic, as if I lay on a loom being woven warp by woof from somber January to bright June in one colorful pass of a shuttle held in the hand of the good fairy.

After a week, Daisy was told in meditation that I would go to Amy's for awhile. "She needs the help right now and it will be a good experience for you, an opportunity for you to be of service, right, chicken?" So I babysat nights for Amy while she went to Daisy's and Art's to talk until all hours. How I wished I were there.

It was hard to think of Amy and Daisy as sisters sometimes. "Amy and I weren't raised together," Daisy had actually confided in me one day. "Mom said Dad was drinking a lot after Amy was born and threatened to hurt the baby. So my aunt took Amy. I grew up thinking we were cousins until I was a teenager. Then one day I found Amy's birth certificate in our attic."

"Then what?" I'd asked. "Then, nothing...except I guess that's why I feel like a mother to Amy half the time." Even though Daisy wouldn't talk further, this story explained a lot. In their dealings with me, the sisters couldn't have seemed more different.

Still, though I was resentful about all the housework Amy made me do and at her indifference to me most of the time, I had some of the sense of belonging I'd felt at Daisy and Art's. "You're good with children," Amy decided, "that's your thing." It was not. So I got to discipline the children, to sit at the end of the hallway near their open bedroom doorway and do what Amy said: yell at them to go to sleep and threaten to spank their butts if they didn't. It sounded so definite, not like the way I was raised.

During the days, while Amy slept on the couch, I took the children, two skinny boys and a plump little girl, to the tiny round apartment swimming pool. The pool was locked inside a cyclone gate, so the many children of the shabby complex slung over two or three blocks pleaded with their mother every day to get the keys to it. Even on the whitest, chilliest days of winter, the joyful sound of shivering children could be heard splashing and paddling in the unheated waters around its algae-lined circumference.

Today, the younger boy took the little girl they called Sissy back to their apartment ahead of Jimmy and me. When I finally convinced Jimmy, whose legs had turned purple from the cold, to go back, I found Amy still asleep on the couch, rousing and then turning in to the pull of much-needed sleep.

Robin, the youngest boy, half falling off the old divan, was perched next to her, and Sissy cuddled into the crook of her limp outstretched arm. "Mom," Robin whined, "can't I go to the 7-11 and get candy? Can't I?" he pleaded, wrinkling his domed forehead. (Vitamin "D" deficiency caused rickets in children, I'd read; Amy rationed milk to her kids, but drank lots of it herself with her favorite sandwiches of hot dogs split open on white bread.)

"All right," Amy murmured, her face scrunched up as if it were wounded by the intrusion of his words. "Be back before dark," she managed. Amy turned and rolled over, dislodging the little girl who clung hopefully as though on a ride. Knocking Sissy to the floor, Amy turned over and buried herself in the divan. She tugged at the comforter Daisy had sewn for her and pulled it over her head with one slim, pale hand. As a form under the comforter, Amy looked like a little girl herself, defined only by the bulge of rather large hips.

"I'll play outside for awhile with the kids; we'll go on a walk."

"Ummmmmm, uhuh...." Amy could care less, I thought. All right. For a moment I felt superior. Later, when the nightly, "I'll spank your butt" had silenced the children's voices, I remained in the hallway still under orders from Amy. With nothing to do but stare at the dirty dishes waiting for me in the alcove kitchen, I glanced at Amy who was pulling up her underwear getting dressed to go out.

Her stomach bulged a lot I thought, probably because she had stretch marks from three kids and everything. Her belly pooched out, but she looked sexy to men anyway from the reactions of the ones I'd seen around her. (One night, left alone in her apartment as usual, I'd experimented with telepathy, trying to will a certain man at the periphery of our circle to call me. Throughout the evening, I'd evilly and eagerly intoned his name. Only the next morning, he called Amy, convinced she'd been "thinking about him," and asked her for a date.) And she told me she'd been a kind of call girl while she worked as a waitress at Lyons, said it matter-of-factly like "I'll spank your butt," like that was it and you couldn't ask questions.

So I thought men liked her a lot. She slipped into the slim-legged, full-hipped pants, struggling to button the tight waist. "You look pretty, Amy," I fumbled as usual for things to say. I hated myself for that. It was like doing calisthenics, sometimes, just to talk to her. "Uh huh," Amy smiled into the mirror, then stared at me directly, flat-eyed and unanswerable.

"You're going out," I ventured.

"Yeah. I thought I'd go over to Daisy and Art's. There're some things I really have to talk to them about. You know how it is." She smiled, picked up some long strings of amethyst colored costume jewelry from an open lower drawer to her jewelry box, which formed an altar on top of her white-painted dresser. She had a picture of James, Jimmy's father and her high school sweetheart, on the dresser. To the left of the box, several fancy lipsticks stood straight up next to Jimmy's picture near a tall swan-shaped perfume bottle.

To the right of the blue box lay two books Daisy had given her to read about reincarnation and dreams, "to deepen your understanding, sweetheart, that's all," Daisy had explained when Amy looked miffed. The books lay hopefully on the ever-important, dresser; I knew Amy hadn't read one word.

The picture of Jesus Amy had placed on top of the jewelry box in the place of honor looked down at me with disapproval in the soft Sunday school face.

"Um...I'd like to look at these books while you're out if that's ok."

"Sure." Amy could be unexpectedly generous. She looked right at me in the darkening bedroom, her lavender eye shadow melding with the splices of light from the amethyst beads. She flashed a soft, pencil lead blue-eyed smile at me, the kind I guessed got Daisy fired up to rescue Amy from her first marriage (Jimmy was illegitimate) to that man in Daly City.

Daisy had confided to me one day when she was annoyed at Amy, "I found the toilet overflowing at Amy's house, with day old diapers stuck down inside it, no baby food in the cupboards, and Amy living to ram around with that man in the city at night on his bike—with just the next door neighbor lady looking in from time to time. At night. Big Robin never wanted to be a father or work or anything, but it was hard as hell convincing Amy that the marriage was really over."

Now Amy's button popped. "On the refrigerator there's a needle and thread. Would you go get it?" I hopped up. She called after me, "I can't get up myself because the drapes are open and I don't know that guy who lives across there—you know, the one playing the Elvis music." Amy loved Elvis. I wondered if the guy was playing it for her benefit. I got the needle and walked in on Amy feeling her stomach. Odd.

"All right," she smiled up at me as though she wanted me to realize something. "You know. Right?" She gestured toward me like a conductor suddenly bringing up the oboe.

"Ummm." I felt stupid.

"I'm pregnant, right?" She flashed the smile, as if she were happy to tell. "You know it, don't you? Daisy and Art do too."

"So that's it."

"They said not to say anything to anybody. So we don't, right?"

"Right," was all I could say at first; I was fascinated by her stomach from that moment on. I thought I could guess who the father was. There was this Jewish guy who came to see Amy at the classes, and who met with her sometimes at Daisy and Art's. He had frizzy hair, was slight and had an aquiline nose. But when I probed, they said no, it was another guy, an addict, someone Amy had known before Daisy decided I should stay with her for awhile.

Amy couldn't really take on another child. And Art had been "fixed" after he and Daisy had their third boy in an army hospital in Hawaii. Daisy told me this later, and told me that while in the hospital, she'd had a dream about herself and Art with yet a fourth child, a little boy named Todd Allen.

The Jewish young man hovered tenuously in Amy's life for a while, although he lived in southern California. When we went by Daisy's one Saturday to let Amy's kids play touch football in the backyard with their Uncle Art and their three cousins, I caught Daisy leafing through the Bible with Amy attentive. I lingered in the kitchen, listening to Daisy murmur to Amy.

"It said the man of the hour approaches from the south— Bernie commutes to work in L.A. sometimes, doesn't he?" Amy nodded. "It'll be a last minute thing, Amy, if it happens." Daisy snapped the book shut. "Why don't you ask Uncle Art if the kids want lemonade or anything. I'll give you some money and you can walk up to the store and get us something too, sweetheart." I knew Daisy knew that I felt left out.

"Ok, Daisy," I said. "What do you want, Amy?" I asked. "Those little licorice thingies—you know, Candy Cables I think they're called." Amy pressed a couple of dollars into my hand. "Thanks, sweetheart," she said, more for Daisy's benefit than mine, I thought.

When I got back from the 7-11 Store, Daisy called to me from the kitchen where she was sitting with a coffee cup and ashtray and the big black illustrated Bible. "Listen, chicken," she said, "I know we can trust you so I'm going to let you in on something. We think the right thing may be for Amy to have the baby for me and Art. You know, even go into the hospital as me, we think. We believe this baby belongs to us."

"Wow. How do you know?"

Daisy smiled at me. "You know how."

She kept opening the Bible, again and again, as though expecting something. It didn't seem to matter to her whether I understood or not. I guessed the Bible was going to tell her something. Tell her what to do. I wondered how they could stay around here. There were a few pretty conservative people in the classes by now, and this thing was blooming, with two classes burgeoning out of the door of the house on North Redwood Street.

As though in sync with my thoughts, Daisy added, still absentmindedly, for her real concentration was on the illustrated page before her, "We may leave. I've been told in meditation that it's the thing to do, that it's time to move on—that we will journey to the mountaintop. Not because of Amy," she added, looking me straight in the eye and pausing to let a drag out, "but because it's the right thing to do—Art's job at the delivery service has shut down and that's the longest job he's had in a while—and because...because I just think it's the thing to do, that's all." I wondered immediately if they would take me, but I knew they wouldn't.

Daisy jumped up from the table, full of life, and glided toward the open front door, calling Art's name twice.

Suddenly all I wanted to be in this world was pregnant with Daisy's magic child so I too could gain entry to the mountaintop.

Chapter Three

Before Daisy and Art and Amy and Stephen and the children left for Montana, they paid all of their debts, including personal and spiritual obligations. Daisy took us girls to a local metaphysical day-long seminar to expose us to a smorgasbord of other psychics at work. Among these were a woman who communicated psychically with animals (we all wondered about that) and a dapper, golden-haired man so handsome that although we didn't retain much memory of his words, we were still terribly impressed. "Someday I'll work with that man," Daisy commented, and we were sure that she would.

During this time a certain Brother Bill Reynolds made Daisy promise to visit the site of his future City of Jesus. Brother Bill was a paunchy, balding blond man from the deep South with luminous eyes, a long-suffering wife and a passel of kids. He was pulled to Daisy—led to meet her—in the same weird, individualized way everybody else had been—in his case it was by the lure of psychic visions, or "God talkin'", as he put it, and telling him to go to a certain "We and Our Neighbors Hall" where Daisy periodically announced her classes. (That's where I'd first heard about them too.)

There he met the blonde woman he'd seen so often in his little daydreams of "God talkin'". He had this idea that God was talking to him about building a City of Jesus on some vacant property up in Oroville—the City of Gold, the Spaniards called it—on property that had fallen into his poverty-stricken hands in the same miraculous way as he had been told to meet Daisy. The man was freaked out by all this and nice, and fell into our disparate grouping with the same ease of another magnet: negative pole.

"I have misgivings about making this trip, Art," Daisy dangled her new green lapis bracelet against her iced tea glass and rattled the kitchen table. "You'd better do it. After all, you told him you would."

"All right. Come to the store with me, Page, and we'll get some things for the trip. 'It's hot as hell', I've heard some people say who've been."

We climbed into the big old white car and went to the supermarket. Fry's was an unfamiliar store to me, filled with kids lingering in the middle aisles around attractive, color splashed packages of junk food set out to net the willing patrons: hog skin chips, frosting covered cookie cakes and generic cans of soft drinks spilled out of the displays. It was easy to understand how Daisy had become overweight.

She rippled beneath the edges of the tight black cut-off shorts she'd borrowed from Amy, and her hair was tied off into tight little pig tails with gaudy elastics that matched the bright dangling pendant that slipped in and out of her still plump bosom. Exposed by a low-cut nylon peasant blouse, Daisy's bosom was an eye-catcher. In the store, men slipped her looks and some darted in and out of the cookie displays to keep their wet reddened gaze on her chest.

Oblivious, she grabbed bologna, beer, white bread, cookies and some of the effusive soft drinks: all the fun things, forbidden in the house I grew up in. "Anything you want, chicken?" With this manna, what else could I need?

"Nope."

She stuck to the hot upholstery when we got out of the car at her house. "I guess I'm not ready for these shorts," she apologized.

"Hey, you should've seen me in that picture Stephen took from the top of the car yesterday. He says he wants a picture of each of your girls for you to keep when you go up north. From that angle my nose looked smashed, so wide-bridged and fat."

Daisy gave my nose a cursory glance. "God, don't feel bad. Up until lately I looked like I weighed 500 pounds from any angle."

She filled a cooler with Art's favorite bologna sandwiches and beer and we trucked out over the low outlying hills east of San Jose into the heat of the Sunol Valley. We drove a little faster than I'd known to be safe, but it was Art driving and although I'd had some bad experiences in cars, I felt ok. Whenever you were with Art somehow you knew everything would be all right.

After an hour we were on a dry, same-terrain-forever stretch of road past Livermore, listening to the radio. I didn't notice that the engine was knocking until Daisy switched the radio off and told us we'd all better be quiet for awhile because there could be some kind of problem.

And then, the strangest thing. Art thought he had a bad fuel pump that caused the engine to rebel, but when he backtracked to the service station we'd just passed, the engine caught with full power. A guy at the station who knew about alternators on '60 Chevrolets, opened the hood and checked it out. "No sweat," he said after a long, hot wait. "I can't find nothing wrong with it."

But after a mile or so back up the road to Oroville, the engine knocked again and pooped out and died. Art jumped out, threw open the hood and glowered at the Chevy's insides. Even Daisy's naturally curly pigtails dropped in the wait. The boys, playing on a sheet in the hollowed out trunk, bellowed their complaints. Art, a policeman at heart (he later became one), cut that off one two three.

God, it was hot. At about 4:45, after three false starts, when it was too late to get there to swim or to see or bless the grounds, which was what Brother Bill had in mind, the idea came to us that we'd better turn back: that "something" was stopping us from going.

We turned around. The rebel car ran smoothly all the way back to San Jose without a rumble. Wow. I saw that there were times not to fight the flow, that all material things obey a law of movement in currents generated by a universal principle of rightness: by a creative Father/ Mother God who protects children firmly from the things they don't know can hurt them. Years later I would run into Brother Bill near the county mental health and alcohol building. Bill's eyes, far away because of the subtle chemical changes effected by the dose of Lithium he had just taken, came to luminous life when I mentioned Daisy and those days.

A week after the aborted trip to Oroville Daisy transferred the group to the Campbell Hall, a rented public hall that was used for dance classes during the day. The numbers of followers had become too great to meet in any one person's home, and that night Daisy helped Rebecca, to whom the meetings were entrusted, begin the weekly evenings. Vicky intended to be an active participant in Daisy's absence, and Brother Bill said he'd felt the "call" to help out. His wife Lurine didn't like this one bit, because Bill, and Vicky—restless in her boring marriage—had found each other and at the very least, Lurine observed Bill's lecherous gazed fixed, from time to time, on Vicky's abundant bosom. Daisy dressed in unusual ways that flattered her bust in an off-hand manner, but Vicky naturally surpassed Daisy in this area—hands down. Gearing up for one of the first meeting nights at the hall, Vicky was shouting at some of the lesser lackeys from the group to come to order so that Daisy, attired mysteriously in her sole remaining wig, could speak.

New people had found their way to the Campbell Hall as well, among them a very tall, big, broad-shouldered ivory blond-haired young man dressed in navy whites who stood, hat in hand, next to his tall, broad shouldered, statuesque young girlfriend as the meeting was brought to order. My first memory of them is of a light colored blur of blond breadth and height.

Although it was barely June, the press of people in the Campbell meeting hall crowding about me made the evening seem particularly warm. Lurine, after thumping out an opening number on the rattling old piano, now stood next to me, close to Bill, whose eyes were still on Vicky's chest that had heaved spectacularly in time to the strains of "How Great Thou Art." Lurine, sensitive to some alarming change in the two tempted ones who were piously clasping each other's hands during Daisy's opening prayer; suddenly shoved me to the left where I was indelicately thrust up against the bright, navy white chest of the young blond man near the door.

He looked at me and smiled, infecting me with his amusement in the glorious solemnities of Daisy's speech. I tried to push away from him in irritation, but Lurine was ruthless in her desire to break Vicky's hold on her husband, and we remained like that, looking into each other's eyes—his eyes still dancing with suppressed mirth—until I concluded that he was impossibly juvenile, and wriggled around to face Lurine and Vicky and Brother Bill—which was worse?

Everyone else in the room seemed to be enthralled with Daisy, just as I had been. Her beautiful, carved-looking bosom was draped by a cheap, empire waist dress from the lingerie section of an inexpensive department store to be sure, but her cornflower blue eyes looked cool and interested in all she beheld, despite the cheap finery and stiff headdress (doubly odd in California in 1970 when long hair and relaxed clothes inspired by the sixties, had begun to be the accepted fashion).

And to be sure, despite her entourage of some equally hard-looking women—Rebecca and Amy and Vicky, to name a few—and some pomaded looking men, something in those eyes held her audience throughout the night, and when she rose shyly, majestically, to ready herself to take questions and attempt to channel intuitive answers, hands from an eclectic group of men and women, boys and girls, gathered about her, rose en masse.

The tall blonde young woman standing next to her irritating boyfriend asked Daisy eagerly about the dilemma she was experiencing between her feelings for this young man and another, dark-haired boy who lived in another city. "Have I known them both in past lives," the girl inquired, "or what?" Her young man stood quietly beside her, his head inclined toward the navy issue sailor's hat that dangled casually in one massive hand.

Daisy commented on the past life connections of the three. The large, pretty, strong-looking girl looked thoughtful and as if in agreement with Daisy's impressions. The young man looked solemn and indrawn but I sensed that he was still smug and impatient. Now he stood, feet apart, weight evenly braced as if against the force of these foreign ideas, and folded his big arms across his chest. He stared down at Daisy, his sea-washed blue eyes scoping her like the beams from a bright lighthouse.

"You could be twin souls," Daisy told the two. "Look at them—they look like brother and sister." The group peered at the similar looking couple and murmured agreement. Daisy echoed the concept of twin souls that she had read to us from that Elizabeth's book.

When we sang the closing song, "Let There Be Peace On Earth," Lurine was at the piano, and somehow the young man had hold of my hand on one side and his girlfriend's on the other, where we stood with the entire group in a circle. All the rest of the newcomers in the compressed, snake-like circle that doubled back on itself in the meeting room seemed excited and hushed. Even the muscular skeptic to my left clenched my hand warmly as the final tones rang out quickly—Lurine needed to stop playing to get back to Bill and Vicky—and I assumed that this handsome, irreverent young man had at last felt the magic.

Daisy called a last, secret meeting at her house on North Redwood Street to impart special knowledge to her original girls before her journey to the mountaintop. The night was hot but we didn't notice. Wearing the shimmery gowns now popular with us, we just sat and smiled and shivered in the late spring warmth. Daisy was going to speak to us about the earth changes prophesied by Edgar Cayce and others.

"I had a dream," I broke into the silence.

"Go ahead," Daisy waved her hand, appreciative of the support from my over-eagerness. It highlighted her importance, I guess; at that time we operated in symbiotic unison. I broke the crusts of some of the more skeptical with my intensity and enthusiasm and Daisy gave me a focus for those energies, a funnel for a kind of inner power that I could not then recognize as having been with me all my life.

"I dreamed that you, Daisy, sent me to the store with Davy, who was both your son Davy and a strange little man I once knew in Palo Alto named Dave. When we returned from the 7-11 store, everyone I encountered—all of you were there," I gestured around the room inclusively—"looked up at me slowly, one after another, and each of you laughed a diabolical, maniacal laugh that sent chills down my spine!

"I went to you, Daisy, to tell you of this; and your back was turned to me. I tapped your shoulder, and slowly you rotated toward me and lifted your head—you smiled, but your smile widened along with your eyes and you laughed, that same laugh, like...like a demon!

"So I grabbed Davy and plunged out the door into the white car. I drove and drove, impelled to leave you and San Jose and the whole San Francisco area behind. As I drove I 'knew' that the horrible laughter was part of a 'laughing sickness' that could occur once in a blue moon, the precursor of some great destruction or cataclysm.

"As I crossed over the Golden Gate Bridge I felt as if we were racing a great earthquake rising up in our wake. Then Davy and I were over the bridge and I thought we had escaped the coming quake—escaped the laughing sickness. So I drove rapidly, headed due northeast. 'We're free Davy,' I shouted.

"Davy's head was bent toward his lap, as if he were asleep. Suddenly, he tipped his face and looked at me as though shyly. Then the maniacal grin broke across his face from ear to ear.

"I leaped out of bed and ran out of that dream, Daisy, my heart pounding. I ran into Cassandra's room (that's where I've been staying since I left Amy's," I told those in the class who didn't know) "and I looked terrible, didn't I, Cassie?" The usually, dour, skeptical Cassandra nodded, wide-eyed, and hugged her arms to her chest as if freezing. She remembered my bounding into the bedroom she shared with her schoolteacher husband Christopher—who spoke with a Kennedy accent he'd perfected in front of the bathroom mirror—and blurting something to them about "once in a blue moon." That's how the dream had announced itself. Lying in the main room beneath a curtain less window open to the blaring moon that lit the mountainside above them and the ravine beneath, my nightmare had given credibility to the Cayce warning about sleeping unprotected beneath the power of the moon.

"What do you think the dream means, Daisy?" she asked. "Do you think it's telling us there will be a great earthquake, or what?"

"It means there will be some kind of a great"—she stressed the word—"shake up somewhere," Daisy answered thoughtfully. She seemed stuck as to how to go on, troubled, puzzled as though the answer were right there on the tip of her tongue. I knew Daisy well enough now to feel that something nagged at her. She sat, poised, waiting for something to jog her from the inner planes, from within; but something did not.

"There's no doubt about it, Page is plugged in," she finally concluded, "we've seen her accuracy before."

Many years later I wondered why neither of us used the keys we'd compiled to decode all other dreams—the "What does this mean to you?" approach Elizabeth suggested in her dream book. If Daisy had asked me that simple question, or if I had asked it of myself, the answer would have been an easy one.

To the question, "Who's Davy to you?" I would have answered, "Davy is Daisy's youngest child—her baby."

Then Daisy would have said, "Listen to the play on words: 'her baby.' You're talking about 'my baby', as in my pet project, my 'work', or something like that."

"Yes, that's it, Daisy," I would have said. "And right now your work is in your classes, your mission to lead, to guide us, to"— Daisy would have broken in—"And where did I guide you in the dream?"

"To the 7-11 store." And then I'd 'get' it. "'Seven,' means the mysteries. 'Eleven,' spiritual mastery," I'd say, ever proud of my quick memory for the meanings of the signs and symbols Daisy had taught. "And the store is for food—that's love," I'd have continued, "or 'store' might mean 'storehouse' for all of the spiritual mysteries in the earth."

"And if my child was both a child and a man in your dream"—it all would have come together then for Daisy—"then maybe your dream is prophetic; for we often say the babe is the child of the man. So Davy would be my 'baby,' or my work in the future."

"But Daisy!" Then I'd look at her and we'd both stop in our mental tracks, shivering, "What about that awful laughter? All of your people had...gone insane! All of them—and you and Davy."

"That means something in all of this...could turn to madness," I wish she would have said.

"And the laughter, being the madness...would mean that...this...joy...could turn into its opposite, sweetheart, into something terrible."

"But why, Daisy, why?" I would have asked, adoring her, believing she was the sun itself.

And then Daisy would have contemplated with us, and we all could have tuned in together; could have reached for, fished for, fished out the thread of what must already have begun to be wrong.

Instead Daisy abruptly said, "Let's take a break," although the meeting had not really yet begun. She pulled herself from the dark recliner chair—rocked like rubber forward and back before the chair would tip to release her. Ashen under a gay blue, yellow and orange flowered acetate robe, she walked slowly out of the living room through the hallway into her bedroom where she shut the door. Fifteen minutes later we resumed the meeting but never once spoke of the dream again.

But at 10:30 at the end of this very last class, when Daisy announced that we must all celebrate the space in time we'd shared and not cry too much—Rebecca, stoic, dark, Madonna-like, had begun to leak tears—then Daisy looked at me especially when she announced brightly: "I must take you—each one—to Asilomar to meet Elizabeth before I leave next week." Frowning at me she added, puzzled as if something weren't right, "And I mean especially you." I wondered as I slid into the driver's seat of my Mustang with Cassandra beside me, ready for the drive up to Black Mountain Road to Cassandra's ramshackle cabin beneath the Santa Cruz Mountains, did Elizabeth have something to do with my dream?

From the curb I stared into the night sky above the little house as though the answer were up there, as though God had gathered

Himself—Herself, in the very air about Daisy's house. I caught Cassandra peering sadly back and squeezed her hand. Maybe it seemed to us that God was about the house because in the hearts of each one who had come across its doorstep, He was already living.

On the morning of our long-awaited trip to Asilomar, we all packed into two cars, Amy and Daisy and Art and Stephen and Cassandra and Cassandra's friend Lily, and we trekked down Highway 101 past Watsonville to Highway 1 and the Monterey Bay Peninsula, with Rebecca and Vicky and some of the others close behind. As usual when I was with Daisy, I noticed no scenery and time fled by us like the wash of the Pacific that became visible once we passed Castroville. "See—look," someone murmured, but I was looking at Daisy. "You'll love this, Page," she said and smiled enigmatically. I sure would. I could feel it, and Daisy had taught me, already, to trust what I felt, as if I were a little child.

The highlight of the gathering was to be a "Come As You Were" party, held on the second night of the conference in rustic Nautilus Hall. This was a nighttime conference in so many ways: the important events unfolded under moonlight. Readings of every kind were available from a plentitude of clairvoyants, intuitives, astrologers, numerologists, palmists, sand, Tarot and rune stone specialists, to name a few.

By night number two, I was an old familiar, a regular. Early that morning, during Your "Personal Psychic Experiences Hour", I'd shared how much I loved everyone there. "I've been on drugs," I confessed into the microphone, "and this is like coming home," I brimmed.

It's hard for me to imagine now, but Elizabeth remembers that I really did say exactly that, adding that I stole the show and her heart. She told me how for months after that day, she prayed for me, for the little girl who had the drug problem. She was relieved, at the next conference, to discover that I was no heroin addict but years earlier, had dabbled in some sped-up combination once or twice but with horrifying results.

And later, when we grew back to being the sisters we really are, she told me she'd taken a certain drug a few times and loved the experience: that it did nothing but send her back to King Arthur's court—so vividly that she could feel the heavy thicknesses of the drapes on either side of the window seat where she found herself,

and that she could see and breathe the dust motes playing through
the air of the castle room.

Not so me—I was a pretty screwed up kid in those days:
drugs, sex and world shocked. But I must have said those words that
morning because I went to the party that night in love with every
man and woman in that room, as though I were the darling of a great,
enormous royal family, and not the outcast of a rich pack of
successful materialists who scorned me and adored my sister—a
sister who shopped regularly at Saks, and discarded her newly
purchased bathing suits in a heap on the floor of her poolside room
before selecting one to wear with cocoa butter for the important
daily ritual of gaining a tan.

No tan did I keep, no boyfriend, no family, no cat even
seemed to stay in my life in those days: no love. At the conference, I
read more of Elizabeth's books hungrily. Self-bound in baby pink
and blue and goldenrod, the booklets were sold only through Fate
Magazine in those days—they should have been sold by Harper and
Row, and read on television during prime time across the land, I
thought—here was the truth, and not just in abstract precepts but
presented as a living book, though stories. Stories of karma, of the
man who would not hear the tortured cries of others in the dungeon
in the Middle Ages—in this life he suffered too—stone deaf; of the
woman hardened with bitterness and resentment who'd grown a
cancer: a hate harbored through lifetimes. Karma operated in
reverse. I read Elizabeth's psychic insight received during World
War II, after nightly prayers for the Jews. "Why, God?" she'd
anguished. She awakened one night to see words about the long arm
of karma scrolled over her wall: "The oppressor must become the
oppressed."

Had I once been like my sister then: vain, selfish, jealous of
her father's house—had I made a Cinderella of someone else? I
hated to admit it could be true. But inherent in the idea was an
original wholeness, from which I had, perhaps, chosen amiss. If so, I
could choose also to understand, to forgive, to go home to the grace
Elizabeth demonstrated in her stories, grace within the awesome,
perfect law of karma. For every action there is a reaction. God is
alive! I thought. Well and just. This world is a little while—but God
lives!

And Elizabeth wrote of twin souls. So one did not have to be
lonely. She told that wherever you might find yourself, you were not

alone, that you were of God and that the Creative Forces had given the closer companion: another soul, a complete soul, not identical, but the complement. Where was he? My heart rose like the majestic redwoods that watched over the deer-filled grounds of Asilomar on which the Philosophical Round Table Conferences were celebrated —in that instant I knew him again, in feeling, and resolved to search for him, first by asking Elizabeth, then Daisy, and then by wishing and praying. So began my long, long journey toward that one who is, who will ever be…another portion of my own entity.

Tired of who I was, I was never happier than on that second, festive night when I got to come as I had been in happier times so long ago—and all because Daisy had invited me to Asilomar.

Emerging from the room I shared with Amy, I bolted across the courtyard in a flame-colored acetate dress, my long light brown hair flying behind me, and stopped short in front of the gurgling fountain. I brushed away strands that fragmented my view of the evening sun setting over the ocean as a sizzling globe, floating the folds of waves that washed up on Asilomar beach. Around the fountain now were blue shadows, the afterimage of the trails of reddening sun. Everyone I saw was in costume. Two nuns approached, crisply fussing with the collars of their newly basted habits. One smiled at the other. I looked up in awe—Daisy? I shyly studied every detail.

"C'mon, Daiz," Amy nudged her sister toward the doorway of the meeting hall at the end of the fountain courtyard. Not sure of whether or not to presume to follow them, I hesitated and the moment was lost. The two nuns glided through the sunset-gilded doorway into the Nautilus Hall. Nautilus and Triton Halls were the twin realms in which Elizabeth's conferences were held. Pine and Monterey cypress trees brushed the rustic rooftop of the Nautilus. I sank to the wide cool stone bench before the fountain.

A beautiful older man and woman, carefully dressed as figures from Palestine, strolled in a manner so familiar out of the sparkling shadows to my left, passed me and disappeared through the golden doorway. I stared after them and felt a leap of happiness, as if I'd come home. I wondered who would see me in the copper and pink dress Daisy had fashioned to change color with the light. "An Atlantean princess-priestess, that's who you'll be."

Room at Asilomar

The Asilomar Conference Grounds—ocean view

"What's that?" I'd asked before we began the trip from San Jose to Pacific Grove and Asilomar Beach. "You'll see," she'd intoned, sewing merrily. Now a tall young man with a yellow, coiled Grecian coif, walked by on the arm of an older woman.

"Hi," he smiled through beautiful parted lips.

"Hi."

"We'll be promenading together at the costume judging," he tossed. Daisy had said she'd see to it that I would have a priest to compliment my dress, but I hadn't any idea that.... The amber robed "priest" regarded me lightly through yellow-green eyes. "Won't you accompany us, dear?" he asked in a faint drawl, or was it a lisp?

"Certainly," I replied, every inch a princess.

Then I clasped his extended arm and glanced at him slyly, thought he caught my look, wondered if—

A little boy dressed as a page darted before us through the doorway followed by a gypsy lady in pursuit. Her perfume and silver satin petticoats, the indigo swish of her skirts, resonated with the fountain's splash and sparkling babble, so that when the music of a piano and flute began from beyond the doorway, I too rushed within as though impelled to enter another hall remembered only in far memory.

Inside, the room was alive with ancient presences, some attired frivolously, some fiercely malevolent. I was alone in a swirl of transcendent beings, it seemed: here a scythe-carrying shepherd, there a cyclopean, third-eyed master magician. When the shuffle of fabric and the footsteps ceased, and the glow of gilt and scarlet, mirror-hued auric bustle lapsed into a quietness and an anticipation, then Elizabeth, our dear mother, dressed as a great lady from an indeterminate time, swept quietly up to the podium at the heart of the far end of the room.

"Thank you all for coming, darlings, to the Come As You Were Party of this thirty third Philosophical Round Table Conference here at our beloved Asilomar. Such an array of beautiful faces," the silver-haired lady spoke. "Our conference this memorial day weekend is dedicated to Edgar Cayce, whose life's work has so greatly helped show a troubled mankind that life is eternal. We've been blessed with some wonderful speakers this time, Dr. Gina Cerminara—where are you Gina, darling, can you stand up so everyone can see you?"

Gina Cerminara, tall, dark hair pulled sharply back in a Grecian coiffure, smiled with great poise. She's the one who'd written Many Mansions, the book Daisy had mysteriously found again in her couch.

"And Jeffrey—Jeffrey Furst—his new book, The Story of Jesus, is the most beautiful account of the Palestine land I have ever read."

I had read that book last Christmas—suddenly Jesus' life had made sense to me—that's why I had come to Daisy's classes in the first place.

"Jeffrey tells me it's going into paperback next month," Elizabeth continued. "Where are you, Jeffrey?"

A round-face man, whose hair was beginning to thin, came up to the podium and announced solicitously that Jeffrey Furst wouldn't be arriving until later that night.

"Thank you, Ambrose," Elizabeth rejoined. "Ambrose will have his slides on Atlantis this time, too—won't you, Ambrose?"

"Well, Elizabeth, they're not my slides, really. It was Edgar Cayce who gave the Atlantis story in greatest depth—although I've read them all: Plato, Ignatious Donnelly, the Theosophist—Scott Elliott in 1896, Louis Spence, 1924, James Bramwell's Lost Atlantis in 1937...I just hope that, in my humble way, somehow, through the slides, that I—"

Gently, Elizabeth interrupted him, addressing another, older man in the back. "Colonel Adams?" Elizabeth continued, "You'll be showing us your slides about the Shroud of Turin, too, won't you, darling?" Edgar Cayce—I'm sure he's present here tonight in Spirit—would be so pleased.

Addressing the audience at large, she asked, "Will each of you beautiful ones write just one question and put it in the baskets that are passing among you. We will attempt to answer all your questions if we can."

As she spoke, she gathered each one to her—we were a sea of bright and shining magical children, from the little boy who'd beaten us into the meeting hall to the handsome, Palestinian-garbed man late in his sixties. Children all, we were enthralled, as the powerful lady spoke to us eloquently, anecdotally, of her life as an interpreter of those readings left through Cayce. As she spoke, we were woven into the broadest perspective imaginable. "Why has there been no love in my life?" She took the first question. "Who wrote this, darling?" Elizabeth held the slip of paper and scanned over the audience. The cyclopean man raised his hand sheepishly.

"If your higher self has chosen a karmic pattern to be worked out in one lifetime, and if this is necessary for your soul's development so that you can eventually leave the earth plane—and there is no happiness in earth life to compare with the experiences in the inner planes, darlings—then a day must be lived at a time until the karmic pattern is met. As Cayce gave, day by day, here a little, there a little, karma is met.

"We seem to fast after a feast. We seem to enter a karmic life—a life without love," she added, looking compassionately at the man—"after a life that has been fulfilling and happy. Conversely, Edgar Cayce indicated that if love had been denied for a complete lifetime, then the tendency is to marry early in the following lifetime. Moreover, in one reading he indicated that at death, the lonely soul journeys immediately to the 'environs of Venus'—the planet of love...especially those who have been torn by love, and hurt through love, and where love has been denied.

"Death comes to all of us, and the karmic pattern of the life is ended, but the eternal pattern—the eternal relationship with the beloved of spirit—is never ended. Even in earth life, if the readings are true, we know that in sleep, we journey out of the body, in other realms of consciousness, and are one with 'the other portion of our entity'. In dreams, we have glimpses of this...and in meditative experiences."

Elizabeth's words comforted my own heart. One and all, great personage from the past and small, the peace of her words seemed to reach through each solemn countenance and touch the core, or what Cayce called the soul entity.

"Who is this darling girl you've brought to meet me, Daisy?" Elizabeth asked the next morning when Daisy and I slipped into empty chairs in the common dining room with a view of the ocean after the breakfast crowd had cleared.

"This is Page," Elizabeth.

"Although I don't know your name, darling, I know you. You were the one who said that you felt as if you'd come home, being here with us at Asilomar."

"That's right, Elizabeth," I answered when spoken to, in awe.

"I was very touched by that, darling. You are—someone."

"Page had a dream last night," Daisy related. "I think you'd better hear this one. It may pertain to you, Elizabeth."

"Go ahead, let's hear it." I glanced at Daisy. Her blue eyes were unclear. She nodded.

"Well…I guess the dream might be about Egypt. Daisy, isn't that what you said earlier?" It seemed necessary to defer to her.

Daisy smoked, impassive and far away. "Can I get you anything, Elizabeth?" was all she said.

"Yes. I'd like some lemon for my tea, if that wouldn't be too much trouble."

Daisy swept away, self-contained.

Elizabeth sighed audibly. "There goes my golden girl. Watching the way Daisy arranged the Come As You Were Party and her contribution to the whole conference—bringing you to see me, darling—you'd think Daisy was a forty-five year old woman and not a girl of twenty-six."

I nodded appreciatively; feeling as if I were having an audience at once with a great queen, and, strangely, an old friend.

"Tell me your dream about Egypt, darling."

When it was done, Daisy reappeared. "You're right, Daisy," Elizabeth confirmed. "Page did dream of Egypt, of the great procession to the Temple of Hat-shep-sut during the time of Ra Ta. This dream links her directly to Isis and to Amen Ra." They looked at each other seriously, then at me with respect. I didn't know what they were talking about. Daisy smiled. "Are you ready to go, Elizabeth?" Daisy fastened the frog clasp at the neck of her new Florence Nightingale blue cloak, helped Elizabeth into a smoke black coat and offered her elder an arm, leading her down the wide wooden steps that led from the dining hall.

I watched Daisy, her golden hair damp and curly from the fog, bent in deep conversation with Elizabeth. I remained rooted, just watching out the dining hall window—until silver and yellow, navy and smoke, blended into one blur as they walked up the long, foggy path leading toward the Nautilus hall.

Rebecca Schemansky (Buchanon)

Chapter Four

Three days after the Asilomar conference, Daisy and Art were packed and made their last stop in San Jose at Rebecca Schemansky's. Art remained at the curb, repacking boxes in the back of Amy's new station wagon. As the last confirmation of the rightness of their decision to depart, Amy's separated husband had died suddenly on his motorcycle and left Amy an insurance policy sufficient to purchase a new station wagon and to fund the trip. After he died, he had appeared to them as a shadowy form in the house on North Redwood Street, and Art particularly, found it difficult to be as somber as he thought he should be, when he could see the dead man grinning at him from the livingroom corner by the floor heater.

"Why did you see him as a shadow?" I had asked Daisy.

"For a while after death before going on, someone appears in a…denser form—like a shadow of themselves," Daisy explained.

I heard them discussing his death among themselves, deciding that the only way he knew how to help them was to make his transition now. He'd been in the picture when Daisy had first seen Miriam and was exposed to some of the happenings that followed—he could have gotten involved in their spiritual search they believed—but he'd "blown it," and chosen, on a soul level, to help the only way he knew how.

Wow. Now I could only accept the "rightness" of their decision to leave. Amy was going, and all of the kids—but they'd decided to take Stephen too. Later, from a feminine point of view, I could see the logic of taking Stephen and not myself, though I'd made it clear I wished I were going. Also, Amy and Stephen looked almost identical and were suspected of being twin souls (although Daisy and Amy's mother cleared that up years later—after Stephen stubbornly refused a relationship with his "twin"—by connecting the miscarriage she'd had just after Amy's birth to this "brother").

Now they were laughing, drinking coffee and smoking more cigarettes in Rebecca's apartment. It was June outside but cool inside Rebecca's kitchen. Daisy laughed, preoccupied with something, fiddled with her hands then crumpled her empty cigarette package thoughtfully, releasing it, then pressing it back into shape again idly— it crackled, then sprang back.

"Hand me your Bible, will you Rebecca," Daisy asked, looking into Rebecca's eyes with her own unveiled and brimming. Daisy held the Bible, caressing its black textured cover. She closed her eyes. The book fell open. She read silently, looked up and then read it one more time.

"We're going," she sighed. "God told us to go and we're going." Nervous laughter all around. She stood up slowly, linked arms with Rebecca and me and we walked out of the dark apartment toward the curb. In the brightest sunshine, through a blur of new green leaves on the apricot trees and on the acacia and on the amber wild rose bushes that burgeoned in the open place between the apartments and one solitary farmhouse, we said our goodbyes. Art hugged me to him hard; they slipped out of the brightness, inside their cars and were gone.

"Crying won't work," Rebecca chided and then shut her front door behind us. "It just clogs up your psychic centers." I knew something about emotions and about therapy, so I was letting myself cry. But her words reassured me, cheered me. It was so simple not to cry, and her living room felt warm now though it was dark and stale cigarette smoke hung heavy in the gloom.

I would like it here—I might as well like it here. Daisy had arranged for me and another girl named Mandy to help Rebecca because she was recovering from surgery. I didn't mind leaving Cassandra's when Daisy had hinted it was time to move on: the drive up unlighted, one-lane Black Mountain Road above Lexington Reservoir in the dark with our third eyes open and our imaginations sparked after late-night sessions at Daisy's had been nerve racking. And Rebecca had the care of two year-old "twins," her own daughter and the daughter of her shiftless sister. So I agreed to help with Becka and Brooke. Since I really didn't live anywhere anymore I felt it was the thing to do. Mandy was a heavy sixteen year old runaway Daisy and Rebecca had befriended at the Campbell Meeting Hall. Daisy had "read" for Mandy and told her she'd been an Indian in her last life:

when she left home at thirteen to live with her hippie boyfriend at the bottom of Montalvo Canyon she was "repeating a pattern."

Mandy showed up the next day in a leather fringe jacket with the belongings she'd recovered from the bottom of the canyon wrapped tightly in an old grey blanket and tied to a stick. Looking into her solemn brown eyes staring at me between curtains of waist-length, thick reddish hair, I knew I could like her. The main thing was that Mandy and I were to stay out of Rebecca's husband's way, and sneaking about to avoid her dark pasty mole of a husband—who ran a pornographic bookstore—was something I enjoyed.

We stayed out of his way, stayed in the back room of the large, darkened bottom-floor apartment and learned about the psychic from Rebecca, who was its living demonstration and the embodiment of some of its strangest aspects. If Rebecca woke up in the middle of the night with "rain" that there was something in the apartment—like a thought form or some kind of astral entity—we would wash down her closet with rags and a bucket at three a.m.—thoroughly. We were educated in wall washing if nothing else. Rebecca told me casually years later that she realized the closets or whatever were probably her own subconscious after all. Rebecca had had surgery for cancer, and although I didn't appreciate the seriousness of that surgery, I knew that cancer was caused by resentment, and I imagined that Rebecca resented sleeping with that dark mole.

Days started late, the mornings were a blur of cold sugary cereal fed the little girls—"They won't eat anything else," Rebecca asserted at the white-lit supermarket when I tried to interject health foods into her shopping cart. I kind of liked living at night, shivering with rain at her Formica table in the smoky, low-ceilinged kitchen. During the bit of the day I saw, the opaque refracted light of the sun only peeped in, politely dim and removed from us, through the curtainless slit of window that overlooked one of those raggedy grass "common" apartment patches that are so common nobody wants them at all.

At night we would scurry about, like moles ourselves, and ready the mole's semi-burned piece of meat, his over boiled patch of frozen vegetables and then wait—hushed in our room—for him to disappear into the bedroom, usually by himself, for the climax of his lightless day lived out of the darkened box of a store called the Red Cat, from which he hustled confusion and nightmare dreams to the lonely.

He was a nuisance as far as I was concerned. I was more Rebecca's mate than he was. I shared her ideas, her psychic experiences, shivered more climactically at the kitchen table with Mandy and her when we "knew" something to be true in a way no books or philosophies could ever convey.

One night an "older" man—perhaps in his mid-forties I would guess now—and a maverick realtor in the burgeoning San Jose market, came by for a consultation. That was an important night for Rebecca and me because we'd been given "messages" about him. I'd had a dream, and we'd spent the night before shivering, rained out, shivering out of our skins until four AM, not even minding that the mole might be disturbed. Or maybe Rebecca knew that he wouldn't because she'd been in the bedroom with him earlier for the lifeless bi-weekly enactment.

Anyway, here was the man of the hour, summoned by us to receive our oracle. Daisy approved of, had even helped arrange our contact with him by phone from Montana. It was part of the psychic sisterhood that was developing, with Daisy listening in from Montana, as diva or mother hen. It was clear by now that Rebecca was to be Daisy's right hen in San Jose and that her dim mole's apartment—this dark den of imitation Mediterranean furnishings with phony royal swords on the wall—would be a seat of fabulous happenings and psychic confirmations for Daisy. (Indeed, last Friday at dusk at the grocery store, while I waited for Rebecca, reading magazines in the racks outside the checkout line while she fished cash from her new white chain purse to pay for the mole's dinner meat, a man who had been crouching beneath me and appearing to browse a "Time," abruptly leapt up, swung around and caught my startled expression in the flash of his camera before he sprinted from the store. And a portion of the first tape Daisy agreed to send to us from Montana arrived erased, so now by long distance telephone the latter advised Rebecca, and through Rebecca ourselves. Were we wanted by the FBI? Who knew or cared. Outside the bounds of time and space, we were beyond their jurisdiction.) Surely, we were privileged to live here in Daisy's dark shadow.

Rebecca was as much a winter type as Daisy was summer. When we studied numerology and the meaning of names, I read that Daisy—Dais—meant "the day's eye" in the original Celtic—and she looked it. Rebecca was slender, with long, thick black hair, a porcelain complexion and dark eyes. She often wore a black brown fake fur coat to go out, even in summer with a snow white collar that fanned out from her slender throat. She was quite pretty to men, but was innately suspicious of them in a way that relaxed as she unfolded under Daisy's tutelage.

Rebecca told me all about her life, I told her of mine. She was one of four sisters spawned by a hardy, Oklahoma-born mother—tough-looking and wizened. Rebecca's mother came by the apartment sometimes. I looked into her San Jose dust bowl eyes and at her garden-hardened skin and thought of the beautiful faces in the "Family of Man" photographic collection. All of the sisters had married or given birth early. The younger one—Lou—fascinated by her pretty-boy husband, periodically left her baby with Rebecca, who had been dubbed "the responsible one" in childhood. Rebecca's mother shared the notion, with many parents, that each of her children should be engraved for life with an idiotically simplistic identity.

That Daisy meshed very well with Rebecca—"the responsible one"—was not surprising. Daisy, herself a child of hardship, was left responsible too early for too great a burden, for the care of the brother who remained after Amy was given away. Now Daisy made herself, and Rebecca, responsible for all of our progress in the movement she'd conceived. Although indefinitely defined, it was unmistakable by now that this was a movement, and that we were moving somewhere.

Jerry Ross rang the bell at 11 PM (that was early for us). I liked older men during this period, so I peered into his expressive face as he hunched over the grey Formica tabletop to hear each word spoken by this strange oracle. Dark eyed, Madonna-like, Rebecca faced him quietly, calmly. Mandy and I—junior oracles—flanked her elbows. We were excited, free and easy in the sleeping mole's cave, and uplifted because by tomorrow's dawn, he would be away on a trip to fetch films for the Red Cat's sleazy owner.

11:10 was probably later than Mr. Ross was used to for visits, but was the perfect hour to make such a venture. Ross wrung his hands lightly, listened; brushed black hair back from his temple, scratched at long thin grey and onyx sideburns.

"All right Page," Rebecca turned to me—proud like the oldest sister introducing one of the youngest—"now you tell the rest." I didn't speak right away so she nudged me. I took a deep breath, proud too that she trusted me now to be the spokesperson.

"Ok. Last night Rebecca and Mandy and I talked about my dream about you—the one we told you over the phone. The dream was heavy enough, but I felt there was some danger to you. Of course…um…I associate the dream symbol of windows and doors left open at night with psychic attack." I smiled at Rebecca, my teacher in that. She smiled back. "But anyway, when we sat down last night—"

"We got tons of rain," Mandy piped.

"Yeah. And between the three of us a picture formed, a scenario I guess you might say, over and over in different ways. It went basically like this: Somehow we kept seeing a man—"

"Oooooh," Mandy shivered. "You'd better believe we saw him—felt him—"

"Well, anyway, this man was climbing, sneaking through your window, the same window you'd left open, unguarded, in my dream. And then he'd walk over to a trunk—and sometimes he did this before he opened the window—"

"But you weren't there so—" Mandy broke in again.

Rebecca, with a look, made Mandy defer to me and then I went on.

"In the trunk were masks, reel creepy, and this man rummages through and pulls one out and puts it on and—"out of breath I rushed—"we felt we had to warn you."

Schooled just these short weeks by Rebecca, I was pretty well convinced by now it was an astral entity we were referring to. Living indoors and with that mole—Rebecca said she'd felt suicidal around him and wanted to leave this world—all this perhaps made Rebecca an expert regarding planes just between here and there. But Jerry Ross took our counsel differently; I could see that right away. He mused for a minute and smiled. He didn't seem shocked, and I knew the dream meant something to him.

"A trunk," you say.

"Yes. Like a steamer or maybe…"

"Maybe an Army trunk?"

"It could have been," Rebecca answered him quickly, perhaps more familiar with Army trunks than I who had no experience with the military. We looked at him, intensely interested, waiting for some kind of tangible confirmation of the midnight visit from the ghostly source anxious to guide this man.

It was obvious he understood and finally, looking up at our eagerness, he spoke, though softly, briefly and generally; but I got the picture—or thought I did.

"Well, when I was in the Army I…had some experiences let's just say—that could be a part of myself that I've locked in a trunk, something that might come out if I.... Well just some part of me that I was then and...."

Rebecca, older and wiser, asked suddenly, softly, fixing her deep shadowy brown eyes into him:

"Would you like some coffee, Jerry?

"We all have things, parts of ourselves, girls...and I guess that's what our message is for, to make Jerry aware of something he needed to look at...and I think he's got it now," she concluded significantly. "Mandy, see if there are any cookies, please."

Jerry looked relieved and smiled at Rebecca, sort of knowingly. I thought I knew the secret too.

"Do you want to lead me into spirit?" Rebecca asked me the next day. "Sure I do," I answered.

She lay on the long black vinyl couch, her slenderness swallowed up in its cold depths. I led her gradually, by light hypnosis, step by step.

Her little girl Becka wandered back in. Mandy was supposed to be watching both children outside. The mole was away, of course; it was daytime but you couldn't see that in here—the drapes were always drawn. Ever tolerant, Rebecca allowed the child to pass in and out without a word, although I sensed by the ashen cast to her already pale face, that she was at least three feet—or three hundred feet—out, away from her body, journeying to the Temple In The Stars, Daisy's favorite meditation get-away spot.

When the child was out and away and had closed the door, I continued the soft suggestive drone. "And now you'll find yourself lifting above the housetops of this area, looking down perhaps." (How neat that she trusted me to lead her spirit like a helium balloon into other realms—mentally I surrounded her in the brightest white Christ light I could before I tugged her along toward the outer stratosphere.)

"Now," I picked up, "you see the blue of the bay like a finger forming the Bay Area, from San Francisco to San Jose. And now you're drifting up, up, up away even above our area, looking down now on Northern California. Now the Northwest comes into view and now the nation—send light to the nation—" I invoked "and now float up, up, until the earth passes back away and you see it as a globe turning slowly beneath you—you who are in the deep, deep, star-pinpointed, darkest indigo recesses of space.

"On, on," I continued into the ears of her emptied body until I had her walking up the interstellar steps of that temple still existing in consciousness—one built in the physical in Atlantis, during the long, latter age when women ruled as the supreme priestesses, leaders, and as psychics. Suddenly it seemed that Rebecca and I were two temple initiates again, in training to span the stars with our minds, to become again as children, and to travel the worlds within.

When she found her way, found her guide and sighted the great viewing screen in the upper hall, I asked her certain questions—the ones we had agreed upon before she "went up." The questions were about her, of course, some were about the earth, and at the last I asked one or two eagerly about myself, for I sensed something special about the tone, the quality, the depth of her visit.

I was very lonely in the man sense, and asked who; or if I would meet someone to marry, and I suppose, by implication, about my twin soul—a concept taught mainly by Elizabeth—but one in which I fervently believed.

"I.... I see him as the man around the corner...." Rebecca whispered. "If you miss him," and then she sighed and drifted in a way that made it sound as if "he" could be possible, "he will come back for you."

Wow. Neat. I led her back again after that, because she was very tired. The doctor said she should not overdo in any way, and she did—daily—some of which was our fault—if youthful inexperience and insensitivity can be faulted. Even at rest her more fragile physical strength could be over tapped by the effort of pulling through this information. My God, that's what killed Cayce during World War II: he tried to read for all those fellows overseas whose families frantically requested readings on top of the mail sacks full of desperate requests that came pouring in every day as Cayce's reputation grew.

By the time I had her back over the housetops, my mind began to play over and over again the delicious promise, "the man just around the corner...just around the corner."

One day the mole said "no more," and Mandy and I crawled out the back window by night and left. Mandy went back to her boyfriend in the canyon, and Rebecca had passed me off to stay with a middle-aged man: Harlan Lewis was a hypnotist who'd come recently to the meetings Rebecca and Brother Bill still led by proxy at the Campbell Hall. We communicated the comings and goings of the meetings on tape, sending these through the mail to Daisy on the mountaintop (hoping they would also be instructive to whoever else might be interested en route).

Harlan told Rebecca that he wanted me for his ashram: "It's part of your next step," Rebecca had rationalized, looking over her shoulder at the ominous, you've-worn-out-your-welcome, mole.

The next day after Harlan picked me up outside Rebecca's apartment was Saturday, the start of a three day weekend and another Asilomar conference. I left my belongings in Harlan's Sunnyvale apartment—it didn't look like an ashram to me. "The rest of the members have yet to arrive," he oiled. Harlan drove me to Asilomar Saturday morning. Rebecca would join us on Sunday: it seemed the mole would only release her one day from the hole. One day was enough. Daisy and Art were going to fly down from the mountaintop near Billings.

Saturday afternoon at Asilomar, after we'd unpacked our bags, deposited them in separate rooms and entered the lodge with the leisure to walk around and observe, Harlan asked, "Who is that fat lout?".

"That's Art!"

"That's her husband?" Harlan went on. He'd heard plenty about Daisy. Harlan had a grungy way of seeing things, but he was 45 or so. I didn't like him and I would only let him bring me once to the Round Table.

I wove through the crowd, exulting. Art clasped me to him. Daisy, slenderer, and surrounded by well-wishers, her golden hair worn loose down her back, smiled obliquely at me between the faces bobbing closer to her and obscuring my view. "That hug is from all of us," she telegraphed. "I'm proud of you." Proud of me too, I didn't break the moment by pouncing on her. With a matching, oblique smile, I filtered back to Harlan, temporarily resigned to Rebecca's prediction, that he would be part of my destiny. And destiny was spelled D-a-i-s-y.

Harlan had a way of opening me up to embarrassment. A Spanish woman, rumored to be a noted psychic, and her young, male assistant, stopped us on the way to the Nautilus. I wanted to move by them. I had hoped to find Elizabeth's cohort Ambrose setting up his magic Atlantean slide shows in the Nautilus Hall. How remarkable that his five dilapidated shoeboxes contained one of the few accurate histories of the world.

"You must let me read for you, dear," the Spanish psychic, Catarina, insisted. "I have so much to say to you." She looked acidly at Harlan.

"He weel gat you preg nant," she insisted in private in the "reading" late that afternoon. She talked to me as if I were an innocent little girl. It felt good. At Asilomar I was a little girl again. I gave her a reading in exchange. Later she said something about me being a great psychic—to someone, I can't remember to whom or just what she said, but I felt as if I were being discovered.

After the reading I walked alone, swirling into a chill wind, hugging my shawl to me. I rushed over the path toward the dining hall. I didn't know who I would meet there; such excitement about this place! A knot of walkers converged with the path. Elizabeth. That plain, almost dowdy figure I saw emerging toward me through the fog—this was my mother, my great queen huddled under quilted robes of velour, emerging from the swells of fog as if from within a great halo, her breath white and crystalline in the cold, pure; this woman knows the secret of the ages, I thought. And yet isn't this face, this someone (whom I had to admit I could hardly see, for the fog, the excitement and the enveloping overtones from previous lifetimes)—me?

I walked further along the path with them, listening to the foghorn braying through the overcast night. My soul flies, I thought. This is my home. More characters, already dressed to come as they were, emerged out of the wet air from invisible tributary pathways. Cypresses glistened unseen and from behind them, between them, emerged the faces of fakirs, lovers, authors, makers of homes, keepers of dreams. All these met and mingled in the fog. I was so glad to be home.

"What did Catarina tell you, darling?" Elizabeth asked when we were walking together toward her room after dinner so that she could change into her outfit as the hostess of the Come As You Were Party.

"It's nothing," I deferred with false modesty.

"Come on, darling. I can see that it meant something to you."

I told her.

"I don't doubt that you were a famous psychic. You…have been something." She looked into me with that same Piscean all-knowing puzzlement. I told her how Catarina warned me against Harlan.

"She's not in a position to judge," Elizabeth commented wryly. "Did you see that young man—her consort of the hour?"

We laughed.

Flying around that night carelessly on Elizabeth's arm, I didn't notice Daisy when I halted with Elizabeth in a throng of seekers on the path to the Nautilus. I assumed Daisy too was waiting to talk to Elizabeth, and I sensed Daisy had been watching me a long time. Our eyes met. She shot me an oblique, "no need," turned on her heel and retreated.

In the registration hall after the conference, Elizabeth seemed to try to make up for this slight. "Darling," she drew Daisy out as Daisy counted the conference money for Elizabeth who was not of this world and, according to Daisy, frequently lost the little she'd made. "I was in the library the other day Daisy," Elizabeth mentioned, "and the strangest thing happened. They have a portrait of Annie Besant of all people in the main branch of the Los Angeles City Library, and when I was standing beneath it once in the section devoted to Theosophy—"

"What's Theosophy?" I inquired.

"The Theosophists, darling, were the metaphysical group of the last century. They were the grandparents of almost all new age thought today."

"And Annie Besant?"

"Annie Besant was 'It'—she was the golden girl of Theosophy —just like Daisy is my golden girl today." She talked to her as if she were a child. Daisy counted the money, seeming indifferent.

"You are my golden girl, aren't you, Daisy?"

Daisy managed a minimal smile, preoccupied as she was with practical details.

"Yes of course Elizabeth, I am," she finally said, tapping the stack of checks into a neat rectangle. Then she took Elizabeth's arm as though to reassure her.

"Tell me about this Annie Besant," Daisy asked professionally.

"She was…physically…just like you darling. She had blond, curly hair I believe, blue eyes, was a charismatic speaker, and quite…mental in approach." I wasn't exactly sure what Elizabeth meant by that but I sensed it wasn't entirely complimentary.

Daisy went on to research that lifetime of Annie Besant's and when I told her at the next conference that I had a hunch I had been with her in her lifetime as Besant, she came up with a picture of an Indian girl who was associated with the Indian youth Besant had thought to be a reincarnation of Jesus or something—certainly a great avatar. I looked into the Indian girl's dark eyes and felt a pull, but coming from within, from some other memory and not from that picture. I told Daisy that then and she said indifferently, "Check it out; I think you'll find I'm right." I did and discovered that the Indian girl was still living in the 1950's—that it was impossible.

Somehow Elizabeth had soothed Daisy because Daisy sat by me at the lunch we took hurriedly before her flight back to Montana from the Monterey airport. She toyed with her bread and looked out the wide windows in view of the thrashing ocean. "It's been a good conference, hasn't it, chicken?"

"Yes," I beamed, glad of a moment with her, of the flow between us that an hour earlier had been at ebb. "That's pretty exciting, Daisy, that you were this Annie Besant."

"Well, we'll see. There's another lifetime I've been working on over this conference," she added, gesturing widely at the tall, distinguished man in his sixties who stood saying his goodbyes to Elizabeth at an adjacent table. "Our wonderful Alden has been a Viking leader—Amy and I got the whole thing last night—and anyway we were all there. I was called The Rainbow," she looked up nonchalantly and I could easily imagine it: drops of spray from a recent walk on the beach had dampened Daisy's cloak and the brilliant sunlight flowing through the pristine window glass bestowed the suggestion of a rainbow all about her head and shoulders.

"You were," I cried spontaneously, wound up in her enthusiasm.

"Yes, yes I was," she pronounced, looking at me idly then blurting happily, "and you, you were—you are—The Rainbow's daughter."

Chapter Five

Even though Daisy had agreed with Rebecca that Harlan was to build a spiritual ashram and that I was to be part of it, as "my next step," I withdrew tranquilly to whatever awaited me in San Jose, overriding my plain misgivings with the hope Daisy's last words imparted.

When we returned to Sunnyvale, Harlan's "ex" wife Helene was the only one present at the ashram, i.e. his upstairs apartment. She mysteriously disappeared, leaving me alone with Harlan, who taught me a little hypnosis, but who moved faster than his belt of avoirdupois would have indicated. In three weeks, after mutual hypnosis and plenty of training in resisting his suggestions, I fled.

Those were beautiful days, halcyon days, but for me those summer days were a parade of longsuffering and forgiveness; I was learning to put things to right in my life—I visited my parents' (dreaded) home; kept up, as by a buoy, by the consciousness of doing right in the Christ, I stayed out in a little unheated poolside room with my six stray cats and was introduced to my sister's high school teacher, a young man of only twenty three or four himself and one whom I liked very much. "Nothing this good's come along in a long time," a psychic reader my mother had seen once before her divorce and who had ironically led me to Daisy, said when I visited her again. I wondered if he was the man "just around the corner," and agreed to visit him in the vine-covered house he rented with two others in the hills above Menlo Park. The pool in the rented house was smaller than my father's and covered by deep dipping trees; it was late July. A cacophony of zinnias and daisies, jasmine and sunflowers shadowed the deep, cool water.

I lay on the diving board, feeling picturesque, conscious of a new virginity, of the importance of doing as Daisy had advised when I told her that I was lonely at Asilomar and that I'd dreamed of the card of the ten of cups in the Tarot deck—didn't that portend a happy union? I'd asked. She told me then to save myself for what I really wanted. That did not stop a hungry, dripping foray into the young man's room; a

Cancer, he had the kind of charm that lighted men and women alike. His best friend, a neurotic-looking, pale fellow, had followed us about during the day, and himself laid an unspoken, jealous and entangling claim on me, which put off Mark, the one I liked so much. After we'd gone to bed, I had to sneak from my room, so that Mark's shadow, who slept in the room next to his, would not see.

In the dim, nighttime cool human mist that hung about the room, Mark slept, dark hair disheveled on his pillow; or did he sleep—he was so still. I was the princess who would wake him with a kiss. On a pretense, I began to speak. He was not asleep after all. He told me he'd always known he would meet, maybe marry someone named Page. I touched his arm, its hairs alive like livid, turning snakes. In the next room over, his shadow, his incestuous brother-friend, coughed. The air fairly sparked. Through deep indigo shadows, pale bleached moonlight streamed in from above through an ivy-clotted skylight, streamed in, made mottled patterns upon his upturned face, over his dark tanned, plushy breast and brown nipples. His hand stretched out for me like a vine's tentacle slowly crawling towards the sun, so I bent down to kiss him, somehow knowing that would be the only conscious gesture of this flowing, ebbing moon man. Caught under his spell, my body, warmed over by its light sunburn, active and vigorous from swimming and diving all day, ached to complete itself inside this stubborn cubicle. We touched each other's breasts and sides; I lingered, my long hair down about his face and neck.

But Daisy's solemn admonitions rang out into the lovely debacle of human heat and breath (strewn about with moonlight and sun dried sheets beneath posters given him by his high school students—my sister included—for his birthday just passed).

I stopped short of laying my long body beside his, slipped out, away from the room and from the man of the moon with maximum effort, muscles and bones and fluids taut and hardened and alive. Soft tissues melted around me, sliding in and out of me like a soft diaphanous skirt. It hurt to leave that room.

Divided from him by a white stuccoed wall and the cooing, chirping garden sounds and the stillness of the house settling in on itself, I was proud of what I had not done and rearranged the folds of my covers and struggled to go to sleep, peeping into the forbidden—hope— something I did not usually allow myself, especially in the presence of my parents or my sister, peeping into a midsummer night's dream carried into the daylight with me as the maiden fair, him as the answering knight, into a marriage blessed with multitudes of children. Maybe here was where I would put my sails down. And so I slept, wakened at four AM by the most horrific of visions. I "saw" Harlan and his rotten wife Helene as plain as day even when I opened my eyes. Bolting half out of the bed from fear I watched them beckon me in the strange wan light that wove about them a sheet like entanglement of ectoplasmic foam. Helene crooked her finger like a witch and Harlan read from something he held in his outstretched hand, a tablet that seemed to smoke—or was it the reflection of the moonlight through the curtains that gathered up the small white "thing" in his hand in light?

In fright I blinked my eyes and, watching him, on some screen in my brain when my eyes were closed, shunting a lurid song to me, an invocation to come back to him. They were doing a chant; I just knew it. I blinked once or twice more and through clenched eyelids forced myself to see—they still appeared, working their dark mouths in unison over the word "Beelzebub." Over and over they said it. That was enough. I jumped up, straight to my feet and wide-awakeness. They were gone. I ran toward Mark's room, but stopped short in the hall and paced. That would never do; he would never understand what was happening here. And what would happen to the vision of the moon man and me and five smiling children under the arc of the rainbow on the card of the ten of cups in the Tarot? No, that would never do—never. I stayed up in the kitchen until the light came through—the daylight, no full moon's crazy wan face, but that of the smiling day—and then I slept.

I returned to my parents' house after that night excited. My sister entered the kitchen for lunch when everyone else was away—she was circumspect, snooty, distant. I looked at her, her hair done with baby pink ribbons. "What have you been up to?" I asked. "I drove around last night," she answered glumly. "Because last week was my birthday, I went to Stanford hospital and gave a present to a baby born on my birthday." She looked deadly serious, as though she had put flowers on a shrine. I had to suppress the grin that wanted to bubble up.

"How sweet," I said, knowing that's what she would expect to hear from her parents who regarded her as "generous".

"You saw Mark," she inquired, still sullen, looking away.

"Yes, I did, Susan. And he's really nice. Thank you for—"

She stood up.

I knew what the matter was; or thought I did. But how could that be? He'd only been presented to me as Susan's nice teacher. Oh, nuts. He had said at breakfast, as if feeling guilty, or to emphasize something to himself, "Your sister Susan's quite special." In her baby blue and pink bows and Saks Fifth Avenue camisole and blouse set with baby blue shorts with Rose's pink nail polish on her small fingers, she looked nonetheless to me, aurically black, or mottled, damp green—deep olive, with little blood red points aiming right at me.

I tried to implement what Daisy had taught. Daisy and her sister were so close. It seemed for a moment that Susan looked just like me.

"We're the same," I spoke up impulsively, "aren't we? We're sisters, Susan. Aren't we?"

Susan got up from the table in the breakfast nook, clattering the cold white-painted wrought iron chairs over the no-wax parquet floor. Then she walked out of the room, through tthe open doorway and into the living room without a word, looking at one fingernail which I guessed was chipped. Poor thing.

That night she got Mark to meet her, and, I found out later, they made out at the Stanford bell tower. I tried to stay "above it" (as Rebecca might advise) sleeping alone out in the pool house, but it was cold on the shiny linoleum floor and I could see the shadows of midsummer slip in and out of the glass door that opened out onto the patio and the quiet pool. I looked up at the gnarled oak tree that bent to touch the water—oak leaves clogged the pool filter, my father complained, and I knew one day he would tear it out. Still, its somber, quiet, shadowy strength seemed to reach into me, into the rising, too-quiet waters that bubbled up into tears as I lay alone in the dark.

There was no peace for me in Susan's home. I'd been offered a job by Amy's old foster mother—a woman she stayed with after she got pregnant in high school by her sweetheart-and I decided, lying there, to accept.

My room at the group home was small and sparsely appointed. I was to be the woman Ida Hess' Activities Director, driving teenaged girls who respectively had one foot in the more serious correction camp (prison, that is, for juveniles) and one foot in this last-chance-at-a-home home. Ida ran the home frankly, for the money. Oh, she liked the girls enough generally, but she was lonely, and had she not needed the money…I don't know.

There was one girl, Polly, who Ida did not like. The girl's only crime was that her father kicked her out of his house to marry a woman younger than herself—her mother was dead. Polly had a boyfriend, George, who was in the service, who said he'd come back and marry her: he was like her rosary, a hope against which she counted the minutes, the hours. She stroked the memories of their time together as if she were running her fingers over the fine slim glass beads her dead mother, a Roman Catholic, had given her to hang onto.

We really weren't so different, Polly and me. My sister Susan used up my hopes quickly, like the discarded Kleenexes Susan used for makeup removal and then threw about in the four-poster, ruffle-covered bedroom at the end of the house she used to receive her court. By now Mark must be a retainer of hers I thought, content to rub cocoa butter along her wide sun browned back as if he were anointing the feet of the master.

I tried to shield Polly from Ida Hess because I knew Polly was as fragile as the glass in the beads and that she could shatter without some hope.

"Let's tell George about what you've done today, Pol, I just think I will," said Ida cruelly, referring to some minor infraction of Polly's— that she'd left hair in the bathroom drain. "You lied about it Pol, you said Rita Chacon did it. I think we should write to George and tell him what kind of person you really are: that will prevent him from making a terrible mistake after all. And we don't want that—it was you who left the hair there, wasn't it Pol, and not Rita. Because that hair isn't Mexican hair—it's white hair and you know it." Her quiet voice fairly quivered with delight in reaching into Polly and turning the bones of her personality about in a way so fierce I feared the skin, the organs of Polly's inner life that somehow stayed healthy enough for the blood of her life to flow still through them, would fall in a useless heap at Ida Hess' feet.

"No," I said, affecting a false laugh for Ida. "No," I said, knowing I was the only other white girl who used that bath: "No," I lied, "it was me. I mean I." Ida gave me a quizzical look. "It was I," I continued, "but…what are a few hairs among friends?" I joked.

"Oh, all right, Page. See that you don't do it again," she twinkled wryly, with a little smile between a mock and an emblem of friendship. Although above the inmates at Ida Hess' but a step in station, I had at least the dignity of being a philosopher—Ida imagined she shared my interest in the unknown, and would talk to me for hours about her personal problems. Sometimes I would entertain Ida with my dreams of other times in which the group of girls and herself had been together.

One lifetime was in Spain. I could see it as we gathered at the table for our meal. I knew that Polly must have done something terrible to Ida because Ida hated her so. More often Ida spent these sessions asking me what I thought that grey-haired man who attended the Friday night meetings at the Campbell Hall might really think of her. Then I would have to listen politely for hours while she spun dreams to lift her out of the pool of thankless duties to which her womanhood was bent.

Still, when payday came, the $100.00 I received—besides my being allowed to have a room and eat with the rest the rationed food— came grudgingly away from Ida's hand. Once I had to ask until the next $100.00 was due, and she seemed to forget the one missed, so that I had to outline this simple event on a slip of paper while she answered the phone in the crowded master bedroom and talked for protracted periods. But she knew how much a girl was eating, down to the half dollar.

During that interminable year I dragged around there, lonely, waiting for Daisy's scattered letters to arrive. But they came—and I imagined myself her emissary, keeping high the ideal of service; understanding then that I was meeting and working out karma.

I lay on my bed one night after the girls had gone to bed, lonely. The room was very clean, and had something of the spare monastic cast I had come to like of late. The bed was smoothed out and I lay upon the cover. I had brought my sister's discarded, beat-up stereo on which I played old records of piano concertos in the absolute quiet after the enforced bedtime. At those times, I could have been alone in the house rather than with seven others on the second floor.

I thought about parallel souls just as I drifted off—Elizabeth told me that my twin soul was out of the body. That left four brothers (and four sister souls), maybe I would meet one of them, or someone. The thought of the twin soul was too delicious to allow myself, and somehow the things I really wanted never seemed to happen. So I was careful what I thought, held certain hopes back from the surface of my conscious mind like you held your breath sometimes. I lay and drifted to the almost absolutely inaudible music—except to me—I had sharp ears for the Baroque music which hung its sweet, sad strains around the room like a gossamer bandage. I supposed I was building patience, I felt so sad: I knew I was doing well, somehow, to do this, and that made me glad. I relished the romantic image of myself doing all this, so that compensated, but not really, because as the outside bushes swayed and rushed against the bottom of the window, I knew the sterile room had no love in it, no love at all; and here I was disliked as much as in my sister's house—not hated though, just avoided. And in the repelling of unlike energies there is at least the possibility of one's own peace. The delinquent girls left me alone, inside, and I served them, or tried to, from a completely different vantage point than they could understand; on the surface I just seemed like a fool to them.

I lay on the bed. Outside, the fan of moist palm leaves swished and thudded softly against the window, lulling me into a deep sleep. The little record player stopped eventually, but by then I was far out, and away from all of this. I woke up after what must have been half an hour or so. I didn't know where I was when I woke up, but was in the most wonderful kind of peace anywhere—like a silence, so like being in a colored cache of light deep within, at the center of the ocean, or borne by winged angels holding the trumpet of morning on the light winds, on the breath of just beyond here.

When I awakened, it was for a moment as if there were nothing else, no sense of self, of where I was and what must be wrong with it, nothing, no thing, just the peace.

Then I felt the warmth, lying now on my back, one hand stretched up over the edge of the bed, of the hand that held mine, tender, reassuring. Its warmth fed my body/mind and in comfort I must have lingered long until the thought of what it was brought me back suddenly and I flexed my hand and tried to grab the "hand" by checking first to see if it was real at all…and it was gone, not there. But I smiled, very happy.

Secretive at breakfast in that comfort, I might as well have been the cherished daughter of a royal house than in that place where Ida Hess rationed out the bad-for-you sugary breakfast cereal as if it were gold.

The feeling lingered long into the day, and prepared me, perhaps, for the dream I had that night, in which I flew over the outskirts of San Jose, toward the country and farms, but where you could still hear the muted roar of an occasional airplane or two. I drifted over a house in the dream, not a house, but some kind of ranch or barn, and into a young man's room. Propped up on one elbow in his narrow bed he said, "I've been in your neighborhood for a long time and I've wanted to meet you." I looked at him in the inner way one does in dreams, and knew he was 22 or 23 years old. Then we were outside going through an orchard of small trees to a tower or a well. In the deep face of the water was an old woman's face; a face that looked like Elizabeth's but was not. The youth pulled up the old lady from the well by a wooden bucket, and when she appeared he was quite deferential to her, as if he were somewhat fearful of her. Then I woke up and the dream was gone.

Was the young man in the dream he who had held my hand the night before? I didn't think so somehow. Yet each of these experiences held for me the feeling of promise, and for weeks to come, I walked around singing inside, oblivious to some of the things that had bothered me before, as though asleep and awake at the same time, as though waiting, watching for something that would surely happen.

The way I met Doug Mitchel was simple: I went back to Asilomar over Labor Day weekend, fell asleep the first night and dreamed I sat at a harpsichord in the 17th century with my younger brother. We played Scarlatti. I woke up, went to the dining hall, saw Daisy at the table sitting in the sunshine. (This time she'd flown in from Billings alone—to rendezvous, it was rumored, and tryst with the golden Atlantean "priest" she'd introduced me to that first Asilomar party night. We all knew she remembered him as her winged protector from the Barbarellian world of her Lemurian regressions). As soon as I saw her, I ran to her, refueling with the warmth of her glamour. So it wasn't until evening that I was alone long enough for an acquaintance of Elizabeth's to approach me.

"I want you to meet someone. This young fellow—well, his parents think he's quite queer—I've known his grandmother for years—I just think he's psychic, don't you see?" Maybe you can help him. She led me across the Nautilus and placed my hand in the warm, moist hand of a light brown-haired boy who looked to be 22 or so. He apologized for shaking my hand with his left, and showed me the rolled up sheet music—Scarlatti—he clutched in his right hand. That was enough for me. It hardly mattered that he sprang from his grand-mother's "cot" ranch in Hollister south of San Jose, but not so far south, I knew, that you couldn't hear an occasional plane wending its way from LA to the San Jose Airport.

"Who's that handsome man?" Daisy asked at breakfast the next day before her flight north, "I'd like to see more of him." That sealed it.

My courtship with Doug was spent at Ida Hess'. No matter. A year later we would be married, with Marshall and Jane, the young blond couple I'd met at the Campbell Hall as best man and matron of honor. Since Doug and I both had light brown hair and green eyes and medium builds, we believed we might be twin souls and easily identified with blond, six foot five inch Marshall and his look-alike bride Jane who towered even above my five feet nine inches. Marshall warmed to Doug right away and confided in him (and no one else) the few psychic experiences even he had known. Jane gave me a shower and opened her home to me as if I were a real sister. For a change I was also by my relatives, who seemed to approve of me marrying anyone at all, and indeed I was enveloped by the unusual attention others were bestowing upon me. Most significantly, the camaraderie developing between the four of us seemed to compensate for the doubts I should have had, and festive moments spent holding Doug's and Marshall's hands while one or the other of them also clasped Jane's, seemed only to lend a warmth that unified us all. It never occurred to me to ask, whom was I marrying?

Only in the dark quiet of the attic landing where I slept at Doug's grandmother's large converted barn—"The fire we had in '33 destroyed our house," she complained bitterly—did I dream disturbing dreams. Awakening from one of these dreams—about fleeing from Doug who had gone berserk and was chasing me through the Santa Cruz mountains in a long, light-colored station wagon—I found myself trying to tear the engagement ring from my finger.

By telephone Daisy encouraged me against these fears and during one trip out she made to Rebecca's, she rode me about setting the wedding date sooner and marrying on her and Art's anniversary as she and Art had done: she seemed sincere and sighted. Referring to the troubled states of mind I'd known when I'd first entered the group, Daisy told her "chickens" gathered in Rebecca's living room, "Page is none of these things when she's with him." It took me until fall to suppress my doubts. In September we were married and set out to follow Daisy at last.

To Montana! Full of hope and bright promise we set out (after waiting a day or two in record breaking heat for a bit of money Doug's grandmother had promised him; during this brief time, we decided, soberly, to stay at a motel rather than to share Marshall and Jane's king-size bed as Marshall had invited—was there no limit to his great hospitality?) The marriage remained unconsummated until two nights out of the bay area in Lovelock, Nevada; worry crept around me, but who cared, we were off! Off to fulfill the Cayce prophesies, we'd escaped suffocating temperatures—105° even at the Golden Gate

Bridge in San Francisco. Crossing the bridge, it felt as if the great earthquake might happen anytime and send the whole sickening mess behind us into the Pacific.

What a relief to hit the cool Nevada desert at night and just DRIVE. We were off to join Daisy, off to pioneer a new land that would one day, according to Cayce's readings, feed the world, would someday be a safety area. Livingston, Billings and Butte, Montana would be a portion of this area, forming a living, sacred triangle. Daisy had written to Doug and me and told us that she and Art, Amy and Stephen and a few newcomers were raising the roof off the house at the mountaintop, in the stand of trees outside Billings that she had named the Grove of Peace.

We drove up through the state of Nevada into Idaho, up the frontier like Salmon River and over the Montana border. All this was new to Doug, to be away from his home, from his grandmother—all of this was new to him.

We stopped for chili just over the border. Elk horns hung in the rustic way station and the forest hushed deep around us. We were in Montana. We cut off the road to an 115° hot sulfur spring, boiled red, breathed deep and moved on.

We stayed in a spacious motel in Helena, wildly spending the wedding gift money, the last bequest—I wished I'd known that—we'd receive from anybody. Doug watched a program about lighting put on by Montana Power and Gas. He was hypnotized by commercials, dreamed about being a real radio announcer. (To that end he'd taken mail-away announcer's courses while at his grandmother's and made her pay for lessons to improve his voice: hence the Scarlatti sheet music.) I was just as glad he was watching TV and not "doing it". His sex was an abrupt pummeling, like a little boy wrestling, and he couldn't come. Still, I was in love with being in love—he did everything I suggested and seemed to be the man my dreams had promised me at last.

When we got near Billings and the Grove of Peace—strange, I didn't suggest we stop. "No," I urged. "I have a feeling, don't you?" He thought it over. "Sure," he said, pleased with the freedom and travel and affluence we were enjoying. "Sure, let's go on." So, "psychically directed," we passed to the left of Billings and wafted our way to the west of the state, leaving Daisy and her sister—and my actual nightmares of them taking Doug from me—to the east. Finally, on the rim of the bowl of low mountains that surrounded Missoula, Montana, we paused and looked down. "I have a feeling," I said, and I did. "Me too," agreed Doug, "let's go."

Down we drove, found a little boarding house room in that small college town. Sure enough, driving out that morning for food, Doug heard an employment ad on KMTA Radio. They wanted someone for sales and a nighttime spot. Doug had hit the jackpot. He wanted to stay. We got a little house and set up housekeeping and wrote to Jane and Marshall about the land of milk and honey. Night after night I dreamed about a huge, snow-covered highway between California and Montana. The highway was beautiful and clean but truncated—its northern end silent and buried in heavy snows. I knew Jane wanted to come to Montana, but Marshall's mother held him in her iron grip. "You'd have to sell your antiques," she warned, "and if you stay put, your father can get you a good job through Mr. Manor at the cannery."

I could feel them itching to come up too.

Then Doug lost his radio sales job. It was nearing Thanksgiving and Daisy lured us to Billings for a visit. On the road from Missoula to Billings through the mystical triangle formed by the cities Edgar Cayce described, we encountered black ice on the first bridge we crossed, and skidded to the guardrail. We bought expensive chains in an all-night service station and crept on, traveling the whole way at 25–40 miles an hour. The difficulty in reaching Daisy made me wonder paradoxically if I should have been with her all along (now she emphatically wanted us with her) and was avoiding my destiny in fear for my new marriage. Finally, I dropped into an uneasy sleep in the back seat. I dreamed I was little Eva picking my way across a river of broken glass ice floes, slipping southeast and into Amy and Daisy's outstretched hands. Only at the end of the dream they reached for Doug, not me, and spirited him off.

Amy Buchanon (Taylor)

Chapter Six

After seven hours total we arrived. Daisy greeted me outside in a fur-lined coat, ice crystals clinging to her hair like delicate winter stars. "Come in." She clasped my hand.

"Twin souls," Amy murmured in awe, regarding Doug in a purple shirt and me in a matching purple knit dress. Waiting for the birth of Daisy's baby, Amy was without a man, and ran the house and looked after the six children. I could see that Amy was honestly learning humility, playing quiet accompaniment to the high notes of Daisy's flashy retreat in the north woods. People in Billings found Daisy warm, like a wood fire or a dry electric heater on high: they reached out to Daisy from past lifetimes, thawed frostbitten etheric hands over her world view. She responded and they were drawn into the circle too.

For dinner that night, we had individual acorn squashes and a ham, both basted in the sweet juices that bubbled up in Amy's mismatched baking pans. After dinner we toured the cockeyed house that spiraled upwards into three stories or more on the north side and two stories on the south. Daisy and Amy bundled up in layered shirts beneath their fake fur jackets and led us through fresh snow to the corral where Daisy tethered the horse she'd always wanted—Diamond Lady. Art, still broke and just getting by, had brought Daisy's horse and a companion steed home to her as a surprise. Delighted, Daisy renamed her Sunshine. "Pick a name for your pet that you'd like to have yourself," she had suggested to us at the classes in San Jose.

Admiring Sunshine under moonlight, I was touched when Daisy confided to me that she'd missed me when she rode Sunshine—that she'd missed a young girl to go riding with. Concerned at Daisy's cold lips, blue under the pale, white-pink lipstick still popular then, I linked my arm in hers.

"C'mon. Art will have a fire when we get back. I want to meet your new friends."

Gathered within the small new group about the fire Doug had proudly helped lay in the grate, I unleashed all my latest dreams and unraveled my thoughts and laid them like a cord of wet wood in the shiny wood catch of Daisy's understanding. Like the rest, new and old, I revered her and shone and basked in the special attention Daisy bestowed upon me here. I was one of her chickens from California, and that carried clout and emblazoned Daisy further in the glory of a reputation which had followed her all the way here in the form of these two hopeful young lovers.

Here in the Grove of Peace we felt special, specially blessed, and we were. Amy put us up in her bedroom. In tumble of comforters and homemade quilts we made love and it was almost like it should have been. Doug's quiet generosity, his goodness, whatever was good in him, came out, and we felt awfully in love and proud of it. It was good to love.

The next day, Art led Doug to the shed out back to show him the beginnings of his repair service—"Peace Grove Repair," the handmade billets read, decorated by Daisy with snowflakes and the star of new beginnings.

"You could start a branch of the business in Missoula," Daisy mused, accepting her sense that we resisted settling here just yet. Then too, I told her I'd been invited to speak over the air on KMTA Radio about Daisy and the Cayce prophesies and my beliefs, and that later in the month we would be staying with a Unity minister in Livingston as part of further proselytizing and networking these ideas.

She counseled me all afternoon and carefully helped me clear away personal debris, so that I could be a channel in the living chain. I asked her if I'd have a baby. She said, "You will—you want one." "Does that mean I'm supposed to?" I countered, inflated with a sense of biblically proportioned destiny.

"It means I know that's what you'll do, that's all."

I unloaded the contents of one disturbing dream I'd omitted from last night's fireside discussion.

"This one comes and goes, and it's really yucky," I said, borrowing one of Amy's expressions. Amy, who'd broken free from the laundry or whatever to join us, sat transfixed—a switch.

"Anyway, it's like this: I dream that I am in a temple—that part's good," I laughed nervously. "I am covered in a thin veil, thin gauzy cloths, and emerge through filmy, light-colored curtains, several layers of them, like a web. I am sitting on a little dais—that rolls—and men come to me, to learn of their fates in battle. You see, I am a dream oracle and I dream purposely for those who seek, and in this way I am a force in matters of state—"

"I don't see what's bad about that dream, Page," Amy sighed.

"Yes, I'd like one like it myself," Daisy joined.

"What's bad about it is—that I have no arms or legs. I come out on that little stool thing because I cannot stand."

Daisy sighed and stared deeply into the fireplace where a log or two burned merrily, warming the late afternoon.

"You can't help feeling the scars of an experience like that; Elizabeth says 'the scars are on your own soul'", Daisy mused, "but...but it's a beautiful dream," she brightened with Gemini cheer.

"You did your thing," Amy added significantly.

Art and Doug lumbered in through the front door laden with wood to rebuild the fire for evening.

"There were other parts of the dream, Daisy; I'd like not to talk about—about something that happened before I got to the temple.... Oh, I don't know," I brushed this aside, denying that I'd dreamed anything else, "I must have imagined the rest."

Daisy reflected. "That first part, seeing yourself as a girl dream oracle with no arms or legs—where did all of this take place?"

"In Egypt." Art's strong voice rang out behind me.

"What'd you say, honey bear?"

"I said Egypt, Daisy."

Art lowered the wood to the brass woodbin in front of the fireplace and sat down beside Amy on the couch. Doug lingered, standing, happy in Art's ambiance.

"Over the last few weeks, Daisy, I've had a dream. You know I don't dream that often, but when I do—" He lit a cigarette. His hands trembled, and his faced looked pallid—not ruddy from the cold like Doug's.

"My dream was that I had this little sister—and she had no arms or legs—" He ran the words together rapidly. "I was away at war and got home somehow and in the yard behind our house there she was, strung up in some kind of sling and these men were waiting—their turn, and..." His voice retreated deep into his throat to reemerge as an angry whisper, almost a hiss. "I ran and cut the man down who was on top of her with my knife—killed him lying on her and—" Art's face broke. "She was my sister, Daisy, only a child—my little sister—and it was...Egypt. Then I took her to the Temple." His voice broke.

I looked at Art, lifting off the rug where I'd been sitting at the fireside at Daisy's feet. "I love you Art," I cried and wrapped my arms around Daisy's honey bear, impelled to thank my protector.

We had to leave on Sunday; Doug wanted to be back Sunday night because the station manager at KMTY promised him he could at least host one all-night show weekly if he would climb up to the top of the transmitter and fix it, and Doug was eager—who knew where that could lead.

We came downstairs wistfully Sunday morning. At the door, Amy popped up behind us. "Here, this belongs to you two." She held out the painting of a young boy and girl that had hung outside her bedroom door on the cramped third floor landing.

"It's ours?"

"Yes. You are twin souls, aren't you?"

"We could be. That's very nice of you, Amy." I touched the textured surface of the framed print, touched the daisy the girl held in her hands. "I'll always keep it."

The drive back was swift, the weather bright and the road ice-free. "I know the roads were clear," Daisy stated when I called her from our little house in Missoula to thank her for our stay. "I asked for good weather for your journey." I was impressed. Afterwards, flipping through the Bible Doug had brought with him from his grandmother's, I asked it idly, "Should we go to Billings?" "Beware the woman who has built an idol in the wilderness," it warned. I clapped the volume shut and put it away.

There were many conversations back and forth during the early weeks of my pregnancy with Veronica. Daisy was having a strange series of dreams—"not dreams really," she said, "but visions, as I understand them." Now she couldn't sleep without the light on and later Art told me he'd thought she was losing her mind. Amy, only days away from delivering Daisy's baby, didn't care about the dreams, so Daisy talked to me over the phone. And across the state, hiding out from her in Missoula and becoming increasingly more ill with my pregnancy, I began to have parallel visions. Lying on my back in the dark in my heavily blanketed bed in a small, unfamiliar room, I repeatedly saw stars connected to us on earth by long threads of light. I shared these experiences with Daisy. "Yes," she mused. "Yes, that's it." That's what? I wondered.

During this time she flew to California to stay at Rebecca's and deliver a message to her other chickens. Seven years later, Marshall sarcastically told me about her trip. "She was into this 'creation' thing," he said. "She told us that in the early earth—that gal had it figured that we all had lived even before what we call the prehistoric past—there were elves and genies and imaginary worlds sort of, and we had psychic powers or something because we had been 'light beings' was the way she put it, descended from stars or something—or God, I don't know. It's hard to explain that stuff to someone in the bold light of day, but you know what I mean."

"Yes Marshall, I sure do. You don't have to explain. And I believe it too, but there's more to it than—"

"Well you don't believe that I was what she said I was, do you? She laid some story on Jane and me—that we were giants, who grabbed planes out of the sky with our huge hands. I had nightmares about that for weeks. I could feel, not just feel but see, touch, hear that time she described. I felt guilty all the time for going around crushing all these little people."

He laughed. "Have another glass of wine. Listen to me, wallowing around in this horseshit."

I also heard about the trip at the time it happened because I called Daisy the day she got back to ask her about our new friends Jane and Marshall. On the phone Daisy was caught up in the vision she'd had coming back in the plane, triggered by a real life event. Frontier Airlines was still the pioneer of the airways up here: one of the outer doors had flown off the plane, and as Daisy watched it sail past the wing she "saw" a Being of Light in the clouds.

"Oh Page, the vision was so full of promise, of hope—I just knew I had done the right thing to go down to San Jose and tell them what I've been shown. I know now that there's no turning back, that I must follow when I am called. And the amazing thing was that I wasn't afraid, and you know how petrified you'd be if a door flew off a plane you were in. As soon as I saw the Being, I knew everything would be ok, and it was. We didn't lose pressure and I was home in five minutes it seemed. There was a feeling of timelessness, as if I were lifted—can you sense it?"

I could.

"And I've been feeling that way ever since.... Oh, Jane told me to tell you her dream. She said she dreamed that she was standing in the doorway to her place and she and Marshall were all packed as if they were ready to go to join you up here in Montana. There was a rainbow just outside the doorway, a beautiful, glorious rainbow. But she and Marshall...didn't want to leave their furniture, which was all crowded high up to the ceiling. Isn't that sad, Page? Not to leave, not to follow the rainbow that calls because of things, because of furniture?"

"Yes, it's sad."

I knew Daisy must be right in her interpretation, because Marshall treasured the few pieces of antique furniture—so similar to his mother's—the couple had managed to acquire, and even the second hand couch and chairs Jane had picked up seemed of substantial importance to him, coming as he did from a family where middle class values reigned. I thought Jane might be freer from these attachments, but Jane wasn't always honest with herself and I wasn't sure.

In 1972, when the weekly radio announcer's job fell through and broke Doug's hopes, we capitulated and journeyed back to California to join Marshall and Jane. Immobilized and finally hospitalized with nausea, I had become too weak—and, responding to the severe anti-nausea drug the Missoula doctor insisted I take, too incapacitated—to consider Daisy's offer and follow my personal rainbow back to Billings. I was so ill that I had to go by plane; Doug drove alone through the mountains with all of our belongings packed into my old Mustang. When we lighted at Marshall's and Jane's they seemed delighted to take us in though neither of them understood how sick I really was.

I remember standing helplessly at the stove in Jane's kitchen while she boiled vegetables in pans with the lids off—southern style. Aware that I needed every nutrient I could retain, I tried to get her to steam the vegetables, but she was (perhaps understandably) offended, almost belligerent. Doug and I slept on a pallet in

Marshall and Jane's spare room across the upstairs hallway from their bedroom with a new king-sized bed. Doug and Marshall stayed up late on Saturday nights watching "Creature Features" and laughing. Marshall rocked vigorously in a big new colonial style chair Jane had bought for him as a surprise from the local furniture store. He rocked, unconsciously grinding the suppressed anxiety he felt over Jane's impulsive purchases into the worn, over cleaned apartment carpet beneath him. I tried to recover my health by taking the little money my father donated through some concern for my plight, to the bright new tile-roofed shopping center that had been built across the street and buying quarts of kefir to drink in the courtyard where I looked at the rainbow-colored spring flowers planted in a circle about my feet and prayed for the child within.

Doug would start some minimum wage job and Marshall would rock and urge him on at night, but Doug would lose the job, always through no fault of his own it seemed, and he grew more desperate. Still, he tried to catch the brass ring of his vocational destiny, and since Marshall had secured his own future through a job in sales at a prominent restaurant supply company owned by a man his dad knew through the cannery, Doug hung on Marshall's words in the vain hope that his friend could root him out of his hole of failures and finally advise him on how to get the one right job. Even after we managed to rent our own, smaller apartment in the same building, Doug spent most evenings with Marshall, letting Marshall pump him up for another success. I withdrew with my private struggles and sought solace by walking in the orchards that bloomed to the left side of our building. Barefoot, I carried a little canvas board and some stubby pastels with me to a spot in the dirt I liked very much. Sometimes Marshall watched me with a worried, confused look from the upstairs window of the spare room in his townhouse apartment. I didn't look up. We were worlds apart in our thinking and I knew he couldn't understand.

While I fretted over the baby to come, enmeshed within my soured and sickened body, Marshall was enthralled by his newest acquisition, an Airedale dog they'd captured as it wandered in danger on the freeway. The dog was clean—appealing enough I guess, with the personality of a teddy bear, but I feared it jumping on me in greeting and could in no way share their enthusiasm. Marshall wanted us all to take trips, which would have been wonderful had I been well, but the anxiety over the baby increased a tendency to be agoraphobic and I put a damper on all of his plans.

Marshall and I generally irritated each other. Jane was friendly towards Doug, calling him "Douglas" in a way that made me minusculey jealous, and dreaming about him, as a brother of one sort or another—a monk in one instance—it was always as a brother, or so she said. However, as nauseated and depressed as I was, when Marshall rocked in his infernal chair to emphasize right wing political points or criticism of Daisy's ideas, I sprang heavily into combat and let him have it. His already florid, Nordic Arian face would flush with blood and I really think we could have strangled each other, his size and my pregnancy aside. At those moments every muscle fiber, every physical cell it seemed, strained toward annihilation of the enemy.

Only once, when Doug was out on a Saturday to fulfill the demands of some new employer, and Jane hadn't yet returned from Oroville where she'd gone to help Brother Bill and his wife, were Marshall and I thrust together outside the arena of our disagreements.

I needed milk that day and he gave me a lift to the overpriced market he favored. Over eight months pregnant, I wore a long, Daisy-like dress in her favorite inexpensive style of a shiny lounging gown converted for outdoor wear. My long light brown hair lay fine and slightly tangled over my back, and I looked up at Marshall curiously when he insisted I buy whatever I wanted and bent over my pregnant form to swoop the half-gallon carton of milk from my hand. Doug never did that.

At the checkout stand, the clerk, a man, looked at us curiously—as if in admiration. I guessed he thought we were married, that this was Marshall's baby. Suddenly embarrassed, I drew back when Marshall brushed me when he reached to get a package of cigarettes. Then we looked at each other, and at the clerk. As he gathered up the grocery bags Marshall whistled shyly, almost painfully, but he smiled directly at the man as he led me by one silvery sleeve away from the store; and I walked lightly, despite the imbalance of my weight, as if I were ever so slightly, subliminally, protected.

By nighttime Jane had returned and I watched her brew the richly sugared iced tea she favored—"like her cracker folks in Georgia," Marshall had commented more than once, unkindly.

Then she made popcorn so that Doug and he could eat it while they watched their infernal "Creature Features". Marshall particularly annoyed me tonight, rocking, rocking, advising Doug as if he were a guru—the diva of materiality I thought—how dare he criticize Daisy. When we all, eventually—finally—said goodnight, Marshall came near me where we stood talking in the little imitation tile foyer the townhouse builders had placed near the front door. He accidentally touched me. I held my breath until he was away. Oh how he irritated me.

At the end of the long nauseated wait of the pregnancy, the baby was born in late August, a beautiful little girl who appeared perfect at first, and we got word that Daisy had left the Grove of Peace with Art and Amy and the kids, including Todd Allen, her new mystery baby.

After Todd's birth, the good feelings at the Grove of Peace would not sustain the family financially any more and they'd gone to Silver Summit on Lake Washington in Washington state for the summer. Art's mother ran an environmental camp on the lake and there they were sure to eat regularly. "That was a horrible journey," Daisy confided to me later. "I only agreed to go because Art demanded that we do things his way for a change so I told him I'd give him six months, that's all. So up to the lake we went—first in Amy's station wagon pulling a trailer, then up the last leg toward the summit on motorcycles on a one-lane road—a path—with whatever we could take and the baby strapped to us, and then, we walked." Since I'd known Daisy and Amy, most of the action had taken place when their bodies were comfortably ensconced in living room chairs; I could see that this would have been an ordeal.

She continued: "As soon as we got there, right, Art proceeds to dump all this resentment on me—about how it was my fault that he hadn't been making a living during the last few years, in the old way to which he was accustomed. I told him, 'Art, you're not succeeding because you want success in the old way, not communally and in the spirit like we've been directed.' Oh Art likes all you chickens—"there could be no doubt of that in my mind—"but...he liked to do things for me in the old traditional he-man fashion sometimes, and that just didn't work out at the Grove of Peace. For example, he bought me a stereo that Christmas after you visited, Page, and he wanted it to be mine, a symbol of his ego's achievement, I guess, to make up for doing so 'poorly'. I couldn't withhold the stereo from Amy and Stephen and whoever else happened to be living there now, could I?—I mean everything was ours in my mind, and Art couldn't see." That she said sadly.

I heard nothing more about Daisy until Rebecca stopped by our apartment one day so that I could show her the baby. Then Rebecca confided to me that they had all left Washington and settled in Utah, and that changes were in the air.

"What kind of changes?"

"Well, for one thing, Amy's got a new man."

I didn't want to seem uninterested, but somehow I knew Rebecca wasn't touching the heart of the matter. Rebecca's mysterious Madonna-like smile leaked through her lips. I was suspicious—for no reason I remembered that Rebecca was inordinately fond of Art.

"Well, enough of this. Let me see your purdy bah bee," she defeated my curiosity. I lifted Veronica from the baby carrier, unwrapped her blankets and she peeped out at Rebecca beneath sleepy eyelids. "I haven't seen you in a long time," Rebecca murmured to the infant. "I think Veronica's only problem will be that she's going to want to do things faster than her body can." She couldn't know how prophetic her words would become.

"You seem different, Rebecca, what's up?"

Rebecca demurred and stifled her Scorpio moon's excitement, but an eager smirk escaped anyway.

"You've noticed. It's really not something I can talk about now." She hung her head.

"Are you going to leave Mr. Schemansky at last?" I asked with hopeful sarcasm.

"I wish I were—I wish it were that simple. No, I think we still have some things to work out, but, we...ell, there has been someone around." "Brother Bill?" He came on to everybody; I felt sorry for his wife. "Well no, not—yeah," Rebecca answered, "I know what you mean about Bill," she broke out in a telepathically induced giggle.

"Anyway...no, it's not him and Doug should be getting home soon anyway, shouldn't he?" That inflamed my curiosity.

"Who is he, Rebecca?"

"Tune in," she whispered wickedly.

"I...don't get anything—Oh, Rebecca TELL me!"

"What do you get?" The desire to tell overcame Rebecca's usual stoic self-discipline.

"All I get is 'Todd Allen'. That doesn't make any sense."

"Yes it does," Rebecca whispered.

"Todd Allen? He's only a baby."

Rebecca retreated.

"And he's far away anyway," I went on. "You say that there's been somebody around."

"There has been somebody around. And he's been keeping me up nights." "You mean somebody as in somebody out of the body Rebecca—somebody astral?" I tried to sound respectful, but managed a disappointed "Oh," that erased the quick-rising dreams of "someone" who would lead Rebecca out of the mole's hole once and for all.

"Not exactly. You were on the right track before and I guess I have to tell you since you tuned in. Todd Allen was right...not Todd Allen, that is, but his...."

Art! Rebecca had a thing for Art, I knew, but....

"How could Art be around here when he's in Utah with Daisy?"

"He's a strong projector," she murmured, reddening. "He's been here...at night. It's been really hard not to notice. I've woken up nights with the bed shaking so hard I thought Don would wake up and—"

"You're kidding."

"I'm not. Once, when I woke up there was a big dent next to me on my side of the bed—it's real, Page, it really is!"

"I believe you."

Did I believe her? Probably. I believed that the bizarre could occur in Rebecca's apartment as nowhere else on earth.

"What are you going to do?"

"I've been feeling like I need to deal with this. Telling you, Page—right here and now I've decided to fly up there. Will you drive me to the airport late tonight after he goes to sleep?"

She didn't question whether or not she could get a flight. I waved her off at San Francisco International late that night. Rebecca's ink black hair sparkled against her fake fur jacket. Her little girls clutched her hands on the windy walk out to the plane. Her plane took off and she disappeared, winked up by the night sky.

Rebecca came back ashamed but more a woman and would not talk about the changed goings on in Utah except to say that Daisy admitted Art was ripe for an affair but that it wouldn't be with Rebecca, and that it was really the love between them, between Rebecca and Daisy, that was creating this strange situation and the new tension between them. Still, Rebecca walked with redoubled grace, and her usual Madonna's modesty was only a thin veil that separated her from red-auraed lusty yearnings that weren't quite satisfied by Daisy's insight.

"Was she pissed?"

"Daisy said when she'd met me at the airport, she 'knew'."

"Did you meet Amy's new husband?"

"I did."

"What's he like?"

"He's handsome, for one thing. They're happy, I guess, except she says 'the sexual thingie'—you know how Amy talks— needs some work. There's some past lifetime in the way, they all feel."

She made it sound like group sex, so intimately entwined their lives had become. I was envious. If some "lifetime" were in the way of Doug's and my sex problems, and if Daisy and her family all were interested in those problems, it wouldn't seem so lonely lying beside him in the dark.

"They're doing really good, really really good, they say. They've made some contacts in Utah. Art and Sam—Amy's new husband—work together, so in that way things are better. Still, I did hear Daisy say she was angry at Sam for no apparent reason. And Daisy had said that when Sam rode his motorcycle into the camp on Lake Washington this summer she'd liked him right away and thought he'd make a good husband for Amy. And when he rode down to Utah on his bike, she helped with the wedding, but she finds Sam an irritating brother-in-law—"

"Isn't Amy happy with Sam?" I asked.

"Oh, Amy seems happy to be married again and all, but something's missing there, Page."

"Maybe Amy rushed into things, who knows."

"Yeah, who knows."

Rebecca gave me their telephone number in Utah and I called on the weekend.

Amy answered. "Art and Sam and Daisy are gone fishing. I'm...watching the baby for her—I just live across the street, so it's easy." Watching the baby? That sounded odd, that she would watch the baby she had just delivered up out of her own body as a gift to Daisy and Uncle Art. Mighty strange.

"How's being married?"

"Oh, you know," she said significantly. I laughed, anxious to be in on the joke, particularly since I was so far away.

"How's sex?" I tossed.

"I have no complaints. Sam's unusual, if you get my drift—" (that was Amy the prostitute talking) "except that we don't do it—" she blurted, "and it's ok, or Daisy says it is because we're getting the spiritual thing down first. Daisy's been counseling Sam about it, trying to get to the bottom of it. It seems like there was this lifetime—Sam finally had a dream that holds the key—in which he and a group of people, women mostly, were 'tower trained' as they called it then, in the psychic. It was really a long time ago. Atlantis maybe, or Lemuria—Daisy said it could have been.

"Anyway, these people had developed psychic powers, and if they blew it and had sex with someone they didn't love, they blew up like—like a fuse!"

"Intriguing, Amy." I stifled a laugh.

We chatted about nothing, about Todd Allen, and about Veronica and said goodbye. Amy sounded wistful, held in, as if she was still pregnant and waiting, only the creative part of the inner unfoldment of pregnancy belonged to someone else and not her. As if she were disowned. And I could relate to the feeling. I was sick of arguing liberal politics against Marshall's right wing politics beneath the yellow lamplight cast by his new antique Tiffany lamp. "What a find," his mother had said. Jane dusted it every day.

A bore, I thought, content with India print bedspreads thrown over hand-me-down furniture from Doug's mother. I longed for Daisy to return, and return I knew she would.

Samuel Kingdon Castle

Chapter Seven

At last word filtered down through the waxy silences of recent weeks. "Daisy will meet you girls in Southern California at Elizabeth's New Year's Santa Maria Philosophical Round Table Conference," Rebecca announced. "I told Daisy we'd all be there, right?" she affirmed. "Daisy has some important new concepts she wants to discuss with you girls and she's bringing Sam with her," Rebecca added as though unaware of what she implied. "Daisy 'got told' Sam should meet Elizabeth—something about a reading."

Was there a new man in Daisy's life? What about Art? I wanted to meet this Sam. Waiting for the Santa Maria New Year's conference to arrive I dreamed that a tall, thin, sensitive man entered through the front door of the rustic old duplex apartment Doug and I had recently taken to have room for the baby. I knew when I awakened from the dream, that we'd loved each other in some way once—this delicate man and I—and I thought the man might be Sam. Reluctantly I continued to unpack our belongings, set up the apartment, and somnambulated through Christmas, dominated by the thought of Santa Maria.

Finally we piled into cars and embarked down Highway 5 toward Santa Maria. Marshall was excited to "blast off," to take a trip with Jane and Doug and especially me. All during my pregnancy, he'd been unable to pry me loose to try **his** style fun; he was very frustrated. I was willing to oblige him in some way—the well of our friendship seemed to run dry after Veronica was born and they had remained childless. Jane, obsessed with her desire to get pregnant, took her temperature every morning, and no one was as ebullient at just being "twin souls" anymore.

Down Highway 5, the road ebbed and flowed over the low hills in easy swirls like a silver ribbon stretched out in the morning sun. Below San Luis Obispo the atmosphere changed, as if we had rounded that strange bend in time, between the old and the new year. The road dropped us to sea level and affected winding turns, nauseating to those of us in the caravan who were stuffed into compact cars. I was sure I could sense a lower vibratory rate.

After all, we were entering the southern end of the state, closer to L.A. From Cayce earth changes predictions; I knew that L.A. was prophesied to sink into the sea even before San Francisco if ever Mt. Vesuvius in Italy, or Mt. Pele in Martinique had "the greater eruptions." Even L.A.'s dense coagulated smog was known in these circles an emblem of its potential destruction. Nearing Santa Maria I could feel a distinct difference. But was my sudden claustrophobic sinking feeling connected to my knowledge of the earth change prophesies? What was it? "It" tugged at my awareness. I ascribed it to the darkening afternoon sky. We drove. Down.

One thought intruded: I felt as if we had dropped suddenly into a strange realm where the old rules might not apply: the realm of the Lord of the Dark Face, maybe. According to Elizabeth and her co-worker, Ambrose B. Wales, certain coastal California lands were the remnants of an ancient Lemurian civilization. "Roll up the windows please, Doug. We're going down closer to sea level and I'm getting cold."

"You're cold? It's only fog. Are you coming down with something? I thought you liked fog."

Marshall and Jane's sedan lit the way to the Santa Maria Inn, its amber taillights meandering through the gloaming in a series of turns that seemed unsteady, undefined. Even though I thought I could count on Marshall's enterprising Aries sun to take charge and on his Taurus ascendant to bull ahead, watching Marshall's red taillights dip in and out of the mist I became anxious. You're just afraid because you've never been here before; I reprimanded myself.

At half past five at the first edge of the dark, we pulled off the coast highway and wound down a short stretch of road into Santa Maria proper and pulled up before the stately Santa Maria Inn, a resort from a bygone era. Marshall parked first and waited for the rest of us in front of the hotel entrance.

"Come on in," he invited us, as if it were his hotel. He led the way, taking charge, clutching Jane's heavy bags in one hand like a bouquet of balloons. Marshall was our guide but he was the last one among us to become aware of what was happening.

Of the half dozen or so marriages, ours was the only one to withstand the trip. No one can say why this happened exactly, except that Daisy was at Santa Maria that three-day weekend, and with Daisy nothing happened once but that it happened ten times over. Ten is the number of the universal law of multiplication, Daisy had taught, "as in the Bible—tenfold". Daisy was the law of multiplication incarnate.

Night fell. We waited on Daisy. She would arrive any minute, Rebecca told us. How did Rebecca know?

Jane and some of the women slipped into the hotel bar. Doug and Marshall broke from the group and wandered around the cordoned-off west wing and pilfered two matching milk glass antique lamps from one of the deserted rooms. Doug felt guilty; Marshall believed he got his due.

"The place is going to close down anyway, old man," Marshall chided Doug. "We've got some mementos here of a glorious era". All weekend, Doug was worried about someone catching up with them. Marshall's actions angered me. He was vain, materialistic and ambitious; his adventurous ideas always ended with somebody feeling uptight.

By contrast, Daisy was sure social magic. She liberated the fuddy-duddy in a situation and turned it into such fun. Oh, yes, the stakes were high in Daisy's games, but Daisy believed she was right and that we were playing to win the highest prize in creation—"Truth"—not milk glass lamps. Risks for a reason, not for personal greed: that was Daisy's creed.

The hotel seemed carpeted on every surface, warm, old, linty and hushed. It swallowed up secret voices; Marshall and Doug going after another memento? I couldn't hear exactly. I couldn't hear Jane's voice either when she left the bar to get something from her room, bent in conversation over a thin, dark-haired woman who looked drunker than one should be at a spiritual happening.

Perhaps I should have listened more closely. Seven of the eleven women at Santa Maria left their husbands immediately after the first of the year, the remaining three followed—the last of these had an interlocutory decree in May.

I waited alone in the softly lit, red velvet hotel lobby on a settee of burnished walnut with gold brocade, waited for Daisy and my next step.

Elizabeth arrived before Daisy, bubbling, glad to see us "darlings," oblivious to the strain in the air. She asked us to sit quietly for the musical interlude and the opening invocations to this intimate Round Table—there could not have been fifty people in all. We did as she asked; Jane, Vicky and her cute, upturned-nose protégé Kelly, Cassandra, Rebecca and the rest listened to the announcements of the schedule for the informal program and to Elizabeth's lawful words on karma and the purposeful life lived "here a little, there a little, with the Christ ideal in mind." The sweet musical strains and Elizabeth's words flowed about us and comforted us. For a moment, our lives seemed all right—we could live them a day at a time. Jane smiled at the impervious Marshall, I squeezed Doug's hand. Never mind that it was the hand of a younger brother, we could set things to right in our lives indeed if we only tried....

Enter Daisy. From the moment we laid eyes on her, the humble presents from Elizabeth's wisdom seemed plain and compact. Daisy's whisper—"Wait 'til the first break, chickens, we must talk"—spelled Spirit elaborately trimmed.

At the break we abandoned Ambrose Wales' Edgar Cayce's Earth Changes lecture and crowded into the bar.

"First of all, there's someone I want you all to meet. He's showering—that was a long bus ride." Daisy, on a bus? She wore a British mod cap too and was a full thirty pounds lighter with curly golden cropped hair. Her blue eyes blazed through the cigarette smoke that rose from the tabletop.

"I've learned something valuable I must share with you all." Daisy synthesized and universalized her experiences, her found truths, by passing them on tenfold.

"What I've discovered is simply this: when we become 'spiritual' we seek to give and give, to live according to an idea of service and we often renounce in ourselves those things we consider not to be serviceable, not spiritual."

She twiddled with the brim of her jaunty cap. "What I need to say to you now is that—at a certain point—that is not the way, not the only way, not even the best way.

"At a certain point you must be willing to follow Spirit wherever it leads you, into whatever hidden parts of your nature, as it seeks to fulfill itself through the desires of your heart.

"Sometimes that means saying 'no' to things you might have said 'yes' to because you thought you should, and sometimes that means saying 'yes'...."

She took the cap off, laid it on the table and looked into its depths.

Vicky boomed ungraciously, "Does this mean you're leaving Art for what's-his-name up there?"

Boy, I wouldn't have said it, it never would have occurred to me to—I wouldn't have dared to say it—but we were all wondering the same thing.

Daisy ignored her question. "What's he like?" Cassandra inquired practically. "Do we get to meet him?"

Boy, were they missing the point. I agreed with the look on Daisy's face—how banal. ("You have more than all those girls put together," she had confided to me in Billings.) I focused on Daisy's new truth, letting the words sift through my thought processes for greater understanding. Still, I was curious.

"Sure, all you girls can meet him if you want. He'll be down in a few minutes." She put her arm around Vicky's shoulder. "Nice to see you again, honey." Disarmed, Vicky and the others dissolved into easy conversation.

At eight o'clock the door to the bar swung open. It was such a disappointment. I had expected to see a man of men and maybe someone who would like me. Instead, a sullen, swarthy, full-bodied man uttered "Hi" from deep in his throat and then nothing else.

Daisy rose and extended her hand to him and Vicky bounded between them. "This is Vicky, Sam." Vicky and Daisy were about the same height, but I thought Vicky had to look way, way up. For a moment, Sam's obscure, heavy-lidded gaze met Vicky's. Then he turned, and opened his arms to Daisy. She stepped inside them. For once, Vicky's booming voice was silenced. The chickens crowded around.

"Sweet man of my heart," she spoke against his tanned cheek, "this is Cassandra, Page, Jane...."

Collectively, we fell in love. Not that any one of us liked him first off. At half past eight Sam said "I'm tired. Let's go upstairs for awhile."

"Yes," Daisy answered him with a casual, secret smile.

We followed them out of the bar to the foot of the massive, red-carpeted, oaken stairway that led from the lobby to the second floor landing. No one dared follow from there on. The bell bottoms of Daisy's black cotton pants embroidered all the way down with green leaves entwined around little yellow daisies were the last sight I saw.

"Where are they staying?" Cassandra whispered to Jane. "Marshall says that they have the only room left in the wing that's cordoned off," Jane replied. How they got that room I didn't know. Doug's and my room was at the end of a hallway of rooms that formed an "L" with the mysterious wing in question.

Awake with the baby at three a.m., I opened the door a bit to express excess heat from the radiator into the hallway so that she could sleep. Rocking her in the dark, I watched transfixed as moments later, Daisy swept naked past my room into the bathroom at the end of the hallway and across from our room. She reemerged in a flash and ran back. Her hair curled tight around her head as though damp. Boy. I guess she was the hippie now. I heard a tinkle of laughter, then a heavy door closing. I was left there to speculate. No one knows anything, I thought, unless they are there to feel the embrace. In it two people emerge as their true selves. I thought that if we had been with them we would have been surprised.

By morning, however, I had returned to my original doubts about what that pool hustler—that's what Amy had said he'd done before they met him—wanted with Daisy.

I went to breakfast in the cafeteria across the street from the hotel while Doug took care of the baby. Groggy, but on time, I pulled up a chair. Daisy was ready for the day, and peered over her egg and juice and toast keenly into Vicky, Cassandra, Jane and all the faithful through her puffy, powder blue, eye shadowed eyes. Sam's eyes were blue too, but paler than Daisy's, washed out. His body, I grudgingly admitted, was broad and muscular. And his cool, white-sky, clouded blue eyes looked out of a comely, masculine face: his square jaw, broad neck, trim nose and black, curly hair made him look less than swarthy in the morning light.

Daisy, less her thirty-five pounds, was beautiful. With pert nose, forward-cast jaw, deep blue eyes and strawberry blond curly hair cut in a wispy shag, she was not the hard madam anymore, but a bright child off to see the wizard.

She still held her little finger aloft to lift her juice and coffee in the overly delicate gesture characteristic of the plump dumpling she had been who was afraid to show her weakness for food in public. This time there was no need to restrain herself, I thought.

At last she lit a cigarette. At that signal, Vicky pushed Daisy's plate aside and plopped her dream notebook in its place, folding it open to one page covered with large dark handwriting.

"I'll talk to you about this one later," Daisy murmured to Vicky after she scanned the page.

"Pardon me," I addressed Sam, who had turned his chair around and straddled it, facing the table from Daisy's left. "Pardon me, but I think I dreamed about you—that I knew you before." My heart pounded. Sorry at once, I hoped for someone to speak. Jane sensed my discomfort and asked after Todd Allen and the children still in Utah with Amy and their Uncle Art. That question was designed to throw them off guard, because it didn't look too good to any of us chickens that Amy and Art kept house in Utah for seven kids while Daisy and Sam basked in the admiring light from eleven pairs of eyes here in the dining room at the Santa Maria Inn. Daisy and Sam laughed with nervous bravado.

"Well, I doubt anyone's missing us—the children that is—" she fumbled, flicking the index and middle fingers of her right hand rapidly one against the other. "Todd Allen calls Amy 'Mommy' too, of course, and she and Art are used to dealing with seven kids you know, I mean that's how it's been ever since Montana."

If I were she, I would have laughed—maybe—but I would have been ashamed and confessed my embarrassment, my qualms, my guilt, to the circle of inquiring eyes. But not Daisy.

Softly she recounted their story in the tone one reserves to tell a young child a Bible story illustrating the divine destiny of the chosen people—the true story of why she "had" to leave Art and come here to bring Sam to see Elizabeth.

"It started in the Grove of Peace," she began softly to recount the story of the stereo Art had bought for her at Christmas time and how he wanted it to be hers. She told the girls how Amy and Stephen and the others there were a family in spirit, how nothing could be part of one person without belonging to each and every other one, and how Art didn't understand this. At this point in the telling, Daisy and Sam looked at each other sadly, and sighed for Art. "I mean Art put me through hell. He said I was going crazy.

"And it was crazy, being there with him while he was trying to be 'earth man' and live up to that old, earth-male image—while I was giving things away and releasing possessions to the universe—to God." I remembered how in Billings Art told Doug and me that Daisy had pleaded with him to buy her an elephant after she succeeded in getting him to buy her the horse, Sunshine. She'd needed an elephant, she'd pleaded; to recreate the consciousness of the Indian lifetime she'd spent with Krishna. Never mind thinking about that now, I chided myself. Daisy didn't mention the elephant here in the cafeteria across from the Santa Maria Inn, so it must not be right to talk about it—not in the energy at all.

When Daisy was done with the story about Art's limitations, we were all more or less convinced she was right, and too excited to dwell on inconsistencies. Sensing this, she moved swiftly to a known chatterbox.

"Well, chicken," she asked me, "what have you got to report about San Jose?"

"Not too much." I shaded my eyes. Then Daisy would know I had a few things to tell her about people who were here and then I could get together alone with her later.

Daisy maintained her "mother hen" policy to the end and always needed deputy hens to keep tabs. When she wanted something done, she usually sent an emissary to the lucky recipient of her concern. It was unnerving. What could anybody say when Daisy sent a right hand—wing—usually Amy or Rebecca, to tell you off, or to honor you with some token? What could you say when you couldn't say it to Daisy directly? Although frustrating for you, this system tended to enhance Daisy's significance.

Your next achievement, you inwardly swore, would earn you an audience. So your next act of service was bigger and better. And if you were not good at noble acts, your next faux pas was certainly a doozey. (Art, for example, later got into the habit of these negative, attention-getting acts until one day he woke up and removed himself and the boys 700 miles away from Daisy's presence, never to return.)

Now the other women cut over me disdainfully, thus lured into direct personal revelation. And revelations they were. One by one they "confessed" that they had been planning to tell Daisy they were leaving Marshall, Don, Herman, Christopher or Scott, after the holidays, or at least early after the new year. This was all news to me and news I couldn't even have hinted at to Daisy in the private session I hoped would follow. With the exception of Rebecca, I wasn't aware of any dissatisfaction much greater than average levels of boredom, in any of these marriages shortly to dissolve.

Never mind that. Daisy was apparently aware of the real truth, because her wide public eyes were fixed knowingly on Sam, who fed back her latest line in syncopated time.

"Yes, girls," she elaborated, "you get to a certain point on the path where you must follow spirit, follow your heart wherever it leads you, must do what's right no matter how it appears, no matter how others may view you. Sometimes you may even appear selfish. You discover your allegiance is to spirit," she reiterated, toying with a bit of leftover toast on the pushed-aside plate.

"Yeah," Sam came in, "Spirit is all you live for, for that truth is wider than whatever you came from, and that carries you to a next step and…it's like an adventure, a game, with rules you only find out as you go along. It's all right," he rattled, interrupting to use a toothpick on his teeth. As I glanced away disdainfully from that disturbing gesture of punctuation, I noticed Daisy's feet. Her sandals had slipped off and she wriggled her toes idly against Sam's ankle, caressing his instep and his shoe in time to each overly enthusiastic word he spoke.

That made me mad.

"I'm sorry Daisy, but I have a lot of questions; a lot of things just keep running through my mind."

"That started a long time before I entered the scene," Daisy retorted, not looking at me very deliberately. "I didn't get you going." Vicky tittered. I wanted to complain that the new concepts were not as simple as the old—that it wasn't clear anymore—but her answer and the laughter that followed all around shut me up. Reeling with the coldness imparted along with her answer, I knew I'd met the new Daisy.

"Who wants to go see Elizabeth with us?" Daisy inquired distantly. (Who was Elizabeth?) Uncertainly, we rose as one and wobbled along behind them from the cafeteria back into the hotel across the street, where Elizabeth, equally fascinated and ever polite, managed to break away from the conference to give Sam a "private" reading in our presence, where she pronounced him— looking into Daisy's eyes—a reincarnation of the poet Percy

Bysshe Shelley. "I knew it," Daisy sighed with satisfaction. Later, however, Elizabeth remonstrated me sadly. "I hope you won't leave Cayce, dear—promise me you won't." Elizabeth believed Cayce was the world teacher for our age, spokesperson of a timeless "Christ" attitude that ran like a thread through all the great religions of the earth. "I hope you won't leave Cayce, dear," she repeated. For a moment I was a little shaken.

After the Santa Maria conference, Doug and I watched in horror as Marshall and Jane separated. Why? We remembered an incident that had occurred the summer before, something that we'd pushed out of our minds. When Jane was away on a brief weekend trip to Oroville to see Rebecca, who was spending some time near Brother Bill's "city" (to be near Brother Bill?), she told Rebecca that she had a premonition that Marshall, who resented her involvement with the local meetings and even more a trip such as this, might take his revenge by being disloyal in some way. "Let him get it out of his system," Rebecca advised.

Left at home at the apartment building where we all lived then, we were privy to Marshall's plans to invite two groupie girls from the meetings by to talk. "Renee has problems," he announced to Doug, "and she's bringing her girlfriend too—maybe we can help them out. What do you say, buddy?"

I waited for Doug at the upstairs window of our apartment that looked into Marshall and Jane's bedroom where the drapes were pulled shut. Doug returned quickly. "I told Marshall I had to get going, and suggested we call it a night—I think those girls wanted something else from him," Doug reported. Marshall told Doug the girls would leave, but Doug joined me at the window anyway in worry. The light in the bedroom was turned out once, and then on again, and after an hour or two we decided that Doug would go back over. I followed him shortly, too restless to wait behind.

There I found Marshall rocking frantically in his living room, pallid and remote and highly talkative. The girl was gone. "What would I want with a little runt like that," he announced after I voiced my concerns, "when I've got a big beautiful woman like Jane."

When Jane returned from Oroville that Sunday night, she opened the door, stood silently in the fake foyer for a moment and called to Marshall who bounded down the stairway that led from the bedrooms, "Marshall, change the sheets." ("You're a psychic detective," Elizabeth once told her.) Afterwards Jane asked Marshall to be truthful with her and he denied vehemently that anything at all had occurred. Somehow, talk about the incident ceased and things seemed to be all right, except that Jane was consumed with the desire to have a child, and that she spent money with heightened Sagitarian impulsiveness, and that the purity of twin purposes, the sparkle of geniality and hospitality that had quickened their home was dimmed, and even the flurry of expensive Christmas ornaments and tinsels that adorned their apartment that holiday season, could not give back the brightness.

Then this must be why they were breaking up, while we tried impotently to interfere. I was confused, because Cassandra and Christopher, Vicky and quiet, mind-his-own-business Herman, Kelly and Scott, Lurine and Brother Bill, Rebecca and her mole Don…all the couples in Daisy's radius were collapsing into the dust of dissolution, whirling in individualized sufferings and confusion like hypnotized dervish dancers. The eventual suffering in the wake of Daisy's grand pronouncement was so great that some loyal members were permanently lost from the group. Cassandra, for example, retreated from Daisy after she lost her beloved only child to her husband's kidnapping attempt—she discovered that Christopher had kept diaries concerning her activities in the occult over several months before their break up, only to present the diaries in court to secure custody of their son. Lurine and Brother Bill, as well as Vicky and Herman, were casualties of this wave of relationship rearrange; but Lurine and Herman, who I thought were hapless victims, made out surprisingly well. To this day, remarried to each other, they live in quiet oblivion, hidden somewhere out on the outer rings of the suburban sprawl of San Jose, which has eaten away the orchards that still bloomed in the spring of 1973.

Cassandra Stevens

Chapter Eight

A curtain of grey rain separated the villa on the Lake of Geneva from the mountains. Daisy—was it Daisy—and I wrote poetry by gaslight. The scene shifted. She asked me, "Why did you marry Doug?" I answered, "Because it was the thing to do; but I always loved you, Daisy, and I still do." Closeted in the duplex, caught up in daily routine, I began to dream dreams like this one that might be about Sam's lifetime as Percy Bysshe Shelley—the lifetime that Elizabeth had "given" him.

Daisy reminded me over the phone from Rebecca's, "Remember, chicken, Elizabeth wrote that when you are dreaming of a past lifetime, it always has a relevance to today." I called her there at least once a day when she would answer—Sam had begun to shield her from our calls. When I called on a Saturday afternoon after they'd stayed with Rebecca and the mole only one full week, Daisy told me—to my jubilation—that she'd "got told" she would be spending some time with us. I scarcely dared to ask her if that meant she'd actually be staying with us—it did.

I relished the company. Jane and Marshall, divorcing each other, were alienated from Doug and me. We were sailing along rather acceptably as sister and brother sharing the romance of a first baby.

By Sunday night, we'd put Veronica in our room and Daisy and Sam were ensconced in her room. On Monday morning, Daisy awakened before I did to let Stephen, the first of her visiting entourage, in through the front door at 6 a.m. Now she lay blissfully in a khaki sleeping bag on the floor part beneath Veronica's crib with her great new love, Samuel Kingdon Castle, who was still asleep, while Stephen, young, blond, gay and saucy, sat cross-legged beside her on the floor and chain-smoked. I remembered how she'd confided in Montana she'd "go green" sometimes when Stephen walked up behind her in the kitchen and touched her shoulder to see what was cooking. When did I hear she'd had to get him drunk in order to sleep with him and get it out of her system?

Winter light streamed through the now opened curtains. After an hour Sam got up to make coffee. By this time I waited, deeply curious, folding diapers in the living room. I overheard laughter, felt "full," complete, nervous. She was in my house.

On the third night I dreamed she slept with my husband. It was long, lingering, passionate. Or was Doug me? I was afraid. I smiled up at Sam when he passed me that morning with the coffee. I wished they would leave. When she said later that day, "We make a nice family, don't you think?" I smiled through tight lips, wanted to say something but much more wanted her to go. Then she said it again, unusual for her to repeat herself, looking up at me from the wash she was helping to fold.

Sam complained later, "You even had us help you with the housework." I resented that. Why shouldn't he help me. Stephen parked his ashtray on the old, rich brown piano in the living room. The ashtray spewed irregular white burning clouds at the baby lying on her back in her playpen beside him. I feared the smoke would hurt her, read somewhere it could. I love you, Daisy, I thought, in between being paranoid about her. She entertained people all day. It was always purposeful. I folded. She helped me. Zipporah, a Jewish friend of mine from Palo Alto, showed up with her sister and a friend.

She and her friend sang "follow the yellow brick road" up to the duplex door left open for the smoke in this wettest of winters. Zipporah stepped over the rain filled gravel-rimmed chuckhole in the driveway to protect her odd slipper like shoes. Daisy gave her a reading: "You will always be different—the way you dress, your friends. You're an intuitive, not a psychic. The intuitive path is the closer...to the heart." After the reading, I asked Daisy if I were intuitive. She said that I was psychic. She said it didn't matter; it was just different. "But I follow my heart too," I said, wanting desperately to be an intuitive today.

"You pick up on people, on world events, right, chicken? You know what I mean." I felt silly, big, dumb, awkward, abashed. "You know what I mean," she consoled. I backed down, quietly folded more diapers. Daisy read for Zipporah's sister and for her friend. During the readings I sat transfixed. Right, right. That's a hit. My pride in introducing Daisy to my friends outweighed my jealousy and confusion. Zipporah, answering some unspoken invitation, followed Daisy into the bathroom after the readings. "Bring me a Tampax, sweetheart," Daisy called softly to me. I delivered it and lingered, listening at the door.

"I've had three children and I still use 'Regular'." Later Tippie, as Daisy nicknamed her, told me Daisy had invited her to meet her for a weekend in San Francisco. I couldn't quite believe Tippie then, although certain possibilities had crossed my mind. (Since North Redwood Street I'd learned that Daisy wanted to sleep with a lovely young housewife next door to her there—only the woman's husband wanted to watch. But nothing had ever happened. The man's attitude had disgusted her utterly.)

"You're the one with a figure, even with your weight up." We stood side by side; streaming wet, in the partition less showers at Jack LaLanne.

I beamed inside, so worried that I was fat after Veronica's birth.

In the steam I couldn't see her, just a curl of light, reddish brown hair between the legs.

At home we folded diapers again—she helped me as if this were her house, got me working at a swift pace, and we talked about things, talked things over.

That night Sam brought home a great sausage. Had he hustled the money for it playing pool? I didn't know, accepting it with the grace a disciple might have, his meal of leeks and boiled rice and fish on that last night. Again rain pummeled the little duplex, pelleted its tar roof, dropped from the leaves of the tall tree in the sideways half-yard of grass near the street, then collected and coursed over the roof and down the gutters. I straightened up Veronica's crib in the room where they slept, and saw their blankets neatly folded under the Tarot poster of the sun on the wall beside the crib. They still slept each night on a rug I'd swiped from the garbage bin at the edge of the lot between C & C Carpets and the Jack LaLanne health club for which I'd stretched our money so unmercifully. Stephen came in mornings, let himself in now and left late, late at night.

Then Sam and Daisy made love; separated from them by three feet of hardwood floor between thin bedroom doors, the almost painful sounds she made carried. The rain streamed over the little house, over Doug and me. We made love too, although we didn't do it much on our own. I had cried out a couple times, weak, tried it out. Now we were singing together, like rain, a love song of four, a concert of dripping tree onto tarpaper, cooing baby, steaming noodles and sputtering sausage.

"Come in, it's ready." I had some sour cream. Daisy found an onion in the cupboard. "Wait. Let's chop it up and make some dips for the chips Sam got."

"Should I? I can't, I'll be fat."

"That's all good food. You're nursing a baby, sweetheart."

We licked the fresh onion and sour cream off the chips, ate the hot pork and pasta (I pushed from my mind Edgar Cayce's warnings about pork).

It was delicious. It savored of Sam, of bike wandering, of pool and the low-slung British rock hats he wore, of his hand that wandered up and down Daisy's back during the meal, as though to wipe from it the ache created in doing the biddings of the faithful—hitchhiking to the shelter for strays across town run by an old man who rubbed feet to heal, "reading" for the seekers who flowed up my walkway like the rain, and for the affluent who invited her by their places. She'd return from those "readings" later with five, then, fifteen, sometimes, twenty-five dollars stuck tucked in one of the embroidered breast pockets of her pale denim jacket, and wrappers from a fast food place stuffed in the other. She didn't bother us for food. They slept on their jackets for pillows until I realized it and gave them one of ours.

Tonight was a treat, like the sounds of their lovemaking under the door—forbidden and private, like premature spring blossoms lighting on the rain soaked housetop, something you should forget but couldn't.

After dinner Stephen came and tinkled the old piano.

"Please play 'Over the Rainbow'", Daisy requested. "I tried doing what you taught me, but it just won't work yet...I know I can, I've played piano in other lifetimes, but my fingers won't translate my thoughts. Stephen, please."

Stephen played the introduction slowly like rain tinkling down the gutter outside the front door. His cigarette streamed white smoke upwards towards the stucco ceiling that looked amber above the low lamp light. (We couldn't afford much of anything then.)

"Somewhere," he began, "over the rainbow..."

Daisy looked up with the rapturous look of a child thinking "I can do it," like the little baby in its bed who would grow up to be handicapped—smiling, with the most beautiful face, cooing—in the smoke and everything—rapturously at Daisy; in her first year, nothing more than a beautiful baby.

"There's a place that I dreamed of—once—in a lullaby..."

I looked into the baby's eyes, full of pride, worried about the smoke, walked over and picked her up and rocked her from side to side on the edge of the falling-down couch. She grinned up at me. Nothing could hurt this baby. Not smoke, not pork—would the onions I had eaten bother her?

Her eyes, wide and new at six months, the color of a marble with threads of green and brown and blue running through round glass; new, yes, still blue about the iris, as if she had not fully entered her body—a bright baby, I thought, the brightest baby lay at my breast and drank milk. "Somewhere..."

Daisy smiled at me, Doug puttered, glued back the turreted walnut edge of his grandmother's old clock and genially placed the clock on top of the piano where it toppled over again when Stephen played.

"We make a nice family, don't we Page?" she asked again, her eyes still on me.

"Page, sweetheart?" I couldn't answer. Like a dummy, like a horrible fool, I looked down, wanting to, but afraid I would lose Doug in the cosmic relationship rearrange, afraid that she would take him from me somehow. I said nothing, though the words started up from my throat again and again. All the years of inbred middleclass death trampled over my feelings as I looked into her eyes. I rose to change Veronica.

"You're wet, baby," I said, trying to sound casual and as though too absorbed to answer Daisy. But I was a phony and I knew it.

The next day when Daisy called Art and Amy and told them about the new girl she'd met, "Zipporah—I've nicknamed her Tippie," and how she might stay with them all, I longed to be the one she was speaking about.

Later when Daisy talked for an hour to Amy, it became startlingly clear to me that she really did plan to go back to Art. Feeling terribly sorry for him, knowing what I did about Daisy and Sam and the bedroom and all, I interrupted them to suggest, to ask

Daisy "Why? Why are you doing it?" Sure enough by now to be ready to make a decision, Daisy replied thoughtfully to Amy, "She's really got me. That's the first time Page has ever 'nailed' one of us. Why am I going back to Art?" Oh sure, I knew Daisy had talked nobly about going back and "being all you are at each moment with each one you love—physically, spiritually, living at the razor's edge—"but I didn't think she really should go back, as Art would be the one living at the razor's edge, because he really loved Daisy—of that one thing I was certain.

Amy confessed to me over the telephone that she'd tuned into the realization that it was Daisy she loved all the time and that the marriage to Sam was just that, a living expression of her love for Daisy and of her sense that her sister felt it was the right thing for her to do. Years and years later, Amy told me, "That's how I got into all of this in the first place. Daisy had a belief and I loved her and decided to support her belief." Amy would fare all right being back with Daisy again, even if Daisy was sleeping with her husband, but it was Uncle Art I was really worried about. "Why don't you and Art pack up and get ready to move out here," Daisy concluded the call. "I think it's time."

The next day she greeted me early, "Good morning."

"What are we going to do today?"

"We have to be going, chicken. I dreamed it. Will you drive us out to the highway where we can hitch a ride?"

"Sure," I answered with a pang, "I'll drive you out, but where are you going, Daisy?"

Sam came out of the bathroom with a towel wrapped about him.

It was raining lightly and the windows of the house were steamed up. Inside it was as warm as Daisy's Montana fur collar coat.

As though she'd read my thoughts she asked, "Mind if we leave a few things here in the garage?"

"Oh no, I don't," I said with relief. "I'd rather you did that than…be bothered moving them somewhere else."

"But where are you going?"

Daisy caught Sam's wide, muscled arm.

"We're off to see the wizard, aren't we, Samuel Castle?"

He looked down into her eyes, his dark wavy hair damp, and curled about him in the manner of a Grecian or a Persian statue.

(Was this the man I had last night dreamed to murmur distorted words in her ear?)

"Yes, Daisy Forrest. We're off to see the wizard indeed."

She looked at him and talked into his ear in her whisper soft voice. I backed away, around the living room corner into the kitchen that seemed drab and stacked with dirty dishes in her pending absence.

"When will you be coming back?" I called to them, feeling helpless and lonely as the sun that pouted back, beyond and over the house, sullen on a day when everybody preferred rain.

"We'll come back after we reach the rainbow's end, right darling?" Sam asked her. His tenderness washed through the room in which they stood and enveloped my imagination. I peeped out, infinitely enthralled and curious.

"You are the rainbow's end to me, Daisy," Sam said. "You know that, don't you?"

"You are to me, Sam, but you must be willing to surrender to Spirit that which you love the most. I've surrendered you," she murmured. "I must—every day—that's the only way to have anything, Sam, to keep it fresh and living."

"I don't know that I could stand surrendering you to Spirit, Daisy…anything but you."

"You just haven't loved anybody this much before, have you, Sam?"

Sam left his filled notebooks behind and I moved them into the garage. I opened and read one, just one paragraph. He always wrote out odd ideas and drew decorative patterns as though weaving a web around his life, as though interpreting the design of his life and dropping it from him like a warm cloak down on summer's dewy grass. He was a Renaissance man, poetic and full of contradictions, street-wise and tender at the same time. I wondered when I read his inspired treatises after they left, read just the part the notebook fell open to: "And our truth shall be lik\e an umbrella to shade them—we will shelter them in the circle of its purity, and they shall stand free before the elements within the nimbus of our love." I wondered if he had indeed been the poet Shelley, the way Elizabeth attuned. Later, standing there in the dim light of the garage and missing him a little, somehow I knew it was true.

As I drove them to the intersection of Highway 101 and the antediluvian, uncompleted, amputated hand of the freeway slated to one day become 680, I had tears behind my eyes. Daisy's eyes were as far away and beautiful as I'd ever seen them. They were so soft and glimmering, so pale and translucent, their softness eclipsed the overcast background of the sky with the sun peeping now insouciantly through its folds. She wore the light blue denim jacket that she'd embroidered, a faded denim cap and a loose shiny blouse cut down into her cleavage. She clutched her purse casually in her hand. Her new hair was cut short with rosy blonde waves and blew as free and easily as the two of them would down the yellow brick road. I had her few things—I hoped she would return to me for them—and I had the pair of black embroidered pants she'd outgrown to these smaller-for-her-slimmer-body jeans. She smiled, wan and perfect and mysterious—was she thinking I wished I were her?— and Sam wrapped a dark, leather-jacketed arm about her and held her to him. But her eyes weren't on him, they were on the road and on the sky, and she looked through me when I said goodbye and then stepped out. It seemed inappropriate to linger until they were picked up.

"Goodbye, Daisy," I said. "Until we meet again, huh?" She wouldn't tell me how long that would be. They were both outside the car now, facing slightly away in the direction they were headed.

Cars whizzed by and I thought she couldn't hear me.

I started the engine, forcing myself to leave for home. In the split second before I pulled the car around, when it was too late to turn back, she called over the noise of the engine, through the wind, "Keep dreaming, Page, and dream of me. There is no separation—don't forget what you really know—dreams are tomorrow's memories."

Later that spring, Daisy reappeared in San Jose with Art, Amy and all the children. "Ring the living bell," rang the stereo in the living room of the rental house that was available the hour they'd arrived. Daisy twirled around twice in front of the stereo barefoot, arms outstretched, head up, rocking from side to side, facing out the plate glass window in the house Art and Amy shared with all the kids. It was the household just as she and Sam left it to run off together to California, transported, transplanted; only now Daisy and Sam were sleeping together and staying in the garage.

I thought it must be right and admired Art, surprised that anyone could handle this. Now, the first time I'd visited them since they'd arrived, I saw the hole in the hall leading to his bedroom, where he had put his hand clear through.

Sam padded in through the open back door. Flies buzzed in the busy, light room. The boys, Art Jr., Benjamin, Davy, and Todd Allen (and Amy's Jimmy and Robin) played in the back yard. I could hear Benjamin scream "Dad!" I knew he resented Art Jr., the oldest. Davy seemed happy to be seeing his mother again every day. He walked back and forth three times to get another color crayon to sketch a picture of the old dog Tag for his mother. From the hallway leading from Art's room to the boys' bedrooms and Amy and her daughter Sissy's shared bedroom, I could see all the action in the house. Art had asked me to keep the little boys out of the back of the house while he went out and got a mop and some Spic 'N Span. His cleaning stuff had been lost in the move and he wanted the hardwood floors in the bedroom mopped up at least, maybe polished before Daisy's first return-to-the-area class would start at eight tonight. There would be mostly friends present, friends who understood, but everyone who knew Daisy was a friend it seemed, and everyone understood and most had followed suit, surrendering to new relationships.

In the living room Daisy and Sam didn't seem to see me, or didn't care that I stood in the hallway behind them. Todd Allen started toddling through the living room and I almost called out, but Daisy, sensing him, swung around and pulled him to Sam.

"How's it feel to see your son?" she murmured at Sam's breast looking up into his eyes. That thrilled me. I looked at Todd, golden highlights glinting off his dark, curly hair. Todd tilted his head back to look up at his new daddy, Sam. Sam smiled that elusive, mostly mental, affable smile he now had and swung Todd up into his arms, curly head against curly head. It seemed plausible to me, a romantic, that Todd had been born for Sam, that they belonged together after all.

I never would have thought that they would keep him a year or two or three and then lose interest when their own child was born, or that Daisy wouldn't even appear in court when Art finally sued for custody of all four boys she'd left with him. I never would have thought it watching them, because I believed what Daisy was telling us; that destiny was at work, that Spirit was directing her to

Sam. I thought that everything would fall in place again soon, and be as it had been, only better.

How earthy and limited Daisy would have deemed my sentiments had she heard my thoughts. I should have known that Daisy, a changeling, really a child of the universe as she gaily professed, and ultimately the child of change itself, couldn't still the dance of life she saw all around her.

"Ring the living bell," she sang along with the record on that historic stereo in her whisper voice. She, Sam and the boy looked out on the quiet little suburban street as if it were the gateway to the Nile, to the conquest of strange worlds afar.

During the next few weeks, Daisy lived true to her new creed—to be all that you are honestly to each person you are with—and Art punched more holes in the wall. All were glad when the leaflet came from Elizabeth and Ambrose B. in southern California, announcing the next conference and inviting us to participate in a play.

Daisy was equal to a new challenge. "Bring costumes," Amy relayed, "Elizabeth's note says we're all invited to take part and Daisy wants us each to look inside and decide who we want to be." We looked, but it wasn't quite true that we could decide. Art chauffeured Daisy and Sam and Amy, and little Tim, the slight young man who'd stayed with them since Utah, and the rest of us followed in our own cars. Daisy assigned parts to us when we arrived at Asilomar and we spent the first night and the next day rehearsing in spare moments. On Sunday night, we dressed up in sheets, cardboard foil crowns, bright scarves and bits of lace.

As usual, while under Daisy's tutelage, we were quite convincing, and when we stepped "onstage" at the front end of the Nautilus Hall beneath the fireplace, it was as though we'd entered a dream. Daisy played Guinevere; Sam, Lancelot; Amy, Morgan Le Fey; and Art, of course, was Arthur. I didn't come out until the end because I was given the part of a nun in the convent to which Guinevere fled, so I saw quite a bit of the play from without as well as within. In the scene where Arthur is confronted with his wife's affair with Lancelot, tears streamed over Art's face. He brushed them back with one sheet-clad lumberjack's hand, and went on to rise to great acting heights, the audience thought. But I knew that anything artistic, outside of woodcraft—particularly acting—fell far outside the realm of Art's abilities.

After the last act, Elizabeth presented Art with a sword and a scabbard. He lifted the sword aloft with aplomb amid cheers. "You made the Round Table come alive for us, darling," Elizabeth gushed, facing the audience. "You are the king of the hour!" People from her Los Angeles circle rushed around him, but he only smiled sadly after Daisy and Sam who beat a path for the same "dressing room"—one of the converted storage rooms at the opposite end of the hall. During this, the Golden Age of the Philosophical Roundtable Conferences at Asilomar, Elizabeth gave readings that rivaled Edgar Cayce's. Late that night, Daisy whisked a privileged few into Elizabeth's room and shut the door on the rest of us. Before the door closed, I glimpsed Ambrose B., Elizabeth's assistant in these matters and keeper of the "archives"—the tape-recorded record of these readings—clutching a microphone before Elizabeth's face. Pressed up against the door I could hear little but the muted drone of Elizabeth's sleepy voice, tracing the lifetimes of those present as they related to the legendary lifetime of the Arthurian knights. That was the purpose of this reading—Daisy told us we would all get to hear it as soon as it was complete, but that a crowd would interfere with the vibrations, inherently high at Asilomar, but highest on this special night.

After awhile, Ambrose opened the door to give Elizabeth "a little air," and I slipped inside to glimpse Daisy, who held a microphone connected to her recorder, lean over the "sleeping" woman lost in the padded depths of an orange vinyl Asilomar armchair.

"And this one: Arthur Forrest—'Art,' as he is known in the present—was there." Elizabeth nodded as she intoned the words Ambrose would transcribe in capital letters. "This one was there at the time...of ARTHUR, that Arthur lost to legend, but that one who truly lived, once, for one shining moment in that brief, bright, place in time known to all who loved him as Camelot, where unconsciously, subconsciously, one of the purposes of all those who entered at THAT TIME, bringing that known as chivalry, was to uplift the cause of woman, whose station had been held so low, EVEN in that time when the Master walked the earth. THIS WAS karma from the AT LAN TE AN lands, to be sure, when women—the female as a rule, ruled there and dominated those lands, and those activities as THE creative force of the day. So there were those drawn there—to that known as Camelot, for this purpose who had ALSO been drawn to those, the Grecian lands at the time of those who attempted to recreate that which was the late Atlantean experience, as the balance. Returning to THIS ENTITY, that one known as Edward Arthur Forrest in the present," (I was aware of puzzled, impatient glances exchanged between Daisy and Sam at her repetition of Art's name) "Ye were there, Arthur Forrest, for this one—not as those tonight who played a part—no, this one," Elizabeth whispered so that I had to lean forward to hear, "THIS WAS ARTHUR.

"We are finished," she recounted after a moment, "Maria Theresa" (I knew that was Elizabeth's guide in the readings— perhaps her higher self) "is closing the curtains."

Formerly much impressed by Elizabeth's kindness to me, now even more so by her "readings," I hung about her like a cloak for the duration of the conference. I drew closer when Daisy and Amy approached Elizabeth where she sat after her conferees had gone, at the old wooden desk by the back door in the huge registration room. I sensed they wanted a secret session but I was not easily disposed of, so they grudgingly allowed me to sit in while Elizabeth "read" for them briefly amid the din of Ping-Pong balls dropped on the wooden floor, and of new arrivals shouting to one another for nametags and keys and of three boys who kept up an ear-shattering rendition of Chopsticks at the battered baby grand at the far end of the enormous room.

But when Elizabeth was "led under" by the ubiquitous Ambrose—who popped up at her elbow whenever "reading" was mentioned as though anxious to fatten "his" archives—when she began to speak, I leaned out of the din and within the circle made by those listening.

Ambrose asked Daisy for her name and birthday. "Daisy Anne Buchanon Forrest, June 2, 1944." Elizabeth began slowly, "Maria Theresa is opening the curtains. She writes, 'Ye were Arina, who was, with the sister Marina, leader of those women who lived on the Isle of Lesbos in Greece in three separate lifetimes, those drawn together on a soul level—those who decided to incarnate there, so that a civilization of women might thrive, that the arts the literature, the phil os o phies" (she drew out the words deliberately as though reading from Maria Theresa's blackboard or whatever) of the centuries of leadership offered by those women in Atlantis—still extant but buried under the su pres sions of the KARMIC (this she stressed) Judeo-Christian period—might, would, certainly would return and flower and offer a breath of relief to the waiting world.

"But, after this became known, the maraudings of men on adjacent islands, the attempts to rape, to plunder this unusual (for that time) society, there came a turning away from these (men), there came a turning toward one another even for com-pan-ion-ship, for comfort, and these, then, lived much as the soldiers of Alexander."

Arina. Marina. I looked at Daisy and Amy walking away arm and arm after the reading, back to their respective—whose was whose?—men. Maybe this was what Daisy meant by the idea that Rebecca's love for Art was really part of her love for Daisy. Did that mean Daisy's love for Sam was part of her love for Amy? And what of Sam's love of Daisy as part of his love for Art? (Had they lived as soldiers of Alexander?) And what of Art's acquiescence to Sam...and my fear that Daisy might take Doug? From where I sat assisting Elizabeth's and Ambrose's scattered, otherworldly record -keeping, the possibilities were endless.

Art and Baby

Chapter Nine

Daisy and Sam stayed in Art's garage for a month more. During this time Daisy apparently lived on the razor's edge, keeping mostly to Sam, but on occasion, "when I had to," making love with Art in the bedroom while Sam vehemently mowed the lawn. Living on the razor's edge must give you energy, I speculated. Also during this time we had more classes, rather meetings attended by many of the first group on North Redwood Street (less the casualties) and new friends spawned within Daisy's wider network, including Wayne and Mary Grace who had just arrived from Montana.

On one such night when the air was cool and almost rain, I remember walking into the house where they all stayed on a windy, late summer night. I wore a denim dress with bright yellow cuffs and collar. Smoke floated in the room like negligee sleeves. Not everyone was here yet. In the bathroom was the red and blue, kind of psychedelic poster of Jesus. The dark curly hair looked like Uncle Art's. I wandered into his, the adjoining bedroom. Todd Allen was cavorting naked over Art's bed, his little penis white and bouncing, his bottom lean and his hair curly like the picture of Jesus. Todd cooed and did a somersault across the bed. Art grabbed his foot before it disappeared over the edge. "Just a minute, Toadie," Art bantered with the baby. Todd smiled back at him, squirmed to get away on his belly through the cascade of quilt and covers. I came in, feeling less like an intruder than I usually did, although I guessed I really was, and sat near the bed on the carpeted floor. I fingered the edge of the white and aqua quilt that dangled near me. In Montana, after Amy pieced the quilt, Daisy embroidered all of their names and birthdates onto some of the squares. I looked at Todd's section and thought of the events that had led up to his birth.

After Todd was in bed, Art and I joined the others in the living room. Doug was at home with Veronica. He didn't mind. He wasn't very interested in the meetings any more anyway. Daisy radiated at the assembled faces, among them some of the originals: Amy, Rebecca, Art, Stephen and me; at the travelers: Montana's Wayne and Mary Grace, Utah's Tim; and at Jade, a young woman of Basque and Asian ancestry, and at Constance, older, more elegant than the rest. Daisy had met these two women during her stay with Doug and me. She had read for Jade at Howard's shelter and for Constance in a private reading party.

Constance's sleek, four-door Imperial had glided soundlessly up the gravel-pitted driveway of our duplex to pick Daisy up and I remembered peeking out of the front room curtains to glimpse the urbane woman in a tan leather jacket who smoked thoughtfully in the front seat. She smiled inquisitively when Daisy stepped out my front door in black jeans embroidered with a tangle of daisies, and reached long manicured fingers across the front seat to open the car door for her. Now tall Constance also looked impatiently to Daisy, her dark eyes glistening with anticipation beneath the swirls of her beauty-shop-perfect coiffure.

An older man had joined the fold as well, a tall, fair, prematurely graying man named Neil who used to drink when he was a purchasing agent at the company where Vicky's former husband worked. Vicky promised to use her psychic abilities to get to the root of Neil's problem with booze and held him to her during the time Daisy was traveling. Vicky hoped to net long term followers of her own while her mentor was away, but Neil and several others migrated away from Vicky to Daisy, somehow called by the strength of Daisy's negative reputation.

Now these camped with the rest of us on the couch and chairs Daisy had kindly given Amy as payment perhaps for the loss of her husband and son, and some, like little Tim and Mary Grace and me, sat shamelessly on the floor beneath her feet. At last, Daisy began in the style of Elizabeth:

"That which we knew in the Temple of the Stars has begun to live among us after a period of great personal testing"—she shed pregnant looks into the wreckage, at the divorced rearranged couples, at the Daisy-made, stray unhappy singles, out of serious eyes now grey above the subdued lamp light. The incense Tim had lit burned in a brass holder beside him on the floor—his last defiant testimony to the split from his Mormon past. The smoke wafted up and surrounded Daisy like a parted veil. "Yes, that which we knew spir-i-tu-al-ly"— boy she sounded like Elizabeth now, even when she was awake—"on a soul level and in the higher realms—in the stars—has begun to live among us—is visible, tangible, is OURS NOW." The refugees from comfortable marriages beamed up at her courageously and even the living wounded, like Art, smiled with pride.

"Now we will be called by a NEW NAME, The Temple of Living Water. And we shall have a book this night, and any of you who are moved to do so may sign this living book, may press into it their living signature—testament of the truth gleaned by that testing, by that travail." Then she looked at Sam as though he was the pearl of truth perfected by her great travail. "Travail" was one way to describe the ecstatic minglings I'd heard when Daisy and Sam stayed with me. Sam, the pearl, gleamed and glowed sagaciously, beneath Daisy's reference. He lifted his heavy-lidded, clouded blue eyes as though to exude luminosity. One by one we winked in Sam's reflected light. He grew within her praise, settled in our imaginations as the man. Art toyed with one of Todd's little socks left on the polished living room floor despite all of his admonitions. Daisy had been "told" Todd Allen was to live with her and Sam and that they were "finished here" and must soon move to their own place. Art said nothing in response to the news but was so sad that I could hardly bear to be in the same room with him. If Daisy's adventures with Sam birthed great pearls, then what, what would be the treasure rent from such suffering? "And so we will make plans," Daisy went on, "for an Easter celebration that will be an initiation, with all those present whom have joined in the signing of the Living Book." Did this mean she'd lost her mailing list in the move? I wondered uncharitably. Daisy eyed me telepathically over the gold wire rimmed glasses she'd begun to wear lately. "When did you start wearing glasses, Daisy?" I'd blurted the day before. "I knew when I read by firelight at Lake Washington it would do something to my eyes, but—"she waved one hand—"Art kept me to my promise to give him six months and I had to comply. Still, Spirit must live, and I fed on those books I'd brought up the mountainside to camp on that damned motorcycle. The books saved me, they flooded my spirit with light even if they blurred my eyesight." She'd made it sound as if she'd been blinded by Art for the cause. To how many others did she tell that story? Art sat away from the crowded semicircle that ended in a tight little knot at Daisy's feet.

"Yes, we shall have a celebration this Easter in that park known as Willow Street." Not only more erudite, apparently, from the intensive study of those books that had flooded her spirit with light, but her diction while awake definitely reminded me more and more of Elizabeth's "sleeping" voice. "What is the Temple of Living Waters?" asked the wide-eyed new arrival Yvette, one of those who had obviously not quite gotten it.

"The living waters flow freely," Daisy replied, "free of orthodoxy, free of limitations. The Temple of Living Waters is here, for this moment, because the living waters flow within each one of you who walks with Spirit whatever the cost"—now she squeezed Sam's hand—"through each of you who walk with Spirit freely, speeding up your own growth and releasing yourself to follow your own path." Now she eyed Art munificently where he sat, still, apart, wringing the sock with eyes more blurred than Daisy's had even been on the mountaintop. Daisy waved the new gold glasses that dangled from her right hand.

"We will move where Spirit leads us and those who move will move together, those who accept the pain of growth will know that pearl, that wisdom born of suffering, will know its fruit, will know its flowers."

I sensed then the choral leap of the heartbeats of all of us seekers alike ascending the lofty purple mountaintop of Truth; for surely that mountaintop would be strewn with the fairest of flowers, the freshest, the loveliest, that daisy, and surely each alone would have access to that blue and golden-hued flower.

"And so now, any of you so called, come and sign the Living Book."

I had known about the book. The hopeful crowded around her, but I had misgivings. I had called Elizabeth, and she said that vows should be made privately. "Remember to put your names and complete addresses," Daisy added, idly chewing the end of one gold wire spectacle wing. She looked over and above us, out the darkened plate glass living room window, with eyes like the Superstar picture of Jesus, as though too anguished to note those lower activities of earth, even those she had initiated when touched by Spirit, like book signings, divorces and sundry things.

The Easter sunrise celebration in the park which convened at 5 a.m., was a merry frozen time with Daisy presiding over the greeting of the sun. Wide-eyed, wondering, we watched her greet the great globe that wandered from its wintry sleep into a greater resurrection than it had known.

Afterwards the kids hunted eggs and we ate sandwiches we'd made, drank grape juice and wine and bathed in the light of the (eventually risen) living sun. Lately Daisy expressed an increasing reverence for the sun and talked of days of sun worshippers who knew the sun to be the living representative of a greater son, and of that light in all, known as the Christ. Today Daisy read Elizabeth's book on Egypt, read of Isis, Nefertiti, of Osiris, Amen Ra, and of little Tutankamen. She held the book thoughtfully before her in one hand when she half reclined on the grass, as if there was new life growing out of the already rich pages, new tendrils creeping out to touch our liege, soft as the touch of grass; not hard or clumsy or coarse like the outer world heard here now only as the subdued roar of cars beyond the borders of the park, but soft, velvety, like the touch of a woman's fingertip when it traces up the breast of her man. Daisy's other hand idly stroked Sam's chest; he lay beneath her on the grass, bared to the waist.

Now those who had tentatively followed her into new couplings, lasciviously followed suit, lingering over each other's chest or breasts, and some exchanged long kisses. Couples rolled in their newfound passion over the colored eggs the children had left scattered on the grass and cracked. They laughed aloud—the uproarious, watchful laugh of those caught in the dance of "earth selves" hidden by the veil of new spirituality. Their lesser selves were so glad to have a man or a woman again. The picnickers were, in their way, egoistic males and females preening in the romantic luxuries of this spring day, and at once the shadows of their priestly, priestessly former selves— idly watching the dance while listening, ever listening, to the lyrical song of the inner spirit that surely inspired this tableau.

What followed the Easter celebration was eventually not so much a rush of living waters, but a hiatus, a long splash in their sunshiny shallows.

But first Daisy and Sam left Art's rented house and took Todd Allen to a small temporary apartment where they stayed up all night collaborating on paintings. Daisy would paint the body of the picture—a rainbow, a dove, or whatever, and Sam would outline her initial form, giving it sharp edges and definition. Once they invited me by and we three exchanged artistic ideas. "Can I borrow that," she asked respectfully, gesturing toward a composite symbol I had made with the crayons I'd brought—the union of a bird, a cross and a Christ figure as part of an attempt at what Cayce called the life seal. "Look, Sam, she's the only person I've ever seen do anything with crayons." Daisy borrowed part of the idea and incorporated it into the design they eventually signed "D-S, '73." Watching me work, she defined my style in a way that had never occurred to me. "You're a builder," she remarked. "Sam and I pre-plan, but you build as you go." It rang true, as another bit of self-knowledge allowed by Daisy's insight. When "we" became pregnant a year later, they pre-planned their baby too, saying that she would be a girl.

After Daisy and Sam left Art's apartment, Rebecca, who'd finally emerged from the stagnant depths of her apartment—from the realm of the mole into the relative sunshine of a dilapidated cottage behind Howard's healing shelter, took advantage of her own and Art's freedom to call on him several times. "Rebecca wanted me," I overheard Art brag to Tim during that time. "She was ready, as ready as any mare for her stallion, and I told her no." "You told her no?" Tim inquired in awe. Nobody had coupled with him. "Yep. I'm just not ready." But for some reason he needed to brag. That didn't seem like him and I wondered why. Usually Art was the soul of chivalry where women were concerned, making the plainest feel special and respected.

And Cassandra; painfully separated from her husband Christopher, and now fighting for custody of her son, speculated about Amy and Art. "You'd think they'd get together at least. It's only logical. Art's a nice man." Art seemed unable to separate from Daisy in that house, so he gave it up and he too took a small apartment. Amy, unable to afford the rent on the house they all had shared, filed for welfare at Daisy's suggestion and moved her kids to a dumpy upstairs apartment in Santa Clara.

One summer afternoon after Art had moved, Daisy suggested that a few of us stop by and visit him as a housewarming. I was glad to go. After Jane and Marshall's divorce and without being part of the heady excitement of the relationship rearrange, I felt somewhat bored. Marshall and Jane's rootless wandering at a time when we were so settled was unsettling. Many times Marshall would try to take Doug out or look at me longingly. This didn't fit. Jane confided her troubles and borrowed money from me for booze, but it wasn't the same. We tried to bring them back together. Once they even slept together in our bed, but it didn't take. Still I was reluctant to admit that the halcyon days as look-alike couples had passed.

For the boys' supper towards the end of the housewarming visit, Art cooked bacon and sausage and tomato sandwiches in the small sterile kitchen. Daisy had decorated the apartment for them with whatever he could afford: plastic patio chairs instead of furniture, a modern globe lamp and that popular picture of Jesus that now looked to me exactly like Sam, with curly dark hair above pained superstar eyes that looked out over full, expressive lips.

We watched an Elvis special on TV. "I'm going to meet that man before I die," Daisy affirmed. "He is the essence of male charisma," she pronounced. She named it right. Seen through her eyes, I agreed, though I'd never liked him much. Amy, usually ecstatic to see Elvis, seemed calmer than usual, more inner directed and did not immediately agree and augment Daisy.

After the special, most people left. Daisy and Sam took Art Jr. home with them to watch Todd Allen as they were going out again. "A built-in babysitter," Artie grumbled when his mother couldn't hear, but he left with them anyway. Doug was tied up doing an odd job somewhere and Art said he'd drive me home later if I wanted to stay and dip Veronica in the pool. I stayed because Benjamin and Davy already had Veronica at the pool and I didn't want to spoil this moment of relief—she had begun to cry a lot of late. Daisy and Amy's half-brother Rexford Buchanon, who'd just returned from the service and had moved in with Art as a roommate was out at the pool with all the children, so I felt comfortable about it and hoped they would stay awhile. The children called him Uncle Rex, and he was very thin with thick glasses and curly hair—he seemed nondescript. I didn't know much about him then—or care.

After they all left, Amy sat on Art's broad lap. His head lay on her shoulder. He looked sad and droll. They ignored me as if I were one of the kids. The TV played electrical shadows over them and obscured their voices somewhat, but I could still hear.

"How was it for you last night?" I thought I heard Art ask. Living here had made a difference. Art's eyes were closed and he looked very still and anxious waiting for her reply. The white light of a Bud commercial flashed over him.

"You know how to make love!" Amy, former prostitute, answered him with a laugh so loud I couldn't help but hear.

A little smile lit the corner of his lips. His face slipped in and out of the light and shadows cast by fast flashing scenes from Mission Impossible.

"Do I?" he murmured. "But I thought…" And this was so soft I wouldn't have heard, except that Barney was cracking a complicated safe that held the plans for chemical annihilation with his space age microtool, and that took a few seconds.

I could see the intensity of Art's question, because the insidious safe exploded in a flash of light that lit Art's face like swimming-pool-side sun, and I saw sweat glistening over his 1950's Elvis-handsome features. Then he whispered something into Amy's ear, head downcast as if he expected to be slapped. Jim and Hank found Barney and dragged him out of the cubicle a few seconds before his impending death. The music picked up. Amy answered Art softly.

"Size has never mattered to me."

"But I thought…not…not even after Sam, the KING OF MEN?"

She kissed him and they went in to the bedroom, leaving me staring at some female's slick, shiny lips sliding back so that her tongue could caress her teeth and consummate, "MMMMMMMMM, I get that clean, shiny feeling." I resolved to find Veronica and leave, even if I didn't have a car!

Marshall showed up just after I got home.

"Doug isn't here," I said.

"I didn't come to see Doug, I came to see you."

"Ok. Wait a minute." I settled Veronica into her crib. She'd fallen asleep in Rex's car on the way home.

"I've been thinking about things. About all this stuff about past lives," he said. (Strange, I knew Marshall was a non, or a sometimes-only believer.)

We sat across from each other, me on the couch and him in the chair by the door. Outside the late summer night reigned, inviting. Inside it was dark and subdued.

"I should turn on the light."

"Don't. I like your face this way."

"Why?"

"Then I can read past lives," he joked.

"You? Marshall, what's the matter?" I sat stiffly on the edge of the couch. "Have you seen Jane?"

"No, and I don't want to," he murmured into a blousy windbreaker that made him look shapeless. He rubbed his ash blond eyebrows with one hand. "NOOO," he cut off further conversation about Jane. I was still trying to get them back together.

"Why can't we talk about Jane, Marshall?"

"I don't want to, that's all."

Even after the interlocutory decree, Jane kept stopping in despondent, full of bravado and self-blame. She didn't stop us from talking about him. She wanted to run into him I knew—she still hoped.

Now Marshall lived with his mother and father again in the family home in Los Gatos. That meant (to his mother) he was upper crust and Jane was shit, only his mother wouldn't have put it that way. Nothing could have been further from the truth. I continued to hope they would reunite. The new couples in Daisy's group were erotically charged, but tenuous, still turbulent. People in her group were exploring each other that year—nobody was sure. In Daisy's circle, only Doug and I were stuck together, firmly married, and there was no one to share that with.

"No, but I plan to ask Doug if he'll go to San Francisco with me—I know some people up there—"

I felt a pang. "You're going to meet women?"

"Not exactly. Well...I don't want to talk about that. I haven't really seen anybody lately. I'm working. Paying the debts Jane stuck me with"—his mother's words, I was sure—"and I'm advancing at the company."

Who cared about companies? "You wanted to discuss past lives, Marshall?"

I felt bored, tense. What exactly did he want?

"I think you and I have been together, that's all."

Together. Like together together. I stifled a giggle. "Oh well, maybe. We've all known each other somewhere," I said and sat up straight, conscious of my commitment to Doug and the inappropriateness of this conversation. I was hell bent on being as monogamous and devoted in my marriage to Doug as I had not been as a free spirit in Palo Alto. I felt Marshall was trying to violate me somehow. A picture of Art and Amy together flashed in my inner eye. I fiddled with another of the insidious washed, but unfolded diapers that lay around the place. Since Daisy left, I hadn't regained any enthusiasm for that pursuit. Marshall's mother would find my house a disaster. What was he doing here?

He stared at me in the gloaming. The only light was the bare outside porch light backlighting him from beyond the front window.

"I'll say it again. We've been together."

"Marshall, I hardly ever talk with you and you don't really buy past lives and here you are…to find out more about them or what?"

He rubbed his chest sideways, back and forth slowly, and looked beyond me into the darkened archway leading to the kitchen that I knew to be full of dirty dishes. Then he settled his gaze on me. Lit from behind by the porch light, he could have been a Viking apparition. His pale blond hair atop his big ram's head caught the light and gave semblance to something more devilish than an auric halo.

"Marshall, I'm going to turn on the light."

"Hey—no." He crossed one great arm across his chest and supported his other arm, bent at the elbow. He cupped his chin like the statue of the thinker.

"I know what I feel Page, maybe not about Atlantis or whatever you and the others are into, but I know my own feelings—what I want. I follow them at work now—and I usually get what I want. You and I have been together before."

"Marshall, knock it off. Do you really want to explore past lives? Are you serious? Well, if you are, I've been doing a lot of research lately. I could show you some pictures. They're quite uncanny, and the other night I had a dream. After telling it to Cassandra, I proceeded to the Campbell Library to check out the references to a Shakespearean play—a fragment of dialogue from that play was included in the dream. And that led me to check out pictures of Danish royalty and of the Princes of Wales. Both of these leads were implied by the dream you see," I rattled on awfully fast. "How can you tell if these leads are real or correct?" I continued primly, every inch the teacher I longed to be. "You can tell because the scars are on 'thine own soul,' as Edgar Cayce said, but it's more than that— things just start to fall in place. You make uncanny discoveries—just as I found Doug's picture among the Princes of Wales—can you believe it, Marshall? There was his picture. Staring right up at me— and Doug has been really freaked out ever since. Really freaked out." Marshall sighed and I knew he wasn't listening. I went on anyway. "Ok, so Doug only lived 16 years in that lifetime. He didn't become Prince of Wales. He either died from an illness or he was poisoned. But the discovery, the thrill," I went on, enraptured, conscious only in the teeniest back part of my mind that this rapture would only make Marshall want to tell me more that we had been together.

He sighed indulgently. "Page. You know it's more than that. More than just research, or discovery, or whatever you call it. I know that I've known you before, because I know now that…I…feel something for you. And um.…"

I giggled. Watch out for the ego, I thought, and stiffened on the couch. Truth. What was the truth of all of this?

Marshall switched on the light. He looked embarrassed and then penetrated me with Viking sea green eyes that looked like guardians from inside a cave beneath a heathered bluff. For one moment I had to suck in my breath.

"I can go." He began to pull his mass up off the couch.

"No. Doug will want to see you. He really will."

"Where do you think we've known each other, Marshall?" I asked, on the surface the teacher, pleasant, an aspiring minister like Daisy, ever available to help the needy, a leader like Daisy was in the Easter morning park. "Perhaps we knew each other as Vikings. You looked that way
a minute ago, Marshall. And no subtle sense like that occurs by chance."

"I…uh…feel there's something special between us. Don't you?" he asked. Under the blatant light from the lamp, now switched on, I did not want to consider this. "There might be," I conceded. "But arising from and belonging to a past lifetime only—and that's it."

He laughed nervously. I laughed too.

Doug came in moments later and they planned their trip to the city. "Want to come?" Marshall eyed me.

"I don't think so. It would be hard to take Veronica along and I really don't want to—I think I died in San Francisco not too long ago."

After that Marshall continued to tug at Doug, involving him in his forays into the world of bachelorhood. I grew fearful. Even Art, apparently "finished with what he had to learn" from Amy, as Daisy euphemistically put these things, hit on Doug to go over to Santa Cruz with him and got him rummy in a bar one night. Then I called Elizabeth in Los Angeles, in distress.

"Single men should respect men who are married with babies," she reassured me practically. "Besides," she said, venting a penchant for psychology, "alcohol is often a cover for tendencies toward one's own sex. Men who drink and prove themselves with numbers of women may be masking a bias toward men." That eluded me, so I called Daisy, Art's guardian, and she chided Art. "I'm sorry, sweetheart," Daisy apologized for him. And Doug said I shouldn't have been so upset about Art, who had really only taken him there to talk about Daisy.

Late in the fall, Marshall came by one night and brought up the subjects of our past lifetimes together once more, when Doug was in the kitchen making coffee. "Please, Page, when I dream, I really do remember a time," he breathed heavily, tapping broad fleshy fingers on the arm of the couch and leaning closer to face me head on. Ruddy hair leaked from beneath his neat sideburns towards his cheek. He smiled, pained, but Viking lights danced in his eyes.

I got up angrily, deciding Elizabeth must be right. But I let him take off with my husband again, in a spirit of infinite self-sacrifice, releasing Doug to his own growth, imagining that I at last understood the razor's edge. Late that night, Doug returned and assured me, laughing, that Marshall hadn't lured him into anything untoward either. Just to be sure I asked him a flood of gratuitous questions about Marshall, whom I just now resented with great irritation—just to be sure. Then we made love with greater vigor and I honestly felt that I loved Doug the better for caring for him freely and releasing him to his own growth; but the bittersweet satisfaction felt when loss has been confronted and delayed pervaded the bed—that, and the memory of the light beams emanating from Marshall's eyes, coupled with Cayce's suggestion—I thought of it because I used no birth control that night—that a child was best conceived with the heartfelt wish to be a channel. Odd that it occurred to both of us at once. Afterwards I cried, feeling somehow irrationally that what we had to learn together—as Daisy put it—was done.

Although Art's affairs with Amy and Cassandra—and I didn't know who else from the bars—must have done wonders for his ego, nothing came of them. After he returned to his apartment one night and found Rebecca in bed with Daisy's brother Rex—they'd been spending a lot of time together—he joked that two greyhounds would have taken more room under the covers. His bitterness toward anybody who loved was becoming more and more evident.

Chapter Ten

Finally, on Valentine's Day in 1974, Daisy and Sam married. They did it in the Campbell Hall and Amy and Rececca and all of us made streamers; red and white—and pink flowers lay upon the table that held the cake. People gathered, not family mostly but tighter than most families at weddings. Art came, proud and gaunt, his face seamed. He gave Daisy away. He insisted on it. The procession flowed up the aisle like a little class—a show about the love of a man and a woman, "follow the yellow brick road" style.

It was a California spring night, balmy, but cold at the center of the light gusts of late evening wind. There was no moon. We stood outside on the cement walkway that ran around the hall. I looked up into Art's darkened, colorless eyes.

He'd been crying. He looked out of place in the froth of heart-shaped decorations and lanterns and streamers, like the dark, harbinger of fall in his suit jacket, too heavy for the season. He wasn't the only one who lacked appropriate dress-up clothes—when did we wear stuff like that anymore?

He looked up and toward the outside wall; his right arm braced against it, hung his head and brought his other hand over his eyes. I looked up and then away and turned my back to him and stayed there, pretending to rearrange my shawl so that nobody could see him. He was like my father. I made a shield for him but he was my shield too, against the emptiness I was just now beginning to feel, away from the smiling admiring faces of the other young kids who now followed Daisy. I looked up at the sky to give him more time.

The sky was unusual, crystal clear, but dark, like winter was coming, not going. I hugged the shawl to me.

"Art?"

"Page," he murmured against his hand, "tell me something."

I was thrilled. He wanted me to tell him.

"You dream true sometimes—have you dreamed about me?"

"Well," I said self-importantly, tripping over myself in my eagerness to fulfill this praise, "let's see."

Then he asked, sounding far away, "Will she come back to me?"

"Oh, I did have a dream once—this week I think. But…I…."

"Tell me. Tell me."

"I saw you as a man on a shore—no one there—an empty shore, as though waiting. Yes, it seemed as though you were waiting…always waiting—like a man who waits forever. I'm sorry, Art. Here, let me do a reading for you. I…I could, I'm getting better at channeling. When Daisy stayed with us, I watched her."

He nodded. I looked back up and inwardly grasped at the thread-thin clouds passing over this dark of the moon night sky as if I were a moon maiden in the Temple of Diana in ancient Greece, skilled to attune to the subtlest changes in the reflections of the moon on the silver waters of Lake Nemo.

Something seemed to come, a feeling from the center of my solar plexus as we had been taught—or was it from my heart that ached for Art?

"I…see you more as lovers than as friends. Those are the words that come, I don't know why…why, do you think?"

He didn't answer but I knew I had offered him some encouragement. "Thanks," he said, still muffled. I didn't try to follow him when he walked away. Alone under the dark sky he tied the pink crepe-paper-covered cans to the car Daisy and Sam had borrowed for their honeymoon trip to Disneyland.

After they sped off, the awestruck young kids hung about Art in their wake. Art made jokes for them with himself as the butt. His own thunderous laughter followed each punch line. I listened uneasily until one by one, the kids broke away and went home, sated and spent by so much fun.

Then he refused my help and swept up the crepe paper confetti and broken Styrofoam cups, stuffed the garbage cans and locked up alone.

We next saw Daisy and Sam at the Easter celebration in the park. Again we greeted the sun as long ago we had greeted it. It was cold before dawn in the park. Doug and I, with Veronica in her carrier on Doug's back, looked around through the dark, damp, wide spaces for the sun's rays, but we didn't find any. I was the coldest—my feet were bare, with wet grass slushing between my toes. We were waiting a long time for the sun. I had remembered only the heat of the late day last Easter here when the infant we'd brought had rolled reddened on our blanket upon the grass in the warmth of that sun, reaching for the one rainbow egg we'd found on the hunt. So today I'd worn my sleeveless purple and white velour dress with the white braid ribbon—the one I would wear in the upcoming play about Egypt to be presented at Asilomar. I'd dressed as if I were in Egypt, in Isis' Temple. Seeing this, surely Daisy would assign me an important part.

"Places everyone," Sam joked, but we took our places, lining up to face the rising sun. One long orange tendril—a finger of light—stretched across the length of the park up to Daisy, who led the group that faced her. All of us stood on top of a grassy knoll at the opposite end of the theatre from the sun, where it could illuminate us. "A R E O UM," we chanted three times, and then the "OM" seven times, each chant intended to open one of the sacred charkas spoken of not only in the east, but in our own Biblical Revelations, each charka represented as one of the sacred seven seals.

Then, as one, all thoughts of position and personal jealousy aside, we opened our throats and sang to the one, the living God, "Alleluia."

Each person singing, each man or woman waiting to sing the chorus in this impromptu choir called upon the hillside, had prepared within herself, himself, throughout this irregular year, a place, a personal theater wherein resurrection might occur.

Yvette, one of the most dedicated of the new crop of youths devoted to Daisy's cause, stood barefoot in the grass (was that why I wore no shoes?) holding to her toddler Gideon, with a cloak of dun drawn about her hair and face. She was lonely, but unable to find a man who wanted her little brood, unable to find a tough, rough, manly man, and was stuck in a house full of wanderers she took in to share the rent, doling out organic peanut butter sandwiches in a kitchen with smeared windows and wandering Jew shoots in bottles on the windowsills. Since she seemed too poor to afford even a plant, the group, who usually liked Yvette, poured out plant clippings and cast-off, but still pretty dresses and robes to her, but it was really not enough.

Now Yvette looked at Daisy, whose arms were significantly, symbolically encircled with Sam's. To Yvette, I somehow knew, they stood as avatars of the truth they actually wished to convey, they demonstrated co-rulership and co-creatorship with the loving, Father/Mother God. Maybe by worshipping Daisy and Sam, the rainbow dust of their blessed relationship and idyllic Valentine's Day union would spill out on her, too. Yvette's crucifixion this year had been to surrender that desire for a man in her life (Daisy's suggestion) to the dedication for service. Yvette had tried, taking in the strangers, and watching Todd Allen for Daisy and Sam when Artie was in school so that they could go to Santa Cruz to "renew" themselves from the superfluous exigencies of Daisy's divorce, so that the two could come back as good shepherds must, with new directions for the developing flock. And Yvette had suppressed her baser desires whenever she could; for the rough and tumble sort of no-good men she liked, for drugs, for anything but the simple songs that led her through her disorganized work at home.

But now her Master, whom she loved from long ago—wouldn't He come bless her too? Now it didn't have to be with a man, she realized, as she looked into the bright sun over which the little half moon still hung clear and visible, it didn't have to be.

I knew, staring over Yvette toward the sun, all of these things. The joy of standing still, of hearing Sam's prayer ring out over the little glen was enough for Yvette. As Yvette stood tall, the tears began to pour out over her cheeks. "And who is my brother," she asked the sun. "Who is my mother, who is my husband?" she cried harder.

Watching Yvette I suddenly thought that Doug's brother Clay or his sister-in-law Emily, whose house was a block away in the old Rose Garden section of Willow Glen, would still be asleep under their fashionable blankets from Macy's. They might say, "No, you couldn't have known another person's thoughts," but I could. Not just because Yvette and I were close in age and in unhappiness, but also because I was just for that one moment, suspended, in one mind, in one body, just as Daisy had said we would be this morning.

When the tears ran down my face too, in the echo of knowing this, my faith in Daisy was increased because, for that one moment, I lived in the love of the one God, the God of the sun and of the fragile moon that stayed to hear our songs, of the one star suspended beneath it—symbols of Zoroastrianism—and to me, a sign that we would be working through the threads of that lifetime between this Easter and the next. But who had taught me to see, in the subtlest of symbols, the truth that ever emanated from within, and who would make me love Yvette—whom I already perceived as my rival in Daisy's affections—as myself? I knew it must be the one God we greeted with the coming of the sun, but to me, young and unable to sustain this joy outside of her presence, it was Daisy too—it must be—wasn't it her magic that could take me over the rainbow to myself?

Sensing the beckoning of new magic, Daisy decided we should all depart early for this Asilomar conference with Elizabeth. Arriving before Daisy, I decided to introduce the newcomers, Wayne and Mary Grace, to Elizabeth myself. After the couple left to unpack and change for dinner, Elizabeth asked me to stay with her while Doug took our bags to our room. She made it clear that I wasn't a newcomer. "Don't go, Page, don't go," she repeated dramatically. "I'm so glad you're here, darling." She stood back and took a long look at me. "I've thought of you so often, Page. It's as if you're a younger version of myself." Excited and immensely flattered, I felt buoyantly confident. We chatted merrily. Taller than Elizabeth, I bent my head conspiratorially to listen to her amusing gossip. When I glanced up, Daisy stood behind us as though accusing me of something. I deferred to her, guiding Elizabeth in her direction, and left quickly to join Doug in our rustic room with shared bath.

That night, we saw slides of past lives that further stimulated our thoughts about our lifetimes in Egypt with Isis and Osiris and the rest. Daisy orchestrated the play on the following night. To my dismay, I was assigned the role of a serving maid. Daisy had played a queen before, but this time she was a reborn goddess beloved of the Egyptian peoples—Nefertiti. Doug played an extra, a soldier, and we dressed in the bathroom of the luxury suite Daisy and Sam shared with Rebecca and Rex.

I helped the others make up and pleaded with Daisy that Doug should have a greater role. I didn't speak for myself, but oh, how I would have loved to play Nepthys, winged embodiment of the principle of the mysterious sky. A new necklace made of stars dangled luxuriously down Daisy's breast, culminating in the gold winged figure of Nepthys, the Egyptian sky goddess she claimed as another of her own past lifetimes. She had begun to teach that as the minister of the Temple of Living Water, she represented us—the body—and so her affluence was ours. Daisy's affluence had increased of late. Lapis beads, bloodstones and moonstones mortared the gold stars that winked beneath the simple stage lights we had devised, as if they were the stars themselves.

Doug had to run in the main entrance from the courtyard wearing only a towel and a cardboard sword, and then out again through the opposite side of the Nautilus and around the building in the fog as one of the pack of soldiers. Newcomers and those in disfavor played these parts. Sam was illustrious as Akhnaton, of course.

Daisy castigated me once we returned home—in front of the Tuesday morning business meeting that she impulsively called at Amy's low rent apartment near the freeway. She shamed me for the over eagerness I'd shown in the bathroom at Asilomar—for insisting that Doug play a greater part. Then she looked past me with an icy sadistic avoidance that unveiled to all present my "ego" problem. Suddenly I was nothing more than a buffoon, like Art, and I went away humbled, my arms laden with boxes of empty three-by-five cards she pushed my way, and with lists of names from the Living Book to be transposed to the index cards.

I didn't know my success as a spiritual leader in Daisy's burgeoning movement was to open and shut on the hinges of those little boxes of three-by-fives. Veronica was crying more and more, throwing herself from her crib onto her head. We'd visited the emergency room of the county hospital twice in fear of a concussion, and I was depressed, about Veronica and now about an eerie sense that an invisible iron door was swinging shut, closing me out of what I wanted most in the world. When Amy returned for the three-by-fives, they weren't done. She took them back and I wasn't asked to help again. The ice cold, imaginary iron door shut tighter, and although I continued to involve myself intimately with them, we were all aware of it—me because I was up against it, Daisy because she placed me there, Amy and Rebecca because Daisy gently pointed out my deficiencies to them and they had come to follow Daisy's spirit rather than their own.

Still I haunted the business meetings that became a regular practice, offering leadership only from the realm of dreams. I was resigned that it was to be denied me for a time in the earth and

Key players in Daisy's presentation of
Elizabeth's Egyptian Play:
Elizabeth, Art, Cassandra, Alden, Daisy and Sam

concentrated instead on building thoughts that would attract a bright, hopeful child. Daisy always began the meetings by consulting my dreams, indulging me as the kid oracle. And for a time I was satisfied, lost in the rising influence of a golden summer and in my hopes for the expected child.

On one of these early summer, balmy mornings, we gathered at the big, Daisy-bequeathed Formica table in Amy's apartment. Everyone was there, everyone who mattered: Daisy's mother, in from "Vegas," as she put it, along with Rebecca and Amy, Connie and me. (It seemed that all of Daisy's physical as well as metaphysical relatives were converging around her.) To be present with them, to be included in the rarified smog less early morning atmosphere of the business meeting was enough. The rainbow-patterned kitchen curtains Daisy and Amy had whipped up from cheap sheets filtered the glorious new summer sunshine, and that elevated orb graced the table and our faces with muted light.

"What's on the agenda for today?" Amy brought another chair for me. I supported Veronica on my lap. She would not stop crying, so I couldn't tell my dreams today. "Shut up, Veronica," Daisy admonished her after awhile in a way that was funny and not unkind. I didn't know anything was wrong with her then and they never really knew. Thumb tacked to the wall above us, an art nouveau poster of spring showered the table below it with the impression of gently dripping foliage. We could be on the terrace of a French restaurant in the last century, I thought. But we weren't. It was 1974 and time to plan the psychic symposium to be presented by the Temple of Living Waters at the San Jose City College. Ideas were thrown around. Overly eager and frustrated, I repeated my ideas ad nauseam and didn't offer to do what I probably should have done—transfer names from the old mailing list onto the new stickums.

At 11:00 we started talking about dreams and whatever other problems arose. Daisy announced that she'd had a dream that told her that six people must sign our new agreement with the City College for the Symposium in Consciousness. "Rebecca, that's your baby," she added. "Who else do you think should participate?"

"Well, there are six of us here."

Daisy and Amy and their mother, Blanche Anne, and Rebecca and Connie and I quickly nodded our assent. It was done. With renewed confidence, I decided to confront Daisy with a nagging problem.

"Daisy, you said at class last week that the men probably had control over the weather in the beginning. Why men?" I asked.

"Not men, really, but co-rulership. You know Page, like the president and the first lady."

"Who wants to be first lady?"

"I'd much rather be that. It's all the same," she tossed out. "The first lady is creative and handles beautifications."

"Daisy!" I couldn't believe it. Daisy was an absolute monarch and was going to be more of one.

"Women are capable of leadership. I say they should lead," I persisted.

"Who's saying they aren't? What you want, Page, isn't equality, but female supreme, isn't it?"

Amy nodded. The blind sycophant, I thought.

"No…I.…" I was confused. She said one role was the same as the other and that the woman was the more creative, but seemed to imply a do-nothing position. Oh, I didn't know. I felt bad, clenched my fists. After the other two left for the post office, I remained sullen. How could my argument mean I wanted female supremacy?

As though reading my thoughts, Daisy said, "That's where we went wrong, Page—on the Isle of Lesbos." I remembered the lifetime Elizabeth gave her. Since then, Daisy's meditations and our group reveries had expanded the story.

"Remember, Page, we came into the body during that period with the intent to elevate women. But when the men tried to take the island, to rape and dominate, some of you turned to violence."

"That's why we had to use the men to procreate and just kept the female babies, right, Daisy?"

"Right. And some of those men are with us today."

"I…think I must have castrated Doug in that experience, after toying with him sexually."

"Sounds right to me, Page."

"How I know…besides from the past life reverie you taught us is…he has a funny thing about his testicles," I blurted. "Yesterday, in meditation, I saw the strangest scene. In this picture I made him do it with me in front of a circle of people, as if I were exhibiting him before these women you know, and at the moment of fulfillment, someone came up from behind at my orders and—it was done! What do you think—could that have happened?"

"As Elizabeth tells us from the Cayce readings, the scars are on your own soul."

"Well, they are—only I don't know if they're scars for Doug because...he's kind of a closet exhibitionist. He'd secretly like us to do it once before a circle of people...and he has a funny thing about his testicles. They're sensitive and he likes them stroked a lot—he's remembering, isn't he?"

"Yes."

"Boy, I hope he doesn't remember the rest."

"I agree. Anyway, sweetheart, I think you've got it." She picked up her keys from Amy's table and got up to leave.

That precocious summer brought intense heat by the third week in July. The heat at the Tuesday morning business meeting was unseasonably oppressive. A white block of unbroken sunlight pressed through the thin-clad kitchen window. One fly touched off a stream of others. They danced through a fluid rainbow made by bold sunlight penetrating the weave of the sheets Amy had transformed into curtains. From time to time, the sheets were ruffled by a sullen breeze that came like hot breath over the lip of the aluminum window to surround our sweaty bodies like a cloak.

Daisy seemed a goddess, an Adonais. The wax cast gold Nepthys swung lazily at her breast when she reached for her coffee or swept away a fly. And we were goddesses in the making. Rebecca wore a small silver Nepthys, Amy one identical in brass; otherwise they were the reflections of their mistress. I hadn't managed to catch up, I didn't have a necklace and I felt increasingly more desperate to be included in the business of the day. Struggling to record my dream on a wadded piece of scratch paper, I lapsed for a moment as if I were a scribe from a former time, set within this unlikely temple to record...what? The rise of a goddess?

The "girls," as they called themselves, drew their coffee cups close in a klatch and leaned over them, glancing now and again into their ink black depths. How could they drink coffee in this heat, I wondered. Daisy played with a rolled up match book, then sat back in her chair, knees wide apart, the skirt of a shimmery blue halter dress flowed between them. Replete with stars, splashed with rainbows, it flowed over her body, imparting greater dignity than the gaudy, red-orange daisies of earlier days. As if she had never been the quivering conservative former pizza hostess, Daisy, sans 35 pounds, tan, even bronze under her casual short, golden haircut, drew her head up all of a sudden and waved her pencil in the air.

"I think, I think it's time to begin something new. We are ready. There is a greater commitment here. You look at the people who are coming through the new symposium and especially the regulars at the class we hold here at Amy's. They're a different group. Not one of these is going to quit before going the distance—do you think, girls? The ones who came before, came because their lives were a mess. They took the understanding, the universal laws, and ran. They wanted to improve their personal lives and they did, but that's all. But we're dedicated to something more. And the ones that are with us now, want that." She stated it as a question. Maybe I was one of those other people she was talking about.

"My life was really a mess, Daisy," I spoke up. "I was at the bottom of the barrel."

"You're different, chicken. You have that drive within."

"What do I have?" I wondered aloud, insecure. If I had it, why wasn't I ascending and contributing like the others in this room?

She wouldn't answer.

"It's simply a matter of letting the next thing come in," she continued. "You can help us, Page, by asking for a dream. That would help." I was appeased.

"But for today I have an idea." She traced the bare toes of her left foot lazily over Amy's ebony and peach kitchen linoleum. "Let's go swimming!" "Where?" laughed Rebecca.

Daisy looked at me. "My father has a pool," I answered as though it had been prearranged.

"Won't we need suits?" Rebecca inquired. Daisy lifted one reddish wing-penciled eyebrow and suddenly we became aware that we would not.

"Call the others," Rebecca murmured grimly to Amy.

"Let's go," Daisy invited me.

An hour later, Daisy and I rounded the corner of my father's house in Menlo Park and I pushed open the dark wooden spike gate that led to his swimming pool.

Daisy followed me into the backyard. We emerged behind the low ranch style house. She stopped short. She stared across the L-shaped pool shadowed by the hundred year oak and back to the freestanding pool house, where I spent that lonely night the last time I was home.

"Look at it!" she exclaimed. "I always wondered what I would have been like if I were raised in a place like this." I tried to tell her, "I wasn't really raised here at all. I left home before they got this. This belonged to my sister and brother, not me."

Daisy spread out her towel and didn't see, didn't hear. I knew what came next. We undressed…all the way. Daisy lived, at the moment, that other philosophy she'd recently acquired, companion to the philosophy of the sun—that the body is beautiful, a representative of the living spirit. I admired Daisy for that.

"Rub my back with lotion, will you, sweetheart? Page, remember way back when I got after you for going without a shirt on North Redwood Street and all—I was wrong about that."

By the time the others had arrived, it was as though Daisy owned the place. She directed each one happily to a spot in the glowing expanse of new May sun. Birds called intermittently from the oak tree so huge it barely rustled in the occasional breezes that made the heat pleasant and inviting.

Although summoned on short notice, virtually all of the women were there, from Pegeen, the very oldest of our group now, who took the day off from work, to Yvette, the youngest and most pregnant. Although I was pregnant too, I didn't show much and I felt quite free and indeterminate.

Daisy and I set the pace. Daisy lay face down on a bright beach towel over the redwood chaise before the pool house and I lay at her feet. We talked casually while the others undressed before us.

Yvette stripped away her hippie-soft, nondescript clothing and took the only remaining chaise when Daisy offered it to her. She also took the towel Daisy directed her to and let it fall to the vinyl pad of the chair. Then she stepped onto it and reclined, half seated before Daisy, her mentor, looking to Daisy through wide, lost, Keene-type eyes. I looked at Yvette obliquely from the side. To me her body was less appealing without clothes; stretch marks from previous pregnancies lined her elongated belly like the vertical stripes of a watermelon. Her legs and arms were slender and unmuscled, and her fawn-soft, sorrel hair fell about her shoulders. Somehow I sensed Daisy accepted her in her entirety and I thought Yvette sensed it too. For without words she'd grown instantly comfortable under Daisy's casual gaze.

For the others who'd never been hippies, the journey from full work dress to utter nakedness seemed tedious. Although it took minutes, thought forms hung heavily over the yard as each one shed layers of protective gilding with loose summer fabrics, and stripped away society's introjected sense of imperfection and shame imbued into them at early ages with the final layers of slips, underwear and bras. Daisy had no underwear to shed, I suddenly realized. I lay beneath her, confident in my awareness recovered from earlier days, and in her trust of me as an ally.

People look different without their clothes. That's a simple thing to say, but stripped of coverings, I seemed to see into personalities in a different way.

Connie, always cool and slinky and elegant before, was boyishly thin and looked like a little child. I "knew" she must have thought her breasts were too small at one time or another. I thought of the little girl trapped with the alcoholic mother she'd coolly alluded to once, of the pathetic child she had once been who loved to go to school because it was so much better there.

Pegeen's body refrained just short of voluptuousness. I remembered the affairs with men to which she alluded once in awhile, and sensed a mature sexuality that I perhaps had not experienced, precluded just by the lack of years. Nora Paul, a new member of the group, was quite a bit older than I was too, but her body looked tough like the tough little life she'd led with her good old boy husband who sold carpet. She seemed open and natural naked, every bit the contradiction of humble Kentucky accent and broad Theosophical horizons she appeared to be in class.

I don't remember seeing Rebecca's body much that day, although we lay out for hours. Perhaps she constructed a mental veil and froze up behind the pristine veil of Virgoan virginity.

Amy lay as directed on the white cement at right angles from us just above the steps leading through sky blue waters into the shallow end of the pool. She trailed her arm into the water and guilelessly let her legs splay behind her. Walking by her later, it became evident that she had indeed been a prostitute, or knowing this did I just imagine that I got a stealthy glimpse of a long slack opening between her legs. Surely I was not looking but seemed to see. The unkind comments of Art's cronies, scruffy little Tim and someone else who claimed to have made it with her, stuck in my mind perhaps. More than anyone she showed the marks of many children. But she wore the relaxed belly skin well on her graceful, slender frame and seemed right away to have unquestioning pride in herself under Daisy's new law of the body. So great was her loyalty to Daisy, she could have bared any flaw before the world of strangers and not been ashamed, so fixed was her visage upon the sun emanating out of Daisy's proud-that-we-had-all-done-it eyes, so light was she, so buoyed by her sister's ease, that she seemed quite…beautiful to me. Yes, beautiful. They all did, at least those who had begun to let go and assume the dignity of a spirit incarnate—that was their right.

The rest of the day was glorious. Light and lively we all felt, close and warmed by the happy karma from some forgotten age. Strange ancient names came to mind: Daphne, Chloe, Lydia and Zandra; Nina, Athina, Arina, Hypatia and Zoann. "Take some salt into your body," Daisy admonished the group. "This sun is hot." She passed around potato chips. We ate obediently and walked nude into my father's house (good thing he was away) to get drinks to go with the sandwiches Rebecca and Amy made while waiting for the others. Returning from the house, I stooped to retrieve a paper napkin that floated across the grass. "You walk like an athlete," Connie commented. Daisy nodded and looked at my long limbs critically. "Page has always been statuesque," she allowed.

We rotated around the yard throughout the afternoon like the shadow of a sundial, spreading and re-spreading our towels to have the greatest advantage from the sun. Though I was not visibly pregnant at the time, I'll bet the impressions of sunlight and water showered on my developing body and through my lilting mind to the baby's, made just the difference in turning the child's eyes white blue, in sand dusting her hair to gold, and in stimulating the dramatic, dreamy creativity she now possesses. "Caw!" called a crow from the old oak tree. Todd Allen, the only child allowed in that afternoon, splashed the surface of the light, crystal clear water. Daisy and Sam had him now, of course, and were giving him the benefit of their enlightened philosophy—at least before he would reach his seventh birthday, widely known as the demarcation between a clean slate and programmed. At that time I thought Todd Allen was lucky.

"If I teach you nothing else," Daisy said to the small group of women gathered that afternoon at my dad's for potato chips and swimming and nudity, "it's to think."

Chapter Eleven

It was during this swimming period that Rebecca's mother Gwen (she pronounced it "Gwin") rented Daisy one side of her duplex near the foothills above San Jose's smarmy east side. How she got the money for income property I didn't know, but she had bought it a long time ago when it must have cost nothing and now it helped her "git by." Once Daisy and Sam moved there (and Daisy always moved quickly) the smoky late night classes and meetings were held there, and even Art attended each one faithfully. Rebecca's mother didn't mind—"I jes let them all be" was the way she put it—but she was taken aback somewhat when she stopped by to get the rent and found Amy there alone watching Todd Allen while Daisy and Sam were on some purposeful jaunt over the mountains to Santa Cruz.

Amy answered the door stark naked. Gwin complained to her daughter later, "What does she think she's got anyway?"

Rebecca relayed this to us at the Tuesday morning business meeting. We all laughed. We knew Rebecca's mother had missed the point—the naked body as the temple of the spirit.

"Amy really throws herself into each new 'piece,'" Rebecca added. That was the new word for concept or something.

The duplex Daisy was renting on Eastside Drive was in a neighborhood of a few straggly untended apricot trees, lots of children: Mexican, Black, Vietnamese and White, and gargantuan parked truck cabs that waited like coaches for the drivers who slept inside the shake-roofed, concrete-floored houses and duplexes, oblivious to the chatter outside. These low dwellings appeared to have been slung here at the outskirts of the city before the rise of olive drab mountains that crouched low around the valley, in morning shadows foliated by scrub like a mangy black beard.

One two-story apartment building—a cacophonous note in this inspired design—flanked the backyard on Daisy's side of the duplex. Actually, the apartments ran diagonally along their backyard. Daisy would often lie out naked with Sam and the kids or alone but for the company of the big, part human-dog, Tag, who was sedate amid the bizarre activity around him. He often drank from the toilet bowl when his dish was empty. Even though the bathroom was clean and fresh, with an arrow plant cascading down past pottery, plaques and posters, only a pile of laundry out of place if anyone came during the day, I wondered if that could be good for him. "He's ok," Sam said, and I knew he must be. Despite the downtrodden neighborhood, everything felt so "up" in Daisy's place, like the tip of a wave on a Santa Cruz beach in summer, before it crashes over the dun colored sand like shattering glass.

I eagerly happened by one day when Daisy lay outside. She got up to go in and take laundry out of the washer, putting on an aqua robe that hung casually closed. How easy she was—clothed or unclothed. It didn't matter that the robe might swing open in the next breeze. She returned and tossed the embroidered comforter and a few sheets over a line Sam had strung.

Bright sun glinted around the rim of the Diablo Range crouching low in one body like a sleeping sentinel—from Morgan Hill past nearby Milpitas. Foil covered the apartment windows next door. Daisy glanced up. "They can't afford sheets," she joked.

"They can't afford movies either," Sam winked at me, bringing out freshly washed jeans and rainbow sprayed white tee shirts in a hemp basket. "They hang over the back fence and watch Daisy instead."

Daisy floated into the house one more time, absorbed in a paperback copy of The Last Temptation of Christ that she'd picked up from the lawn. She got lettuce and sprouts and a package of mushrooms out of the refrigerator and murmured, "How do you make that wonderful dressing we had at the meditation seminar, Page—make some, will you?" So I rummaged for buttermilk, mayonnaise and a lemon.

"Have any blue cheese?" I called after her, but she was gone out in the yard. I watched them through the sliding kitchen window, hidden behind a pert piggyback plant that floated in the open space above the window like a mobile. She lay on her left side, burning her skin to the rust red hue of the Atlantean Great Priestess whose skin was the color of Atlantis' earth, whose eyes were as blue as the seas that surrounded Poseidia in the last age where the feminine force still held sway. Now her face was like an amber glass, absorbing the light of whatever truth might flicker from this latest book.

"Feel the energy of this, Sam," she read a passage from the Last Temptation to him. He sat hunched in the shade, drawing paper spread out over the short-cropped east side weeds. The pressure of his body had pulled up his white drawstring pants almost to his browned knees. At ease, he listened to the ripple of Daisy's voice, quiet, lost in her feelings about the book.

I watched, piggyback on their dream, drawing a picture of marriage I would keep.

Before I left I managed to invite Daisy and Sam to come with Doug and me to my dad's the next weekend. "No, I don't think so," she murmured, still preoccupied in that book Maybe I'd done the wrong thing; so far only women and children had attended the nude poolside days in Menlo Park while my dad worked or was away on business trips.

But at the Tuesday morning business meeting she allowed, "We'll go. Is it still ok?"

"Oh sure!"

I had visions of Daisy and Sam and Doug and me as two happy couples in the vein of Marshall, Jane and us in earlier days. No such luck.

It became evident that this was a test, a step in consciousness for Daisy only. I sensed she was a little intimidated by my body somehow—even when it was pregnant—that she admired and enjoyed it when we were only women, but like most of us, was afraid in the presence of her man.

So she forced herself. But far from being the free, glorious foursome—of Daisy, Sam, Doug and myself—that I had hoped for, at first our outing appeared to be mainly a successful test of Daisy's resolve to overcome fears of competition with other women in front of Sam. And in addition, even though it was a weekend and I was assured my dad was away on business, and I thought the pool would belong to the four of us as something I could give to Daisy, my sister returned to the house later in the afternoon. I didn't even know she was staying in the house, or that she was up from school in Santa Barbara, but I should have. As always, she had free reign of the house and brought a "valley girl" friend along who regarded the tableau of Daisy and Sam and little Todd Allen splashing nude in the sheltered shallow end of the pool with something less than graciousness. They leaned close—to get a look at Sam perhaps, I didn't know. I hadn't looked at him once and despite the proximity, didn't yet know much more about him nude than clothed.

Daisy could have cared less about my sister's attitude, but I felt inclined to leave, to protect the sweetness we were sharing with Daisy from her shallow gaze, to retrieve a sacred freedom from her angry jealous patronizing. And, in truth, a few weeks after my sister saw us, it became impossible to use the pool, and it was hard for me to attribute that to my horny teenaged brother's hypocrisy alone. He didn't enjoy having "his" space invaded—the unused pool didn't belong to me or any one who might enjoy it, was the their philosophy—but he'd had more than a little fun viewing our group from behind the living room curtains with his friends on more than one occasion I was sure. I'd seen the edge of the curtains pulled open and shut by unseen hands on the days when we were bathing.

It seems—retrospectively—that my sister's assessment of our pleasure was that—were we clothed or unclothed—we had little right to "her" pool, and that it should be saved for her biannual use in all its pristine splendor—should she have occasion to return from Santa Barbara for a dip—and then it should be free from troublesome riffraff like myself and my acquaintances.

So this became the last day Daisy and I could partake of that pool, and it was no great loss, because synchronistically, she alluded to a new change when she reclined with me where I lay uneasily on the grass after my sister's hostile stares had driven us out of "her" water. "We may be going to Santa Cruz for a while," Daisy said. "There's a church there that has invited me to try a stint as a resident psychic and part time minister. Isn't that exciting?" she asked listlessly.

I knew she felt she must follow Spirit wherever it led her, and apparently she felt that this was an offer made in the final analysis by Spirit itself.

"Sure," I answered. I doubted that we could move there just now, as Doug was finally working at a job for more than just his two to three month average. Sensing my reluctance, she changed the subject. "You do have the body of an athlete," she soothed, speaking apparently from the happy vantage point of another inner obstacle overcome. At last my sister and her friend made noises about going to Stanford Shopping Center to look at some darling tops that had just arrived at Magnin's. Hoping to pique my sense of deprivation perhaps, she lingered. Then, sensing no response, she departed. What did I care right this minute if she intended to throw any quantity of my father's money after overpriced outfits that would end up discarded on "her" bedroom floor at his house. I lacked the money for a box of Pampers for the new baby at the moment: Doug's new job was little more than minimum wage as usual, but Daisy was leaving again and there was no room for emotional inconsequencia. I got up when they left and articulated a few sloppy dives off the board.

"God, that was gross," I apologized, sounding like a valley girl myself. "I shouldn't show off," I apologized and tried it again. Again bullets of water stung my eyes. Was it that I hadn't been let in by my sister—the duenna of the homestead—in years, and was out of practice on the diving board, was it that I was slightly out of balance from the pregnancy, or was it that I just couldn't show Daisy up in front of Sam in any way? After the last aborted dive, my loyalty and sadness drew me like a stone to the bottom of the pool. There I lingered, not wanting to come up, feeling that the sun had gone out of the day, that it was just a yard, just a pool in someone's yard, and that I had nothing now to give Daisy that she would want.

At last I floundered up from the bottom, heaved myself up over the side and plopped down beside her, boyish, conflicted.

"I've been watching Doug," she said.

"Those were stupid dives," I apologized. She waved it off. "Well...you say you get in trouble when you try to show off." She seemed satisfied. I had given her something. I restrained myself against my desire to jump back in and swim laps with Sam. I took it easy, the way she did. Maybe I would have my magic-two-couples day in the sun yet.

Answering my thoughts she suggested, "Doug is a lot like Art, isn't he?" I wasn't quite sure what she meant, but then I noticed that, as he slept on one side, his penis, otherwise ordinarily ample, had retreated, shriveled up from the breeze. Actually his whole personality seemed retreated all day, just like his penis. Was it fear of something or indifference? Uncoordinated to the extreme, he stayed far away from Sam's cavorting and seemed to help himself to the respite from Veronica and his already disappointing job, by lying inert and watching—what was it?—clouds going by perhaps, or just…nothing.

"He is like Art," Daisy persisted casually, "even in that way." I felt ashamed, as if she were looking into my sex life, into the poor choice that I had made, disrupting the artifice created by a semblance of pride—that things were even halfway ok between Doug and me. She felt sorry for me, I guessed, and seemed understanding. I totally forgot that she had vehemently recommended the marriage to me, not only when "we" met him, but also by phone during that first year of courting when I worked at the home for wayward girls. She'd encouraged me to marry him sooner than I did, likening Doug and me to herself and Art. At that time she'd described herself and Art as "one person in every way." She even explained that there could be occasional attractions toward (or even affairs with) others outside their marriage because they functioned as one person. Such oneness wasn't my goal with Doug, in fact I literally held my breath in the presence of handsome men and hadn't, to date, felt the slightest anything, or at least in holding my breath, I had successfully held back the possibility. But I felt she was telling me something, suggesting something, and, well…it felt uncomfortable. I was cross with Doug all the way home, nitpicky and testy, as if I were trying to quicken that in him, so that it could flare up and I would feel ok at last.

At the next intense nighttime class meeting on the east side, we continued working with an idea called "concept living." I admitted to the group I wasn't at ease with "concept living." "You'll always find it hard, I think," Art whispered to me. "You feel things so deeply, don't you?"

"What is it?" I asked stubbornly, although I must have known.

"It's just that you act on the concept you have mentally recognized to be true. You act on that principle irregardless of anything else," Rebecca instructed me once again. I focused on Rebecca's grammatical error and once again blocked out the offending idea.

It wasn't that I didn't understand the concepts. Daisy had handed out a little schoolish quiz on universal laws as described by the group of late, and of course I got the equivalent of "A's."

"You have all the mental understanding there is," she said tonight. "But you must live the concepts, manifest them. To know them intellectually is to be able to teach; to live them is to minister."

By the end of the class, Daisy told the group she was moving on to Santa Cruz to work for a time. "I don't know for how long, but this is something I have to do, you know?"

They knew. Staying "in concept," there wasn't a wet eye in the place. Summer was only beginning but there would be no more parties.

Daisy handed me a flyer and passed one in turn to each person there gathered, now including Nora Paul and her husband Kenny and the ever cool Connie hanging around with Neil, and Jade and Tim and Mary Grace and Wayne and Art, with Amy Rebecca and me and Doug and several hangers on from here and there. What could Pixy Talbott, a middle-aged, self-appointed, ex-alcoholic minister Daisy had met on one of her jaunts "over the hill," have to recommend her? Could it be her connection with the glamorous man we'd all seen lecture that first year on North Redwood Street—the man called Patrick? Pixy and Patrick seemed to be part of a chain of events that were leading Daisy to an unknown destiny. On the strength of Pixy's recommendations, Patrick was already asking Daisy and Sam to come down to see him in Hollywood, carte blanche, as it were. Daisy was considering it, but first had to follow spirit to Santa Cruz to the congregations and doings of this self-appointed ex-alcoholic minister Pixy, whom I knew Daisy didn't particularly like.

The tract Daisy handed about was quite sentimental to the tune of "You've all given me more than I've given you. To me, each one of you is the teacher," etc. It was hard to stay "in concept," when it sounded as if she were leaving us forever. Was this a test?

Before Daisy left, she married her brother, Rexford Buchanon —to Rebecca, in the park, on the authority of a mail-away minister's license she'd had in reserve (as legal protection) for a while and as technical backing for the Spirit-directed Temple of Living Waters.

For me, the highlights of the wedding were that Daisy and Rebecca spent the night together in Rexford and Rebecca Buchanon's bed in their newly rented house while Rex stayed with Art. I stopped by to give Rebecca a present and they let me into the bedroom where they were gossiping like sisters. Also, Amy showed me snapshots of the wedding after Daisy and Sam disappeared over the hill to fulfill their destiny in Santa Cruz. There was a streak of light (honest to God) leading from the sky over Willow Street Park onto the

Daisy at First Communion with her younger brother Rexford

proceedings in the photograph. Rebecca was fairly content with this manifestation from Spirit, and she and Rex embarked hopefully on a new life. Rex had once been gay, but that fact lay submerged in the "rightness" of this inclusion of Rebecca into Daisy's family. At last Rebecca became Daisy's sister-in-law, somewhat anticlimactically, since Rebecca's favorite story to recount at Elizabeth's Asilomar conferences we all continued to attend, was that Daisy had been her "sister" since the first night the two met in a bar just before the classes began on North Redwood Street.

Rebecca told the Asilomar audience without embarrassment, that this blonde woman kept flipping a coin down the bar where she sat having a drink with some girlfriends, and that she was pretty irritated until the blond woman asked her "sign". Before Rebecca knew it, the blonde woman had told her that she'd lived before as her sister in Italy, and then Rebecca had gotten chills all over—"rain," she told the audience—and that "the attraction started there and has gotten stronger ever since". She meant attraction at the deepest, soul level, apparently; but I would have been more than a little embarrassed to say that publicly. Maybe not, if Daisy cared enough about me to say, (as she did of Rebecca) "I would murder her if I had to—if I knew it were for the good of her soul."

Santa Cruz appeared to be a steppingstone for Daisy. I should have known she'd be back with us soon. Toward the end of the summer, Daisy began to come back over the hill (what a relief) to Rebecca and Rex' rented house in a run-down section beneath the city college. There Daisy held business meetings I got to attend—why, I didn't know, since I'd almost accepted that I wasn't to be part of the business. Maybe they were just being solicitous since I was so close to giving birth. They drank even more coffee, although Daisy was pregnant, and ate delicious crystallized sugar doughnuts and smoked. First we listened avidly as Daisy described the certain events of her future daughter's conception. She told us that the child had "come to them" after they came together in the duplex on Eastside Drive. Was it on that sunny day after I had watched them on the grass through the kitchen window? I was thrilled at the thought. "She will be a leader, an expected one," Daisy announced. We listened breathlessly, and the child within me moved insistently to the rhythms of Daisy's words.

Then Daisy told us she soon would be finished at Pixy Talbott's; that she had learned what she'd been sent to learn, and that

now she intended to accept Patrick's invitation to visit his center in
L.A. (Would she see Elizabeth too? I remembered how Daisy once
remarked that she would gladly "go sit at Elizabeth's feet, and help
her"—like a humble devotee, I had interpreted the remark.) Daisy's
eyes sparkled. We snapped out of the listless, heat-saturated period
of her absence and sat up. "We'll be staying with him for a week—
'carte blanche,' he said—I'll tell you all about it when I get back. So
much is happening for all of us now."

After innumerable cups of coffee, we took turns using
Rebecca's bathroom. Daisy went before me. "Bring my notes from
the table, will you sweetheart?" she called to where I stood outside
the door she'd left open. I brought them and stayed to scrutinize the
plants perched on Rebecca's windowsill. Daisy was even more
enthralled with plants now, influenced by the "organic" mode of the
Santa Cruz culture. She brought each of us plant slips on trips over
the hill. Rebecca's things had a little of Daisy's flair but were dirtier
somehow, and the leaves of the plants on the window looked dried at
the edges, yellowed and curled. Rebecca hadn't watered them. Now
Rebecca got some of the best of Daisy's pictures and gifts. A cheery
embroidered hanging was strung sadly at an angle on one plywood-
paneled bathroom wall. Outside, through a plastic window, in the
house behind a half-covered porch, I saw an old man working on his
car. These were the things that always irritated me at my apartment
—around Daisy unpleasant sounds like metal against metal were
muted into nothingness. Rebecca's plants definitely weren't watered.
She's probably watering them later today, I thought. I had to trust
Rebecca—all of them—to know better than I did.

Daisy chatted with me from the can. My admiration rose.
Casual. Dignified. Strong. Daisy was being a Being in a body, as
always. Art said at the end, that she only consciously deceived us to
the degree that she projected an ideal as though she could live it,
before she actually could. Daisy on the can was the projection of
casual dignity, a thinker, no pretensions. We discussed the conversation at the table. Or rather I discussed, having the advantageous
position of Daisy's total attention. The bathroom was rather large for
the size of the house, but close enough to create a self-consciousness
I hadn't felt nude swimming or out of doors. When asked for the
toilet paper, I passed it from the top of Rebecca's overstuffed clothes
hamper, not dwelling overly long on the paper passing, meeting her
eyes freely but not too long, only long enough so that we could both

see that I was free enough to meet them. I certainly did not dwell on her body or even look at it, but scanned the air around and over her body lightly and with neither obvious interest nor disinterest. I was exhausted by the time she finished, though cheerful.

I got up to water the plants with a decorative cup from the fake marble sink top. Daisy smiled, absentmindedly but appreciative. She had given Rebecca the plant after all. I didn't say anything after that but gave the plant a little soddy tuck into its moist blue plastic container. Daisy reached up to touch the tendrils of the "Creeping Charlie" after she'd flushed. "Poor baby," she said to the browning tail of unwatered foliage. "Would you water this too, chicken?"

"All right," I said, almost tumbling over myself. Usually I talked too long when I finally had an opportunity. This time, thankfully, I stumbled into graceful silence.

She checked her notes. When she was washing I asked her, "Do you think I could have the baby at home? I want to, you know." "I don't know," she replied. "As strong as you are, I know Veronica's birth wasn't easy for you—I wouldn't, that's what doctors are for." A straight, discouraging answer, but perhaps I was relieved. I wanted to deliver at home—but....

"I'll help you," Daisy promised brightly as we left the bathroom. (And didn't she dream of my labor on the night the baby came nine days before the due date, dream she was walking with me when I stumbled over the one, rough spot in our otherworldly walkway. Didn't she announce these facts to Rebecca on the night after her dream, on the morning I would return from the hospital three hours after a delivery easy save for one rough spot?) Not knowing at this moment what form her help would assume, we returned to the others and planned the Temple of Living Waters service Daisy said we should undertake in her absence.

She called a meeting after her return from Los Angeles. The night was extremely hot. The room was packed with Daisy's followers. Yvette sat as near as she could to Daisy. Rebecca made coffee. Eight months pregnant, I was choking from the cigarette smoke around me and sat nearest to the door. I complained, so every so often Sam would perfunctorily wave the door open and shut it again. It was fun otherwise, all huddled up together in Rebecca's small house. As usual, the street noises, the shouts in Spanish from next door, were subdued and then vanished. Everyone listened to

Daisy. I wiggled to a more comfortable position on the hardwood floor, leaning against the back of Yvette's chair. Then Art emerged from the far end of the room and brought me a stool.

"You know why I've called you all here," Daisy began. "You know I felt led to stay for a time at Patrick's church down south—and we did. I honestly believe they are a sister group." Her face was alight. She smiled up at Sam positioned near the front door. He winked back and urged, "Go on, go on," he gestured with thick, tanned hands. The wide loose white sleeves of his shirt fluttered, a shirt hand-made by Daisy and embroidered with rainbows and a star shower along the open V-collar that revealed his heavy, handsome neck and bared, bronze chest.

Daisy could barely stifle the excitement as she stood, bare feet on either side of the floor heater between the kitchen and the tiny living room, swaying, gazing up beyond the low stucco ceiling, swinging her right hand, skywriting with cigarette smoke. "Now I know why I had to go see Patrick. We're going to be working together." She dropped her cigarette into the ashtray Art provided her and left it to cloud and burn against the other butts in the dish. She smoothed her blouse a little over her pregnant form and twirled the gold, wax cast Nepthys pendant she wore so often now, recovering her authoritative voice from the burst of childlike enthusiasm.

"Listen, I've got to tell you all something before we go any further. You were fantastic last Saturday. I listened to the tape Neil made of the service you held while we were with Patrick. This is the beginning of something greater, believe me."

I broke in, "I had a dream about them—about Patrick's group—I'm sure now it was about them. Um...do you remember, Daisy, last year when I dreamed there was a parallel world or something, and there were others of us in this parallel world?"

"Right. You got it," Daisy bestowed a brief, benevolent smile upon me and went on. "They're where we were two years ago in some ways—we have something special—but they have it together. Really. Don't they, sweetheart?" Sam smiled. "Go on, don't keep them waiting."

"They have ministers and a real church and a choir and money. They support their ministers." (This she stressed.) "And their ministers support them. They have singers who sing sometimes at the Hollywood Bowl, and whatever they need, they manifest. Tell them later, honey, how they got the materials they needed for the new church they had been told to build on faith."

"It's pretty far-out, you guys. Some really far-out things—**really** far-out things happened there.".

"They're not into that conventional religious thing—you know, 'Re-joice, Re-joice—'"she pronounced in a funereal monotone, "or anything like that." Sam continued after the laughter had passed, "But they're manifesting, guys, they're manifesting their beliefs and…"

Daisy picked up that thread and looped it through the fabric of her remaining message. "It's time to **manifest** what all of you have been sowing up here"—she pointed to the ceiling—"it's time to make it happen, to reap the rewards. We're beginning to act as one body now. We were able to be in L.A. making the contacts necessary for our next step and you sustained yourselves without us, manifesting those energies necessary to send out the call that must follow." I wanted to ask, why didn't you see Elizabeth while you were there? But I didn't.

"And because of that," Daisy continued, "I've accepted Patrick's invitation to become co-minister of his church here in Mountain View—and you're all going with me."

"Whew," Rebecca gasped, grinning expectantly at the rest of us gathered in her living room. For a moment, all were quiet.

"What are we getting into, Daisy?" Art asked from the back of the room. "A church? Won't there be some problems with this? You've repeatedly said that when a group becomes an institution—a church or whatever—they fall, they crystallize around some idea and they lose the truth, the energy, the spirit. Didn't you say that? I'm not saying I agree with that, but isn't that what we've been operating on all this time? Isn't it?" His dark, slate blue eyes looked small in a face that was gradually jowling. "You shouldn't hide that beautiful soul in a heavy body, Art," Daisy had been chiding him lately. Art was a hassle in a way. Poor Daisy, it was awkward to have him here. People were beginning to like him less. Even me, I thought; what did they do with the last consort, when the goddess cast him out for a muscled poet with sweet eyes? "My darling man," Daisy called Sam now, "sweet man of my heart." It made Art look more dour and sour daily, as if he were yesterday's style, like a ducktail or pegged pants, when earth shoes and unisex haircuts were the vogue.

Daisy regarded Art over her reading glasses and answered him patiently, "Yes, that's true, but we haven't become orthodox or crystallized. We've remained true to Spirit. But in remaining true, we must be willing to follow Spirit wherever it leads us—without preconceptions—even into a church." Art sighed and receded.

"Before we can embark on this next step, there are a couple of things: we have to make some decisions about the Temple of Living Water and its future, and there are a few little problems we need to clear up before we can proceed," she tossed as if it were an afterthought. "Now, however, I want to share with you some of the messages, the prophesies I received in L.A. A lot has come through —and about some of you."

I shifted. The stool was as uncomfortable as the floor, but I wanted a better view of what was to come. It was better than opening presents to hear Daisy unveil such messages.

Daisy recounted her vision for the destiny of the group. I became aware that she was staring into me through her new glasses that widened the wide vistas of her eyes even more. She looked, I was sure, into my soul.

"I saw, at the end of this vision, a being holding a staff writing over a very large gathering of people listening to one person, a young woman who might be you, Page—I think it was you. The staff wrote, 'And the last shall be first.' You may have a great responsibility ahead of you, chicken." Smoke swirled around her head. I didn't mind the smoke now. "Let's take a break." Sam sprang up. Daisy walked toward me. As she approached, the Nepthys winked at me. She pressed her cool hand on mine and walked off to stand close to Yvette and talk confidentially to her in the kitchen. I didn't even think to wonder what they were saying. Wow.

I preened under the words, twirled around inside once or twice. I could wait.

Chapter Twelve

Daisy resumed at half past ten. Rebecca told us we had to stay longer in order to clear up certain relationship problems that would hold us back if they weren't "fixed." Neil dutifully switched back on the tape recorder, fed by a black cord that snaked off to a mysterious plug somewhere. He looked smug and nervous at the same time. "If you're going to say something about relationships, don't look at me, Daisy." Daisy smiled at Neil. An unclear image in the smoke, I thought I saw him bend his knee, a courtier, the tape recorder symbolic of a pledge to his liege.

"We've come to a point where most of us can deal with a relationship in our lives," Daisy began. "Those of us who are in these new relationships have worked hard for them." She did not look back up at Art or at Sam—or at Amy whose Sam he had once been. "But there are some of you still without a relationship right now in your lives," she continued, "and some of you are playing games, little girl games." She looked at Jade, whose pretty dark Basque and Eurasian features clouded, and at Yvette, who looked paralyzed, staring down at the grain of the wooden floor, moving only to draw her bare feet from the spot where they almost touched Sam's golden muscled calf. After that she froze. "Little girl games," Daisy continued, "and little boy games too," she said, but didn't look at anybody in particular.

Neil coughed then, as if she had directed her remarks to him, and looked sheepish, as if she would accuse him. Also he looked pleased. But that stuff never bothered Daisy—that is, the men who wanted her. She explained that it was the love of Spirit that flowed from her, and that these men were clicking into past life memories, momentarily the gateway to memory had opened, returning some of the lower charka feelings known in past lifetimes. In all fairness, Neil was quite shy and if it seemed his half-lidded gaze was aimed at his lower charka between his legs as he sat tailor-style, he really didn't have anywhere else to look but up and into someone's face. Daisy went on as though unaware of his behavior, zeroing in on Yvette, who by this time had everybody's attention. Phony, I thought. That's a sweet little girl look if I've ever seen one.

"Now listen, honey, I'm not singling you out." Yvette began to cry, quiet, childish tears dripped out of her wide, Keene-type eyes.

"I really don't know what you mean," she whispered. "I haven't done anything. Ask anybody."

Rebecca sliced, "You didn't think she'd find out, did you?" Then she included Sam in a penetrating third eye assault. Sam looked down and twisted his foot in his sandal repeatedly, finally arising, opening and shutting the door once or twice for smoke.

Amy giggled. "You can't do anything in the energy anymore and not get caught—can you sweetheart?" she tossed off the last.

"Oh, all right," Yvette cried. "I didn't mean to. I mean...I mean..." She laughed through her tears. "I don't know why I feel like this—about him. I'm so sorry to have hurt you. I'm sorry," she blubbered now.

Satisfied, Daisy turned to Jade. "I'll talk to you later."

Uncle Art bent down and patted Yvette's back with a wide fleshy hand. "It's ok, doll," he assured her in the same voice he used with Todd Allen. "We all make mistakes." Even Uncle Art is a company man, I thought. I too feared Yvette and Jade, if they were playing little girl games with our men as Daisy had said, but I wondered if there weren't something unfair in this. Less than two years ago, Daisy made it with Amy's new husband, Sam, on Christmas Eve in Utah while Art babysat all the kids for her so that she could test her need for this man Sam who "God had brought into my life," and for whom she longed intensely while she imagined she hated him. "I didn't want to do it, Page, but it got so bad that it hurt." No, I corrected myself, that's different. Daisy and Sam were meant to be together, they'd earned it.

"Those of us who've earned our relationships deserve some respect," Daisy now emphasized. That made sense—yes that's it—just what I was trying to understand, I thought.

Curiosity buzzed in the background. Images of Yvette's sad, pretty, cow eyes and lipstick-less, cupid bow, hippie mouth over Sam's firm lips, floated in the group's telepathic thought pool. We glimpsed her white face like a flower, obscuring view of his bush of soft-looking, wavy brown, short cropped hair over his wan, white-marbled, silver blue eyes which peered down over Yvette's soft, straggly brown head.The adepts glimpsed too his meaty, pared-nail hands, gripping hers to emphasize that it was wrong, his row of porcelain teeth flashing in sequence into her tear-brimmed eyes reflecting her shame as she slanted her serape-robbed, braless body closer to his V-necked, white-shirted trunk. "No hair on his chest," she might have thought, "no one told me that." Some sensitives shuddered at the clairvoyant image of the huge bulge beneath his loose drawstring unisex trousers. "I bet he can do it for hours," we imagined Yvette to speculate when confronted with the fact of his flashy proportions.

Then we imagined Sam's feelings. The confused buzz of our thought forms and images settled more slowly around him. We couldn't imagine what he would have thought, settling uncomfortably within Yvette's pretty cow-like gaze. Probably he thought it wasn't worth it, not now, not here, not yet. And that Daisy was his sweetheart. I wondered if Sam might have been just the least little bit disgusted. Rumor came back later to confirm to me they'd kissed. It was a momentary thing, I guessed, but enough for Daisy to use a meeting to nip it in the bud.

Leaving Yvette dutifully blubbering, Jade dreading her rain check to discuss her misdeeds, and the rest of us highly titillated, Daisy plunged back into what was really important—more important than the human entanglements of babies, indiscretions and the like —and that was Patrick's church.

Next Saturday, we rode up together, squished in Art's beat-up van, to meet the man Patrick, to hear his Universal Singers at Ricky's Hyatt House in Palo Alto.

The room was full. The singers, young men and women, entered wearing matching shirts. They looked out at us. Beyond one glass wall of the crowded, comfortably carpeted room, a fountain cascaded water, shimmering into a white-rimmed pool.

The group began; tambourines in hand, voices beginning crisp and light, brightening, strengthening and straining until there was an almost palpable tension; something, someone, was expected to come. First, a white-suited, distinguished man in white shoes, a Colonel Sanders looking gentleman who called himself Jonas Saul, stepped up and took his place to one side of a center spotlight

ringed in rainbow light, softly tinted with sparkly radiuses like the
fountain water which continuously streamed outside the window.
Now the singers began in earnest: "When the moon is in the second
house, and Jupiter aligns with mars, then peace will guide the
planet, and lo-ove will steer the stars." From the back of the room,
an "ahhh" began. Heads turned. A golden haired man, arms
outstretched, palms open, head up, with a sweet smile and the look
of tears about the eyes, walked in long strides up the thick-carpeted
center aisle.

"Aren't they beautiful," he whispered into the microphone,
not your Lawrence Welk perfunctory buffoon, but in awe, like a
little boy in church. Swinging around to face us, he glanced at the
white haired, handsome man who looked up at him with the
benevolence of a father for a favorite son who was a divine being
about whom he could feel no jealousy; only love and adoration
because of his commitment to protecting this god incarnate. The
girls, the boys in the choir, lapped up his first words as though long
starved, feasted on him with their eyes from behind, although they
couldn't see what we could see, the front of Patrick's satin shirt,
gently bared further down than was usually seen in Palo Alto. I
glanced at the understated cross that slipped between smooth
parted pectorals—how could I not?

"Hello," he said, and tears, it appeared, started coursing
down lightly browned cheeks.

"Come up here," he called to Daisy, seated at the outside of
the front row. "I want you to meet someone—will you, for me?
This special lady, Daisy, will be with you now in Mountain View,
at my church, at our church." He turned to her and whispered the
word like a caress.

"Thank you, Patrick," Daisy answered almost inaudibly from
the front row. Was she too moved by this?

For a moment, to me, Daisy seemed to pale like a wildflower
drooping shyly in a hothouse, but then she turned and walked the
three feet to her seat with the distant, unattached, unseeing gaze she
had that promised—if you could penetrate it fully—all the
mysteries of the universe that lay behind it.

When she swirled about self-consciously as if to quell his
beckoning, then dropped in her seat, I thought she was overly
modest. We knew who she was. But then I noticed afterwards that

the audience, and even the distinguished healer, seemed to follow her even when Patrick was speaking.

All we could talk about on the way home, crowded into the back of Art's windowless van, were Patrick's words. When all of them lit cigarettes, I got openly angry. The baby was due any day and my God, there were no windows.

Daisy said I had something hidden I needed to deal with, other than the smoke, which was a smokescreen. Everyone laughed. I felt dumbfounded. All the smokers stared at me as though I were a stupid kid when I insisted that there were studies now saying smoking could cause premature births and respiratory problems. Daisy said, "If that's what you believe, then maybe you can make it happen," and laughed, puffing a plume of smoke into my eyes. Awkwardly, I climbed out of the back of the van in front of the even shabbier duplex I'd moved into, to be nearer to Rebecca's house—the nexus of Daisy's visits. Only around the corner from Rebecca's at my miserable place, I could still clearly hear the traffic and the macho shouting of the Mexican bikers next door. Now I stood in the smog-charged yard and tried to clear my lungs, feeling sullen and resentful of all of them. Still, I questioned diligently, what does smoke mean to me? I decided smoke might mean mental confusion. They often told me (Amy with particular venom) that I was too "mental." Could there be anything in my life that I was so confused about as not to be able to see clearly or penetrate the smoke of mental confusion?Three stars winked at me in an opaque clearing made by the wind passing through the smoggy film of the night sky.

I sat down on wettened grass—from Doug's hose—and cried. I didn't know why, but I kept hearing a still, small, quiet voice. "I am as near thee as thine own heartbeat." I listened a minute, felt comforted and went back into the little living room I had painted Daisy's favorite color, cornflower blue. The 11:30 newscaster's voice scratched through the worn-out speaker of the Goodwill-purchased black and white T.V. set perched atop the antique, half-finished wooden sea chest Doug prized. He was asleep, the dishes were done and cacophonous music competed from across the breath of space that separated us from a row of run-down apartments. Veronica's cough kept time to the scratchy voice of the announcer.

Flies crawled up a white sore on a baby girl's cheek in a T.V. appeal for starving children somewhere. I watched, because I had to, felt I should. The scene shifted to the brutal image of another baby, brain-damaged by starvation and already blind, whose parents had saved their single banana for the baby that night. That's all it had. God. God. Tears fought their way out of my tight, half-shut eyes. I had to see though. The warm salt tears slid over my cheekbones and slipped over the corners of my mouth. I sat on the wooden box, and pulled my knees as close to my belly as they could come, wishing the scenes would stop. I promised the children I would do something to stop their suffering. God, I asked, let me.

And then I thought of Daisy's words at the last meeting at Rebecca's. This was to be the start of something greater, and I remembered how the mood in the room swelled and rose, blotting out all the terrible residue of the day that hung about this neighborhood: of the screams of neglected children; of the swarthy boys laughter mocking the pale alcoholic woman who wove out of her house each day, knee-highs drooping over bony, varicose calves beneath her threadbare housecoat; of the sound of bottles breaking when she dumped her overfull wastebasket into the can at the end of the yard.

At last I could do something for these people, for the starving children, for the world. A feeling, like peaceful music, like the sound of the one bird that trilled outside the parted window for a second, made me realize this was where I wanted to be more than anywhere else in the world, that all the years of waiting, of giving up, had culminated in this: "And the last shall be first."

When Molly was born, Daisy admired her, said "I want her." Daisy often got what she wanted and I took the joke uneasily. Nine days old at Elizabeth's great philosophical gathering by the sea near Monterey, Daisy whisked Molly off and took a nap with her. When I came to retrieve her from the room she and Sam shared with Rebecca and Rex, I overheard her wonder why she felt so close to this baby. Rebecca asked, "Daisy, are you sure it isn't because your own baby will be here soon?"

"Maybe," Daisy responded. "I don't know whether I'm relating to her as if she were Anne (it had been revealed that the child in Daisy's womb would be named Anne) or what?" I walked into view. Daisy's eyes looked dark and watery, suboceanic blue. She lay coiled about the baby like a sea goddess who, at the bottom of an undersea lagoon, was unwilling to relinquish her yet; the two seemed lost in clouded waters. I felt flattered, distantly angry and shy, almost as if I were the intruder.

Daisy had announced quite early on that she had had a vision of Anne, her daughter, at the moment of her conception and so it was accepted that she would be a girl, that her name would be Anne. Daisy stuck her neck out on that prophesy, but her confidence was up. She had the church now—at least part of one; many of her personal prophesies had been fulfilled. For eight months they referred to the baby as Anne.

When Anson was born, I was asleep. The call came from Amy at about 2 A.M. I asked, "What about him being a girl?" Amy cut me off, nonchalant, distant, as if it had all been planned that way after all. Nothing was ever said about it to anyone. Except once, when Daisy remarked to me apropos to nothing at the maverick new hall she established after splitting from Patrick in Mountain View, ostensibly for philosophical reasons. She had had a vision, she said, where she was shown that we were sheep innocently subjecting ourselves to a wolf in sheep's clothing. Daisy was well trained (by osmosis) at Patrick's church and may have felt strong enough to break off. Certainly her rumored tactics at the end—long after I had left the group—showed the gossipmongers that she had learned well. If there were suspicions of the sex-linked murders of pubescent boys linked to Patrick (Steven's slanderous rumor), there were beginning to be 3 A.M. Gestapo-type raids by Daisy (now the irrefutable reincarnation of Mary Magdalene, she said) and her newest consort, a twenty-year-old kid whom she flatly declared to be Jesus. (Amy's distorted rumor.) On the hot August afternoon when we sat around discussing parenting children in new age consciousness, it would have been hard to predict allegations of raids to unearth traitors betraying Mary Magdalene and a new son.

"If I'd gotten pregnant earlier, Page, Molly would have been born to Sam and me," Daisy said when no one important was listening. I thought about that quite a lot. It unnerved me the first time Molly painted a rainbow with watercolors at preschool and then added the little star of new birth in a fuzzy, little kid technique to be sure, but the star nonetheless, Daisy's most characteristic signature. Molly was only three when I left and has never seen Daisy since. Her rainbows and flowers and stars have accelerated and she once—probably nobody would believe me if I told them, but it's God's truth—signed Daisy's three initials to one of the works. She looks, in some ways, more like Daisy and Sam than she does me. She has a short pert nose, wan, water blue eyes and a mouth set in an attractive, forward-cast jaw a great deal like Daisy's. I suppose her physical appearance shouldn't surprise me, because Daisy was the focus of my admiration during my pregnancy and the late, great true psychic Edgar Cayce did say that the impressions gathered by those about the soul of an incoming entity, particularly those of the one carrying or caring for the child, do have an effect.

The situation of my motherhood, which even I could see had bought Daisy's envy, as quickly brought forth its dark side. By now it was clear that something must be wrong with Veronica. She had stopped walking and dropped to her knees. At Molly's baptism, Daisy almost stepped on her. "A floor baby," she said kindly. Plucked out of complete denial by a dream that warned me to take her to a chiropractor or a neurologist, I chose the latter. I was still a traditionalist when afraid. The wonderful holistic Cayce health concepts were further from my mind than ever, now. Elizabeth's importance to the group seemed to have subsided as Daisy led us elsewhere.

Doug's mother, who'd just been with us to see the new baby, returned six weeks later when Veronica was to be admitted to a local hospital for a neurological workup. After the initial office visit with a doctor who assured me that something was definitely wrong, I returned to the business meeting at Rebecca's so crestfallen, so weighted, that I literally hung my head over and dropped it on the bright orange-painted hexagonal table that had come with the ramshackle furnishings of the house.

After awhile Rebecca chided me. "What's the matter with you?" I'd already told them what the doctor told me about Veronica. I repeated it. "That's what you're upset about?" Rebecca looked puzzled. I was too sad to be ashamed.

While Veronica was being seen in the hospital, I dreamed a dream I sought quickly to repress. I dreamed there was something in the water that stopped her from developing past a year. In horror, I shook it off. The results of the tests were inconclusive.

Without further invading her body, all that could be determined was that she lacked balance. She shared a hospital room with a little girl who was hydrocephalic and had come in to have fluid drained from her brain. (Why had they chosen this roommate for Veronica?) I wondered in a panic.

After Veronica had been there for three days, she managed to get up and begin walking again and I attributed it to the strange scent I'd smelled after she'd had an x-ray series the night before. I told Daisy about it. "Could she have been healed? Is that what that odd, sweet odor indicated?" "Possibly," Daisy mused, "I think you're right." I clung to that and took Veronica home, deciding with Daisy that her soul just wasn't fully in her body yet. I took the stance of positive thinking, of mind over matter, and deferred the only remaining test—the CAT Scan—for a time. I had other appointments with that doctor but could not return. For this I felt guilty, although in the final analysis he had nothing more to offer. I decided we should move again and tried to find a proper house more to the north and nearer to Daisy's new church, rather Patrick's existing church in Mountain View, nearer to the mid-point of the San Francisco Bay peninsula.

Before I found the overpriced, overgrown, haunted, "real" house I thought might mend my problems, I enjoyed a few brighter days, buoyed falsely by the hope that Veronica was entirely ok after her "healing" with the x-rays. After all, she could walk again, even though the falling had resumed and I was buoyed too by Molly's presence. She was a rose growing in brambles, I thought, just like the rose that had bloomed outside the front door of the duplex, next to which she'd been photographed on the first day of her life.

One of these brief, happy days of denial dawned blue, with unusual white waves of inland clouds washing over San Jose, washing through the inner city and out toward the more affluent suburbs beneath the western edge of the circle of mountains that formed the sentinel range surrounding the Santa Clara Valley.

I put the children in a single stroller and wheeled them down the long street and around the block to Rebecca's house. The early morning wind whipped chill and unwound Daisy's hand-me-down wrap-around skirt from my calves. Molly cooed at the wind. Veronica was, for a moment, content to watch leaves fall to form a carpet under the metal wheels of the baby carriage. I approached

Rebecca's with last night's dream in hand and a bitter squall of blackbirds fluttered out of the gnarled tree in her front yard. When I'd awakened, I'd put the dream to paper in a rush. I'd dreamed I was Annie Besant. Instead of the blond, blue-eyed Besant, I saw myself instead as a middle-aged, dark-haired woman, saw the face clearly—the serious eyes and strong nose—saw that they looked like mine.

The crumpled sheets in my hand felt dry, like the brittle leaves that floated from the stooped tree across from Rebecca's front doorstep. Her door was left unlocked. All of our doors were left unlocked now because of the power of positive thinking transformed into Daisy's latest concept, "You can't lose anything that really belongs to you."

I hauled the baby carriage up the steps into the living room and called for Rebecca. To my left, the door that led from the tiny living room to Rebecca's bedroom was left ajar. A curly male head protruded from under the bedcovers.

"Rebecca's not here," a muffled male voice reported.

It was Peter Taylor, a friend of Daisy and Sam's from Santa Cruz, and Amy's new boyfriend. When I had taken Molly to Elizabeth's Labor Day Asilomar conference, I was present in the courtyard when Peter first laid eyes on Amy, the former prostitute. "You look like an angel," he'd whispered sincerely. I was touched and knew that he saw true. So was Amy evidently. Now they were very close. I left the children in the living room and entered Rebecca's small, close bedroom.

"Hi, Page."

"I'm sorry."

Amy broke from a titillating entanglement beneath the covers and addressed me with unusual gaiety. Peter, similarly freed and snuggling in the crook of Amy's arm, smiled at me with the broad mouth and wide soft eyes of a former jester. He was a short man with broad shoulders, a very young man, but poised and intact.

"Come in."

"Are you sure?"

"Don't be silly," Amy sniffed. "We're not uptight about these things. Not us." By that I guessed she meant the magic three: Daisy, Amy and Rebecca, now Amy's sister-in-law. "We've never minded before," she repeated, more for Peter's benefit than my own. Peter. Amy's suitor at last. It was hard to escape the magic. I was happy for her but somewhat embarrassed. "I had this dream. I dreamed I was Annie Besant," I started inappropriately. "Well, I know I wasn't," I said quickly, because they weren't to think I was putting on airs. "You know I'm not Annie Besant..." (Elizabeth had discovered that lifetime for Daisy four years earlier and I thought she was right. Daisy looked like Besant and there were many life parallels. For example, Daisy once took up the piano without training with some success, and, during the last throws of the group after I was gone and she'd lost Sam too, Daisy discovered a very young man she believed to be Jesus reborn—the pattern, Elizabeth pointed out, of Besant with Krishnamurti. "We tend to repeat the pattern, baby—or do the exact opposite," Elizabeth had told me. "But maybe my dream about Besant is a clue to something," I continued to Amy and Peter. "Rebecca has a book on Annie Besant around here somewhere, doesn't she? That's why I came over," I defended.

"Sure." Amy nudged Peter under the covers. Their toes lifted the rainbow afghan at the bottom of bed. Daisy had made it for Rebecca and Rexford as a wedding present. Amy and Peter's neatly folded clothes lay over the back of an old chair, contrasting with Rebecca's cluttered bureau in the low, stucco-ceiling room. Daisy's artwork hung askew next to the bureau. The windows, steamy and smeared, isolated the two guests in Rebecca's bedroom.

Eager about the dream, I remained a captive, like a lady-in-waiting in the next-to-the-great-lady's bedchamber. "Where is the book, do you think?"

They giggled, oblivious to me...or maybe glad of an audience. Peter tipped Amy's head backward and kissed her under her chin. Then Amy mumbled something. Evidently there was a joke I didn't understand. Peter laughed, patted her head and hugged her to him, but his eyes met mine. He pulled the afghan to his chest. The blues and purples on its outer edge reflected in his eyes, blue too, an odd shade of cornflower similar to my duplex walls. Then he ruffled his curly hair.

"It might be on the coffee table, I think," he said politely, sensing my discomfort. Suddenly Veronica rose from the stroller and stumbled after one of Rebecca's cats. I turned from the bedroom. Through the doorway, I warned Veronica not to touch the hot grates of the floor heater between the living room and the kitchen.

On the coffee table among two or three other books was a plastic-covered library book simply titled, "Annie Besant: Her Life And Times." I searched inside, flipping through the first few pages idly. Then I opened it abruptly about half-way through to gaze at a full page photograph of a 40 year old woman with black hair, serious eyes and nose similar to mine. I shivered. "Eleanor Marx," it read, "youngest daughter of Karl Marx." I carried the book with me out the back door—Amy and Peter still giggled—and let the baby loose on the overgrown pathway. In the yard just behind us, the old man hit a hammer to the bashed metal hood of a rusted-out car. I dropped to the rickety steps and read.

I read that this Marx person had lectured for Socialism and that she was associated with Annie Besant before Besant became a Theosophist. Ms. Marx was a persuasive lecturer, interested in mobilizing the oppressed child and women workers of the later nineteenth century factories, and in elevating the economically downcast.

The thing was, apparently she and Besant were interested in the same man in that lifetime, only he chose Eleanor, leaving Daisy/Annie Besant to her own devices. It was after this period that Besant entered the world of the occult and became one of the Grand Mothers of Theosophy. Apparently Besant's effervescence was lost on this man.

I wondered why Daisy, in researching the Besant lifetime that Elizabeth had discovered for her, hadn't noticed my face staring back at me now from the pages of a book on Daisy's own past lifetime. Hadn't Daisy recognized this dark-eyed, half-Jewish "slovenly amanuensis" (the book said Besant degraded Marx thus in Socialist trade magazines after the incident with the man)—as me?

When I approached Daisy about my discovery, she rattled over something to do with the new church and I don't honestly remember how it was we never came to talk about it, but somehow I felt she saw to it that we did not. Excited and slightly terrified by my further reading about "myself," convinced beyond any doubt of the visceral reality of reincarnation by the abundance of coincidences regarding Eleanor's and my personas, I was happily quite distracted from Veronica's condition and from Daisy's latest dream, until she assigned Amy to go to Patrick's church ahead of the group and "cleanse it," and Amy, desiring to have someone to whom she could happily babble about Peter on the way, someone who wouldn't check her feminine pride against "concept," unexpectedly invited me along.

Half an hour later, we turned into the darkened drive that led into the little church in Mountain View, parked in the back and got in through the kitchen door. The church was virtually empty now except once a month when Patrick appeared from on high off a plane from L.A. We couldn't find the lights—was that significant? —but walked soberly into the darkened sanctuary. We were forerunners and feeling it, serious about our work for Daisy. Even after Amy found the lights, the high corners of the opened-beamed ceiling in the little chapel seemed shadowy. Amy sensed things where I did not. I went along with her, mentally vanquishing those forces that might not belong. I felt honored to be chosen for such a work. And I noticed later, on the night we began services that the pristine sanctuary actually glittered. It gleamed and glowed from the moment Daisy walked in and her soft voice rang loud that night through a building that was all—light. Was that because we had come before and sent antagonistic thought forms or forces out of it beforehand? I didn't know. When Amy and I were finished with the cleansing, two heavy ladies (part of the small contingent who preserved the flame when Patrick was away) showed up and welcomed us with tea and cookies. We returned to Daisy with the good news.

Jade Avila

Chapter Thirteen

The temple was cleansed, all false thought forms swept away. Daisy radiated. She was now ready to inhabit it. She and Sam left Santa Cruz and rented a house halfway between Rebecca's and Patrick's. Convinced of an impending exodus to Mountain View, Doug and I followed, renting a house beneath the mountains in a direct west-east line to the church. It was a peculiar house and the month's rent took half of our meager paycheck.

Convinced also that better surroundings might bring Veronica on track, I didn't look back and deposited all of my belongings in the yellowed house beneath a wholesome looking pepper tree, quite expecting Daisy's high to carry us to the crest of a great new wave that would roll us into the future.

While Doug and I and some of the others (Art, Wayne and Mary Grace among them) moved to Mountain View, the magic three made last minute preparations. Resentfully, I noticed the magic three were now four: Daisy, Rebecca, Amy and Jade. For each of these, Daisy had lapis five-pointed stars cut at a rock shop in Mountain View. A fifth star had passed between Connie and Yvette thus far. "They are stars of initiation," Daisy murmured in response to my anxious inquiries. I longed to wear one, even once. After all, Rebecca said Daisy cut them as gifts for the women originally responsible for the Psychic Symposium at the City College. Shouldn't one of them have been mine? A sixth star, her mother's, Daisy explained, lay unclaimed in the rock shop. It was maddening.

After Daisy was formally installed, Patrick came up for his regular monthly lecture and service. Daisy was excited; so were we. I offered to be Daisy's astrologer for the evening and gave us all a reading while we waited for Patrick to arrive from the airport. Saturn was at the top of her chart, at the mid-heaven, so I knew that she was at both a karmic apex and at a peak period where career was concerned.

"I told you, Page, didn't I—seven years ago when I first heard Patrick lecture—I told you someday I would work with that man." (It had been less than five years since Daisy took us chickens to that seminar where we encountered Patrick, but somehow Daisy had expanded time.) The biographical blurb Sam (who worked off and on now as a printer) had printed up for distribution for Patrick's church, introduced Daisy as a minister with seven years' experience. She spoke in terms of seven years at the City College Symposium also and at the Psychic Fairs where she was invited to "read".

Patrick arrived, exactly on time. He stood shyly under the bright ultraviolet lights in the church kitchen and asked for Daisy, who'd retreated to the little "minister's house" Patrick used on his visits up north. While Daisy was summoned, several of us gathered around him while he mused and collected his thoughts for his talk. Patrick's hair was strawberry blond like Daisy's, wavy and charming, although I wondered if it might possibly be dyed. Blue-eyed also, he was well built and trim and at the beginning of middle age, carefully dressed. Our attention was drawn down white, slightly tight pants that just masked what lay beneath toward white shoes with taps. Yvette almost swooned in front of this new hero.

Patrick. Daisy entered the kitchen shyly, as if she were meeting her father or mentor, but she winked at him as though they were two of a kind and had some private understanding.

I was impressed by his lecture that night, not only because of its humor, but by insightful "hits" in a style apart from Daisy's—but real zingers. By the end of the evening I was no better than Yvette and caught myself hoping he would look at me, or something, acknowledge that I existed. Doug acted odd too. From that day forward throughout our time with Patrick, he seemed happier and more involved than ever before. I noticed Patrick smiling at him, joking with him, in exchanges of the type from which Doug was usually excluded, by his very nature.

Patrick said things that I have had a chance to think about from a distance of many years, original concepts like "being psychic isn't supernatural, it's super natural," and that "recreation means simply re-creation," and "you call yourselves spiritual people," he chided his audience once, "but when I come into your homes I hear your plants screaming for a drink of water." (Like Daisy, Patrick adored plants and was often more solicitous toward them than children.) Sure, I realized later Patrick said things I could have said myself, but Patrick was boyishly clever and he had a cute, head down manner that invoked thundering applause and laughter after a "hit." Like Daisy, he had an appeal you couldn't account for, and as tock follows tick, Daisy's congregation grew between moons when Patrick was away.

It was a winter day. All around us people prepared for Christmas but we prepared in a different way. The bustle and the excitement were with us but the way was different. People thought deeply: What will I bring tonight to the Christmas party at the college? Even though this was where we shared Christmas with "them," the people, the public, and the church was the inner happening, we took the gift exchange seriously. You were to select something you had cherished all year, something you were ready to part with, and leave it under the tree and then pick up the gift you were led to, and the select understood that gift was symbolic as well as actual, that it heralded the new year to come, that it was a material reading of coming vibrations. Christmas was the culmination, Daisy said, the Christ mass or celebration of the Christ within, the indwelling spirit; it was a time when those who had sought to listen and to understand and to act according to its dictums, really felt the miracle of the season.

I had one special thing I thought I should give away: it was a ring, a gold-flecked lapis oval supported by a silver band culminating in twin daisies. We had bought it in a moment with 20 dollars Doug's mother had given us when we left her house in Northern California after a visit. Just out of Santa Rosa we saw a sign that read "Rocks, Gifts." We swerved onto a roadside rest area and then doubled back to the shop on the other side of the road.

Inside I was drawn to it immediately. It sat among some other touristy type jewelry and the usual polished treasures of the rock hound.

"How much do you want for this?" I had asked the older woman who sat self-absorbed on a wooden stool behind the counter.

"It's not new. Twenty dollars I guess." I paid it—no tax even—and ran for the car, jubilant. All the other women had the matching lapis stars, but this was mine.

"It's be-u-tee-ful," Rebecca said casually when she saw it.

Daisy asked, "Can I see it?" "Sure," I answered, proud. Many times afterwards she mentioned it and even said she'd looked for one like it in the art shops in Santa Cruz but she could never find one.

Tonight I debated deeply about bringing it. Ok, I thought, I'll do it. The real sacrifice of something I'd loved. Maybe I was finished with it. Maybe it was to belong to someone else now. I felt a pang. Was I sure? Follow the energy. It seemed to be sweeping me toward the dark back room of the new house where I found the Christmas wrapping paper in a box with some give-away clothes to be taken to the church nursery. I wrapped the ring quickly and put it in my purse that I carried under the shawl I wore over my long dress.

After Christmas carols and a short talk by Rebecca about the truer meaning of the season, we were free to "psyche out" our choices among the gifts we'd laid beneath the big tree. People cradled the little packages before they decided, trying to do what Rebecca had suggested, "See which ones you're drawn to." I remember the exclamations when someone who had given away his beloved picture of Jesus in the garden, got in exchange a lovely picture of Him walking on water, and someone who'd given away a treasured wooden Buddha, picked up an exquisitely crafted brass one, in exchange. Some found gifts that were different in every way from any they might have hoped for, but the gifts seemed to speak to them and to herald the coming year.

I listened more to hear who had drawn my gift from the pile, than to my intuition in selecting my own gift. I watched Jade pick up the package I left beneath the tree, open it, look at me deeply then walk away. I bore down on my inner self, asking it which gift would be mine in return. Which is it? I'd been attracted to a little box that most resembled the size of my ring. I opened it. A necklace with a single pearl. I didn't like pearls, hadn't until now. I resolved to look at it when I got home. Jade Avila, Daisy's new favorite, danced up the aisle of the college auditorium with her little gift in hand, eating cookies and flirting with two men I didn't know, who'd come together. Oh well. It was "right". I knew.

A week later, after I bought myself a cheap, polished, reddish-stone ring at a discount store, and after Daisy consoled me, saying, "That's really pretty," Jade came into the nursery at the church one afternoon where I was putting up Christmas decorations for the children (no one had thought to), and pulled the ring out of her purse without a word, looked me deeply as before and gave it back. This belongs to you, the gesture said. After she left I floated around the nursery, laughing to the babies, swept through the clutter of last night's dishes at home and managed to make Doug a really good dinner. It was Christmas and I put the ring back on my finger and I knew I would never take it off.

"You had to give it away to know it really belonged to you," Daisy said later. In a sense, she was right, she knew. In another sense I knew better, for the still small voice told me it meant something more—this ring—that I would have another, different kind of purpose than the girls with the great big star necklaces. The flower on the ring had five points, "the number of humankind in the earth," the Edgar Cayce readings stated, and also the number related to writing, Elizabeth taught, and communication and travel; she associated five with Hermes, former incarnation of Christ. Was I a scribe in their midst, as the voice within now suggested? Was the voice a comforter, or a compensation delusion? I didn't know which, but somehow the ring became an emblem of hope in separateness.

I looked up the meaning of the pearl anyway, in the new booklet Daisy had compiled (and Sam had printed), that was based on the handouts from the earliest classes. Under Stones, I read about "The Pearl: Sentimentality in sorrow or joy. The mark of pure and virtuous faith." I lived the meaning of the pearl that year.

Christmas Eve night 1974. One infant in a carrier, another (the floor baby) crawling on the floor of the hall before the sanctuary; its carpeted floor had been brushed clean by Mary Grace's vacuum; the nap was up. The baby felt it slowly, caught a microscopic speck up in her fingers and inspected it.

On the table above them, pyracantha boughs and brass candlesticks decorated the midnight buffet. Light salads and glitter cookies ornamented the table. The ladies who came with the church, already sat eating the white anise square cookies and coconut fudge mounds they'd made. Moving among them I wondered if Daisy and Sam had come yet. (Seven months pregnant, Daisy sometimes took a nap before a service.) Amy wore all white, except for an emerald package ribbon behind her gold barrette. She greeted me by shaking my hand. Christmas was in the air.

Earlier, Doug and I had stopped off with the babies at my father's. All he did was talk about Susan at college, showing pictures of her having a slumber party in her room with two college girls sporting beer and T-shirts. It didn't matter that he seemed strained. I knew he wanted me to go after the lonely hour we all spent trying to be Christmas. Relieving him of his duty by me, we went out into the California-cold night, drove through the wide black suburban streets into a darkness broken only by the wink of rainbow tree lights on flocking, refracted through impenetrable plate glass windows. Like ships in a bottle, ships we could never sail, they did not beckon.

Our car with one fender bashed—who cared, our insurance was the energy—rattled down toward the freeway where people lived in cheap apartments. In the bright black Christmas night no longer sullen, life like a star aurora danced out to us as we drove closer to the church.

Now, before we went into the sanctuary, Amy handed each of us a poster, giving mine to me with a special smile. "Many are called..." read the archaic letters of the poster through wisps of fog that camouflaged an angel with a trumpet on a mountain dark and Christmassy. "Many are called...But few are chosen," it said. I have it still with tattered edges and many creases. It was folded once when we moved here, twice when we moved there. I look at it and remember Amy smiling at me with that crisp wrapping ribbon bow low behind her ear. I smiled back at her that night. The suspicions we brought with us from our lives subsided.

"All is calm, all is bright." Under winsome candlelight we came into the sanctuary to light our tapers from the great Christmas candle on the altar. "Beneath the silent stars the town is sleeping." After the holidays, my mother wrote a jagged letter to me, "Your sister Susan is so normal, so caring—away at college and so normal she keeps her high school room just as it was. I had to beg your father to let you come to his house," she'd seared, tearing away the illusion of belonging just a little more. "Susan said you came too late to see them—normal people sleep." "Beneath the silent stars the town lay sleeping." The silent little minds, asleep dreaming of Emporium boxes could not torment me. I had Amy's gift and the lapis flower ring on the finger of the hand that held a candle. Within the sweet silver, pooled light of our candles, the undersea whispering of the voice in the hush of each of our hearts, joined us together as a silent chorus...none of these could hurt me.

At the first Sunday service in February, Daisy intoned through the sanctuary, "In each of us there is a babe wanting to be born, an I

AM presence seeking nourishment and nurturing from the fruit of our daily living. Give sustenance to the child that is the indwelling Christ" she said, herself big with child. And when her child was born, a boy, we made a daisy chain and blessed the child, each person in the chain laying hands on the back of another. It was Patrick, up from L.A. for his monthly service, who called us together to do it. "Maybe someday this blessing will return to us and walk among us," he said. I wished that Molly could be blessed (by the church group)—after all, she was the child Daisy had boasted she and Sam would have conceived if they'd begun earlier. Still, the moment was magical and intense but my resentment simmered underneath the joy.

Holding the baby after the service Patrick joked, "I want him, Daisy." By now I knew Patrick was gay.

Daisy started me off early one morning with a song—a laughter, a little bubble of the music she felt. Life was just a bubble, just a song, just a "follow-the-yellow-brick-road" melody for her now—and for me. I would ride on her coattails to "over the rainbow" and be with them yet.

She whispered, the little bubble breath coming out like a sparrow's song in the new dawn for baby and me. "Anson, not man's son, but son of Spirit," she sang to the baby, to her "man-child," to her "child of the universe."

The crisis was past; her baby was home again and would live. Vines and ferns and flora of every description crowded her little house in Sunnyvale. As if in a sunny vale, she'd slept the last of the night through in peace and dreamed new dreams for us. The church was new, her first real (shared) church, and the baby Anson was home at last in her arms.

The whole week through the baby had struggled for breath in intensive care and Daisy had bitten her nails, smoked and worried. The night before, while he was still in the hospital, she'd called me over to tell me of a dream she'd had. In the dream, the baby was going over an embankment. "Rebecca was on one side of me pulling at me, and you were on the other, Page, and I couldn't get to him."

"What does that mean?" I asked.

"Rebecca..." she twirled her blonde hair pensively, "Rebecca is the me, the part of me that can't..." Here she murmured, so I knew it was serious stuff. "The part of me that can't...have any children again, you know?" I knew Daisy had herself "fixed" as we liked to call it, after this last one. Flesh didn't control us—we were Spirit, divinity in expression, as Daisy had said, and we could play little games with flesh, little tricks on it.

Daisy dragged real deep on her cigarette. I'd wondered at how healthy and rosy Anson was at birth, as though the hopes thrown around him—the ego too, maybe—for her son was the son of a veritable goddess—as though the thoughts and hopes had imbued him with a fiercely protective aura. During our pregnancies I'd tried to warn Daisy about the smoking, and she'd rebuffed me, made me a buffoon. Choking in that windowless van where they'd all smoked, I'd tried to warn her, but I wasn't sure of myself. When her baby lay for a week in Valley Medical Center with respiratory problems that had set in after he'd been home, I remembered my warning.

Incredibly, Daisy had blamed me for Anson's infirmity. The first time she brought Anson to the church nursery, I held Molly near him to greet him. Molly had a little cold—possibly from our poor diet—and Daisy saw it as the cause. Of course Daisy forgave me for giving her son these problems. "Don't worry about it," she said sullenly, after he was rushed to the hospital, barely breathing. I pointed out to her that smoking might be the culprit. "Molly had a cold and you were both near him. No, I don't care about what you did," she forgave me again, "You didn't know, and there's nothing you can do about it now."

How nice of her to have let me come by last night to hear her dream, to sit with her while she kept a vigil of excruciating worry for her child. I knew what it was like: I knew from that agonizing business with Veronica three months earlier. "If Rebecca represents the part of me that can't have any more children," she'd asked last night, "then what part of me are you?"

"You feel I got the baby sick, don't you?"

"No," she said in a hushed voice, "No. You're the worry, my fears, the fears that might pull me overboard in this thing."

"Oh."

I felt her respect for the seriousness of my own situation with Veronica now, underneath the blame. United in fears for our children, she allowed me to come close, to sit with her on the green couch underneath the flora and worry the night through in silent prayer.

Finally Sam called from the hospital at half past two. "He's going to live. He's going to be fine. There's no more fluid." Daisy looked up at me, eyes brimming. I went to her. No more fear—I would hug her. She turned instead and went to the record player. "Ring the living bell," she sang with the record she put on, her face turned away from me. No one would see her cry, I guessed. She picked up the bright flowers someone had sent, and arranged them on the shelf above the stereo cabinet. She stretched up her hands to the poster of Jesus as Amelius, his earliest, androgynous incarnation in the earth when he was one with his companion soul—who became Mary—the Beloved Mother. Elizabeth had taught me about Amelius, from Edgar Cayce's creation story. When Daisy turned around, I was still, gently, offering her my arms and she looked right through me, as if I hadn't spent the night in her worry too, as if I was caught down on this earth in the muck of personal emotions, enmeshed, mired in my concern for this particular child and for my own. Once again we were alike transported through the cool stare from her "above-it" eyes to the realm of higher purposes. Elizabeth once told me that Rebecca confided in her at Asilomar regarding Daisy's aloofness. "You get just so close to Daisy," Rebecca told Elizabeth, "then you hit a wall."

"Has Mary Grace washed my white altar cloth for Sunday do you know?" she asked. Mary Grace, burdened with her own babies, often talked with me in the nursery during Sunday service when we were trapped there with our fussing babies and could only hear the lilting voices from afar.

"She finished hemming your new over robe too," I answered in the affirmative. "It matches your white robe. It's really beautiful, too."

"Oh good. Would you pick it up and drop it by later on? You are going to see her today, aren't you?"

"Yes. Sure." I answered, anxious to come back, to be part of her dream in whatever way I could. "I'll be back."

By midmorning I'd returned, after I fetched the white Irish lace altar runner and Daisy's new cover robe from Mary Grace. Daisy's relief about the baby and enthusiasm for her new church homogenized with that kind of heedless ego that captivated all of us, and she sang in her lilting whisper voice, "Shine the living light," and I thought, nothing can stop us now.

"Vu-lu-ra-ma. I really wanna feel you, Lord…"

Buoyed by the rhythms, by the rush of voices we all made, we projected ourselves past Sam, our choir director, who stood in front of us facing Daisy—the only audience at this practice. Sam's heavy shoulders swayed in a circular rhythm away from his hips. He threw his big head back and sang to the open beams of the sanctuary of Patrick's church.

Shiny new aqua tops that looked metallic clung to various size bosoms and wide, white shirts covered the men's dickeys. Auburn, curly, black, wispy, blond and red heads bobbed behind Sam's crisp dark curly one. "Vu-lu-ra-ma…I really want to feel you, Lord, but it takes so long, my Lord." When Daisy took over the daily ministry of Patrick's church in Mountain View, I overheard the one older woman who'd asked to join the choir because she'd once been a member of the Sweet Adelines, talk about how others in the old congregation might react to us. She said, "You're all so young and good looking." I thought that was a dense, "out-of-the-energy," irrelevant thing to say at the time, but it was really true.

I was willing to be in the choir, but I longed to be a minister, so I sat in on the minister's class held before choir practice the following week in the empty, late-afternoon church and listened to Amy apparently channel from the overall "energy" (that word was just beginning to be used but not with the tremendous popularity it later enjoyed.) She smiled demurely in the way I always thought was phony somehow, and clasped her hands, one over the other, over the bird's egg blue gown she got to wear for this instructional service, with just Rebecca and myself and Jade listening. She got kudos from Daisy. "She's really ready, isn't she, Rebecca?" Daisy affirmed. Rebecca giggled, holding her inevitable coffee cup and later hugged Amy in the archway between the minister's office and the kitchen. When I passed through the archway to find Daisy, Amy looked through me as if I were transparent glass. I had to find Daisy. If I told these two my feelings they would laugh, as they usually did and their soft detached laughter would underscore my insignificance.

"What is it, chicken?" Daisy asked in the anteroom where white robes and necklaces hung. A thick Bible lay spread open on a podium in the corner. Daisy took off her silver robe and un-tucked her blouse from her skirt. She looked at herself in a small oval mirror on the wall nearest the door. "This won't do, will it? Everything wrinkles under the robe." The smooth skin beneath her eyes broke into curved wide rays. She tucked the blouse back in. "Now, what is it?" she asked without really listening for an answer. She hummed "Long Live God" and righted her necklace from beneath her shirt collar to drape over her breasts that emerged just above the blouse.

"Ummm…I'm wondering if you wanted me in the class…to learn to do the channeling…or whether you wanted me to just— support the others."

"What does it matter, Page? You know better than that. I want you there to support the energy, that's for sure, and to support your own energy."

"Uh. Huh." I acted stupid, as if struck by something obvious that I only dimly understood. "Oh, sure…"

"Long Live God, Long live Go-o-o-od, Long Live God," she sang.

On Sunday the choir sang the last "Long Live God," staccato. And Daisy glided in, hands up, heart pounding I thought, big smile on her face, eyes downcast. Then she looked up, a calm, serious, energetic-looking gaze and the crinkles around her eyes came up. "Now let's be seated. Let's feel the energies as one mind, one body." "Long Live God," the new choir quavered, uncertain as to whether to go on. "That's fine, thank you," Daisy joked. "Sit down already." Laughter.

"Seriously. We are all here because we are all committed…to our own calling within and it rings out…from around the earth today as it did in His day…" and so on.

"Long Live God," the choir concluded when Daisy left. "Long Live God." It was becoming her theme song.

Shortly afterwards, Daisy was called to a Psychic Fair at the San Jose State College. I got in somehow I think, on Daisy's coattails. She had a table by the wall. I had a table in the middle of the room. Daisy was in one of her good moods toward me. But I overheard her say to someone who bent down over her table, and who I guess she didn't want to read for, "Try Page, her readings are **different,"—she** stressed the word—"but good in their way." It was a lot like the other time recently in the little house behind the church when she talked about the group's understanding of universal laws regarding money, with the purpose of chiding Uncle Art, who wasn't there. She cited his inability to surrender to being out of work as the reason he didn't get another job. Now he was the black sheep. Even I was coming to dislike him just a little bit. Of course we all thought as One lately.

"The rest of us," she said, "have our shit together about money, even Page, although she has it bass ackwards." I smiled at the compliment. And another time, just recently, she had announced she'd discovered a new psychological technique, called "Reassociation," which she said was given to her by the space beings visiting from another dimension this year, beings who had visited us in a long ago past lifetime. They had showed her this method, Daisy explained, to rectify a karmic debt from that earlier encounter, a debt owed to Daisy and the group. Everyone got involved in the new technique; she had an overload of people wanting to reassociate with themselves and she needed people around who knew something about psychology to get them started, so she asked me to take Thea, the older lady in the choir who had once sung with the Sweet Adelines, and a couple of others to my house, and start them.

To thank me, I guess, she told the group at the next smoky inner gathering at the minister's house behind the church, "Page's the best psychic psychologist I know...even if she is dingy." I smiled more at that one, but sat uncomfortably frozen when no comments emerged from the group, until someone abruptly changed the subject.

Today at the psychic fair was different, I thought. I had arrived. I always thought that, but like a snail laboriously crawling up a drainpipe, too sluggish to have learned that the rain runoff gathering in the gutters on the roof will wash it off every time, I hoped without reason or rhyme that this time would be different.

At a break after giving my "different" readings to only two people who seemed to like them quite a bit, I walked over to Daisy's booth where she too was free. What a relief to see that there just weren't a lot of people around, rather than, that they sensed something lacking in me. Were my readings different—what did Daisy mean by that? Maybe she meant that my readings were intellectual only, or self-seeking.... I thought about it all day, but could only get a vague sense of what she might be saying.

Daisy fiddled with the pink flower in her vase casually, and as if she were a snowy wind drifting across a slope. Beautiful, careless, she bestowed her lovely snow queen looks on no one in particular—we were all alike blessed.

"Daisy, I tried to talk to Sam at the last break. He's funny with me, argumentative, or I am with him, Daisy. I just can't get along with him the way I can with you. He gave me a reading with his new cards and I felt as if he were putting me down."

Daisy looked down at me from a great snowy height. "I'll tell you something…"she was quiet, thought for a moment, "because I can trust you, chicken. Sam and I were talking the other night, about who we could imagine ourselves married to…if we weren't married to each other. And he said you…you were one of the ones he mentioned."

"Really?"

"Don't you think that's what you feel when you're around him? I mean you've probably been married or something in a past life. And maybe you're just a little bit unhappy right now in your marriage." The snow flurry melted, it unfolded me like a warm, white, furry parka. "Right, chicken?"

I looked up into opaque blue eyes twinkling at me. "Right."

"Where is Doug anyway?"

"Well…he's…I don't know, working on a car or something."

"And I know you have a babysitter. You told me last week your neighbor said she'd watch them so you could come here. Why isn't he here actually? You tell me, Page."

"He's not here because he's not into any of this and he's not going to be, not ever, is he Daisy?"

"No, chicken, he's not. I've watched you trying to buy him new clothes like Sam's and Peter's," (they were into silk print art nouveau shirts) "but new clothes aren't going to make a new man, Page. You think about it."

I asked Sam for another reading the next time he and I had no customers. Daisy was busy for the rest of the day. He spread out the new set of cards he'd designed and printed himself like a child with bright new toys. He was tickled with himself I could see, but he said very little that helped me, and he laughed, a queer backhanded laugh as though amused by my discomposure.

"Your psychic thing will open up…after you take care of something in your life that has to do…with a man. This jack, here. I feel that's Doug. You know what I mean? You'll get there, kid."

I felt a pang. Annoyance?

Children with Angel:
Todd Allen, Jimmy, Art. Jr., Sissy, Benjamin (on horse), Robin

Chapter Fourteen

On Sunday next it was my turn in the nursery for which I'd come to assume the greatest responsibility, assigning turns and keeping a schedule of duties during the services. Molly played with her toes while Anson—"not man's son"—slept fitfully. Yvette's baby, Desiree, pulled herself up to inquire over the bars of her crib at Molly's engaging play. Veronica sat sullenly at my feet, looking as listless as a hopeless prisoner at Mary Grace's towheaded boy and toddling red-haired girl who ambled about the nursery, hauling out all the toys there were in turn. Rain pelted the little house to the right and behind the kitchen door that led into the church building proper.

I heard the clatter of heels on the wet concrete step leading down from the kitchen door. Daisy burst in the children's shelter and swung a necklace of lapis beads connected by a silver chain in my direction. It was a good thing I was at least quick enough to receive them or they would have tumbled onto Veronica's head.

"Here dear, you've earned these—for the nursery…"

"Oh O.K., all right," I said.

"And for the astrology thing you do." I gave her horoscope each week now, and since she was the "head" of the "body", we considered it all of ours too. How naive. Couldn't we see what this was leading to?

After she left, a thick, natural hemp plant hanger Sam had made vibrated in the window to the tempo of the rain. Winter bare branches swished against the steamed up panes of window glass. Hypnotized by these rhythms, soothed by the chatter of the babies (now even Veronica laughed out loud at Yvette's little daughter Desiree, who grasped through her crib at wisps of Veronica's blond hair), I thought, this is all going too fast. I guessed the happiest time of my life was passing me by…as if it were rain on glass…choir notes sung high and fast…

Sam stood above me beaming. "So this is what happens to ladies left alone too long with babies."

"I didn't know you were here," I apologized. Then I realized Daisy had said Sam would be back for their son after the choir had finished singing the opening. Daisy hovered over Anson since he'd had his sickness, hovered as near him as her nature allowed, usually sending Sam or Rebecca or Amy after him if she imagined any danger. Tonight he was fretful. Sam would take him to the sanctuary—that special baby—that he might be healed of whatever ailed him through their favorite modality, the strains of his daddy's music and the hallowed syllables of his mommy's channeled intonations. "Draw from the overall energy, from the filaments of Spirit," she'd counseled Amy at her ministerial training session, and I'd taken notice. "That way you meet the greatest need, answer the questions embedded in the hearts of the people." It all sounded so grand. Did a lapis star—instead of a chain of rough little baby's beads—indicate the readiness to answer those questions within the hearts of the people? "Just like the bread and fishes," Amy's big sister had suggested to her when she looked puzzled, "He fed them with the bread and fishes and there was enough. And you shall feed them with the bread of Spirit and answer the inmost questions of their hearts— posed only in The Within; when the Watchers of Spirit bend low to touch man in his enmeshment. Understand?"

It seemed a grand task for Amy, but she demurred, honestly sobered by the task. I understood; I understood exactly. Should I be given a chance, I would find those filaments by magic as the three had been trained to do and I would...

It occurred to me that I was alone with the babies and him whose broad chest looked better than all the rest in the thin muslin choir shirts the men wore even in winter. His broad neck and large head emerged from above the ribbed dickey like the thick trunk, dark-crested tree that bent to bash bare apricot crops against the window glass.

I watched him quiet his son, but he didn't pick up the baby or start to leave right away.

I imagined for a moment he needed me, wiped the thought away just as he wiped his thick, broad hand across the window to look out at the storm, at the patch where the garden would be soon. (Bread and fishes and garden fruit to feed us, I wondered.)

"What is it you need, Page…Can I give it to you?" He looked away from the barren patch of ground outside into my eyes and back to the window, where he caught the trembling plant and stilled its movements between his hands. He remained puttering with the plant as if he had nothing else to do. I let his question resonate within, then a filament of Spirit touched the question that lay embedded in my own heart and read that Daisy was my love. We were all spokes on the wheel that was Daisy. If we touched, it was incidental, but sweet somehow. Sam and me.

"Rejoice in the Lord always.…" The rain had quieted and we could hear the choir. Sam leaned toward the window, hands pressed into the painted corners of the jamb, legs braced wide apart. He stared into the dark. After awhile he swung around.

"Um…I must be getting on. Page. Anson's fine with his bottle." I agreed with him. "Bye bye, 'son."

"Page." The dickey was hung up beneath Sam's latest ornament—a Star of David. I pointed. "Oh," he acknowledged. He smoothed out the dickey and his clear, night's-blue eyes were opened at me a moment too long.

"Come here, Page." He embraced me. I watched each of my muscle's movements. Did we remain too short a time, too long, in this exchange of the love of Spirit? I flinched as though to pull away. He held me still for another moment. The rain sloshed, and the wind swooped down over the ground where we would plant our seeds. The dark March sky encased the little house, held the nursery and Sam and me, still. "Hmm…" He wriggled his big arms away, then tensed them and pushed me out to arms' length. "Page…Page. We—ah—love you." Somehow even I knew he meant it.

On a nice day in the warming spring I brought a bag lunch to the church and settled the children in the nursery. I was excited because I didn't have to sit for the children as I had during so many of the winter services. I was one of six women selected to be recipients of a seminar in child rearing conducted by Daisy—"New Age Parenting" it was called. I was thrilled. It made me feel really included because the warp and woof of my life now was children. Always one to be conscious of wider purpose, I thought this training might contribute to the rounding of my preparation for the ministry, the dream of some of us "lesser mothers" who gathered there on the grass at Daisy's feet. Yvette sat nearest to Daisy, almost touching her bare, golden calves. "It's like...like I can't get close enough to her—" Yvette had confided in me innocently. "It's something I feel...Do you think she feels it too? We must've known each other in a past life or something." Yvette wasn't riddled with the ambition to become a minister, but she ached to be near Daisy for some other reason.

In the fresh, warm sun the kaleidoscopic patterns of the green leaves of trees and their shadows played on the faces of the rapt young mothers who listened to Daisy's counsel. One of the points Daisy stressed in her formula for ideal parenting was the need to relate to the child as an individual. For that I was praised. It was acknowledged that I regarded children as persons and related to them respectfully, something that Daisy herself almost admitted she hadn't done with hers and Art's first boys.

I lingered in this dalliance, stood reprimanded on my need to "discipline." I supposed they meant by this, Veronica, who, poor thing, grew more and more troubled and distraught. Now and again I awakened from a sound sleep in the house we subsisted in by picking oranges to eat after we'd paid the rent, with the eerie feeling that the man the neighbors said had died in the house before we moved in, still prowled about. But in the back of the back of my mind, buried under denial and anxiety and belief in faith healing was a nagging concern for Veronica, a concern that I should take her back to the callous neurologist, or to someone.

On the grass in the lovely, new heat we talked in abstract principles and applied them to each personality predictably. No one reflected on Veronica's disturbance beyond the pleasant implied warning to temper her personality with "discipline."

The "New Age Parenting" seminar bled into other folksy fun activities that kept my mind away from the terrible exigencies of my daily life.

On the Fourth of July we conducted an outdoor rummage sale in the parking lot in front of the church. Heaps and heaps of brown-bagged clothes lay on card tables and any other kind of table anybody could muster up. I sifted through the clothes and found a few things that I liked, eagerly, for we were very poor at that time. Yvette, my competitor for refuse—and for Daisy lately—somehow seemed to go for the things I wanted, and I felt obligated to defer to her because I thought she needed them, and I wanted to be fair and also because I felt degraded digging through the bags of clothes. Daisy and Jade (who was an almost minister now too) took things casually with flair as though it didn't matter to them, and I gave Jade things, because adorning her with the hand-me-downs was like putting rings on Daisy's left hand (for I guessed Jade was that by now), or at least it was like shoeing her right foot. Daisy picked up a gaudy (to me) tapestry bag. When she picked up anything though, it kind of glowed or took on new meaning. Looking back, I wonder if some of the cheapness never left. Daisy was raised by her mother, Blanche Anne, in unheated apartments, left later with her brother Rexford alone on weekends while Blanche went off with men and Daisy had to beg food from the neighbors when the cold cereal she and Rex were left with, had run out. Blanche was, if nothing else, proud.

Daisy excused herself early from the duty of the burgeoning tables (it seemed that there were very few customers), but some of the young, poorest women, like me, ended up with paper bags full of baby things and a pretty cast-off dress or two for church. I remember how thrilled I was to get Daisy's discarded dresses or the pair of black, flower-embroidered pants she'd worn two years earlier. She even gave me a pair of shoes that day, said I could stretch them out with the end of a broomstick when I said they wouldn't fit because Daisy wore shoes a half-size smaller than mine. She said lovingly, "When I'm done wearing a pair of shoes they're just right for you."

Piles of old clothes at a rummage sale are an exciting challenge at first whether you are rich or poor, but after awhile the old smells and the odor of stale Avon perfume that emanated from the garments baking in the July sun, and the pervasive lint, and the knowing they threw it away because it was stained, dragged you down. I let Veronica toddle unsteadily under a card table draped over by an old, linty chenille bedspread and watched Daisy in her halter sundress and those gold lame sling shoes she bought at the store my mother had laughed at when she dragged me out on shopping trips when I was a young teenager. Daisy clipped across the parking lot to where the men washed cars, spraying water arcs up to the gleaming blue sky dotted with occasional, perfect white cloudlets. It seemed to me that the spray shot much higher and lilted poetically when their minister approached.

"How're we doing?" Daisy asked the men, head tilted back and away to withdraw from her lungs the big drag she'd taken from her cigarette as she'd walked along.

"Not bad, Daisy," Peter smiled confidentially up at her. In the gold sandals, Daisy was just an inch or two taller than her new brother-in-law. (Patrick had married Peter and Amy and even let them honeymoon at his house in LA where they slept in his "far out" bedroom and reported the only discordant note—the picture of his mother staring down at their conjugal bed from Patrick's nightstand.)

Peter smiled into Daisy's orchid blue eyes. "I'll have to talk to you later," Daisy often told Peter at classes. And I'd envied him as the two sat on the wide steps in front of the church scanning the night sky for space beings, almost touching on the cold grainy concrete, but not quite. Peter, Daisy's sister's husband, often came to these classes without Daisy's sister. I knew he loved Daisy. He always said he'd had the same visions as Daisy, such as later on when she announced the newest one—that John F. Kennedy was a reincarnation of Jesus—things like that. Then Peter popped up and said, "Yeah Daisy, I had it too." And then she would take him into her minister's office and they would have a talk, him standing less than a foot away from her and facing her. And he would look up into her eyes, which seemed cornflower, or sea green, or blue heather, or whatever she was wearing at that time or feeling, or whatever he was feeling, and the two would stare close but never touch. I wondered…if she had touched him more, would the visions have kept up? I doubted it. He was held there by some invisible tension. Oh, sweet tension. "You are my consciousness," she told Peter and he loved it, ate it up.

At Christmas time she always gave "her consciousness" special things. A star of new birth embroidered on a silky shimmer of material with a fountain of embroidered starlight flowing across the fabric from the Bethlehem star. He would feel it afterwards sometimes—I saw him once and I'll bet he did it more—feel its slippery smoothness against the light stubble of his beard in the morning. I think she stayed away from him because she'd already taken one of Amy's husbands, Sam, and because she had an uncanny sense of just when to stop, of just when the wags would be able to say she was tacky and have it stick.

He seemed to love his wife Amy, too in a way. He'd said, when they'd first met, she looked like an angel to him, said that again when we discussed how she'd been a call girl. She did look like an angel sometimes now that the clothing styles had evolved, and Daisy took to wearing rainbows and white gowns and long dresses instead of black wigs and acetate clinging gowns from Lerner's. Of course Amy followed suit and on Amy the white star outfits looked particularly delicate, and her hair, now un-teased, now not sprayed—still dyed but no one knew—looked fresh as if she'd stepped out of the rain, draggly but natural and nice, and the dyed blonde made the whole effect shimmer like Miss Clairol cotton candy above the angel wing blouses.

In late summer of 1975, Daisy invited Doug and me along with all the others—this time that meant the men too—to a nude swimming party. Tonette offered her house. My brother, after selling peeks to his friends to see the naked women in his backyard, had ratted to my father, and the pool suddenly became less available to us.

There would be a picnic too—it seemed like lots of fun in store—we even had a babysitter. Jane deigned to take a few hours away from her sad life in the bars where she drowned the sorrow over the loss of Marshall, to watch our babies. Doug and I drove across three undivided suburban towns on a bright sunny day toward Tonette's house in the South San Jose foothills under the huge, over-grand Baptist Revival Church that stood on an enormous mound-like hill.

Could the Baptists see us? I doubted it—they were too far away, but if they did, I could care less.

In Tonette's backyard after the decision where to undress—out on the porch right in front of them, or inside in her bedroom—we had settled for just around the corner inside the house. We were hidden from the group gathered in the backyard only by a plastic drape. Then we'd walked out, towels wrapped around us. I have to hand it to Doug—he was nonplussed at practically anything. He took off his towel and settled his long whitened body, slender shoulders, slightly overfull rear on a towel a bit too short for his five feet eleven and three quarter inches and went to sleep. And since I wasn't in love with him, I didn't have the fear some of the others probably had—that their person might like some other person, or that person's tush or her this or his that—it was a relief, really. By now I was in love more with this group of friends, at least infatuated, intrigued by them enough to be very excited by this demonstration of sexless, platonic Grecian beauty.

And it went off rather well, really. Sam, though, disturbed quite a few. He sat in a deck chair, uncircumcised and of some enormous breadth and mass; casually the thing curled or coiled between his legs and some dark poetic pubic hair. Daisy lay beneath him on a chaise, sporting new marks of motherhood from delivering Anson, murmuring to Yvette who lay on a towel to her left. I watched Daisy's golden back and slightly plumper hips oiled to Atlantean, Poseidian bronze, beneath Sam's casual laughter. Oil drops expressed from the bottle by one of his meaty hands pooled and glistened in the small of her back. I didn't look into Sam's eyes, which I knew were as pale blue as the shimmery pool water.

I knew the color of his eyes but I certainly couldn't look into them because I had this disturbing, pushed-aside impulse. I wanted him to notice me. I wanted to be important in his casual summary of the bathing spirits around him. And certainly I couldn't analyze "it" or even look at "it" long enough to separate the jewel from its fleshy setting—why was I thinking that…no, I wasn't, I wasn't thinking it after all. Instead I called out to Daisy, "You look terrific; you're looking better than ever." Deeply engaged in some conversation with Yvette, she didn't reply.

Rebecca lay on her stomach, slender at 29—she would be 30 in September—tanned, with dark, plush, wiry hair gracing her shoulders. She seemed as cool and tolerant as the Virgo-Scorpio princess she was, but underneath, I sensed she still kept certain Vulcanic fires alive. I remembered the night at her apartment five years earlier, when she'd described an insistent astral lover who was plaguing her, and her reluctant delight when I'd guessed it was Art. Now she had Rexford, Daisy's thin, aquiline nosed half-brother who might once also have been homosexual. She looked quite serene, pristine and cool to me from keeping to the higher realms of consciousness she preferred.

She was cool to me these days, too, believed I was too selfish and emotional for words or something, as if she had transcended that realm of human hardship I inhabited. (The truth of her rejection lay in my refusal to have a baby for her and Rex. She'd been left barren after the operation she faced living with the mole. Even Daisy reproached her, not for the idea itself—Yvette would several years later produce that child for Rebecca under Daisy's guardianship, at Rebecca's house, with the choir singing in the background. "It's not Page's karma," Daisy pronounced recently when she found out what Rebecca had "done"—asking me. Rebecca retorted bitterly, glowering in an unusual show of rebellion at the clot of followers knitted about Daisy's chair, "You've drawn your strength around you." Ultimately though, she too bowed to Concept.)

I remembered the night Rebecca and I'd first really met. "Don't cry," she'd said. "It clogs up your psychic centers." (How different from Elizabeth who believed feelings **were** important.) And now we were deep into Concept Living (as it had been formally titled), lining up our lives to mental concepts we believed to be universal truths, such as the Law of Manifestation—defining the physical as the last level or ring of manifestation of impulses that came to one from Spirit, through the mental body, through the emotional and finally through the physical body, out into the physical realm of the life activity. Very simply it meant that if your kitchen was a mess and if to you "kitchen" symbolized the giving of love to the family, then you were to look to your manifestation as a clue to what was wrong in consciousness, and fix it. Were you angry at your kids, not spending enough time with your mate?

We looked at clothing, at colors, always, as "vibration in motion,"—Cayce said that color was "the spiritualization of sound"—knew that certain colors had the power to uplift or depress in this or that person's wardrobe, because of the colors she might have active in the aura at a given time.

Well. I certainly couldn't think much about that today because the colors presented to my eyes, gazing as if of their own will at the others, were much the same: tans and flesh tones of united hues. I thought of bodies, thought of how they were made and shaped and felt and why, thought "in concept" most of the time because the others were acting from the point of awareness of the essential divinity and common humanity of each other guest. Peter, in his persona as the jester, organized splash play in the pool. I jumped in as the tomboy I had been, on a friendly keel with these men who talked so much more than Doug did. It saddened me that I could not suppress entirely the idea that Sam or even Peter, might look at me a moment longer than anyone else here, so I fanned out my hand and shoved a wave of white water toward Peter. Perched on an air mattress, he whirled his strong arms in mock shock, fell backwards into the water and then bubbled dramatically down to the bottom of the pool. I floated in the ambiance, rid of thinking of them, and then Peter whooshed back up from beneath and wrapped tan hands around a blue beach ball, and chose sides for Keep-away. I could see Wayne's glassesless eyes glint happily under wet sparse hair as he caught the ball away from Peter. Then Sam parachuted into the water from the sun, and gained control of the game. I swam harder and faster, and at the last, only Sam and Peter and I were playing.

"Race you," I yelled to them. I pounded at the surface of the water, breaking it over and over again like glass. I outstripped Peter and came within a length of Sam's meaty arm. I knew Daisy was watching. Damn. I could have beaten him. Sam got out, king of everything he surveyed and I resented him again. Good.

I pulled myself up after him over the corner of the shallow end where Daisy basked on her chaise. I knew she'd seen me. "Sit down for a minute," she invited. Sam draped his rainbow beach towel over his deck chair, straddled his legs into the sun and closed his eyes.

"I hope we didn't splash too badly," I joked, less awkward than I usually was with noonday sun relaxing my defenses.

"Someday," she said, "all of this will be yours…but it won't be with him," she added, pointing to Doug asleep on his towel. "Now go," she brushed me off when my mouth fell open. "Go have a good time."

I leaped up, then stood for a moment so as not to run off and fall over, deeply thrilled and awkward all over again, as though I could not possibly live up to the prophesy of this, the ultimate laurel.

Exultant now, I lay naked on the warm concrete with clear water trickling off my skin and regarded Doug, who'd turned over beside me to lie on his back. I found myself matter-of-factly comparing his body to those of the men. His penis lay cool against his body from the meager waist dip he'd taken when I'd called him to come into our game. Immediately he'd returned to his perch on the side, head slumped with sleep and disinterest. Now he seemed smaller than usual. Maybe he was afraid of something because he wasn't that small, and these men, some shorter in height than Doug, seemed bigger; even Wayne and Rexford and broad trunked Peter, who though an inch or two shorter than I, was proportioned like a David. Or maybe it was the way they played and emanated. I didn't know, but I was kind of ashamed of Doug, and of me for having him, and mostly of me for my nervous comparisons, so stupid and out of the energy and sneaky.

"Who wants food?" Tonette called, never out in the sun too long because she had some Mexican descent and was so middle class and correct and did not want to turn to brown and because she believed we would all wrinkle up in the end.

"We'll help," Peter called.

Tonette sauntered demurely past us to check the pool filter. She frowned at Daisy's back, reddened now to a darker bronze that obscured the motherhood marks, and at Amy, thin, blond, of the broad hips and attractive back, in deep sleep within the sun's oven.

"You girls are going to wreck your skin," Tonette clipped nervously, as though it was very difficult for her to challenge anything we might do. But she sold makeup products for a living since her divorce, and I guess she felt it was her duty.

"Wreck?" Daisy murmured sleepily.

"Yes. I really think you will wreck your skin because they know now that the ultraviolet rays will cause wrinkles."

She said it with a gasp, as if it were important. She too was trying to apply Concept Living, and this probably came under the heading of brotherly love. It certainly was sisterly love, to offer help to keep us from getting old. That word was a pariah waiting outside the life of any woman to suck her loveless. Tonette had told Rebecca, her personal demi-guru; that she wouldn't get old, even if she had to have surgery.

Sam looked up at Tonette with kind and dreamy eyes, and then gazed lovingly at the bronzing back of his wife.

"Like the beautiful old Indian women, Tonette?" he retorted. "I love their faces," whispered Daisy, and I looked at Daisy and Sam ecstatically, like the child I once was, who wanted her parents to believe in something, and to hold and touch and love each other just once.

Tonette disappeared into the house where it was dark and we lifted ourselves off of the patio cement and towels as lightly as if we were now the concept of the law of manifestation in its perfect light: we were Divine Beings.

I took a bologna sandwich Peter offered me and smiled—we stood a foot apart stark naked and started one of our typical happy arguments about space beings, him for, me against.

Under the one little tree on the wide-open patio Daisy and Amy and Rebecca discussed business: when would Patrick need our choir to join with his own Galactic Group at Eastridge shopping mall, etc. We were no longer so much nude, as in the nexus of whatever problems we were currently working on and living out toward the greater glory.

Then Art came, late because of work at a temporary job, bringing with him three giant watermelons. Sam kissed him on the lips, a buss, and Peter followed. The undisputed leaders of the pack and Sam **the** leader, they cheerily undressed the male prejudice against kindness and tenderness, one to the other, with these little loving busses; and the gruff men and those deathly afraid of homosexuality, melted like the cookie frosting Mary Grace brought to spread on Amy's peanut butter thingies—softening now into the cookies under the afternoon sun.

Art didn't undress at first; he left his pants on. His huge, heavy chest was already reddened from maintaining the church garden. As always, he worked tirelessly for others. (Last fall, he'd burned his foot rescuing Yvette's children from a nighttime fire in her side of the duplex on Eastside Drive. Art had taken Daisy's duplex unit, after she'd left for Santa Cruz—abodes were freely rotated as needed among the group members. The San Jose Mercury News had cited Arthur Maxwelton as a hero for his actions in the blaze. "Art's doing his 'hero thing,'" Daisy had commented.)

Lately, Daisy had been working with him on the law of manifestation. I'd heard her remark recently, "You're such a beautiful soul, Art, and your body is your temple. Don't hide yourself under all this weight, sweetheart." When she talked to him like that, I knew it melted his heart, so he ate more, because he missed her so, and hated himself for losing her.

After we cracked through Connie's ruffled chips and smooth green-flecked dip, crunched through Yvette's tabuli salad in pocket bread, punctuated conversation with casual bites of Daisy's delicate egg salad on rye and savored Sam's experiment—stuffed grape leaves with salami and olives, we chunked through the watermelon, spat out a few black seeds and began to meander back to the towels, chaises and deck chairs.

Daisy caught me aside. "I have a bone to pick with you, Page." Twisted up and nervous and ashamed already, I let her guide me through the sliding glass door into the cool dark house. I looked up at her but she looked away.

"You told me I look terrific," Daisy said. "I'm fifty pounds heavier than before the baby." (She must have been ten or twenty only.) Wistfully she added, "I don't look the way I did last summer." That had been the climax of the dramatic, gradual weight loss she affected with dreams and fasts and being in love with Sam.

"Yes, but Daisy, you look great," I said and I meant it.

"See"—she clutched a fold from her golden waist—"you don't think I look like I did then, do you?"

"But—"

"It's not really important, is it?" she laughed.

"Oh…right," I answered, feeling silly as if I had made a big deal out of it or something. "But you look great."

She smiled then. I couldn't help but be buoyed up by the new confidence conferred to me by her beautiful promise. And now I knew she had her fears.

I walked out and lay again on the warm cement. Art lay silently on his stomach about three towels over, still with his pants on.

"Hey, Daddy Art," Peter yelled from the pool, exuberant and friendly in a perfect imitation of Sam's new vogue. The "in" men were all daddy this and daddy that to each other. They shared child rearing because of the interblending of the families, but I thought they were each other's daddies, too. It was all so happy and so pleasant, and Daisy had asked me something and promised me **that**. I wondered if my body temple had earned me the ultimate promise. Strong and athletic, I felt good about my body, but unclear about how I appeared as a woman. No matter. I would enjoy the halcyon, milk breast sweetness of being a boyish child a little while longer. No threat to anybody, I rolled over and almost fell asleep.

"C'mon, Daddy Art," Peter splashed in friendly challenge. After awhile his calls began to bug me. I was surprised that Art held back this long from undressing, and now resisted Peter's invitations. And Sam, always Peter's playmate and co-instigator, stood steeped in the deep water at the back of the pool, strangely silent.

Finally everyone looked up to see what was wrong. All of a sudden Art stripped off his pants and flew to the water, but not before I could clearly see why he'd resisted. My heart ached for him. His testicles, round and strong like the rest of him ended in a diminutive button of a penis so retreated and small looking I could hardly see it was there. He made Doug look immense. In an act of great courage, he hit the water like an enormous statue tippling under siege—of a Samson pushed from its huge height by a golden-haired marauder, of a Goliath slain by a this tanned, daddy-calling David—there to crack, there to fissure, at the bottom of the pool where it would lie in silence for a thousand years.

Peter Taylor and son

Chapter Fifteen

One day after the swimming party Daisy took me into her confidence again. "This thing with Yvette is strong, but every time I'm tempted to move in with her, I think of all those kids and it helps." I knew they'd slept together. Yvette stayed with me for a while after the party at Tonette's because Yvette's mother had the kids for a few days, and she wanted to get out of her house where she took in transients and newcomers to the group as part of her service to the overall body (and to help with the rent). During the time she visited us, Daisy invited Yvette out for what she called "their special day"— something to do with the reassociation process, with "clearing" or "popping desire bubbles"—and Yvette came home late and crept into her sleeping bag on my living room floor without a word. The next day she gave me a little speech about "people who judge other people" and I guess she figured I knew. I did.

On the other hand, Daisy didn't confide in me about her sudden decision to leave Patrick's church. I "got told" with the rest of the group one night after choir practice, that she had had a vision in which we were sheep being led by wolves in sheep's clothing and somehow—I didn't quite understand it—that meant Patrick. We had sung with Patrick's choir at the huge Eastridge shopping center—and it had felt global and apocalyptic and promising, and he'd moved Daisy from her place in Sunnyvale into the minister's house behind the church—but now she was convinced that we must leave, and, like the dry shards and stems from the garden, broken free by the night breezes, and carried past the door outside the sanctuary, we agreed to move on.

One by one they walked in to the last service at Patrick's church. The Cauldwells, one small child, the boy, clutching his daddy's trouser leg, the little girl leaning from her mother's arms, and the baby, the one who would die from septicemia (even after Daisy and Rebecca went out of the body "before the hierarchy" to ask if he could live, if Mary Grace renamed him and gave him to Rebecca), squirming visibly within his mother's belly to the swells of the music, as his parents slipped into the side row, and up to a place in the pew closest to the center aisle and the front. Mary Grace brushed a wisp of Northern, white-blond hair away from her glasses, and sat down and smacked the little girl, too hard I thought because she would not settle down right away. But that's how they were raised up in Montana, I rationalized; that's how it would be up there.

Rebecca came in from the back at the last, wearing a blue cast-off dress of Daisy's, taken in, of course—she was always thin. She looked dark, the scar above her lip was imperceptible except to me—I thought of such things because I knew her secrets, knew that her father had taken advantage of her in a basement once, that her Oklahoma born mother raised her four sisters alone from then on. Here we were homogenized, all of the differences were forgotten, here the energy raised from these disparate people "like to raised the roof," as Mary Grace and Wayne would say.

How I loved them this Christmas, loved every one of them, loved Constance and Neil, elegantly dressed, so different from the Cauldwells, Constance's face pensive and quiet. The gray was beginning to bristle through Neil's wavy hair and a wry, unbalanced smile lined the creases of his cheeks, as was meet for the worldly wise, and he wore a careful square-cut navy shirt—no baloney choir blouse for him—yet I knew that he and Sam had card games and loved each other in their way. Neil juxtaposed his worldly, self-deprecating jokes against Sam's more literary witticisms: "Education without wisdom makes men clever devils," was Sam's latest. I couldn't tell worldly jokes yet, because I hadn't been out in the world, didn't know the trade winds of buying and selling, was as sophisticated lately, as the tables of hand-me-down baby blankets and the law of cosmic give away that I practiced, mainly giving away my few things to Daisy and her family—and I had been raised richer than most here. I looked at Neil's back and didn't appreciate all that Sam saw in him, looked at the elegant Constance—hers wasn't my style, but I loved her just sitting there, loved the back of her head.

In the power of the group we were readied, having all thought long and hard of what this moment might mean and through the warps of too much self-seeking, through the bents of Daisy's increasingly mentalized dream we still stood up that last service; ready for our next step, we still stood for love. We rose up to sing, our voices rang out and the tones were good and loud. And those of us who had never sung before sang out now, and through the hurts and pains—the reasons for having come in the first place—rang out the love of Spirit, the miracle of having someone, if only the back of a head—maybe someone I didn't understand at all in everyday life, nor they me—the miracle of having someone to love—really love—so that wherever they might go, whatever they could say or do, the feeling of them would live, recallable by a millisecond's thought, for the rest of my life, for the rest of theirs.

Jade, swaying, looking like a Eurasian Daisy, chimed the last words to "Long Live God" in her throaty and most beautiful of all the women's voices; Mary Grace who ate white bread and her kids were often in the hospital, and I'd tried to teach her about better food and she'd resented me—my God, how petty; who cared—Mary Grace made the altar cloth with her hands. Her husband Wayne, 35, with two broken teeth and a wisp of blond hair crossing his balding spot, whom I liked a lot—I don't know why; who cared—sang a new song about a cowboy with no blanket beneath a deep and starry night sky. I thought of his early life in Wyoming where he grew up poor and neglected until he was taken in by a doctor and his wife at twelve, with his teeth about to go; Wayne with so many man's burdens as a boy who worked now out at the Ford motor company midnight shift, until I worried his feet and back might go—who cared what was wrong now.

After he sang his solo, he sat back down beside his boy, frowning intently as if trying to grasp the words of the song that followed his, holding the words in thought as he told me sometimes he did, when he thought he'd missed the meaning of the message. I'd often watched him ask Sam, "Umm," hesitantly, brave and serious, "what do you think this thing means here? I mean is this what...umm...." The words were very difficult for Wayne; they came slowly, and sometimes visions of the "fat, old, farm woman" who'd had him first, sprang to mind—of her beating him, not caring about his rotten teeth. "Umm, buddy, do you think we want to say this, that Christ means this? Would He have said this, Sam?" he'd ask, scratching his head with embarrassed laughter. "Umm...you know what I mean?" And Sam would take over, and say it for Wayne, and make it ok, and clap his back and he would accept it. Careful Wayne, I had often wanted to say, it's ok to question, but if you question you'll get too close to the heart of your own dream and then you'll find it doesn't match theirs and you can't sing out and feel at ease. But Sam and Daisy's broad charisma erased the individual differences in people that ought to be erased, and also rode roughshod over the core of dissension—the uniqueness of each one's truth, where I sometimes thought the Christ lived.

Soft music now and everyone was seated, Amy like a graceful angel in lace—white lace over Christmas-tree-light blue—came in with a candle and lit it from the greater candle already blazing on the altar. Lights were dim here but no one noticed because the stage was set for something greater than this building, and nobody, honestly, could see it in an ordinary way. It became an intra-dimensional capsule for travel out of the lonely spaces where each one dwelled toward the rainbows and the stars Daisy and Sam displayed on their clothes, and for some of the more sensitive ones, toward a moment wherein they might lay the mantle of the proud Christ across their Spirit-freed shoulders and drop the burdens out of sight on this sublime and foggy night.

In the back row of the men's choir called forward at Sam's sign, Art's shoulders were bowed. He seemed tired. He bore the burden of shame of losing Daisy to Sam, whatever "in the energy, it's O.K." bullshit they said—and he seemed to believe. "This is the best thing for him; it forces him to grow. Because I loved him, I let him go," Daisy insisted. He carried the shame whose bitter root was being misunderstood, but he still came because he loved the people here and saw the good. Did he too patch together a careful comfortableness with his new situation, by disguising to himself the burned pride feeling with a queasy, confused adoption of some of the newer principles he hardly gave a damn about?

But he was stuck by love, Art was, a big man in a grey shirt that hung too short off his strong, overweight arms and shoulders. What was there to do now but make up a delicious mess of sausage and tomato sandwiches for the boys and his friends and eat too much after we all left? He still loved Daisy and everybody knew it, but I think he stayed despite what he said to us and **despite** loving Daisy, because he knew something was still here, like a flickering candle in a window where there is wind and a crack under the door. I think he stayed because he loved us and we loved him and love has no pride.

Already he had begun to craft Christmas gifts for the boys and a handcrafted, superb wooden box to give to Daisy and Sam, as though he flaunted his lack of pride to show he had never been hurt. But I knew better, and I wondered if that was what finally would bring Daisy to her knees. Elizabeth had loved Art. Elizabeth often said, "When Art enters a room, somehow you feel everything will be all right." She acted protective of Art at the plays at Asilomar where Daisy now subordinated Art's part to Sam's.

I watched Daisy's blue eyes, pale as shadows, look out beyond the congregation toward the luminous, candlelit ceiling. I just knew that from the crest of this wave of Spirit, Daisy could see out to an unmarred landscape of greater events to come, with Sam and her taking the loyal group one step and one step and one step farther, while she and Sam remained two steps ahead, and people like Art and me, whom she could not deal with and believed wrong, writhing like good sinners always do back and behind the group.

Who cared about Daisy? We were all this moment in the arms of the Father/Mother God; the peals and the rejoicing and the peace of the words of the songs melted and melded us: Come away, the voice seemed to be saying, don't be afraid to break the shells of bitterness or power or fearful self-sufficiency; do not condemn, do not worship any gods before me (Daisy!) but listen to the singing, look over the moments when you have fallen into each other's arms, recapture the times, the little times when someone has had a word that has made the day worth living (Daisy). Recapture the prayer you said when you were tired and the answer uttered through the medium of memory by the still, small voice. "Rejoice, rejoice," our earth voices strained beneath us, but we didn't hear them. "On earth it is as it is in heaven." "Service over," someone said, but we just sat and stared at the candle flame, some for five minutes, some for an hour. That was our last service at Patrick's church.

Compelled by an inner command, I drove to Jackie's apartment fast. It was windy. New to the group, Jackie let Daisy and Sam and the rest stay at her apartment (she was away on business) after their "midnight move" following the service, because there was no choice—Jackie was going to marry Daisy's ex-husband Art—she and Daisy "knew" it, and this was a form of gratitude.

I'd never seen her apartment before. Jackie was a sort of an annoyance, I thought. She worked at a big electronics firm and was "plastic" in my estimation, although sweet in an old-fashioned, kewpie doll way. But she was the lady of the hour—she'd given Daisy a place to stay. Plus she actually had a job "in the world," something despised, perhaps, but also secretly admired and used to advantage at moments like these.

I got to Jackie's upstairs apartment through a labyrinth of greenery on paths lit by discrete low outdoor lamps, through dripping fountains. Jackie's cute, gift-shop-bought, glazed ceramic plant pots hung all over the place around the final outside stairway to her porch.

"Well, all right" Daisy said when I entered, "someone else, far out." Rebecca, right hand lady in waiting until almost the end, nodded briefly as though on bended knee; as if she were the physical extension of her mistress's cogitations. "We got out by the skin of our teeth," Daisy said, smelling faintly of alcohol. She had drunk her Christmas Tom and Jerry's past New Year's this year. Baby Anson, whose little penis dangled diaper less and free, squirted suddenly on Jackie's double pile rug. Daisy bent absentmindedly to blot it once with Anson's discarded diaper. The baby peed on, free, and I think he knew he was a noble child, the way he toyed with the baby star of David that hung on his wide, man-child's neck and patted his unisex haircut from time to time as though in rhyme to "Long Live God", which played on a tape recorder in the back room. That meant Stephen—who'd met Patrick through Daisy, gone south and returned as assistant choir director—was here too. Shit.

A weak early rain began outside through the fancy foliage surrounded by expensive, made-to-look-distressed wood fencing. Tonight Daisy drank wine, something also she did when transition periods were really tough. "Here…eat, Page…pretty Page." She stressed the word.

I looked skinnier lately. I was worn down by worry over Veronica and subsisting on our poor diet—how did Daisy always manage to be so flush? Oh, I knew at times in the past between marriages, she'd drawn welfare, explaining that since she supported the country with prayers, she could allow it to support her. I couldn't understand why we were always struggling. Because she was right, I had learned the laws of abundance, even if I had it "bass ackwards" as she had jested to the group. Certainly, I released everything possible, to stimulate the tide—to free the flow. I'd donated my classic book collection to Patrick's church; Doug and I had given our Christmas dish set to Amy and Peter as a wedding present because the design was their favorite; still we were poor, over our heads, often unable to make the rent on that dark house.

Was it the house that was my problem of late? I couldn't be sure. Once, I'd stopped by Daisy's when she held court from her bed like an ancient queen. There she'd told Sam and me to confront the "ego-involvement" of our friendship, which we did publicly at her bedside; Peter played therapist. Sam concluded nervously that it must be the leftovers from an intellectual friendship from a past life. She seemed quite friendly after that was decided, although she let it slip that she had "gotten told" that someone in the group was going to endure a "crucifixion," part of "an initiation of fire." Heady stuff.

Just after that, a strange pattern of night waking had begun for me, coincidentally right after the space beings' reassociation technique had been further worked on me by Amy and an over-eager Peter. After one such session at Amy and Peters', I'd had to be driven to Daisy's on a morning after they'd reassociated me—delved into bizarre sexual "memories" that seemed to spring from other lifetimes, or so Daisy said, calming me at last with her final puncture of the unhealthy bubble that ominously haunted me since last night's reassociating session. Between these spacey methods, our rented house where the dead seemed to walk, and my denial of Veronica's unhealed misery—not to mention certain solitary attempts I'd made at automatic writing to impress Daisy (or myself), I was frequently terrified lately, and consequently, far thinner than I'd been in a while.

Daisy always saw the bright side in the cloud however, in all the misery, personal or collective. Daisy could do that. "We are here, really, to congratulate ourselves. I know we've done the right thing. We had to get away from that. Patrick's going to market his choir and sing at the Hollywood Bowl—Stephen told us. He's slick, but we're not going for glory, are we, kids? We're here to bring the Christ principle into the earth and to follow Spirit wherever it may lead us, and it may not always lead us in man's way." Rebecca's dark silent eyes beamed pride at Daisy.

"Bring me some more wine will you 'Becca?"

"Cerrrtainly." Rebecca slipped off the couch, slender, dark hair bright against the synthetic, cream-colored top she wore over navy slacks, and passed into the kitchen.

"Listen to this, will you?" Stephen's voice preceded him into the room. "Man, I think we have it. I've listened to the tape of their choir three times, Daisy. I think we can do it with one organ and one piano, Daisy…I really do."

"Have some wine, Stephen."

He laughed that smoky racking laugh. Patrick had the balls to talk about Stephen in his zinger-talks at the church. "I've been with somebody recently who put my soul through a meat grinder," he'd said. They had been lovers.

We stood in the living room of Daisy and Sam's newly rented house. In blue, green and white, bright and yet subdued, we swayed to the "rain is on the roof" song—"hurry high butterfly...oh I know why the skies all cry"—and I focused on my right eye. Things looked darker lately since we'd lost the church and I'd been left up north in that house: I had become peculiarly concerned that I was going to lose my mind—yet I knew I wouldn't. Was the darkness in my right eye, an effort to blind myself to the fact that the whole group knew Doug and I had been indulging in embarrassing sexual practices (recommended by Daisy) in an effort to defuse the past life charge I carried? "I've seen more energy between you two than ever before," Peter winked now, encouraging, I suppose, the perverse act I was advised to ask Doug to administer nightly like medicine, until the desire bubbles burst, until I was clear—buggery for Spirit. Once I'd wanted them concerned about my intimate life with Doug, so that Doug and I could grow closer. Now I felt closer all right—to them! The side effect was—that they all must know. I sighed, managed a resigned, "Oh, thanks."

Daisy and Rebecca and Amy scraped chairs up to the Formica kitchen table and planned the group's next move.

In the living room Sam reminded Stephen, "It has to feel right in energy," when Wayne rose to sing the song that was the story of his life as a lonely little boy left to live with that enormously unkind farm woman after his mother died. He sang in a cracked, emotion-filled voice. Sam interceded after three tries to "get it right" in energy. "I'll do it, Wayne" he said. Wayne acquiesced and rocked back into his place with a little laugh.

I protested for Wayne, but he stopped me. "It's all right. It's all right. This is the way it's supposed to be, the energy and all." His shoes squeaked as he rocked nervously on his heels.

We sang, "Every man's got a seed, sleeping deep inside his soul...that's more precious than his gold...to a mother it's her baby, sleeping deep inside her side...to a cowboy it's his blanket on a dark and starry night." Sam's redolent empty voice boomed the words for Wayne. He kept the same pace as the "Our Father", as he did "Stop and Smell the Roses", as he probably fucked Daisy; one, two, three long strongs. (On his back actually—I walked in on them recently once when I burst in, panicked that I was going mad.)

At 10:30 Rebecca brought two candles, lit, into the room slowly, as if there was going to be a wedding. Amy cut the living room light. Daisy entered in full minister's dress. "We have a surprise for you." She blessed the candles, laid them on a shelf that usually held a TV and blessed that shelf—this would be our altar for now.

"Jade's ready—it's time for her to take to her wings as full minister under our new charter as the 'Circle of Light!'" Startled, we sang anyway on Sam's cue, "The rain is on the roof..." Perhaps I would be a minister too. Elizabeth had often asked me when I would be able to begin to teach, or lead a little group at Daisy's church. If Jade had advanced, perhaps I would too. My right eye cleared a little bit. I thought, maybe tonight...

"And there are two others here, who've been ministers for a long time, and who are ministers in essence," Daisy said, quickening my hopes. "All we're going to do is to acknowledge...that essence... already alive and moving in them.

"Rebecca, Amy—step forth." Amy and Rebecca lifted teary eyes, to Daisy and Daisy blessed her sister and her sister-in-law, and Jade—thrice. "And...now...we're going to sing and welcome them."

We finished at half past eleven. Moving by bodies, clothes brushing, I wanted to get to the bathroom. I was focusing on my eye, worrying that my vision seemed darker than before. I was blocked by Sam who took my hand. "Soon for you too," he promised, looking up from under perplexed black brows. His wan eyes winked sadly. I knew he was sorry, but he no more knew that it would be soon for me, or ever, than I did. My eye cleared for a moment. Or did he?

I thought of Sam a lot after that...and of—when? Things remained dark looking out of eye during that time.

In the morning I came early because I thought I was going to lose my mind. I wore the striped Joseph-of-many-colors robe that I had worn before in some lifetime of old. The colors ran down it like bleeding ink. I showed Daisy this robe I'd bought at a brightly lit shop far away from the malignant house beneath the gnarled pepper tree. Daisy—and Amy and Peter—had been telling me lately to get out of "that house" and "rent a little apartment you can afford."

"Go bowling," Daisy suggested today, "that's what I did when I was trapped as 'earth mother'—do some of the things that express the complicated person you are. You paint neat pictures—so paint! Too much of diapers and babies has made many a good woman nuts. I remember taking meat out of the freezer when Art's and my boys were small, and finding it melting on the counter when he got home." Sam said, "Page, you look harried." They didn't know the half of it.

I had come to her house early that late autumn morning because I thought I was going to lose my mind and I wanted to be near her. I told her in choppy, short, fragmented sentences, "See, it happened again—are you really sure that I'll be ok—when I move, Daisy—will I?" Oh yes, I wished she had said, but instead she looked at me with an enigmatic smile. On the other hand she didn't say "if you do go mad, it's meant to be," or, "surrender to it" as she had on one or two occasions when I called her in the middle of the night and interrupted her sleep—or her lovemaking with the King of Men. And so we were poised, delicately balanced as usual between former enmities—the rivalry and jealousies of earlier lifetimes—and a kind of understanding that had sprung up between us.

Sitting at her kitchen table I felt very remote from last night's terrors—the waking up to see a Buddha sitting in my plant even with my eyes open and seeing a woman in a Victorian gown sweeping through the hallway a foot off the ground. Daisy didn't know that for months I'd been channeling more inspirational, automatic writings in an effort to compensate for my problems in the group by contacting the highest source—for what was a life lived out at the lowest level in my particular community, the family of our church fellowship? I didn't connect the night terrors to the automatic writing either, not until later. Elizabeth said Edgar Cayce warned against two psychic practices: the use of the Ouija Board, and automatic writing. Inspirational writing was different, Elizabeth added—she did it often herself. The difference was, in automatic writing, you let a spirit take over your hand. Inspirational writing came through your Higher Self from the Source.

But I'd indulged in automatic writing, and at this point I was fighting for my life against the fear of cracking up entirely. Intermittent, midmorning light filtered through the Daisy-made curtains, white and blue with trellised daisies climbing up their sides. It felt good to be here. Sam was home as usual—the ministers' men rarely worked all the time any more, but as true companions worked "as one" with their wives. He retreated with Stephen into the back of the house to arrange songs for choir practice. All of Daisy's rented houses seemed idyllic. Thinking to move soon I explored her back yard. I noticed the rear neighbors had a pool separated from Daisy's pastoral yard by a high redwood fence.

"You'll have fun next summer," I commented while we lay out nude in the dim, pre-winter sunshine, because I was convinced that the neighbors would be part of her "family" soon. "I had asked God for a pool at my next house." Daisy laughed. "And I got one—only it's over the back fence. Oh well, it's probably better that way, because I wouldn't be doing anything else but this."

She stretched out in the waning sun, warming under the glace of wind like a body would under covers.

Her skin, tan all year now from the many exposures to the sun—representative of "the Light," which Daisy worshipped—resembled the peel of a long, plump fruit, with fullness in appropriate places; hers was a lazy skin, stained iodine, umber, gold with downy hair caught at moments by the wind dipping low into our cache of warmth. Her physical ideal, I knew, was to be at peace with the body—pure of temple, to have a clean vehicle, one in which a hundred and forty-four thousand cells would be uplifted to the Christ of the ages, would be Christed. And her belly, indiscernible from the rest of the gold mirage, had the faint whitened "marks of motherhood", by now quite beautiful to me because she taught they were. A body looked most beautiful to me now when it carried itself from its heart charka out, and hers did today, lying lightly oiled under the morning light deepening to noon.

All of her nighttime cigarette smoking and morning coffee guzzling were offset by this exposure to the "angels of air and light" as prescribed by the Dead Sea Scrolls, true record of the Essenes who had prepared as a group, man and woman alike, for the return of an elder brother, so that He could do what they all must do one day—become Christed within their own body temple. Edgar Cayce had spoken of the Essenes. Now Daisy was reading a new book drawn from the Dead Seas Scrolls, and Daisy applied concepts that seemed true to her. So, there we lay, two beings in two skins bared to the Essene angels of air and light, striving for Mastery in this plane.

I would never go insane around Daisy, and if I did, she would show me that I was doing it for God, for Truth, and lead me back out again away from the flame. That was it—Daisy had been talking of the "initiation of fire" lately, and I wondered if I was taking the initiation of fire during those terrifying nights, so that I might be anointed with oil and become a minister at last.

Just then Daisy asked me if I wanted any suntan oil. Oil? So it must be true—my heart sang. I smiled inside at the beautiful synchronicity.

I wondered if she thought the fire initiation might account for my night terrors. But I was aware that she did not want me to ask why again, why I was waking up four times a night with my heart pounding. I had asked her this morning, and she really did not know yet. She was sure the deeper answer would come "when it was right." But I couldn't help myself. "So why do you think I'm having this fear thing?" I persisted?

She got up slowly and pulled on a light short robe from the clothesline. "Want to help me water the flowers around the side of the house?" was the master's reply to this obnoxious seeker.

Shoot. I followed her and we watered, the spray of crystalline rain like prismatic dew seemed to presage a great new day. I shortened my steps to keep with hers as we slowly made our way around the border of late chrysanthemums, to the cold frame Art had built for what would be her spring vegetable garden. The chrysanthemums got to sleep directly under Daisy and Sam's bedroom window, under the laughter and I imagined, the ecstatic mumblings that must flow from their bed laid simply on the floor when the rest of us finally went home at last after Monday, or Tuesday, or Wednesday night's meeting.

In the umber, garnet, auric river of her skin, revealed after shedding the little robe again, we lay. She told me of a dream she'd received, and I listened intently because I was certain of my ability to dream…at least of that—one thing—I was certain.

At last it was Christmas time and I thought she was going to give me a special present. But she didn't, and I was sad and I walked around for days doubting inside what I had done.

I'd given her something of me—really of me—a hand painted portrait of herself delicately painted with pastel watercolors; and to each of her friends, to each of her closest supporters, I'd given something almost equally beautiful or important. The paintings were special enough, I thought—but then I'd also channeled poetry from the same Dark of Night voice from The Within that spoke to me in comfort against the night terrors. "Many journeys far/Through golden halls," I'd written, "Could not have brought us farther/Than to tame the wild heart within/Nor could we spy in those fair cities/As clear a light/As we find in ourselves."

Dually motivated, I gave of my Self—the Self that cared and gave the words of comfort through the poems to those others who needed the peace, but mostly I gave out of a desire not to go mad, and out of a desire to have Daisy see my spirituality and my giving and recognize me. I had principles, separate principles, but Daisy eclipsed these. To me she was the sun, the moon, a great goddess.

I waited for just the right moment to carry my gift to her at the Christmas party we held at Constance's, because we had, as yet, no new building. She gave me a nativity scene she said she'd made by hand. Later, I discovered it had come from a kit, and was only one of several. Daisy suggested this Christmas, that we find a moment when the "energy" flows between ourselves and another to exchange gifts— that to tear everyone's gifts open at once, was a Christmas ritual sorely needing amending. When new customs were needed, Daisy created them. Her gift would be a talisman against the night terrors, which, mercifully, had begun to recede. Finally, I decided to place it on the dresser in our bedroom and laid it there next to a sweet-scented, slow-burning, pink candle. That was the right spot for it I sighed, and built the thing up in my mind. That was right because it could light the way of new birth in the bedroom, which represented the place of personal communion and out-of-body experiences, and also the marital relationship, which was in need of new birth. That's why she chose the nativity for me. That's why it was so special, more than just a kit nativity scene could be. She chose it because she knew I was ready for a great inner "birth" and was going to help me attain it.

I watched the candle illuminate the flat wooden, painted, glitter-haired family. I was the babe, per her philosophy; or the babe was that Christ within me, within all of us.

The voice, still and small, that wanted me to keep making the paintings and give them to all, even though Christmas had passed, was relaying to me its hushed guidance, too, about the nativity, about her, about the frightening time I was passing through in this temporal and material existence. But I could not always hear it yet because it was so small. And her words were so great and they glittered like the flat wooden cut-out Christ family vivified by her quick artist's brush.

Daisy wearing a lapis star

Chapter Sixteen

I miss Daisy terribly. The days the weeks the months, the years go by. She was a light in my life. Summer cool, the tile blue sparkle of the Bethlehem star in the crèche she gave me, washes my mind with memory. She ebbs and flows as all the values I came to know through her, rise and fall in my adult life.

She is ankh blue, moonstone and emerald. Her foreign white washed indifferent blue eyes haunt me. There was a time when we were true, good friends though we were uncomfortable in each other's presence.

Yet I thought the way she held her cigarette was fine, the way her eyes looked, the way she tapped her fingernails—bare of polish—on the Persian paper-covered desk she loved at her new hall. I loved the laughter about her eyes, I loved the gown she wore that changed with the seasons, her now bare feet underneath the wide robe, no underwear; she'd given it up as a significant gesture of some sort or another—I've forgotten why.

I watched her slip from her seat near the edge of the desk to tip up and reach for an Egyptian statuette given her as a gift to reflect a certain lifetime she had lived. I didn't know what dynasty it represented, but I had a desperate urge to have lived in that lifetime **with** her.

Lately I felt as if I were grasping at wind that was blowing off somewhere without me; first one direction, then the other—why wasn't I too impelling those currents? "A natural born leader," they'd said when I was a child.

"Hand me that, Page." I picked up the starfish set in an oblong glass paperweight and passed it to her. She lifted it to the far corner of the shelf above the desk. She was still getting settled in.

"Long live God, long live Go-o-od, long live Go-o-od—long live God!" They were warming up in the large, low-ceilinged front room down the hall to the front of the building. Jade banged on the door. "Daisy—it's time."

"Someday, Caroline—Page—Ryder," Daisy responded to my lost look. "You're too important to stop...at anything short of..."

She smiled and stepped into thin-strapped gold lame sandals. Even if I knew she'd bought them at Anita's, the low-budget, cheap-made copy shop at the shopping mall, it seemed she had just stepped into Nepthys's temple sandals. She left and I sat in the Persian papered office like a stone.

Mirror mirror. I looked into the mirror and saw white. I meditated in Sunshine Hall on the subject of my inner self and saw Daisy's face; when very still I encountered her...the inner me. She'd asked us to "go in Spirit," had led us through light hypnosis to a garden where a face appeared in a reflecting pool—the reflection of our own inner "best" nature, she explained. When it was my turn after the meditation, I told the group that hers was the face I saw.

Daisy, ranging around the room barefoot in the last hour of this Saturday "Power of the Word" seminar, paused to interpret my symbol. "Oh," she mused, "that means...that's you too, Page," she murmured, surprised. I had hope then. I could be like her one day. Neat. I was proud, but another—resentful—thread wound around the old hopes and choked them. But why was my higher self garbed in her face? Still, my newfound pride stooped to pick up the scraps, and then the deep humiliation bent me low and I chose to ignore it as I always did. Like a water-sodden reed in heavy wind, I bent almost to the drowning.

We broke into separate groups. I followed Sam, the newest minister. Daisy had made him one and met my fury with a patronizing explanation about "oneness in energy—like attracts like and we are each other's manifestation and therefore he is a minister—you see?" Sam took our group into the back room of the hall to make sure that each one was "finished in energy" and had "their piece"—the core insight or realization Spirit provided. He couldn't quite figure out what my "piece" was. He called Daisy in. I didn't know why—weren't they one in wisdom?

"Page here says she got nervous all of a sudden when we came back here to the room," he submitted for Daisy's analysis.

"I don't remember what anybody said to trigger it," I reported scientifically, while clenching sweaty fists.

He whispered aside to her. (Perhaps they were talking about how important this "piece" would be for me.) I had been to their house so many times during the winter to talk about waking up at two and three and six with my heart pounding; they had been annoyed and concerned, and yet we'd come closer through all of it. And I'd found a comforter within—like that described in the Edgar Cayce readings—when nobody would answer my late night telephone calls, when Veronica's undiagnosed screams and head banging persisted even in the new apartment and Doug looked more and more to me like the angry child he really was. I'd found that voice, at the center of me, that said "it is I, little one", that kept me away from myself, from the consuming worries, kept me safe from myself.

Now I felt a pang, a taste of it again—that release.

This was the "Power of the Word" seminar expressing a new philosophy, that what you accurately "named" aloud, was called and dissolved—"popped" was Daisy's word for it—and the energy and the truth would set you free.

She looked me in the eye: "Isn't it—the fear thing—still happening because you want attention?"

I looked back at her. Blam. All right, Daisy. I loved her enough, and the truth, to smile through the embarrassment. The other people in the room didn't matter. We, Sam and Daisy and I, knew it was worth it.

It was a Sunday morning—still winter. Kim Selby stood up in the front meeting room of the Sunshine hall on Hamilton Avenue already dressed in his muslin choir shirt. He looked like all the rest. It really didn't matter here—that he was gay. So was Stephen, and Daisy herself, and now a few of the other women had had forays with their own sex "in the energy", to "pop desire bubbles", "to discover the point of truth that underlay all movement," etc. I appreciate the group's attitude toward Kim now. There are so many tight constraints on what we are, so many simplistic labels. In this Sunday morning minister's class held before service, Kim had the floor. I watched Daisy, who felt close to him during that cycle, urging him, tugging him into heterosexuality, which she still believed to be the better way—particularly for men. (In a desperate move to help him one night after choir practice before we'd gotten the hall, Daisy had met with Kim and his lovely look-alike sister—

believed to be his twin soul—in Daisy's temporary, home minister's office. We all knew—though it was hush hush—that Daisy proposed that Kim and his sister live together freely, as man and wife—just like in Egypt when brothers and sisters married with great dignity.)

Again today Daisy tried her hand at Kim's psychology. Words darted from person to person. We all wanted to help. She asked him more about his mother. It turned out she was a cocktail waitress, very beautiful, and she'd had a series of "uncles" around. They seemed rough from Kim's description, and he didn't like them. Daisy bore through, biting on the square rim of her gold glasses. "Kim, aren't you attracting these men to keep them from her?" It clicked. Kim smiled, the "psychic grin." There was nothing he could say. A hit for Daisy.

My turn. I broke into the space that followed to recount an attunement after watching a program about a French woman singer, born in a brothel, the emblem of a certain part of French culture, who'd died in the early sixties. Edith Piaf, "the sparrow." I said I had the feeling she'd been reborn as someone I now knew, possible one of my daughters, or Yvette's. Kim lanced back. "Why would you think she's one of **your** daughters at all—just because she was somebody famous?"

"Very **good**. Look at him go." Daisy praised Kim, sopping his pride and congratulating herself on his healing.

"Ummm. She probably is Yvette's daughter, Desiree." Sensing he was right, I gurgled my reply in embarrassment. Her daughter had a French name. But I was too quick to be humble and it didn't go over very well "in energy."

We were all aboard now, resettled at Sunshine Hall and I could feel us headed somewhere again with Daisy at the helm. Oh how I longed for the days so sweet and simple when we were going nowhere but listening within.

One Wednesday morning I remembered those earlier days as I drifted and dreamed and nodded out between gusts from Rebecca's and Amy's and the elegant Constance's cigarettes. Their Atlantean-like, proud, pursed lips refilled the kitchen with every puff. Daisy passed in, as ephemeral as smoke. They all looked at her in adoration, or was it only me? I felt like a flea, a longsuffering flea, itched off the greater body, extinguished from the proceedings. How long would I suffer without the vital key? Where, what was it?

On March second, Daisy had said it was time to celebrate Sam's birthday. Now they were all abustle this morning as they waited for him, holding mysterious gifts. Jade, with the one she'd made for her sometime mentor and friend, Rebecca for her brother-in-law, Amy for her former husband—a gift for the gift she'd given to Daisy when she'd given her sister a sharp pricked Atlas with a mind. No one minded those events now—they all gave homage to the queen. But I minded.

Sam arrived and parted the nouveau Atlantean mists. Daisy kissed his lips. Afterwards his lips looked salty through the smoke in the opaque light let in through the kitchen window. When Daisy kissed him again I felt a powerful pull. I tried to meditate. Better to go to unconsciousness than to have lecherous love and envy break through the veil. A gaiety erupted in the women, a conscious gaiety, for him, for their birthday. For anything anyone celebrated was Daisy's too; she was the "day's eye," of the ancient Anglo-Saxon meaning of her name and she was never not in the limelight, nor removed from the sights and sounds of her people, or even from the sexual feelings that boiled and subsided in the strange subterranean heats of the welter world of her people. We **were** her people; we **were** The Body. We moved as a fleshly mass about her as if we were her limbs and belly and breasts, coiling about her like long legs about long legs pressing two hot loins together toward the release.

"Give me your present, sweetheart; let me see it," Daisy asked when Sam unwrapped Jade's homemade gift, two large jars labeled "Pickles Sweet." Sam handed Daisy the parcel. "You can't get 'em like this anywhere outside da East," he chuckled, reminiscent of the biker and pool shark he'd once been. Rebecca gave him a rapidograph pen set, Amy gave him a blanket crocheted by her obsequious unloved sons—I gave him nothing because nobody had invited me to. Constance gave him a belt she'd designed under Daisy's eye. I felt left out, not one of his wives at all, merely a trollop who had eyes for him.

One by one they'd remated and married: Daisy to Sam and then, like blossoms ruffled by the wind, Rebecca to Daisy's half-brother Rex; Amy to Peter who secretly loved Daisy; Constance at last to Neil who gaily stated his onetime fancy—that Daisy would summon him to her bed just once to mate with him "in the energy." And Jade, deemed Daisy's good daughter, responsible, sweet and shy—was linked to Russell, a tall, ambitious man in his thirties, who itched to be Daisy's leading male minister. So far Daisy was thwarting him and he remained a choir member. Still, I had waited the longest, impelled by the quiet remembrance of Daisy's first "in spirit" reading for me on North Redwood Street. "For you, I will open every door," the voice had promised me softly through Daisy's half-sleeping lips. And the voice rang in memory, jogged my belief that the cup I trained each day to carry would, at last, be passed my way.

Suddenly, watching all the others gazing at Sam licking Jade's sweet pickle juice from his lips, I saw that they were all one wife, lesser energies condensed and joined into the best wife that Sam could ever have—his great wife, Daisy. Maybe I was the only one who wanted the cup passed. Maybe the others, even Russell, were content to drink out of her cup. Something different stirred within me, impelled the erratic rhythms of my heart that hammered worlds apart from the great, regular heart pumping the energy that ebbed and flowed in and out of The Body.

Sam cut the cake. After the eating was over, I had to go home. Never formally invited anyway, I'd made no plans and had to retrieve the children early from the upstairs neighbor at the fourplex. Sam walked me out to my car on his way to his own car to pick up his sketchpad so he could try out the new Rapidograph. Walking toward the street side of the building he pressed me to him, arm around my shoulder, when I apologized for not knowing when the celebration would be and for not having a gift. Honeysuckle budded between us—and the Sunshine Hall, physically, a long low house, converted some time ago to this usage. Already the air seemed rife with sensuous whiffs of these and other flowers in the blossom. At the car he sparkled about me like the new evening star I'd spotted lately from the upstairs four-plex window. When he hugged me I felt beneath the awkward—when shall I pull away so he won't think?—the love of spirit coursing through me until I felt my head ringing, the blood boiling out my eyes, it seemed.

So locked into the night of my shyness was I that I wished it were night. I heard his heart under his new muslin star-of-birth embroidered shirt—Daisy's present to him with signature flourish. I heard the thumping melody of my own heart against his. I broke from his embrace, startled to realize it was late morning instead of night. I drove off with my package, the secret inner package of my response to him and the knowing of what was wrong, wrapped up inside the thicknesses of chosen blindness as if it were a bird in a heavy layers of net. I closed off my inner sense so that I could not feel the bird's hungry fluttering, nor hear its cries piercing my waking dream. I **would** be a minister—someday. Everything I'd suffered would be worth it, worth the prize. I hobbled from the car towards the four-plex, stepped over the litter in the streets, not seeing the wino's crumpled bags tossed into the weeds and newspapers and fly-laden dog excreta—pretending it was night in San Jose and inside of me, although it was a bleak, blaring overcast noon beneath a waxing sun late within the Ides of March.

But at night I laid the dream down and found a sleep that provided peace even after the cruddy diaper-soaking day that remained after his special secret hug; just a press closer than that of an elder brother; the hug he was friend enough to bestow so that I would have something, something anyway, to dream on.

That bleak overcast March turned hot and dull by early summer. Doug hung around over at Art's with Mary Grace and Wayne. Art had moved near to Daisy and Sam's after Daisy married Art to Jackie just after Easter time. With the warming of the days Daisy decided she needed a real pool and vacated her house, deciding also that it "was best for the kids" if Art moved right into it and set up housekeeping with all of the boys at once. She'd dabbled at having the bigger boys for a time during the winter—rotating Art Jr., who'd been with her off and on, to help baby-sit Anson—with Davy, for whom I helped her fix up a Mickey Mouse bedroom and as quickly tear it down. That was too bad because Davy, a doll in my opinion and the sweetest of the boys, lived much to himself now in the world of imagination. Benjamin, the second, was a darkly handsome boy who wanted to be a policeman and who already was growing to hate his mother. Daisy attributed this pityingly to Art's earthbound reasoning, but I remembered Elizabeth warning Daisy way back against a sense of rejection in this middle son.

Now Art had all of his boys, including Todd Allen; for Todd Allen he was all too happy to move, or to do anything else Daisy demanded. Art seemed a king at home in his castle moated off from the rest of us by the currents of his unfortunately earthbound energy, but reasonably secure with all his little sons about him. He changed the airy ephemeral colors in the house to earthbound browns, and Jackie brought over her clever expensive ceramic pots and objects d'art she'd bought on her IBM salary. Art was very much out of favor, a new caustic wit regarding Daisy was costing him whatever grace he could have earned by letting Daisy marry him to Jackie, to expiate the awkward situation of his loneliness.

That summer I hung around with nobody—so much more out of favor than Art; I had nothing but the trips to Sunshine Hall and the kids and the miserable bleak apartment. Sometimes, sitting alone on the unstable concrete steps outside of our apartment that Marshall called the "bird's nest," the word four-plex suggested quadriplegic. I felt paralyzed.

Doug smoked dope with Art, who'd added that rebellion to the collection of jibes at Daisy and Sam that left his little audience always in stitches. I would have gone over there more often—even if I didn't like to be in the same room with dope smoke because of some unfortunate experiences in the sixties—because around Art I still felt as if everything was going to be all right, as alienated as we appeared to be on opposite sides of Her disfavor. He was scorned because he did not try to get "in the energy"; I tried and tried but couldn't be let in. Desperate, I even submitted to Daisy's unspoken command to spy for her where Art was concerned and Art was still in love enough with Daisy to absorb her prejudices about people— even me. He was still that much in awe of her judgments—even about himself.

But still I would have been over there more often viewing and being viewed through the dull glass of Daisyisms, just to hear his latest jokes drawn from events that transpired when she'd lived around the corner from him before this last move. He told a great joke about how Daisy condemned him for his lack of faith. Jackie had bought him a big freezer and he stocked it with a side of beef and a multitude of "goodies." (Uncle Art loved to eat.) Daisy helped herself freely to roasts, whole turkeys and the like on her way home from Sunshine Hall. But when the power went out in May and the entire freezer of food melted, she told him it was his comeuppance for his lack of faith, citing the example the lilies of the field that neither toil nor spin nor keep meat freezers.

Daisy marries Art to Jackie
Left to right facing: includes: Rebecca's daughter (Becka), Peter, Vince, (back corner standing: Doug, Page, Yvette (with star necklace), Mary Grace, Rebecca (holding bouquet), Constance, Joel, Jackie (flowers in her hair), Wayne (back standing), Art, Daisy as minister, Rexford. In the audience, Amy (center).

For the jokes I would have gone over there and listened with an ear out to describe his "earthbound" difficulties to Daisy later, but there was the problem of Jackie, ironically Daisy's hand picked successor. I sensed she disliked me, no, just did not like me…well, whatever. It couldn't have been easy to have Daisy gesture at her and Art and the kids in church and wave them off as "my earth family." I stayed away from them and most everyone else for a while and dreamed my own dreams.

Certainly my dreams were still of becoming a minister after I had completed my training—when Daisy would let me in, that is, or when Daisy or God or somebody would let me into Life, but now my dreams were more than that. The scares, the waking up nights with my heart pounding from a cause even Daisy couldn't name and command with the power of the word, had taught me something invaluable.

In the terror that I was going mad I'd had to turn within to what I thought was God. To me it was the kindness of the Christ, the tender handed, patience we'd known at the very beginnings of time, and it was the still small voice within. It was surrendering to that voice during the dark night in the dismal apartment, with the pathetic whimpering child tossing in her sleep, when the dying old woman beneath rattled her broom on the ceiling beneath my bed, when I felt the Fear and thought it would not stop, when a ride in the car with Doug, the half-man, half-retarded boy, and the children set me on an edge from which I feared I would tumble off; then I would listen to that voice, that still small voice. It would comfort.

"Be not afraid, beloved; it is I," the voice said. "There is no fear, no circumstance that can separate you from me. I am the way and the light, the alpha and the omega, the beginning and the ending. Fear not."

"Fear not," intoned the spark from the light place within.

"Will you take Mary Grace's kids and our boys while Doug helps Mary Grace and Wayne get moved out of Mountain View to our house?" Jackie asked me in July. No, I thought at first, no. They don't want me, no; she's only using me. Then I thought more about the voice. Be not afraid. And I thought of the beautiful times, thought of what "spirit" really was. Maybe I could not come in, could not partake, because of ego really. Maybe Daisy was right. No matter. I was lonely. I would take the children. Because it would be a way of being part of the kindness, of the giving, of something I couldn't name—only feel—and it felt good. They brought the kids by for the weekend. There, outside in the carport attached to the natty four-plex, watching two more babies and my own and hearing the shy stories of Art's middle boys, I rested in the sunshine and felt ok, less afraid, content to do what was before me, what was given into my hands, and to bless the children with my heart.

There came again the wondering, "Does Daisy mean this?" Is this what she is teaching? Was it this all along—have I been missing the train, over and over again—self-abnegation, service to the Christ: the tenderness, the passion, the calm, the sacred heart of all of us, even of the dying woman downstairs, eaten up, if Cayce was right about cancer, by the hates hardened over into resentments built over lifetimes. And was it not the Christ emanating from the heart of the child Veronica, so hard to manage, who asked for kindness, who battered at me to tear me out of sloth and self-absorption and sheer misery?

It must even be the Christ in me who, after fumbling and stumbling about carrying laundry down the long concrete stairs that swung and banged against the building that night, dropped my basket to the bit of grass at the bottom and stopped to gaze up into the stars. It was the Christ trying to find itself in me. Oh how could I know? Daisy would know.

In the night though, after all the children slept, in the soft, still, dead night when the pressure of the dark seemed near around me, when fears about myself and for myself began to crowd out sleep, I knew it was the Christ who padded across bare linoleum that creaked to get a glass of water, for it was not I who said all the while; "Be ye not afraid." And it was not Daisy, comforting me so in the hard, dark, open gloom.

After the weekend with all the children I found greater peace in assuming simple duties at the Hall. I scrubbed dishes during the Fourth of July festivities, enjoyed Peter in white face paint, tights and bells prancing in and out of the group as the embodiment of his favorite past-life persona as the jester. Mostly I washed the dishes quietly, talking to Nona Acacia, a new Mexican-American girl—one of many newcomers who hung about the edges of the group and who looked upon me with great awe. Daisy noticed me among the dishes that day and during the week or so afterwards. At a business meeting in the second room down the hall to the left, when there was need for someone to do the mailer, because Amy's greater duties were carrying her deeper into the dignity of the ministry, I said I could. Daisy frowned at me, then allowed, "You can give it a try if you like." Out to prove myself, I plunged into the effort wholeheartedly, drumming up volunteers by "promotion", not always by "attraction,", as she advised, but I always had helpers among the lonely young newcomers and from Pegeen whose wealthy husband provided the computerized address labels.

Early one morning I started out for the Hall. I ran back and forth down to my new used Datsun (the Mustang had been totaled one night where we'd left it by the roadside near Patrick's church. The group didn't believe in insurance—"God's our insurance," we often said—and sure enough, the guy who demolished my car coughed up some insurance money, and this "miracle" used car that I'd found by following my hunch seemed to have rewarded my trust.) Back up the stairs I leapt again for the stacks of inserts to staple into this month's missive, back for the box of labels, the staplers, sponges and the bright blue and orange and yellow stickers. The babies were already in the car hitting their fists against the windows, eager to go. I was careful running back down the stairs the last time, careful not to drop a single sheaf, handled them more carefully than the children who tumbled about the back of the tiny white car in a cacophony of old wrappers, toys and hand-me-down baby clothes. "Stop that. Put your sweater back on Veronica." But she couldn't. I forced her arms into it, stuffed her thin legs into torn corduroy pants. Sleepily, Molly followed me with her eyes, wise and patient in her car seat like a two year old mother.

One more trip. "Mommy will be right back." I hurried, jumped up the steps, pushed open the thin door. It clattered against the wall behind it. I looked around for something I must have forgotten. Oh. "The Magic Meditation Seminar" flyers. A month away, but it was important that everyone got the word. Or was it? More money for Daisy. On the top of the refrigerator were two quarters. Good. One banana, almost too old, in the refrigerator. I stuffed it in my linty sweater pocket. (The sweater was a find at the last Fourth of July rummage sale at Patrick's church.) I've got to wash this when I get time, I thought. Have I got everything? I picked up the heavy little box of half page flyers decorated with Sam's precise (copied) Art Nouveau designs and pulled the door shut, hoped it caught. Worried if anything was undone, and always afraid it was, the fear caught my belly. What was it? Head bent, feet as careful as a ballerina's; I couldn't drop the box. Why would I? I feared that my arms would throw the box to the bottom of the steps, acting all by themselves out of some anger I couldn't fathom. I only had two people I knew would come to help: one to stuff and one to staple. Two more volunteers to call. I wanted to be early, to have it all spread out and ready by 9:30, to be done by one. The steps, concrete and grey. This mailer was a step, only a step. I'd master this, be a minister someday.

In the car the kids seemed restless. They hadn't really had breakfast. I split the banana. But they too, had been born at this time and in this place to serve the overall body of humanity, right? I glanced at them: Veronica's head was scabbed from her last fall; I couldn't do anything about this, could I? Daisy said not to worry, Veronica just wasn't in her body yet. Molly was thin, weak and sickened from a milk allergy. Well, now I had soymilk, and the doctor agreed to take payments every two months and not turn us over to "collection" as had the last. The attendant at the gas station across from the apartments took the grubby handful of change I gave him with disdain. "Deal between yourself and God, Page," Daisy in my head admonished me. Sagaciously I stared the man down and rumbled off a minute later, tired, as if I'd been up a month instead of a morning.

I opened the hall (the second time I'd been allowed to arrive first), darted back to the car, then bundled the two little girls into the back room—last on the left—that was used as a nursery, answering their hungry looks impatiently. I hauled in the mailer materials—Daisy's sacred trust—and rummaged through the virtually bare refrigerator and found some crackers in the cupboard and some not yet sour milk for their bottles. "Here. Have this." I felt as if I were being torn apart. That wasn't enough to eat. No way to go to the store and have enough gas to make it home. Three food stamps left. Those would be used for dinner.

In the deep dreamlike state in which we lived anything should have been O.K., but as time progressed, I felt more and more uneasy, more and more restless, as though something was missing—had been promised and would never be delivered.

Sometimes, the restless, nagging feeling would overpower me. Daisy said I was "like my daughter," with so much of me living on other planes, so little of me here in expression, in comparison with who I really was. And, she intimated, I had those periods of rebellion, just like Veronica.

Was I pushing my head against walls metaphorically? It certainly seemed so. And Daisy was my wall, a sweet skinned, curly cropped wall with enchanting lines around shallow, water-blue eyes. Eyes so shallow you could never get in them, eyes so iridescent you always tried, spent your lifetime it seemed, wading around in puddles of crystal.

Several nights later, I got back from the beauty shop to Sunshine Hall before class feeling bad, as usual, that I couldn't leave a tip—just didn't have the 50 cents. Now my hair, light brown though instead of golden, was cut in the unisex shag that looked like Daisy's, and I pushed my Daisy-like wire-rim glasses back into my face where they looked and felt as if they didn't belong.

The lights in the hall were dim, eclipsed by the last of the daylight. Everything was readied for the Wednesday night class, a lecture series by Daisy, who channeled the energy freeform; nothing preplanned. She took her own messages—when they "hit" her—out of the verbal flow of psychic material she disciplined herself to receive and to channel to us.

I waited for Daisy in her office—the last door down the hall on the right—and noticed the small Persian rug covering the top of a white-painted cabinet that held the water heater. An Aladdin's lamp sat on the rug with an Egyptian necklace laid out across its beautiful pattern. I recognized the rug as one Daisy had borrowed from me—to keep for me, she'd said—when she'd moved me from Palo Alto to San Jose six years earlier. I felt a pang but pushed it aside.

An arrow plant danced lazily toward the diffuse light from the far edge of the sunset beyond the window. The sheer, homemade slip of a curtain shut out the last of the day. Amy slipped in and lit the tapers. When she left I noticed a new picture of Sam, directing the choir, propped up to cover the sprocket protruding through the top of the water heater cabinet.

When I'd first met Daisy she had showed me a scrapbook she was making to leave for herself to find in her next lifetime. "I've already seen the house where I'll discover it as a young girl—about 13 I think—I can't wait to get back in the body again, to live in the New Age, in the millennium of peace predicted biblically and the world over. Now is the time to prepare for that next lifetime, Page," she said. "Elizabeth predicts we'll meet and marry the twin soul, and have our true work. There is so much to do to prepare." That is how I'll always remember Daisy, not the way they say she is now.

The calendar read "Wednesday." Wednesdays were bright, alive—class night. And we were the closest we ever were before I left. After a long while Daisy flounced in, flicked on the light switch and dropped absently into her chair. "What's up?" She brushed the air with her hands when she talked. I envisioned firefly sparks freed by her Gemini fingertips. Her bracelets jingled, the new one with gold and lapis beads beat a rhythm apace with the sparks that darted from her eyes. She'd caught the last rays of sunset into her pupils and threw them out at me in an accusation. She lifted out of her chair and stood poised above me in the cramped office. "I hear you're all freaked out again about taking Veronica to get test results at Valley Medical Center tomorrow." Then she paced, even in that small space.

"Page. You are an eternal being. So your daughter's retarded in this one lifetime. So. So what?" The fear clutched at my solar plexus. The fear. Maybe that was the thing I'd been trying to avoid all this time. "It's not certain she's retarded, nothing like that," I retorted. I wanted momentarily to throw up. She didn't know how hard it was. For over a year I'd avoided taking Veronica back to the hospital because I feared they were going to say she was a vegetable, a thing, an animal, and cart her away from my dream for her, for the little blonde baby who'd said "dada" at five months. They would tie her to the giant grey institutional baby carriers I'd seen at Valley Medical Center when I'd made the appointment. And I'd seen the oversized lifeless forms in those things the day I'd dared to bring her for the battery of tests. (It was a good thing the child psychologist had been called "slow" himself as a child and decided to determine that Veronica was too hard to test. He knew how afraid I was of that label. "You're all she's got," the defiant little man said. I didn't know then how right he was.)

Daisy threw her hands about her; then she adjusted the gold wire-rim frame on her pretty nose. My own glasses—the yearly pair I was allowed on Medi-Cal—were a square version of Daisy's and dug into the hollows between the bridge of my nose and my closed eyes.

"No, Daisy. You don't understand." But I wanted Daisy to be right. I guided my hand to my heart and willed it to stop its irregular dance in its cage of fear. "Daisy."

"Page." Daisy looked deep into my eyes. Her glasses for farsightedness magnified her eyes, mine shrank behind photo grey lenses for nearsightedness, but I looked out at her with the faith of a person who was willing to stop pretending. "Now Page—hear me. What's wrong with Veronica, **as she is**?"

I tried to speak, to utter the clusters of terrible words waiting to enter the space between us from the back of my thoughts, but I looked up at her and I said, "I'll…I…she…."

All of a sudden I smiled and said, "Nothing." From the place where my knotted gut hid with my clotted heartbeat, arose instead, a peace, a flutter fountain of new knowing.

Nothing. The words quietly filtered to me. Veronica—I could see her little head swaying to the music of the choir, slack muscles slumping her head just a little against the folding chair, her deep eyes burnished bright, watching the candles on the altar—is Veronica. Nothing! I couldn't say another word. Amber auric lights and violet and blue pinpoints danced in the minister's office as the last lights of the day outside faded. Finally, when I could speak at all, Daisy let me say a few more silly things in the bright see-true light of our new understanding. I tried to vocalize my worries but they came out transparent, like the dried butterfly wings in the paperweight on the desk. Nothing.

Finally I gave up speaking. Rather the words gave me up. They vanished like the electric light switched off by Daisy so that we could bask in the nimbus of the candle. I folded the new happiness around me like Daisy's white and golden minister's cloak that lay on the back of the chair. Russell, sounding excited, rapped on the minister's door. "Come in, come in." Daisy laughed. "We're almost finished in here, aren't we Chicken?"

Chapter Seventeen

One by one the Wednesday students arrived. These were the students she thought of as serious, as dedicated, the ones who were living the truth, following the pull from spirit like a molten river into each other's lives, through some bizarre circumstances. Vince, shaggy and not my type, sat down in a brown folding chair. Sam sat in the doorway, part in and part out, tracing the intricate Art Nouveau design that would frame a new "Circle of Light" flyer announcing Daisy's classes, and Rebecca and Amy's workshops, to the greater San Jose area.

Preparations completed, Amy floated in wearing a backless, ruffled long dress. Pregnant with Peter's baby, the flutter of ruffles became her. Mary Grace wore a dull colored loose robe she'd thrown together. (She sewed magnificent emerald and cerulean and garnet robes for the ministry, however.) Russell strode back into the meeting room looking perplexed. He slid into a folding chair and let Jade take his hand. As he slouched into the chair inadequate for his length, he absently entangled one long leg with Jade's. His baggy white trouser leg lay against the sheen of her just shaved olive shin.

Wayne sat near the back beside Sam, staring in awe at Sam's drawing, all the while wringing his hands and pushing his thin ruddy hair over the balding crown of his pate. Acacia, new, curious, an outsider; plump with coarse wiry hair flying from her large soft-eyed face, sat in the middle as though soaking up these important sights and sounds in their full amplitude. When all the little seats were filled—each with an attentive Being in a body, Daisy marched up on air it seemed, and slipped out of her gold lame sandals.

"Hi," she said slowly like warm umber, personally, intimately, to each one.

Wayne rubbed his head and twisted his hands for a moment more, then the excitement that had inspired these mannerisms caused them to cease. Caught up to attention, he smiled shyly at Daisy, like a little boy.

Amy adjusted her white and blue frock over the hard chair and looked away from Daisy with a secret, frivolous smile, as if they were so much "together" that they had delicious secrets. Did I know then that they had encountered each other "in energy" and finally burst the desire bubble that led them to share husbands? Did I ever really know for sure? There was a rumor. At Patrick's church I'd been privy only to Yvette's allusions, and a spontaneous talk session with "the girls" and Peter held in the church nursery. It's hard to believe so much of it went over my head but I do remember allusions to love between women being a pure celebration of "femininity," and Peter musing in deep appreciation. After that Amy murmured something about how it had "opened up a whole new world to her," and Daisy told someone how in Montana she had brought Amy flowers, "like a husband," and how joyful she'd felt. Alas, I was not included in everything, and this passage seemed closed to me, and on the outer circumference of my thoughts.

Russell resentfully eyed his mentor. As Daisy spoke she walked slowly, up and down, back and forth in bare gleaming feet. I watched his head turn and dip like a metronome with her movement.

"At last," she began, "we come to a point whereby we realize that we are, that we have been, divine spirits incarnate. Where we are no more of this earth, but a part of it—just as we were in the early days when we overshadowed the animals, the plant forms—when we were the earth's guardians."

Amy sighed.

"With that divine spark alive in us today, we sometimes encounter those earthy, earthly"—she rephrased it as if she were being corrected by some higher source—"conditions that do not line up with the true purposes of our spirit or soul. When this begins to occur, we have that sense of warring"—she stressed the word—"which some of you," she laughed, a glorious shimmering crystalline, gelatinous laugh, "which some of you"—and here she looked at me directly—"have been experiencing, lately.

"And when you are toying"—she stared at me intently—"with lining that up with Spirit, and when the warring gets so bad that you are screaming inside—"

"Should you worry about that, Daisy?" I blurted. "I mean what should you do when—"

She looked at me sadly as if I were an idiot.

"No, silly," she whispered. "You don't have to do anything. Because that desire, that thrust for alignment will carry you. If you sincerely desire this—and it is a matter of evolution really—then cell by cell you line up."

"Cell by cell?" asked Russell, the Leo, too proud for anyone else to take the stage for long.

"Cell by cell, that consciousness—truth—grows. Truth always grows. We say 'truth lives.' If we start with one cell, here tonight, with one little click inside—of the **truth**—it will live, carry light into all the dark areas, and force a process of alignment. That's what we're about now, process alignment. Any questions before I go on?"

"How about an example, sweetheart?" Sam, the reflective battery-supply crystal beamed from the back of the room, his head happily bent into his drawing.

"All right, whatever's right," she flowed, as though acknowledging his influence to be through him from another source.

"Whatever's right," Amy piped.

I felt like shrinking into the tubes of the slender brown chair. But there was nowhere to hide. I basked, too, in the warmth of her attention. She regarded me evenly. "Suppose you had a sexual area that was blocked with guilt or whatever earlier programming you'd had."

"Then what would you do?" Russell asked—to get on the bandwagon I thought. Obviously, he didn't have any sexual problems at the moment, arm curled protectively around Jade's bare olive shoulder.

"You would," Daisy smiled significantly at me, "**want** to do something about it, or maybe your own point of personal growth and evolution would carry you to…I don't know."

Sam coughed. He seemed unconcerned, his deep blue gaze engaged within the intricate surface of his artwork.

"You would," she went on at a stronger clip now, "dive into those dark areas to bring in the light, or simply take one step into any, say, forbidden attraction you were feeling, and bring all of your spirit with you."

I imagined her taking one step into Yvette. She said that adventure had brought her a new understanding—that there is a Love of Spirit that flows between people that is not sexual but that encompasses sex; that is whole and complete in a given moment. (I remembered vividly a scene in the house in Sunnyvale sometime after Daisy's "special day" with Yvette, remembered them walking briefly into each other's arms in front of the whole group, in the kitchen, between arrow plants that dangled and tumbled about them.) That's why lately I had her permission to hug Sam, to enjoy those moments of laughter if we met outside on a path and just happened to want to hug, to say hello. That's why I was getting confused about him, wanting there to be more than just moments with someone. Daisy went on talking about sex.

She must be talking about me. Was I a sex fiend?

As though in psychic answer to my question, she rephrased the dilemma so that we could all see.

"Say the sexual thing is your only block to something else. Isn't it spiritual to deal with it so that the rest of you can flow towards greater truth? When we first 'get spiritual' we put our dark self into a closet: the part that we consider to be dark, that is. We don't 'do' whatever it is—we don't even think about it, right?" Everybody laughed.

"But there comes a point—not for everyone, but there can come a certain point on say, the mystics' path—where self knowledge, where cleansing, where personal freedom from the jams and programming of this earthly earth **must be unblocked**, and a person must break though these, and it's then, at that point, that you might find yourself in a bar doing something unspiritual because you have to, to find out what really is you and what isn't. Often, you encounter some thought form bubble you have carried around with you from early in this lifetime, and sometimes, for centuries.

"Hear me. Hear what I'm saying. It's not necessary to go around suppressed, oppressed. There's an energy inside, a spirit, your spirit, you, that wants to carry you home. Go home, Divine Beings, Light Beings. Go home."

We got "rain" on those last words. They didn't seem to come from her. Sam gestured that it was time to break.

"Wait just a minute. There are some questions. I can feel them. Right here in this room is some reassociating that could be done. Anyone want to try?"

I instantly raised my hand.

"All right, chicken. Meditate, now, pray to unlock one of those memories. All right, got it?" she asked, lightning fast.

"Yes, I...I have one," I said, not knowing where the first image my memory brought up had come from.

I had a nervous stomach.

"What is it?"

"Well," I laughed, "I'm seeing this scene when I was a teenager and I worked as an usher at this little theatre, and my dad showed up one night and confronted me in the foyer when the play was on inside. We were alone and..." "What happened?" Daisy broke in. I looked around. Nobody seemed to be ridiculing me; they were all watching Daisy.

"Well," I went on, "he pulled his hand from behind his back (where I guess it had been since he showed up) and held it closed around something in a small bag. He held that bag as if it was stinking filth. 'Know what I have here?'" He hissed, veins bulging, eyes full of hate.

"No I don't."

"You tell me," he crackled.

I was sure he had a kind of diary I'd kept with a description of a taking advantage sexual scene with the boy from over the back fence who was an actor at this theatre and who wrote radical poetry: a sexual scene in a park that had happened—pretty explicit too. Oh my God.

"Well, I write things," I said to my father that night, "but that doesn't necessarily mean they happened, really it doesn't—anyway it's none of your business—" I pleaded. He let me squirm and hate myself. Then all of a sudden he whipped from the bag a tiny perfume bottle of liquor I had filled from their cabinet. Was that all? But somehow it was too late. He whirled away and drew his crew cut, hating head in close under his grey windbreaker, darted out and disappeared. Oh, dad. I didn't. I didn't, I pleaded in my mind. But I felt I'd told him the real, the horrible truth about me. Filth that I was, I'd nearly had sex. Maybe not real, complete sex.

But I did it, some of it, and I knew, I sensed what he felt about that and how much he hated me for it. A tear started to form as I told Daisy.

"Page," she said gently.

"Look at me," she added sharply.

"Do you feel guilty about it, about this boy, about having sex in that park or whatever?"

"Oh, yes, of course I...."

The room was still, but I felt as if I weren't in it. I was so much inside of me. It was as if she addressed the real me, the one that wasn't, as she described it, entrapped in this earthly earth.

My mind made the little weak words try to come out again, words like "yes, of course," but they were only papery shadows.

Suddenly all I could say in a small crystal clear voice...was..."No. No, Daisy, I don't feel guilt."

I'd never known that before. Relief like a great held in laugh after disaster has been averted—burst over me.

"No Daisy, I don't," I thought in happy bubbles in my mind as she went on talking. And for the first time in my adult life, I knew how I felt, not how he felt about what I had done. And more pictures flooded in, as though she had broken the seal of a secret room. The warm, sweet, innocent scent of the boy's skin. The rushing of the deep green grass hidden in the dark...sounds and feelings hidden from me underneath the fear of that time, underneath the guilty looking for headlights, for my father's head peeping angrily, with hate—I hadn't changed my mind on that— over the park fence looking for me, looking to bring me back to my room where I would be locked in shame, where they, as a hateful unit, would harbor me. Sounds, tastes, lovely thoughts hidden under that mire. Was it mire? Maybe I had misread my father. I had only begun to scratch the surface, I began to think. "See," Daisy continued in whisper shadow tones. She linked my example to a network of other examples and insights that made process alignment a reality. She did not say much more to me or care that I was feeling wet grass or touching a rough cheek in my released long ago memory.

"We'll consider more of the dynamics of process alignment after break," Daisy concluded softly, and we scraped our chairs dutifully and got up.

At Halloween, the night air was bright and crisp and pumpkins winked when I came in dressed like a prostitute, swinging my black, beaded bag at my hip. Peter was costumed as the clown-jester again. We made up in front of a swing out mirror in the minister's office. We'd come as we were, as we had been, and to express new cycles, as Daisy described. Jade, dressed as a Kabuki, borrowed some of Peter's white paint. I stood importantly between them; after all I had "come out", done what Daisy wanted, I thought.

Now I was a prostitute, a whore, now I was really going somewhere. Maybe I would be a minister by spring. My mind flung back to the last class in this very hall when Daisy told Vince, "If you think a woman is going to go around dressed up when she's trying to be sexy, you're wrong," because Vince had said, "You really don't look like you're trying to be sexy," when I said "I'm putting myself out there bit by bit," in answer to Daisy who'd said, "Page's problem is she's afraid to take that step and deal with her attraction, and **that's** what's keeping her from being a minister, from coming into her ministry."

Okay, fine. Here I was, a real minister and everything, swinging my black bag like the past life San Francisco hooker I could have been, feeling ashamed like the sister of the brown order I was in the 12th century, and feeling even more foolish and abashed than usual. But this was important. Why didn't they give me more mirror space? I was pretty, I was cool and I was gutsy. God, it hurt to feel like an idiot.

In the temple room wild faces emerged. Daisy, already dressed as a space age doctor, auctioned off art objects to raise money for the center. Daisy said that lower astral entities were loosed and walked on All Hallows Eve—that it was important to lift the vibrations with our enjoyment of the evening. The benefit art auction was followed by a costume judging similar to the one held at Elizabeth's beautiful Asilomar conferences. Amy, over eight months pregnant, decreed that she had come as a World Mother. Daisy put her white-coated arm around Amy's shoulders and told the group that Amy was, indeed, one of the earth's Great Mothers. Amy took her place in the costume judging to a round of respectful applause.

I got up amid the colorful shuffle, said something stupid and sat down. I knew Daisy wanted Amy to win, and she did. Amy packed the prize, a luminous, float-on-water candle, into her car and went home early after another round of applause.

Stephen and Sam had transformed the back room nursery into a house of mysteries and good-natured horrors. I drifted between the group gathered outside the back room door and the vivid merrymakers in the temple room, feeling almost sexy in my cut off velvet dress and low-cut, raspberry acetate blouse. I didn't know that I could ever be anybody but myself, but I tried a few lascivious trial winks on Peter, who remained ever the indifferent clown under his white greasepaint, and wondered if Vince liked my legs now that he could see them.

Doug, dressed in a voluminous Renaissance blouse and tights, hugged the shadows and talked to Wayne. I could see the pain of embarrassment across his face, but also an unpracticed gleam in the light cast by the Art Nouveau pumpkins that lined the walkway toward the nursery door—there was something more. In the reflection of Douglas' face, I saw the gleam of excitement, as though his foolishness—and mine—presaged a "coming out" of some sort.

By the end of the evening I still felt foolish and frustrated but just a little freed. I clopped up the swinging concrete apartment steps slowly; pausing after Doug had let himself in, to drink in the windy vista of the Halloween-scarred starry sky.

A year later, at another Halloween party, I wandered around another party, dancing with every man in the room. Not a soul was with a church. Who cared. People postured in phony poses. How I dared to be around all those drugs I did not know. I was with Marshall and I was in love.

It first came to me that I would be with Marshall after a disappointing choir performance at a red and black plush rugged hotel in San Jose. It was daytime. People with money I didn't know very well co-hosted the Thanksgiving symposium with Daisy. We gathered outside the door to the huge conference room (waiting to go on to sing) where a heavy, "old guard" woman metaphysician sat to the left of the doorway, selling Atlantean crystals to participants. At last we clumped in, after smoothing our muslin choir shirts and synthetic tops that clung, but not suggestively, one last time so that they would not crease. Once inside, Rebecca appeared before us and led us up the aisle to the low stage. She smoked busily. I hoped the audience—not nearly enough to fill this hall, but a beginning—wouldn't notice the delicate piles of ash she distributed walking up the fine soft steps.

We faced the audience. Sam led us in a rendition of "Let There Be Peace On Earth," to inaugurate the all-day seminar. I had a cold, a bad one. Sam encouraged us to sing even if we had a cold, to help clear the frogs and clogs of jammed up energy in our throats. Peter, now the assistant choir director, had made a bumper sticker from a saying he'd found somewhere. It said "He Who Sings Prays Twice." We believed the singing would bring the "next step" on the path because of our dedication to the Overall Body. More and more, the Overall Body seemed to mean the overall body of the Circle of Light, and not the universal body of earth. That we were to be an emblem, a prototype, a beginning, was the dimly articulated theory I sensed, but now "The Body" was the group dependent upon Daisy and led by Daisy (and Sam, Rebecca and Rex, Amy and Peter, and maybe Jade).

Even Jade and Russell were the dinner guests of these elevated ones, along with Constance and Neil and Pegeen, more mature devotees, who, incredibly, didn't seem to want positions of authority and honor in the group. Doug and I were seldom (almost never) invited to dine with these, our friends and ultimate mentors. We were excluded from the proud, shining, self-possessed select. And today none of the select had a horrible cold, born of exhaustion, none of them had to leave a handicapped child and another baby with the upstairs neighbor's pubescent daughter to baby-sit (it was all we could afford.) No one of them had to leave, lingering to hear the child's unwell cries through the door, and stand hopelessly on the swaying concrete stoop and then go back and try, just one more time, to quiet her. None of came late to practices after interminable scenes like these. Despite my faith in them, none of them seemed to understand, and some condemned.

Peter often called Doug to do some errand for them, to help one of them move, to come over and fix Amy's stove. This had begun after his and Amy's wedding, when Doug and I had spent one whole Saturday re-upholstering their chairs and learning about the law of manifestation. (Certainly they were manifesting well lately, weren't they?) Basking in the special honor of their calls, I would summon Doug to the telephone as I'd done yesterday morning. In just the time it took for Doug to drop the load of laundry he was collecting from the molding cabinet at the end of the hall, Peter had managed to comment helpfully, "It doesn't look like you're doing too well."

"What do you mean?" I'd asked, knowing fully well he meant "in energy," evaluated as acting accurately on the needs and instructions of Spirit.

And just then Veronica, who'd been crying nonstop for a half hour, tottered ataxicly in her fury toward the stove. She had a bad burn on her forearm from a similar venture last week. Baby Molly pulled on my pant leg, tugging at me to pick her up. I leapt for Veronica, clutching the phone and Molly spilled to the cracked linoleum with a sob.

"Why do I think you're not doing so well?" Peter continued into the din. "Why? Because your kids are crying, and c'mon Page, you know what we've 'hit' lately." ("Hit" was the latest Daisyism—it meant a deep discovery of universal truth and it meant a right-on zap from the truth of one person to another—Peter was trying for one now.) "We've 'hit'," he continued, "that when children are quiet and contented it means the parents are doing all right, and when they're all over the place, it's because they feel their parents energy and everything. Get it?"

Humbled, I'd said nothing. "Where's Doug?" Peter had probed. "Amy wants to know if he'll fix the stove this afternoon." That meant no Doug until that night and more chances that Veronica would get near the stove and that I would be stuck with the diapers from the hall laundry closet.

But I'd said "Yeah, I'll go get him," because I knew that it was really important and a real honor to have him ask us. Maybe we were at least manifesting "right" for this to happen. Wowee.

Now, in the cavernous hotel conference room, Daisy, like a glittering August sun flooding the grey November day, swept the audience into her verbal embrace almost instantly. "I've been at this ten years," she tossed at the onset and then channeled smoothly, the energy swirling through her in a Light whirlpool spitting its rays, out into the cavernous room to zap and startle the newcomers with comments so apropos to their own, secret thoughts—how could she know?

I bit my lips against the urge to sneeze and clenched my arms to my sides in the cold air floating down over my head and shivering shoulders from the filtration system. Although outwardly cold and ill, from the moment she uttered that bit about the "ten years"—almost doubling the time she'd been a spiritual teacher—I boiled inwardly in an aggressive, malevolent rage.

I tried to corner her at the lunch break and managed to half challenge her, while hiding the challenge with laughter. When she stared contemptuously at me, her blue eyes bluer and colder than the water in her chilled hotel glass, I swept away and ran to a phone booth to call Marshall, the only person I knew anymore who wasn't a member of the Circle of Light.

He was there in fifteen minutes in a bright shiny car that I hardly saw. I choked unattractively with a cold and my convoluted thoughts. He was courteous and concerned and let me mumble blankly about Daisy.

Before we reached our apartment that he always called the "bird's nest," I knew I had to go back to the hotel. "When you're about to 'hit' a big piece," Sam had said, "you resist, right?" Was I resisting? Guiltily, I foraged for some Kleenex and grabbed a coat. All the way back I contemplated Daisy's remark. Could she **lie**? What was the matter with me that it should matter how many years she said she was a spiritual teacher? In Daisy's purity, in the purity of the energy, surely there must be a greater reason. She wouldn't lie.

At the back entrance of the hotel, nearer the conference room, Marshall dropped me off and I stumbled through a labyrinth of corridors to find her, to receive her forgiveness. I almost forgot Marshall's face pressing back a smile when I got out, oblivious to him, and forgot that he brushed his light, wide hand across his bleached canary hair. I almost forgot, too, that he smiled as if he already knew something that I had only dreamed of.

I met Daisy's easy, forgiving eyes and clung anew to the last words of the last songs of the conference. When it was over, outside in the dusk winds blew across Highway 101 from the Alviso bay lands and swept the last yellow leaves across the black asphalt of the parking lot. I thought wistfully that I would not meet times like these again, nor persons so similar that we could play our parts in perfect symmetry and create a mood, a feeling, that would live after us.

A week later Daisy made us all stand up in front of her as she inspected us before we entered the great shopping mall festooned for Christmas. Sam led us in his white dickey and pressed blue pants. In walked we women, in rows, and the men followed behind us, solemn and circumspect like a group of nuns and monks from before, in sharp contrast to the curious, callow, urbane youths and the young women with unbecoming slit mouths—dark, almost black lipstick was in that year—who paced idly around us where we prepared to sing. Their gaze circled us as though not looking but we knew they were. We seemed pale by contrast, but I knew we glowed because I saw auras, and who doesn't feel a glow when it is present? Poor dead people, I thought, they all seemed afraid of not meeting up to the images prescribed for them by the thick, shiny store windows with their sweeps of shiny disco clothing in the dark, solemn, colors the designers had devised for them to wear that winter. Looked like fly wings to me—but I didn't care what they wore; it wasn't my world anymore. I was bringing something to them and to myself. I saw hearts opening on contact.

It was Christmas. I could feel it; it was all I was hanging onto—these people in Daisy's group were my family—the warmth. Without them I would be just another furtive face wearing the wrong thing: a black slit mouth and a creepy grey-green dress, maybe, and spiked, in-style heels that hurt my back. I depended on Daisy. I couldn't challenge her just yet. I needed her warmth and sureness and golden glow to warm my life. We filed out just as we came in and I didn't look into the shiny store windows and I didn't miss a thing. Not yet.

Marshall was hanging around our apartment an awful lot lately. He often brought wine, a cheap gift for him, rather rich at twenty-six. And Marshall inevitably downed almost every drop himself. I didn't drink, and Doug was so much shorter than Marshall at a mere six feet—and so much less macho that it took very little wine to overwhelm him.

Marshall still looked at me strangely, but I was finding an excitement of a kind—even with him—when I told him all about the experiments with relationships we'd done in the Circle of Light, and when I counseled him about his latest girlfriend. I taught him to tell the truth about his feelings and not to beat around the bush so much, so that he could either have something with this girlfriend or admit he wasn't interested. Since his divorce, Marshall had always made pit stops to see Doug and me between women, and I liked that I guess, although I considered him way "out of the energy" and everything.

We got back late from the shopping mall. But Marshall wanted to come over; it was a Friday night and I should have expected his visit. We scrambled to get the apartment picked up, slowed down by the lady downstairs who banged on the ceiling because of the noise. How could we not make noise when Veronica made noise all the time?

Marshall was "up" that night. "Hel-lo folks," he exclaimed, bouncing his 240 pounds restlessly across the apartment floor. Crud. The lady downstairs. Nothing much I could do, though. Marshall gave off a man-in-the-know air apropos to his "take-care-of yourself-first philosophy" that helped me give guilt and altruistic concerns a rest.

"Let me tell you folks what's happening to me," he said. "I picked up a Model T through my brother and it's a beauty." He recounted the complicated deal leading up to the acquisition where he'd made out and nobody was **really** hurt but then again he got it away from that older couple and boy was he pleased with it—"for $1,000, that's all!"

The numbers were from that other world at the shopping center. Marshall's money was an unreality I disdained except that I intended to sell him two of my paintings that remained from my earlier days in Palo Alto, because I really needed some money for groceries. I'd been rolling the babies in a shopping cart through the bleak apartment-flanked streets, over the broken glass and debris to get to the local Safeway since the "miracle" car had also been in a collision outside Sunshine Hall and its replacement hadn't yet arrived from Spirit. We were low on the money for this week's necessary ordeal because I'd bought materials to make simple Christmas presents for Doug's relatives in exchange for the necessities they'd give the girls. Knowing that Marshall admired my artwork, I offered the paintings to him and he bought them on the spot for $35.00, another good deal for Marshall, like the car. I might have made some observations about his character from these scenes, beyond the sagacious conclusion that he hadn't "gotten" the universal laws regarding money yet and the wondering—who was rich and who was poor anyway?

Asilomar at Washington's Birthday. Elizabeth's Philosophical Round Table Conference. I went as usual. Fog horns brayed two sounds the first night that sounded like "not now, not now." Doug and I had arrived early. We were Elizabeth's special friends, a condition built over the years. Daisy and the group followed; they were less and less interested in Elizabeth's conferences, and more and more interested in what Daisy's Circle of Light was doing. The group presented the Jesus play Peter had written for the coming Easter. Sam was, of course, Jesus. We performed it outside in a stone patio with cypress trees crouching nearby, framing the action. The blossoms from the flowering shrubbery floated down onto the irregular old stone flagging, looking like a rain of confetti. Three cheers. I did not feel very cheerful however, felt tired of hearing the choir trill the backdrop for Sam's "Amazing Grace," felt something was lacking, felt I might cry.

Later, at night—they all left as soon as the performance was through so I tracked down the ever-popular Elizabeth. She agreed to meet me in the huge old lodge that was the fulcrum of the place Yogananda had visited and decreed to have the highest vibrations in the Western world. We always said things came to a head at Asilomar, were magnified, the good—and the bad. "Tell me about Daisy," Elizabeth invited, as though chatting.

"Well, you saw the performance," I answered. "Peter wrote it—"

"He's a good writer", murmured Elizabeth, sipping at the Coke she always carried wherever she went.

"Should you drink this?" I asked her, worried for her health. She told me the story again—did she remember how many times before she'd told me the exact thing?

"When I was a little girl," (*Gee that would have been before 1920,* I thought.) "Coke had cocaine in it, and my beloved Daddy was addicted to it. Whenever anything went wrong, he'd say 'Don't worry Lizabeth. Let's just have a Coke and talk it over'."

I knew her father had been her world and that when he committed suicide during the Crash, that a part of her world ended. She kept his comfort alive with the Cokes, I guessed, although for her, as a diabetic, the compulsion was as self-destructive as he was. One thing about Elizabeth that I liked, that helped us to be friends, was that she was honest about her weaknesses, about the kind of problems in all of us that were difficult to change, with the "energy", with "nailing," even with the power of Daisy's word. And Daisy, railing one day against people who deified her personality, said,

Elizabeth C. Barnett

"Elizabeth is so human, no one has that problem with her." Well I saw it a little differently—that Elizabeth was honest and sometimes the things she got me to see, undercut everything in my daily practice of Daisy-style metaphysics at the Circle of Light.

Elizabeth had forgotten her key, as usual, so we finished our sodas and got another key from the desk at the far end of the comfortable, open-ceiling lodge. We walked out into the fog, me solicitous. Was she warm? She wore mostly old black discarded, elegant dresses gleaned from thrift stores with shawls over them.

"Are you really warm enough?" I asked.

"Oh sure," she said, ever an optimist, impervious to the little discomforts and fears that worried most people I knew, including me, as though some coordinating force, like a smooth gelatin, coalesced it all into something understandable.

I told her, going slowly, slowly up the walk—she was getting older now which made me sad, because I loved her and did not want to see her drawn by that coordinating force away from this world, where she might still be of some help to us. "Comfort ye my people," she had once said to me in a reading given long ago. I remembered it now. Elizabeth herself was so often my comforter. I thought maybe I'd try to talk to her about Daisy, in whom, I knew, she had a keen interest. But I felt guilty, as if Daisy were with us.

We walked up the narrow, paved path, cut between the lodges on the pine needle covered footpath, stepped high over stones and leaves and a potpourri of twigs and feathers and sandy loam. Breakers crashed in the distance and the foghorn seemed to cry "why not" instead of "not now" as I had heard before.

My heart beat harder, not just from the climb. And Elizabeth, coke in hand, seemed both in a deep dream and crisply attentive as I began to speak. "I was in the chorus again in the play, Elizabeth —you know how many times I've had the part of a serving girl in Daisy's plays, from King Arthur on. She says I must learn the virtue of being in the background, that it's only my ego that prevents me from progressing. She told me at first that it was my lack of responsibility, but now I put out her whole mailer—she won't even let me stop now because she needs me through the transition to the new church she's gotten. I've washed dishes. I've tried, Elizabeth, I've really tried—and maybe she's right…maybe it's too important to me. Maybe one day I'll be more selfless like her and Sam and the others…"

Wind wove in and out around us, knitting us together in the dark lilting atmosphere of the still wintry sea. "But someday, someday, Elizabeth, do you think there could be a time for me? I always thought there would be—when we first met—maybe I've failed to...."

"Tell me again what she does when you ask for an opportunity, Page."

"She gives it to me, then says I must wait—she let's me take the class to learn the thing but then somehow I always fail...or she says I fail to live up to my responsibility, to follow spirit right—but Elizabeth, sometimes it's not what she told me to do in the first place, and then I'm a student again, always a student, and they all laugh at me. I know they—".

"Who does she have teaching now?" After interrupting me Elizabeth seemed deeply thoughtful.

"Why, Amy and Rebecca and Sam and Jade."

"I've seen these people here, dear, over the years. They're 'yes men'. Daisy's a kind of an abbess and everybody around her must do things her way. You're not like that, Page. You're too much your own person, even though you do not really appreciate yourself yet. And she has a thing about you," she mused, as if only to herself.

"A thing? Like love, attraction? Oh, no...." I countered.

Elizabeth sighed then began again. "I think she's jealous of you, and Daisy won't let anyone lead or teach who could outshine her—and you would, Page. You were a teacher of Jesus in the Grecian land when he was the young Hermes, Maria Theresa said so." She was referring to a reading she'd given me.

"That sounds very grand. I don't know about that. But, I did have a dream recently, Elizabeth. I dreamed that you had adopted Daisy in Egypt. Later you had a natural child—me. In my dream you loved your adopted child—Daisy—but then, you favored me." Could the dream be true? Surely Elizabeth thought the best of me now, to say I was a teacher of young Hermes in Greece. I did though, long to teach with my whole heart. I'd been studying astrology, dreams, making past life discoveries under Elizabeth's tutelage—all this time. But Daisy made me feel so unworthy.

Elizabeth seemed nonplussed. "Couldn't Daisy let you teach a little class on astrology or something?" she continued. Suddenly it all seemed so simple. Of course she could have!

All the reasons evaporated, the turns, the twists of the self-torture: Daisy's torments internalized. Of course she could have. It felt very dark on the path. The wind whipped and I felt afraid. I left Elizabeth off at her cabin way up the hill.

Oh God. Of course I could have. Then I felt very afraid. I could feel Daisy's jealousy and the ugliness of it like a tangible force. It rained lightly and I felt as if a turgid, demonic fire, a lance was aimed at me from San Jose where she must be…sleeping, planning, plotting? Oh no, maybe it was me; maybe there was something wrong with me. Wasn't there? Wasn't there? Wasn't there, Daisy—mother? Isn't there? Where was Daisy? It was awfully cold. It felt as if a great light went out and all I could see walking farther, farther up the interminable hill to my farthest out, most economy cabin—all our money was going, voluntarily, to help fund the new hall—was the darkness. Plaintive, the foghorn sounded, like a child without its mother, like one of the little deer one saw so often at Asilomar, but separated—as was never the case in this happy place—separated from a mother who was dead. Oh no.

Daisy had told me, "Elizabeth sees through her warps, her humanness." That's right, I'd better consider this carefully, better not jump to any conclusions after all. I scurried up the yellow-lit, wide wooden steps to the cabin, carefully opened the door into our dark room and crept into the twin bed across from Doug's. The floor heater whistled, sizzled menacingly, the bed seemed cold—where was the extra blanket they always gave you? I just wanted to get sound, sound sleep away from Daisy's lance that even now, in thought, reached out to me in an accusing question.

Daisy had a hypnotic power over her people, over all of them, Elizabeth said years later. I couldn't believe that. Daisy wasn't evil, was she? She was just a little girl, off to see the wizard, a little girl who wanted elephants, who wanted her mother to leave food in the house when she went off with some man, who wanted to be patted on the head and told she was a good, good girl for watching her little brother like that when she was only nine and mother was gone a whole weekend, to be forgiven when she begged bread and bologna from the neighbor lady, to understand. That's all Daisy wanted, wasn't it, to have all of us understand her, love her, obey her, always.

Chapter Eighteen

On Good Friday, busy cutting wet flowers that grew on the pathway behind Sunshine Hall to place into an amber bowl upon the altar, I was tuned in to all the currents of life, for I was the Creative Force itself, gushing like rain running from the roof, rain I heard in sleep. I am human, I affirmed, am sentient, am able to apply the laws of my Father, of my Mother, but must keep myself away from doubt, must trust that I came into this world for a reason. With my cutting knife I beheaded the Easter lily. So I would carry the flower back to Daisy. I would be what I was, make my own contribution.

It was almost Easter. Oh, how I longed for Easter, for I hoped, I believed that this Easter there would be a resurrection for me, too. From Christmas to Easter each year now I waited, mature to the promise of the season, secure, at least, that the Christ would meet me Within. And so I sat with head bent later that day just before Easter, and kept Good Friday vigil with Daisy in the sullen-lit hall. The dark breath of late winter lingered all around us, as though to remind us that He suffered and that neither sky, nor winter's last dark breath could pass away until each had competed the karmic pattern, until each had felt the lash of the ego. As Edgar Cayce stated, souls living between 1958 and 1998 would feel the lash of the whip to the ego, to that place where each had violated the Christ within in past lives. The living Christ, Elizabeth taught, rises as the flame of hope within each one of us. Jesus, Cayce said, was the man. Jesus attained to the Christ. Christ was the pattern for all.

Wasn't I living, wasn't I feeling the Christ that Good Friday vigil day? I asked the swirling round amber and dust colored sky seen outside the plate glass window like a mirror of my inner muddle. I looked at Daisy, apparently gathered up by the Light that must be behind this cloud, and I longed to be uplifted too.

When I bent my head, the still, small voice that is promised to all of us (if we would just turn within—for within is the teacher, the keeper, the source, it is said), spoke to me softly like rainwater lying in a gutter or broken crack of the center's parking lot. Go back, go back, it intoned, get back to what you are; you have never left me. *Go back, where?* I wondered, no less certain when I opened my eyes to the sight of the white robed Daisy, with arms up stretched and eyes cast to the dark rafters. And I was no less anxious that I wouldn't be "let in," when I observed the little crowd of Vigil keepers in white folding chairs looking to Daisy as if she were the expected sunshine, the rainbow incarnate, the dawn that would illuminate the rainwater God had brushed over the landscape like crystal jewels—like Easter eggs painted by a master hand. She seemed to stimulate the followers to grace and to purity and light, just as the crystal chalice kept on the altar spun gossamer, rainbow light all around when Daisy held it aloft at the tail end of a service, when she danced in circles in apparent, up stretched ecstasy.

Drab as a wren, I listened instead to a still, small—still there—voice that urged me ceaselessly from within to take faith in myself, that promised me quiet wonders, that patted me with its intangible hand as if I were a small child lost in a dark hall looking to its mother's, or father's, familiar face through an open doorway.

"Little one, fear not, it is I. There is nothing to fear. I am the Way and I am the Light, I am the Beginning and Ending of all, ALL things. No one goes to the Source except through Me. I am with you. Though you know not your own worth, I know and will bring to fulfillment. Unto each is given a season, a time."

Every time I opened my eyes Daisy seemed carried higher, to be in another rapture or something, humming now, so carried away it seemed, that neither we who knew her or those who filtered down the few rows to swell out the numbers for the more generally known noontime service, mattered to her. She looked like a long-ago Catholic martyr. Once she'd dreamed she was a saint—Katherine?—Theresa?—I'd forgotten who she might have been. I remembered a sense of the dream though—that she'd had to carry some impossible mission without support from those around her. Let that be a lesson to us now, she'd implied. In a kind of cold, unhappy awe I saw her closed eyes, heard her murmurings and could not find the threads to link these expressions of one apparently wiser, more favored than myself, to the center within. Daisy was a parade I seemed to watch from beginning to end without joining; I sat in confusion on the hard steel seat, cold metal emanating through my thin robe.

I felt like the mote of light I could see out the window in the ash-banked sky, dark like night at midday. I felt like a child who had forgotten the brightness of its parents—somehow the inner ambers glowing within the gray sky were the parents of this light dot child and I knew the sky would clear in time, the child had not been forgotten, that the backlight behind the sky we stared into through the plate glass portals of Sunshine Hall, would reclaim the bright little dot that stood alone in morbid cowardice at the center of the tableau. *When this happened,* I thought, *the Easter day would be lit from its heart.*

"Beloved, be still and know," came the voice, almost as if spoken aloud. "There is no power on earth that can separate you from me." Daisy came and sat by me—two chairs away. That was close. I felt tender and a sense of honor pervaded me. That was as close as I was allowed to get. But I sensed her approval about me like the crisp, lined-navy cloak she wore, like the soft rain that fell outside the Sunshine Hall, like the petals that tumbled down the March wind from the acacia shielding the front window from the street.

The room was dark and cool. A single candle burned in the happy gloom. Daisy sat beside me, extended her hand to the chair, over the empty space between us. She drummed her fingers absentmindedly and it was as if she had patted me. A bird trilled in the Chinese plum outside.

The sky was all grey except for the white glow low down in the space outside the window framed by the trees. The rain accelerated and decelerated like distant cars whooshing home over the wet, gray, asphalt streets.

"Stay late, Page," she said unexpectedly. Now it was so dark I could scarcely see her lips.

"I'll stay," I spoke the words, trying to phrase them as softly as Daisy's own.

"You need to be at class tonight…" She left off still speaking softly in the wonderful gloom.

She left the room a minute later and I was absorbed into that wood-raftered ceiling, listening to the scatter of rain on the roof, hearing the glass tipped specks of icy water cascading over its apex, like magic hands spraying fire and ice sealant over the timbers and the little seams of the roof to keep me in and secure.

Incandescent, the light wavered into nothing. Daisy came into the room, dressed to go out. She brought the light up slowly with a dimmer switch. "Coming with us, Page?" I noticed Yvette beside her. This was Friday and Yvette always came early to this and any class to sit at Daisy's feet. Yvette wore the dun-colored knit poncho I disliked and smiled shyly at Daisy, oblivious to me.

"I'm hungry." Daisy laughed. "Sometimes I just want a good steak." With a wave of her hand, she invited Yvette and me to attend her hunger. In the doorway she appeared to glow with tawny lights and orange radiances splayed through her aura.

I leapt up from the cold seat, feeling silly about my somber, prolonged prayers now. The lights had shifted; it was the summer to come. We tumbled into my car, cloaks over our heads. (This time the miracle replacement vehicle had come through my oh-so-earthy father, who knew somebody willing to sell him the old blue station wagon cheap.) On the way to the Sizzler, Daisy was concerned about my driving, so I made nonsensical mistakes. I felt like a dummy.

By the time we were inside the Sizzler approaching the salad bar, I'd lost touch with the honor of the dinner invitation, lost my place in the gay tumble of Daisy's words. I let the two of them go on without me, although I tried to redeem myself by being "with Daisy," looking down at Yvette's silliness, hoping to counsel Yvette as though Daisy and I were a unit. But we weren't really, were we? Yvette, by doing nothing, had Daisy's respect and love. I was shut out tight like the frog clasps of Daisy hand sewn cloak shut out the jewels that gleamed at her throat. Nothing to do—but surrender to my awkwardness and listen.

Yvette told Daisy that Gypsy, a hippie girl who looked a lot like Yvette only plumper, and another woman friend who was enormously heavy were staying with her now. "We've been making goodies for the Easter celebration, Daisy."

Yvette took a crisp, flaky bite of butter topped French bread.

"Ummm." Daisy smiled lightly and seemed not to have registered Yvette's news. "Honey," Daisy zeroed in on the girl, who seemed about to cry for some reason, "you don't want the 'munching' to get out of hand…." She paused and looked out to the dark street splashed with auto lights streaking by.

"And what about little Joel?" she asked Yvette.

"What about him?" murmured Yvette, sulking.

"He's staying in that house too, isn't he?"

"Well…yes, he is." Yvette sighed. Now I deduced that Yvette was mooning over her last man, a raw, young ex-con who'd drifted in and out of the classes during the winter. It should have been obvious. She poured a big dollop of the leftover salad dressing on her garlic French bread and ate it, looking up at us with those huge blue Keene eyes that I guess made her so appealing to some.

"Well?" Daisy gazed straight into her, and smiled ever so slightly. "Yes?" Daisy intoned, as though to invoke some response from Yvette.

Yvette forked up the last bit of meat fat on her plate and then, chewing, looked back at Daisy, her blue eyes childlike and unknowing. Then Yvette began to giggle a little. "Joel?"

"Yes…he's a man, Yvette, and he likes you."

And the way Daisy said it, caught both of us. Sometimes Daisy would convey a picture. This time she did. A little "click" in our heads as we looked out onto the dark, shiny night. We felt Joel's sincerity, his essential dignity. What if he were short, and built like a young boy, and gentle? We saw his round wire rimmed glasses under thin, side-parted blond hair—saw him strumming his guitar between breaks at choir practice.

But he was as much a man…. Daisy's word picture flowed through us. Daisy scraped her chair away from the table. "Let's go, girls." We followed. Yvette smiled eagerly, tearfully—more at Daisy's concern for her than for the "revelation" about little Joel, which seemed dim to me when I settled back into my own head away from Daisy's stare.

After all, I remembered another "handsome man" Daisy had urged me to look at almost seven years earlier. I hoped Doug had fed the little girls whatever we had left tonight. I would shop tomorrow, make it up to them after I cashed the food stamps and could get plenty of everything. We feasted in cycles. The grocery store was probably Doug's and my only shared pleasure now.

Doug's aunt, who'd had cancer, had passed away. I felt her presence in the house late that night after Doug and the children had gone to bed. I was moved, felt close to her, lingered long in my chair and felt as if her spirit overreached me, overshadowed me, or was it her? When there was a presence, a spirit, an "angel," it was usually a beautiful thing to me, an unexpected peace enveloping me, to tears, to heights. And now, tonight, the soft voice—inner yet outer at the same time—answered the turmoil of my thoughts about the group. "This won't be important to you soon. It won't be an important part of your life."

Then came the subtlest suggestion: "You'll be married to Marshall within the year."

Startled, I got out of the chair very slowly and walked to the bare Formica kitchen table, anointed with an empty mayonnaise jar and two red peonies stolen from a slip of garden near the garbage cans. *Marshall?* As strange as it might seem to say it now, the thought never occurred to me. Then I remembered him on the other end of the phone when I'd call him lately, awakened from an occasional night fright. I remembered him differently, tried it on. Wow. The swells of imagination; where they could take you. No, that was imagination, because I'd never thought of him that way. I was sorry to be thinking anything at all that could take me away from Doug. But, tantalizing came the promises of Daisy, that one day at the nude swimming party, in the sun. "One day all of this will be yours, but it won't be with him," she had gestured toward Doug, white bottomed, unaccustomed to sun, silent, unfamiliar with the other men, content to do nothing when ideas were discussed. Now I sat at the table with nothing to do—though mailer work was piled up everywhere—but look out the dark, open, wide prefab window and smile up at the spring sky.

I admired Daisy as she stood before us in the little hall, riding a great swell of sunlight, eroded only by the bodies that blocked the view of the sun forcing its way in through the plate glass window to look at us gathered in the hall bearing its name.

Today those who had been baptized under the old Temple of the Living Waters were to be re-baptized under the auspices of the new Circle of Light, with godparents assigned as spiritual guardians of the children. In addition, many newcomers who had not been baptized gathered to receive Daisy's blessing. I had asked Marshall to be Veronica's godfather, and he'd accepted. Doug's brother, Clay, and his sister-in-law, Emily, who'd always avoided us, had agreed to join us at the church. They owned a perfect house—that jewel in the Rose Garden area of San Jose, and ordinarily viewed us with dismay. Elizabeth once told me, "Don't want to be conventional, Page. Be glad you're not. To be conventional is to be nothing, really." But for that day they stood with us as family. I think now that they did it because somewhere behind their conventional personalities, they came prompted by their souls, or by the universal soul. Something was necessary to break Daisy's hold.

Daisy and Sam Castle were to be Molly's godparents, and I heard Daisy murmur before the service began: "A child given to Sam and me is given, is promised to the church and to the Greater Body." That felt like an honor, **and** it frightened me. Doug and I sang in the choir and watched the door for our guests. Clay and Emily Mitchel found their places in the rows of seats early—punctuality was always their habit—and Marshall Hart came on time, but at the last. When he had unconscious feelings about something, it crept into his actions. He looked crisp in his white and canary striped-shirt, and I was proud of him this morning, felt his eyes following me when I sang out; raised by the melody of the song Sam led us in to a taut height away and above the audience.

One by one children were brought to the altar. Marshall stood up alone holding Veronica. I hoped, with tears running down my face, that his great arms would infuse strength into her scrawny little body, and that that's what this meant—that it was truly a blessing.

Molly was the last child, baptized after Yvette's little girl, Desiree, who was also "given" to Daisy and Sam as godparents. Intricate looks wove from Daisy to Sam and around Desiree and the choir sang a little louder. But when Molly was brought before them—Molly, the child Daisy had first held as an infant and joked (or commanded?) "Give her to me"—when Molly was brought up, the significant, this-child-is-given-to-the-Overall-Body look bestowed upon Yvette's little girl, brightened and deepened with the sunny sparkle of personal love. But before Daisy could touch her fingers to the crystal vase and complete the rite, Clay and Emily, who'd been making their way into the tight little circle around the two ministers, put their hands protectively upon Molly in the posture of the godparents. I was embarrassed—they weren't to be "guardians of her mind and spirit" because they could never understand—but Daisy didn't **seem** to mind, as her gaze was carried upward by the chorus of "Long Live God", her theme song. The ecstatic tension increased and then she was Daisy, showman, sprinkling the golden drops from the chalice from the greatest height she could manage; then she seemed carried away from this measly spectacle by the power of The Greater Purpose. It was then that Clay and Emily and

Marshall and Doug and I carried the child away from Daisy without knowing why we did so.

At a coffee shop afterwards, all of us together (Marshall suggested the celebration and paid the tab) talked around the service. Snug in the vinyl semicircle about the anchored table, it felt as if I were on the brink of something, teetering between two worlds.

They all said all kinds of polite things: Emily said that the service reminded her of her youthful involvement with a charismatic branch of the Episcopal Church in San Raphael. Marshall concurred, remembering being an acolyte at another Episcopal church in Los Gatos. Why did I feel tension as thick as the butter pats we stuck onto hot rolls and moved over the surfaces of flaky bear claws? Why then? The children, hurriedly dressed from home and unused to restaurant eating, rolling about on the ends of the long horseshoe booth seat, crumbling things and lunging for the unfamiliar bacon, grated on me. And every time Daisy was mentioned I felt something akin to embarrassment, even shame, although I certainly couldn't identify why.

Three months later when I rushed over to Emily's fine, childless house and unburdened myself to her, she—they both—looked into me and let me talk for hours, with fine, deep, Episcopal looks. And she sent me a card the next day urging me not to be ashamed of anything I'd told her. I felt wonderful then for a whole week—as if I had a real family. But the second time, when Doug and I both went by, they were somewhat, unaccountably, cool. And then one night in crisis, when I needed Emily and appealed to her like a sister, she retorted on the telephone in a white, cool, rose garden voice, "I can understand your feelings **as a woman**, and so does Clay, of course, but we simply cannot become further involved in something that drags out this way—and Doug **is** Clay's brother." Those words were said as heavily as the lead in Marshall's stained glass window. I knew there was no hope of being part of this family either. And later Doug once asked if he might come by their house, just for a visit—"Nothing heavy," he promised his pristine brother.

"All right," Clay agreed weakly; then put the phone down. He returned a few minutes later, relaying in a dim monotone, "I'm sorry, Emily's involved in 'Upstairs, Downstairs.' We always watch it at this time. Goodnight."

But now, glad of Marshall's arm when breakfast was over, feeling as if he were my token to a ride on life with these fine friends, feeling like a person with advantages, I said goodbye to Clay and Emily in the parking lot quite blithely and thought the day had accomplished a great deal after all.

At the last Sunday morning service held in Sunshine Hall, beautiful voices lilted from the square temple room. Lush ferns, arrow plants, philodendrons and Wandering Jews cascaded from the beamed ceiling, suspended in thick, white handmade macramé hangers. Music swelled the room. Near me a young woman reached out to someone in an aisle and asked for a handkerchief to dry her eyes.

Alleluia! The choir ended its moving prelude on a triumphant note; relentlessly, Sam pitched us into "Long Live God". Tambourines beat, feet tapped, Daisy emerged in the aisle in an ice white robe and a white turtleneck. It was still cold outside, warm in here. Acacia's pretty, dark eyes fixed on Daisy. Caught by Acacia's longing, Daisy cast a benevolent smile into her dark eyes and then swirled away from her, passing up the clotted aisle to the altar like a white dervish.

Planted before the silver chalice, Irish lace altar cloths and candles, Daisy radiated great grace and promise. She smiled over us through the sylvan spaces toward the apex of the ceiling. "Long Live God," "Long Live G-O-O-OD—Long Live God!" Yvette's tambourine shivered frenetically. Sam lifted his hands and settled them, palms down, through the air like dust motes dropping through a shaft of light. Our cue. We stopped. No sound but swallowing.

Daisy, now looking vulnerable and a little nervous, smiled up at the group gathered before her. Acacia, hugging her two kids close to see, smiled around the room and up at us in adoration. I twirled my new chain made of bloodstones and unformed moonstones, twirled it and knew, somewhere inside, that I would never come this way again. I pressed damp hands to my sides, clutching the pale, ironed choir shirt. I would have to quit the choir—quit this moment. Wayne and Mary Grace's little boy coughed in the next room over. We all heard him through the thin walls, but we strained, watching for Daisy's first words. Stop, we wished. He'd coughed all through the warm-ups and the prelude.

"Someone go and get that child," Daisy surprised us. "He's part of this energy. You're all trying to get spiritual, and he's by himself coughing. Shame on you." She had the little boy brought up close to her, where he eventually stopped coughing with a little soothing from Acacia. "Suffer the little children." Chastised, we sat in a silence as bright as the new spring flowers laid in a posy across the Irish lace—starched Irises, sticky primroses, violets, daisies and new, dew-wet roses wafting their delicate scents toward us.

"Come with me," Daisy intoned, "on a journey into your own heart." I knew what she meant, strained forward to absorb. "You are the child—hear the child—it is your own true spirit—hear its cry." She wove, with simplicity, the events of the day like the stitched star rays trailing from that emblem of new-birth seen in almost all of her hand-embroidered wall hangings. She stitched commonplace events into the messages of her services. Or did certain events happen within her view to key her to the "next step in consciousness" we needed to take? I knew by now that all life was synchronistic. I knew that.

"Tithe now, tithe in the full spirit of your being," she called out near the end of the service. Graceful plates were passed nonchalantly. People gave. Amy scowled at me. I had a check for $50.00 in my pocket from my dad, a rare thing lately. I was going to ask someone to cash it for me afterwards, and maybe go back and put $10.00 into one of the "tithe to the spirit of your being" baskets.

Sam left the choir to Peter's direction and stood with Daisy. They held hands and reached out their free arms like a fan opening up to us. "Ooo—ahh—" The ooos and ahhs rose higher and higher. More wallets and purses opened. I knew how this could work, how $10.00 could return ten times over. Amy knew I had the check—somehow. She must have. She stared at me. One body. Had we become one body already?

"Give it," her eyes demanded. "Ahh—" the choir sang. I too would be in the circle of irises and red roses and daisies forever if I did. We swayed. Tears brimmed. Oh I wanted it—wanted the full spirit of my being—wanted them…

Peter sang a poignant, rapturous piece aimed at Daisy. He surfaced from the song to applause. Like a well-oiled machine, we all arose in cheap sling sandals and shiny shoes and rebounded the applause with another chorus of "Long Live God". Daisy and Sam surrendered to our love, echoed it by raising their clasped hands to the rafters. Then they faced each other, danced in an ecstatic embrace. This was how it could be. Everyone without love in their lives looked to Daisy and Sam as the hope of the fruits of their struggles to come into the fullness of their being.

Daisy's last child, Anson—not man's son—bounded up the aisle. With his soft, blond, two-year-old's unisex haircut and little choir robe that tumbled around his clean bare feet, he was the image of their unity. He tugged at Daisy's white lace robe. She adjusted her gold, wire-rimmed glasses a bit before she stooped to include him in their merry dance. The baby couldn't quite follow his parents' movements, so Sam lifted him toward the heights of the rafters and spun him about. Someone, Amy, I think, darted into the kitchen and returned to snap a picture of the three of them. I snapped one too, mentally, a habit I had formed so that if I died, certain moments would be alive in my soul's sight. I must not forget. The choir readied itself to file out. Sandals shifted, turning shoes scraped the shiny hardwood floors. Daisy stopped us. "One more song," she mouthed to Peter.

"Today is the day, you know, that we move to our new church, to our own real church. All of you who feel called to do so may help—we'll need lots of bodies. Let's go!" Whipped, as if by the ruffle of morning wind outside, stirred by the music and the tableau before them, choir members and congregation hurried out of the temple room, restless and supercharged after the long service—ready to be put to work all day for Daisy and Sam. It was then that I knew I had to do it. At the last, too late to be noticed, too late to be among the roses, but not too late altogether, I dropped my father's check into the basket.

We had the new church, the last one she ever had. It had bright red rugs. Later I heard her ask Elizabeth about the color. "It's O.K., it's a royal red," she answered. In back of the altar was a big space that Daisy filled with flowers. It was ultraviolet lit. The church had an odd smell even when it was all fixed up. This one was bought for Daisy by some of the older, more fixed friends she had recently attracted. Afterwards, to pay the woman who had tied up the deal, and to encourage more deals, I guessed, Daisy installed the New Age Realty Company on the premises. I was never sure now, exactly how Daisy's finances worked. I had broiled when she posted a public notice at the little Sunshine Hall before leaving, that read, "Spirit has directed me to give over all of my earthly possessions to the Overall Body—and from this day forward that Body will sustain me." I felt low to be so angry, but I sensed something wrong and not just because Marshall said he smelled profit. I felt cheated—and I feared that I would be further separated from Daisy the person, that she would evaporate up into the higher echelons of Spirit or into the bosom of these strange new friends.

The new inner circle was made up of these and others who couldn't remember the little house on North Redwood Street at all, people who'd come into this so much later, after "energy" was all we talked about and the "power of the word" and "nailing" people, after the kindness and the friendliness to the friendless—taught by Elizabeth—was forgotten, people who looked at the miracle life-sized statue of Jesus in the newly made garden on the street in front of the church and saw just a statue—who couldn't remember. Some of these were part of a continuing influx of souls flowing to "the body" from Santa Cruz County—a flow stimulated by Daisy's brief stay there in '74—people who wore Birkenstalks and chewed wheat grass selfishly, minds fixed on their digestions—on what was in it for them I thought—on how they'd make out doing health counseling in the back room, having to tithe half to the Church.

Now Daisy had a new secretary who told me one morning in her dark office in the bowels of the building, a little about herself, including the fact that she and her father—she called him Harry—had "worked something out" by sleeping together once before she'd come to the group. I could only stare ever afterwards at the family photo among the clutter of her basement desk, at this secretary Kendra, at her sweet-faced, oblivious mother, at her sisters and back again at Kendra who smiled wearily while her father's—"Harry's" —hand snaked over her shoulder. Kendra's pretty face was always marred by dark circles under her eyes. Daisy said, when she appointed Kendra the administrative assistant—why not me?—that dark circles meant you had some responsibility you must undertake …or something like that…was she that short-sighted? Who could imagine that, years in the future, Kendra would steal Sam after sleeping with this new "mother's"—Daisy's—husband. Was that the reason, long after I had left, Daisy would believe her new young lover to be Jesus and drive her last followers away?

Certainly, the rules were being broken, principles of karma— what one does unto another returns to one, of grace. "Grace is love," she used to say when she lived with Art. One by one the Cayce principles Elizabeth had taught seemed to lie scattered about in my memory, like the diffuse litter of broken glass by the railroad tracks that ran past the back side of the church. A Pentecostal group had

had the church before. I wondered if their vibes were so high as to drum out the noise of passing trains. Daisy was strong enough. She vanquished the noise on the first night and I never heard it again.

Daisy and I sat in the tiny garden by the statue of Jesus one overcast weekday afternoon in the early spring. It was quite cold, but Daisy, our model and a believer that the sun was itself the Christ energy, sat in a T-strapped halter and white pants, turning her gold sandaled feet to the left and to the right, examining her clean, pared, faintly-embossed toes, tan up to the pearly nails. She was talking about Art and she was letting me be close to her. So I tried to, I **wanted** her to believe I understood what she was saying; yet I had a stubborn sense of justice that made it too hard to lie. But I'd give a friend the benefit, the benefit of any doubt; and just as Daisy worshipped the sun, so I worshipped her, and I was trying to give her every benefit.

But I didn't understand, not even enough to disagree, really, and the resentment, too, was eking in, like opaque white mist that blocks the sun on too many California days and makes it not quite the orange land that people who don't live here always say it is. It's just a place to live, like any other. Daisy was just a mother, just a sister, just a place to live out my childhood, just a heart to enter, just an unobtainable child who could never hurt me—as my own mother had done—because Daisy was a little girl in dress-up off to see the wizard after all.

Now when I talk to Art and I ask him what he thinks will happen to Daisy at last, he answers on the long distance lines with an expensive smirk—"the rubber room." "Oh, Art, you don't think, you don't think—do you?" As if I have to hear it again, as horrifying and amusing as it is to hear him say it—"the rubber room," he repeats.

That day in the garden Daisy smiled. "I had to leave Art, because I loved him and, you know, and Art needs to blame me because…" She looked up at the sky as if she were going mad, or looking for a string of words to patch together the nonsense of what she was saying. "To love, chicken, is to give the light to someone else, no matter what the differences of that consciousness from that of the personality." She seemed troubled, restless, and dug at the dirt where bulbs planted for Daisy by one of her new circle—by a gay guy who dressed like an apostle—popped just beneath the surface. She looked up at the life-sized statue, sprang up, and then slowly,

slowly, reached out her hand over the little fence someone had laid to protect the flowers to be that surrounded Him and touched His hard white robe.

"The greater love…" Daisy murmured, touching His robe, then pulling away dramatically as if He were losing her for a moment…"Page, if you take nothing else with you, take this. Follow Spirit no matter where it leads you."

"What about Art's spirit?" I asked. "He didn't want to hear Spirit, right, because he…I know he still loves you. He didn't want to leave you and marry Jackie."

"It's strange," she mused. "Jackie is married to the same man I was and now he's opposing her coming down from Oregon to attend that dream thing she wants to go to…just like he opposed me. Do you suppose…her pattern and mine…that she's following Spirit… nothing happens but for a reason."

I could see it. Through Jackie, Daisy was, once again, the young woman crusader whose earth-minded husband had given her a new stereo for Christmas in Montana when they were broke, Daisy was again the idealist who informed him that any possession of hers belonged to the overall "body," which at that time consisted of Amy and Stephen and a few other stragglers about the house—including the Cauldwells and a runaway teenage boy. And Art had coughed, thinking perhaps about the hours Daisy spent out in the back pasture listening to Stephen read poetry, or of the two of them riding together on the horses Art had maneuvered to get for her.

When she'd said at Easter in Montana, "Art, I want an elephant because Stephen and I have remembered this Indian lifetime and it's important. Art, while I'm clicked into this, I need her—I need Rasha, my elephant, back." Art slid into the old couch by the fire, looking up only after Stephen left the room to growl at Daisy, "I want my wife back and I don't want that kid—he's got a family somewhere hasn't he?—leaving my stereo on and playing those beat up records of his on it. Daisy, that's a crock and I'm not going to take any more."

"I wonder where Jackie's headed," Daisy murmured, looking dreamily at the darkening sky.

"I don't think Art cares, Daisy, I think he still loves you." Then, softening, I added, "It's going to rain, Daisy, don't you think? I'm cold in this sweater." I looked at her like a mother, tender about her dreamy little girl, wondering if the pressures were too great—a doting mother infatuated with her bright little daughter who once, just once in awhile, worried for the welfare of the bright, brittle, little thing who entertained her so.

"We've been through this a hundred times or more," Daisy said, as if I were opposing her still. "It was the kindest thing; maybe someday Art will confront himself—someday he will, don't you think?" She looked up, hopeful, self-sacrificing, so noble; there under the sunless sky, her eyes cast up to the white concrete impervious face of Jesus. That Sunday when the group had moved Daisy into the new church, we had helped Art carry the statue once again for Daisy, in his old, dark green van. Jackie stayed behind to dust out the cabinets of Sunshine Hall. Finally, Art slammed the heavy metal truck doors shut after he'd pushed His white concrete feet all the way in. "That sucker's heavy," Art joked, and hopped in next to Doug and me up in front. Art patted Him as he planted Him for what he hoped would be a permanent stay in the garden of the old Pentecostal church. Rounding the corner of the white-painted building, I heard Art whisper, tears glistening in his sweat in the bright sunlight, "Watch her, will you Lord?"

Now Art was gone—he'd suddenly taken his new wife and sons far away to Oregon. She had me, her daughter-mother, but I was no good to her, was smitten with her and blind.

"Come in, Daisy. Really, let's go in."

"Page...it was the very best thing, wasn't it? It's the very best thing." She stood and wrapped her arms around the statue as if it were as strong and burly as Art, as if it could bend down and catch her face in its massive palms, fingers splayed back in that expressive, wide-open gesture of humor at himself and at us all. "Knock it off, Daisy," the statue should have said, as Edward Arthur Forrest would have. But it was silent, and we walked back in, Daisy's blue tearless eyes looking white and far, far out like a statue's.

Reverend speaking to group

Elizabeth's musician, Evan Williams

Chapter Nineteen

We had the new church and it was to be a new day, a glorious day, filled with song. Or so she said, but for me it was the same old living hell. Elizabeth and Ambrose B. came to San Jose for a seminar. "You are Cinderella," Ambrose murmured, mild, friendly, when he saw me bent over the deep cement sink at the entrance to the kitchen.

Oh no, Ambrose, you just don't know how irresponsible I really am, I thought. Just as Daisy says, and the very fact that I attracted you to say this to me means that I must be on some kind of ego trip. Yes that's it. A dull, lurking gray-green tinged with yellow eroded my aura from within; deceit, that's what yellow-green—chartreuse—meant; everybody knew that.

At other moments, I felt like Cinderella after Ambrose's comment. And it felt clear, light and shiny, as if I were good somehow, and put upon.

Dish after dish I washed, some still filled with food left by newcomers so excited they couldn't eat. One by one they brought me their dishes; one by one the newcomers had, and would, pass me by—become my minister.

And yet the very last days before I left altogether were the happiest for me in that I had made a chink in the wall and Daisy and I were, at moments, close.

She said I either loved—worshipped—her, or hated her. I wish it had been that simple. I felt a lot of things in between, and always the hope of earning real closeness with her. Rebecca had said to Elizabeth in a moment of confidence to which I was privy, "You just get so close to Daisy and then there's a wall. Do you know what I mean?" Elizabeth had said, "Yes," appreciative of the understanding. She had described Daisy as her "golden girl" in the early days, admitting to us that she had been a little in love with her. Strange, how Daisy brought out that tendency in women, as well as in men.

A heavy girl from Santa Cruz stayed with Daisy then—right in their house, the lucky devil—and she was into health foods. Daisy had come a long way from the potato chip and root beer days. Now she ate hard boiled eggs and cheese and salads mostly, though she did still buy the sweet, flavored yoghurts and the half-white and half whole wheat crackers and thought they were the real thing. But she was thinner, though not compulsively so, and she bought natural makeup, and tried chewing sprouted wheat-grass and everything far-out if somebody brought it to the church, which somebody often did. Cell by cell, she was birthing a new consciousness, and she invited us to do the same. Patsy was one of the continuing influx of holistic health-minded souls flowing to the group from Santa Cruz County, a flow invoked by Daisy's stay at Pixy Talbott's church in 1974. Patsy was natural, from the Birkenstocks on her plump feet to her makeup less blue eyes.

I invited Patsy to come along to swim at my father's house with Marshall and Doug and me. All the way up Patsy showed me stuff about iridology, the art of reading eyes for health indications. She said that if you had had greenish eyes like Doug's and mine, that your eyes were really blue but were clouded with impurities. Well. Marshall had blue eyes but I suspected that was because his eyes were exactly like those of his tall, pale Germanic and Norwegian ancestors. Right now I wished I were a little taller than my five feet nine inches and that my eyes were clear of impurities and looked like Marshall's. Patsy had really blond hair. I hoped Marshall might like her. Or did I?

We pushed open the spike gate to the pool and then Doug and Patsy and I, with hardly a giggle—Daisy would have been proud—disrobed. "Come on, Marshall," I urged. He began to unbutton his shirt, but only after he'd made a big pass around the yard looking for just the right deck chair. Then he scraped the chair about and draped and re-draped his towel until he found the right angle from which to receive the pale sun. Odd for Marshall an Aries always direct and to the point, to vacillate on anything. I can see now that it was right in character. Hell, he wasn't going to take off his trunks for anybody. Down he went, stripping off the canary yellow and pale blue pinstriped shirt his mother bought for him at the big and tall men's shop first. Then he peeled away his jeans and revealed the rock-immovable trunks, and at last he laid his bright white deck shoes and thick socks into a neat pile.

I kept cajoling, "Marshall, take them off—it's ok!" Then in response to a look of his, I stopped. I was kind of proud of Marshall; he was a personal acquisition of mine. Our friendship was different than the sum total of what Daisy—and because of "group-think" everybody at the church—would have thought of our parts. Daisy hadn't been too keen on Jane and Marshall even when they were married and had not queenly reason to revise her opinion since he stubbornly refused to enter her court or even attend one of her meetings in all of these years. Still, he had his Friday nights with Doug and me in between girlfriends and everything. But he didn't exist to Daisy. I could feel her opinion of him. A heavy, material-minded kid. But she hadn't seen him since he'd become a man.

Marshall wasn't as heavy as Patsy and Patsy had whispered something bizarre on the drive up to the pool. She said she'd walked into the kitchen at Daisy's and overheard Daisy telling Sam, "I'm so in love with Patsy it hurts." Wow. That was something. Patsy didn't seem to mind when Marshall kept his trunks on. She bathed with rolls of healthy, whole wheat fat and big, trail-mix breasts bobbing in the unheated water all by herself, as though preoccupied with some other delightful secret. I dove proudly into the crisp blue water; it was a little too cold to swim and my nipples stood up when I shot up out of the dive. I was too uncomfortable to remain in the white blue water. I thought I saw the blurred image of an old black branch at the bottom of the pool but I didn't dive to pick it up. When I got out, I could see it was only a twig. That's more like it, I thought. Dad kept everything so neat. Good thing he was away.

Marshall appeared neat too, like my dad, although he was a half a foot taller and meaty, but somehow the extra flesh was well organized around broad shoulders and above a modest rear. Conservative side-burns burnished red beneath styled hair but stopped short above clean-shaven cheeks that gave way to what he once called self-deprecatingly, a "beefy jowl." He did look well fed, with a calm grace that belied his size. Canary-yellow hair curled over his large Aires head. His arms and torso were massive, balanced by only relatively long legs. Marshall was a big, gorgeous man to some women, I guessed. He'd had a lot of infatuations, since the break up of his marriage, each seeming to lead to a precipitous re-marriage and then to drop off for some reason. Usually he discovered some deeply disappointing facts about the woman, or his mother pointed out to him how squirrelly the girl was. I wasn't clear about what happened. I just thought, *about every new girlfriend—neat, we're going to be two couples again and maybe we can do things together,* and, *I wonder if she'll like me*—and then things would drop into smithereens for Marshall and we would be back at ground zero with Marshall waiting around our house on a Friday night, or occasionally meeting some church friend of ours like Patsy.

On the way back after we had dropped Patsy off at the church, Marshall asked me, "Hey, why are all your friends that you introduce me to lately, fat?" I thought that was a very uncool, out-of-the-energy thing to ask, but it rang somewhere inside.

I was afraid of him at first, I had been afraid of him since he'd told me he was attracted to me after his divorce. But one Friday night before he left—in order to follow spirit—I tried out my "coming from the heart" attitude on Marshall. A little well of the love of spirit lumped up in me for him, and I squeezed his hand right in front of Doug, as we all sat in the living room finishing our wine, me drinking a miniscule drop or two; I was even afraid to drink wine then.

And then later that week when I awakened deep in the night with one of my residual heart pounding episodes, over the phone Marshall seemed so kind, reassured me that it was more than O.K. to call him at any hour. And Doug urged me to go over myself and visit Marshall at his new apartment; he'd finally moved out from his mother's, five years after the divorce. On the subject of anxiety Marshall confessed to me that his father had had to drive him just to go downtown after he'd left Jane. He never said "after he'd lost her," but the unquenchable thought of bringing the two back together leapt up again. You'd think I would learn—he and his mother inferred that Jane had done something to him, that she was from the wrong side of the tracks—it didn't matter, somehow I had less of an urge to quibble with him now—even about my "neo-Marxist" versus his "Bircher" politics, or whatever the mutual expletives were.

We sat on the couch for a minute, his hand so warm and fleshy, embarrassed and guilty, mine strong, dry, unabashed in its beliefs I thought—*so what if he saw this as a pass*—I wouldn't let him think it was one.

On another Friday night in our apartment, Doug insisted, amid giggles, "Kiss her goodnight, Marshall." Why? That seemed out of place, Doug's problem. Daisy said you just act between yourself and God, and don't go into anybody else's space. So I chose to remain incognizant of Doug's suggestion. Marshall left, lumbering down the ill-slung concrete and metal stairway that swung against the apartment house. I went back to the things I did or tried to do. I wasn't very well organized domestically. There was ketchup on the cheap plastic, rented kitchen curtains, but I danced across the rippled dark linoleum, got an empty mayonnaise jar and ran outside to pick flowers at night. I could see the taillights of Marshall's sleek yellow sports car rounding the corner to shoot like a star around the Safeway store.

The next night he was back. Unusual. It wasn't even Friday. This time he bought a better bottle of wine. I wished he'd bring cheese, or nuts, or something we could eat later, but I was patient. He sat on the legless blue couch that was covered by a bird and flower print madras bedspread. The couch slumped further into the floor under his weight. "Ahum," he joked. "Maybe I'll have to have some more of that vulgar, I mean bulgur wheat you made for me the other night instead of the prime rib I've been eating lately." He didn't like my bulgur wheat and chicken. I was a little hurt.

He saw it under the laugh.

"Page, it was very good. And Mom read recently where they're discovering you need fiber. I'd come over and have fiber again, if you like." He laughed. He seemed to be in an awfully good mood tonight.

"Oh certainly, we'll have you again."

I was always trying to catch up with some expected image he had of me, where I was a capable, efficient housewife, as Jane had been. Jane who dyed her hair even blonder to match his mother's and who had bought a slug of expensive, 1950ish dresses with patent leather belts to match his mother's. I could never be like that, but in between serving Daisy and surviving the little girls I sort of wanted to—I didn't know why. But I never made it then. Doug did the laundry downstairs, half-hazardly but regularly, angry with me for not doing it more. But who wanted to carry a baby down cement stairs with another poor little girl who should have been walking but wasn't, crying all the time, with the stairs swinging and the sick old lady who lived beneath—resisting a nursing home—banging the inside of her front door as I walked, or banging the ceiling with a broom. "I never had children," she'd said when I first met her, "I never was blessed." Then, as the animosity sparked by the broom handle banging hardened, I tried to think, think about what it must be like to be her, and sick. I even theorized, perhaps wrongly, that it was resentment about not having children that had brought the cancer.

Once, after an "up" choir performance, I'd impulsively picked a flower on my way up the sidewalk from the car and given it to her. With a puffy, sullen smile she'd retorted, "Where'd you steal this from?" I left with Daisy's "You do it between yourself and God and don't get caught in their personality" smile propping the corners of my mouth.

Tonight Marshall wanted music. Big expansive music that would wake the lady up. "It's your apartment folks," he said, "and it's Saturday night." Nervous, as about everything else lately, I let him turn the radio up and I felt better too. He sat back on the bird couch listening to the turned up radio, and I sat across from him on another falling-down couch set at an "L" angle and was glad I had the other wall in back of me. The bird spread had grease stains, I suddenly noticed, from when Veronica dumped out the natural vegetable oil I used for diapering on herself and in the air, there were oil stains on the wall too, I now realized. I wished I had another one of my sketches to put up to cover the oil stains while Marshall went to the bathroom. The bathroom. Ugh. Doug was in the back of the apartment now, cleaning up. When I'd heard Marshall shaking the bottom of the suspended stairs on his way up, I'd asked Doug to straighten the bathroom. Doug moved quickly.

Cleaning up seemed to be Doug Mitchel's career. Generally, he lived in the kitchen, banging, clanging pots and pans, scrubbing the walls and floors methodically—to little avail, considering the level of mess here—singing bombastic militaristic songs, perseverating commercial messages, simply, driving me mad. He was often in and out of jobs, or would get a job for which he was paid little more than minimum wage and which he eventually lost. "It wasn't my fault," Doug would say over and over as he cleaned. It was just that times were hard and everybody he knew, like his brother who'd gotten him the job in the first place, said that the guy was going out of business because he was so eccentric and nutty. I never asked Doug's brother about this—we were already an embarrassment to them, or Doug was.

Doug's brother had come by one day recently—a rare occurrence. Doug wasn't home. Clay sat down with me on the grass outside and asked me if we were O.K., if the girls and I could live on what we had, and I answered, proud, "Of course." Daisy had taught me, "you deal between yourself and God." I knew I was learning lessons about material manifestation and that I knew things this brother didn't. Maybe Clay sensed this, maybe that's why he was smug—Doug always felt he was, and said he didn't need that guy—maybe Clay sensed he was missing something we had and sensed he wasn't smart enough to really know what it was. Sitting that day on the lawn, Clay behaved the way Marshall was behaving tonight, kind somehow and strong…the way a husband was supposed to be, not like Doug, who was parroting a fragment of a toilet bowl cleaner commercial. "Down, down, down, Bowl-Bright sucks it down!" he delighted in the scatological imagery. He sang it loud now, over and over again until he was shouting like a frantic, frustrated child as he folded laundry fast and then threw it into the sleeping children's room. "Quieter, Doug." I hissed into the hallway where he was. "Please stop it. Veronica will wake up and you know what that means."

Across from me Marshall wore an alligator shirt. How funny. I had on a navy blue corduroy jumpsuit. I loved jumpsuits. I had gotten this one cheap. Marshall said later that I often, on that night and others, sat with my legs open, showing him he said, and then laughed, embarrassed, your.… I did not, I couldn't have. "Yes," he said, "you did. You were, and I had a hard time not showing you I…noticed."

That wasn't the only time; he was by more and more after that, his heavy step in tempo to Daisy's ever stronger admonitions to take the parts of myself out of the closet that I'd been hiding—and line them up to Spirit. She didn't know anything about our visits with Marshall. "Do you want me to have an affair?" I asked her.

"I don't know. No, stupid, just take one step into those parts of you that you know are there, take one step and you'll know if it's real, or what you need to do about it. Risk falling on your face if you have to. You've come so far lately." I knew Daisy applied the philosophy. She'd slept with Yvette only months ago, an event I should have thought more bizarre than I did. But such was Daisy. The drive "to Spirit" took precedence over everything, I thought, and one followed its pull wherever it led, in submission and in total honesty.

But certainly Marshall wasn't a candidate for me to deal with that stuff with. Through the increasing visits I just sat and listened to the diminishing tales of his current girlfriend problems, and tried to apply the philosophy to those problems. He always seemed immensely grateful to me; and I'd never thought of him as that receptive to truth before.

One night I dared to visit him again at his apartment alone, to share with him Daisy's latest insight. "That's interesting," Marshall yawned. His eyes brightened visibly as he leaned toward me in his heavy leather swivel rocker. "And what about us?" he joked. Or was he serious? "How do we fit into the cosmic scheme of things?" I submerged my gaze into the swirling depths of my wine glass. Quaint images of a past life man and woman dancing in a stately ballroom hung suspended in the amber-lit, antique-clad spaces of Marshall's living room. "We had something…once, before," I allowed. "Let's leave it there." I got up, snatched my purse and tumbled down the stairway to the outer door without saying goodbye.

Unceasingly these past few weeks Daisy had urged me to "deal with my attractions and desires." Elizabeth was returning to town alone for a follow-up lecture at Daisy's church. Elizabeth was my friend. I would talk to her about this. Leaving the children with Doug I set out early in the morning, full of gaiety and cheer. The whole group cleaned and swept and vacuumed Daisy's building. Daisy smiled benignly at me and shifted chairs and end tables in the basement room. The room was used as a nursery and emblazoned with the unicorns and stars Pegeen had painted on two of its walls. The periodic intimate moments in Daisy's ministerial office flagged my hopes of one day becoming a minister. There the very air seemed to wiggle and dance with Daisy's manic vitality. Daisy carefully reinforced the teaching, to speak my heart, to express what I was really feeling, to trust and to act on the prime force that moved inside me—to trust myself. But it was also Daisy, I dimly realized, who was pushing and pulling me, invoking my courage one moment, and strangely subverting my achievements in the next. Daisy was more and more like an autocratic implacable abbess, although she referred to "the energy"—of Spirit— as our absolute authority. I'd had no doubt she could have been sainted once—as Catherine, or Catrina, or somebody. Elizabeth said you could have a lifetime where you were even recognized outwardly as a saint, and not have been such a saint on the inside. It took a great deal of effort to recognize that whatever energy there was; was entirely invested in Daisy, and subject completely to her whims, personal tastes and proclivities.

In the beginning, with Art, her undeniable personal charisma, the genius she possessed—in some area at least—her mystical understanding of God, her love, and her sparkling personality had drawn people like lemmings into her home. The phenomena of Daisy might have been related to her most recent reincarnation, too. If Elizabeth was right, Daisy had lived before as Annie Besant in the nineteenth century, so she would carry the unconscious knowledge of

Theosophy —as well as the memory of losing her man to me in that life. When I made the discovery of our karmic tie of the past, I'd wondered if Daisy could have been jealous, and if the feeling could carry over. No, her purposes seemed more ennobled, her love for us timeless and, as she said often, "beyond the limitations of personal ego."

Some of that same past life wisdom, impersonal love and transcendent energy still sparked current followers to take part in her projects. In the early days, magic had flowed from her as from a hidden fountain. Her talks then were inlaid with hushed silences, as each new seeker awaited, and received answers to the innermost questions of the heart; they untied age-old knots that constricted their inner workings. How many of those answers we had brought with us to the gatherings was not analyzed. But the memory of those halcyon, just-arrived-home-after-long-waiting days and nights surrounded me in memory and gave me the impetus to continue with the group, perhaps long after it was wise, and long after it had outlived its usefulness in my life. "But everything that happens, is right," was the newest slogan at the church, the newest group realization. So, when doubt often entered now, I was as often reminded of those days, and my love and gratitude was as for someone who had thrown me a strong rope when I dangled halfway down an abyss. Oh, I loved her.

In the fleeting moments when I was able to speak alone to her about these matters during the seminar, Elizabeth, so much older, though not, I knew, completely removed from worship at Daisy's shrine, kept insisting, strangely, that I recognize what she had come to further understand during this visit. "I can see it in her eyes every time she talks to you, and in her aura. She has a thing about you, a crush if you will." And, cautiously Elizabeth reiterated, "You may not agree now, but when you're sixty—you'll understand that, in a sense, we're both, well, let's say sixty-forty, male and female, each one of us. I won't explain it further," she said lightly but significantly and as though unwilling to dwell to long on the obvious, "but Daisy's aura does change somehow when you're around."

"But you wanted to talk to me about something—what is it?" Elizabeth asked later, after the lectures were over and nearly everyone began to clear out. "We'll talk later," I whispered and then left the building with the last few paying customers. I had gone to great pains to let it be known that I was going home after the choir had sung its last number and people left gradually, talking animatedly in groups. Only after it grew dark could I sneak back to the church. Daisy had made it clear that monopolizing Elizabeth's time could cost me what I most hoped for—that illusive recognition as a teacher, as a counselor —the manifestation of these seven years of study. To this end Daisy had lectured me—velvet gloved—the day before the seminar in the intimate, promising confines of her ministerial office, on the importance of serving the Overall Body.

Marshall, stopping by our apartment again that night, said "Horseshit. That church is no different from any other business."

"That's really true, you know," I'd answered him numbly. How could I know what he was talking about; I hadn't held a job "in the earth" at any time during my adult life. Because of that conversation with him, however, I did felt like a schmuck for having to sneak to see Elizabeth in off hours, and as if, somehow, I'd been bought and paid for by the Overall Body, i.e. Daisy's profitable—to herself and her sisters and their families—non-profit organization run by "the energy."

To monopolize, or in my case, to even speak to Elizabeth was to sneer in the face of the energy, and to be "out of the energy" was practically translated into 25 more hours stuffing envelopes, learning, as Daisy so adroitly put it, "the virtue of humility, of serving in the background." But the rub, the facts, were difficult to ignore: for example, some rumpled looking Jewish guy in his forties who reminded me of Professor Irwin Corey, the epitome of the nonsensical, had recently entered the fold and "claimed" his ministerial degree. He was a great showman and popular with the ladies at psychic fairs, where he made a bundle "reading energies," but his anointment seemed a disservice those others, like me, who drove old cars and who had been forced to live beneath the surface of life, to those sincere seekers after a more substantial way of living, loners often but distinguished by having passed through a kind of "dark night of the soul," a loneliness in which they had found God. And God, or better, the Creative Forces, at this church, were so graciously left in their fullness and mystery that all could keep their own private vision of them, and still look into the eyes of their fellows, with tears oftentimes, seeing the reflection of Spirit.

During the dark drive around the back streets before re-approaching the church, I felt as if I were a thief, about to steal from Daisy, because I intended to voice to Elizabeth my ambivalence about Daisy, and to tell Elizabeth that Daisy's unconscious misuses of power were making this haven a trap, the memories of the halcyon days overexposed, and the loyalty and gratitude Daisy had inspired in me, stretched beyond the breaking point.

Elizabeth would know what to do. Like Daisy, she had a presence and a commanding aura, intermixed with warmth and gentleness and such obvious personal foibles and weaknesses—she was frequently running late or losing keys or her purse—that she was approachable. By her manner she didn't claim to be God, only to know of God, to be only a fellow seeker who had attained to a certain wisdom. Over the years, Elizabeth had told me things she'd never told anyone else, including Daisy, and I was beginning to wonder if Daisy was jealous of that fact.

Although Elizabeth was 38 years older than I, we felt at times as if we were contemporaries, and I had known with her the certainty of easy friendship that is so hard to find. In the dark parking lot outside the back, kitchen door, I stared up into the luminous eye of the church window and tried to formulate my questions, about my deepening friendship with Marshall, about Daisy's simultaneous encouragement that I "take a step" into my attractions. How many times had Daisy told it, that one begins to walk the spiritual path by putting aside certain desires that are unacceptable to the ideal of the developing self. How many times had she revealed the truth she believed; that somewhere, sometime, it becomes necessary for the seeker to acknowledge these, to "take them out of the closet" and "take one step into them," but to "bring all of your awareness with you," so to discover the true meaning of these shadow areas, to "align them to Spirit," and to come, as Daisy often promised us we would, to know the true self.

In some ways I agreed with this, in some ways I didn't. As it was, I felt precariously poised between two positions: that of maintaining the ideal of loyalty in my marriage and the desire to have the courage to confront honestly that which was hidden in me.

Daisy's infernal prodding didn't help. She made a point of bringing this up publicly and of singling me out as a person who could, if I believed it, accomplish a lot for Spirit, but only after I liberated myself and could live in the "fullness of my being." Through Daisy lately, I was beginning to feel more alive and confident and connected to people I loved because I had begun to speak my mind, to act on inner feelings instead of denying then and swirling mentally in circles of confusion. Daisy's courage and concepts continued to be a balm, a hope. But this "desires and attractions" business somehow contradicted what I knew to be true of myself. I had never loved lightly. Just as now I did not love Daisy lightly.

It was dark in the temple room when I crept past the pews towards the room adjacent to the kitchen where Elizabeth was staying. Peeking around the corner into the warm soft light, I saw Patsy and Jade, there by Daisy's command, casually serving Elizabeth tea. There was a little laughter when I came in. They continued to talk about the seminar, the choir, and about tonight's eclipse, for what seemed an interminable period of time. Finally Patsy and Jade left, and Elizabeth, very tired, asked me what I wanted to talk about. I stumbled around it; then mentioned Marshall. "I thought he was really something," Elizabeth murmured sleepily. "I think the attitude of my generation toward affairs is overdone." I continued to try to talk about it but Patsy, remembering her duties, popped back in for something she'd forgotten, and glowered at me to leave, suggesting icily that Elizabeth was tired. So Elizabeth kissed me goodnight and I left, feeling unsatisfied but bravely optimistic. Well, then, maybe this is something for me, I thought, resolving, however, to corner Elizabeth when she was more awake and talk to her about my conflict over Daisy's beliefs.

The next day was busy and Elizabeth was surrounded by people so I kept quiet not to risk her Daisy's disfavor. Even when I drove Elizabeth to the airport we were not alone and she was running late after she stopped to see Evan Williams in his wheelchair. She gave him the most readings at Asilomar now. She felt close to those who had been hurt by life and deserved better. He played beautiful Sufi music for her conferences now; and, though far apart in age, she sensed they'd been sweethearts in a past life.

I could only drop her off at the terminal and drive away. On the way home I decided to return to Marshall's new apartment. Doug and Marshall had both been urging me to visit him there. My heart was beating more rapidly than usual, my solar plexus emanating acid waves, and a pleasant, unpleasant pulling sensation was beginning somewhere in my lower body. I felt excited, daring, and driven. When I got onto the lonely lake road near Marshall's I drove as though drugged, remembering that right now was the moment of the vernal eclipse Jade had told us about.

Chapter Twenty

I pulled the ratty blue station wagon over to the shoulder of the road and looked up at the united heavenly bodies of moon and sun, visible through the front windshield. At that precise moment, Elizabeth's plane, southbound, passed overhead. And as clearly as if she'd been sitting in the seat beside me, as if she owed me a warning, I heard Elizabeth's voice. "This will be the hardest year to year and one half of your life—the hardest year of your life."

I tried to still the voice, to rationalize it as my own imagination. Still Elizabeth continued, "Keep him as the knight in shining armor. He, the husband, will never forgive you."

Now, after all the inner warring I had done it was really too late. Now I wanted him, wanted the experience. I looked into the overhead mirror. I was flushed. I saw hot pink in my aura. Good thing I wasn't at church where everyone could see. This clairaudience beneath the eclipse was no more than fearful imagination born of the lack of courage to really confront myself, I told the wild eyed visage of myself. Daisy was right, I had to take one step into my attractions and desires to become a minister. At the same time I was aware that I had listened to Elizabeth's etheric words carefully, as though remembering them one by one as if to file away for future use.

Moments later, after discovering he wasn't home, I laid a pink Oriental poppy plucked from the terraced garden beneath his upstairs bachelor apartment—upside down over the handle of his door.

The full, shadowy light of the April eclipse, still reigning overhead, reminiscent of Elizabeth's warning—splashed across my face, playing counterpoint to desire too long toyed with. Still, dutifully, I acquiesced. This must mean that it is not meant to be. Sure that I should be relieved, I ran to the car, jumped in and barreled home, apparently freed from that initial, irrevocable step into adultery. But as I drove, a dull hungry pressure bore down from within my lower belly, and so immediate did the sensation become that I tightened and released my legs once or twice to rid myself of it. Unfamiliar, it settled into the hollows of my thighs and there left a nagging tightness.

At home Doug met me with a wry, knowing grin. I told him what had happened, that I'd gone to Marshall's. His back was turned where he stood washing dishes. Casually, he murmured, "You missed your action." He could have been Daisy! I stared at him. How often lately had I tried to tell him that my feelings for Marshall were growing increasingly strong. And how often, then, had he continued driving, or washing, or talking about the price of Venetian blinds to replace the ketchup-covered curtains, or of whether or not we could get an air conditioner for summer.

"Go back," said the strange man. Now the tightness squeezed my legs out of my chair and propelled them to walk the few feet across the squeaky kitchen floor to the telephone hanging on the wall.

Marshall answered and thanked me for the flower and said that he regretted missing me.

"I'm coming back."

"Oh…" was all he said, and that softly.

The bedroom at Marshall's apartment was warm and yellow; a low antique lamp shed a subtle, glowing light on the bed covered by a brown, smoothed spread. Everything appeared still, unmoving, beautiful, and yet barren at the same time.

He sat hunched, unmoving. We joked. A thousand doubts like gnats beat about my head. I flopped on the bed casually, scanning the carefully polished cabinets that faced each other on the bedroom walls. I drew on remembered emotions when I blithely invited him to lie beside me. "After all, we can see what happens," I tossed, the teenaged rebel once again. He said nothing, but flopped beside me and crossed his hands across his breast. I was nervous, sweaty, twisting my toes in my socks.

I heard the chiming of the antique clock from the little dining room; my husband had fixed that clock. Doug did so many things for his friend, gratuitously, and somehow Marshall's walls accrued the greater treasure.

Then there was no sound in the room but the rustling of covers and thin spread and feet sliding on sheets—nearer to me? I felt a brief touch, warm, of what I knew to be his hand. Our mouths covered it over with nervous jokes I can't remember because they were insincere; every nerve fiber was drawn along with the miniscule scratching of flesh on pillowcase, moving nearer, 'til side of finger touched strand of hair. His head moved, rumpling his pillow and mine in parallel, sympathetic motion. We used silence to straighten that out, then silliness, then silence.

Then a brush of warm hand and I, a million miles away to protect against the hand, thoughts spinning guilty thoughts in the dry distances, twirling like dancers over and over in the same patterns, going nowhere at all. His leg had managed to touch mine, its length hard, warm, not too big. Why was my head where his was, my foot with his, if I was nine inches shorter; where was the middle of him; had it disappeared? Or were silence and twirling thoughts the nimbus we'd woven around what we were about to do now?

And somewhere, nestled between Macy's best percale, beneath chocolate blankets, between bare walls off-white but for the refinished brass and oak pieces, were the beautiful pieces of flesh we would use to enact it with, each like a polished gun or a maddeningly delicate cloisonné vase—each like a treasure.

Now the room looked white and amber and wide. Its ceiling swept away. My eyes glimmered. He reached over me and flipped off the light. A hand, trying to ignore his hand, touched it. His hand touched back, his hand gripped mine, then opened like a butterfly, fluttered, and when not rebuffed, closed down hard upon my hand. Eyes adjusting to the dark, I saw an evergreen fur spire high against this upstairs window, its curtain parted a face's width. It scraped the April-cold glass languidly, pleading to be let in.

We lay shyly, listening to the clock chime in the other room. He kissed me tentatively, mouth closed in respect. I tasted the wide lips slowly to overcome my fear. We had nothing in common—we'd fought politics, everything, all these years. Now he seemed preternaturally large in the dark. "How's it feel to be in bed with the king...of Republicans?" he suddenly asked with an insecure laugh—his attunement to my thoughts surprised me.

I put out an arm toward him, wrapped it around him, brushed my hand across his cheek, felt the red brush of beard I'd never seen in all these familial years, touched his lip. He was a stranger. I did not know this body.

I watched as if outside of us, as if I were both of us. He rose, holding my one gripped hand like a pinion to steady the heavy body in midspace as it vaulted because of hunger across the thoughts that he was too coarse for me, that he would not please me, that he would like to wait and not break the dream, that I might leave and fly away and not light again on this long, firm-mattressed bed in this room appointed perfectly like a case to show off trophy.

Now he moved above me like a glider homing slowly to earth, making an entry now more familiar than morning, into his own woman. He twisted himself away from my hips as he lifted me high to meet him, with his hard palm pushing that ancient girdle of Venus as far upward toward my belly as it could stretch, so widening me patiently until I felt he could see it in the night, that I was all—his.

Desperate, lost and half-choking in his own dream he thrust himself into me, found I was slickening with sheen, and knew as I gasped and swelled, that now—now was the realization of the dream.

And his knees, the muscles in his thick back moved to strong rhythms, his body broiled, the thrust was hungry, shameless, the pause to draw back calculated to give the greatest spring. Through his eye slits I saw he was a collector, saw he knew a moment of hatred and cynicism toward me, but when he would rush forward, down as if to impale the percale, then he would drop the hatred, and arch his spine as shamelessly as a cat, down through me, into me as though my body protected him from touching the shame he'd felt when he'd done it in his sleep into the mattress at night, dreaming of me and waking in cream.

Afterwards I lay against him, bathed in the splendor of memory. I saw him in the first of a series of disguises. The masks, the personae of other lifetimes floated to my mind's eye and fled, as quickly. His fingertips trickled up the inside of my thigh. Each touch, each pressure, opened the capstone of a sealed inner chamber, and memories, heady, exciting memories of what must have been other lifetimes together in the earth—spilled out.

He flicked on the low yellow lamp and reached for a cigarette. Lying across his legs, still gently shifting, I looked up into his cat's-eye blue eyes and smiled. I reached my arms out to him and he lifted me toward his chest. We sat listening to the clock chime the quarter hour; he stroked my hair, traced the shape of my breast with his fingertip. I reached over him for a notepad and pen that lay on the table with the lamp. He gripped my waist into his chest while I leaned, underpinning me like an ancient giant—a god, who could support strong women as if they were toys. His golden hair, rumpled and full, curled from his sweat, haloed his head as if he were an archaic Greek. I laughed, startled that the faces and aspects I had seen in the dark would remain beneath the light. "You are Archimedes," I named him, frowning, "you were Archimedes, can't you remember?" I kissed his lip to wake him to the memory. He turned from me and thoughtfully exhaled a breath of smoke. He smiled back at me, shy and delighted, proud of anything I might do, but I could see he did not remember.

The words of a poem tumbled out involuntarily. My fingers raced to record them on the telephone note pad. "May I read it to you, Marshall—Archimedes?" I asked. He watched me pensively, his big face in hand, his eyes illumined with love. "Uh...huh."

"To Archimedes
    Archimedes,
    Golden warrior, father of the sun,
    On what broken homeward ride
    You come I do not know;
    Surely death enchantment has possessed you—
    Flying helplessly behind you in the breeze
    I see the golden dusted feathers of a king.

    Where is the music now you used to play
    When skies were quiet and no one heard you but your soul?
    And where is the God of night who answered
    By blushing the dawn's first light to powdered gold?

    Archimedes,
    How hidden things must haunt you—
    And whispers burn your heart,
    When memories are the cup you put to lip
    To quench the thirsting of your heart."

"That's sad, Page, and I'm not sad." I looked at him mutely. I did not know why I had written it, much less why it was sad. I hoped Daisy wasn't right, and that I was not any kind of prophet. "You've always been able to dream true, Page. Maybe someday you'll write the prophesies for the new dispensation, for the new age," she'd said. Well this wasn't a prophesy, it was a poem...and about the past.

How long had it been since a poem had flowed from me, intact. It was since before I'd known Daisy—definitely since before I'd married Doug. Stretched across this man's belly, all fearful doubts I'd had lately about myself as a woman evaporated. Marshall looked into my eyes as if into a mirror. We both smiled and radiated a quiet pride. It was as if we'd just anointed each other as a man, and as a woman. For the first time in these seven years, I knew that I was a woman and whole.

Marshall took the slip of poetry from my hand, placing the evidence of his ancient personality on the antique night stand. I explored his body with my hands, awakening now, rocking against him, feeling still swollen, suddenly twisting, itching, as if the rivulets flowing from him inside me were not enough to define this new pride.

Where he had hung afterwards like a folded glider would lie against the cool earth against my thighs, now he began to grow. "Ohhh," he uttered painfully, surprising us both. He tore his hand from me to fumble for the light, and that failing, left it. Then he turned me over and began again, until, by morning's light, we had known each other seven times.

Morning. Drapes parted, song issued from the stereo in the living room. He shaved before a fancy silvery mirror in the walk-in vanity leading from the bathroom to the hall. He touched up styled blond hair with the blow dryer, patted it, put the things he used to shave away. He smelled of after-shave. Would he drive me home? I guessed. It was very early, but I doubted there would be time for orange juice. I'd known he was punctual. Daily, ruddy-faced, craving coffee, he had been punctual at the back door of the restaurant in Woodside where he served his first account. He wasn't becoming the top salesman for Farmer Brothers Coffee and Restaurant Supply at 27 for nothing. But today he blended orange juice in the antiseptic kitchen, seeming at a loss as to where things were. His mother sent her "gals" in to clean on Thursdays and to pick up his laundry.

The "folks" lived around the corner on a quiet Los Gatos street in a simple, though prestigious house, known for its good taste, for its formality and attention to detail. Original art hung about in his house too—oh I might have said mediocre before, but now when he showed it to me, it glowed, it looked perfect, like the shining hair on top of his head—the dry look was in—so then why did it shine—shine like the spun angel wings on top of a Christmas tree? I wanted to touch it, to feel and see better by touching, open worlds by touching. There was little we could say. It was just after dawn. We sat with me on his lap in the heavy bent wood rocker on its metal pedestal. We touched new lips never known before, listened to the clock chime. You are mine, cried the cells within us.

"I'll have to get you back," he said. "What time does Doug leave? That's right, he's not working. But I'll have to leave. I have to be up there by 7:30." I was a little hurt. He had to be there—that came first. He poured more orange juice. I sat on his lap. There was music. He liked the rock of now. It grated. "How about some classical?" We were young I guessed. I should have liked the rock. But I wanted to sit on his lap in the stillness of the Kreuzer Sonata on the FM station he switched on. We sat there, swiveling. We were both afraid. Our thoughts, mine I knew, stretched between things like fine gossamer wire; his hung in the balance between the things he must do and the things he wanted to do. He touched my knee as if it were a child's, within his large hand.

I thought of the word "husband," recalling that it was from the old English "houseband"—he who is a band around the house, the woman, the children and their lives, securing them. I wondered if he could be…Doug? Where was Doug? What would he think? How strange for Doug to have suggested this. I said many guilty things, pulling away from him in the chair, like a rose I'd seen, choked among weeds against the tall back fence of our apartment building.

"Page," he broke in. "Today is my birthday."

"I knew it last night," I apologized. "I knew it a day ago, but now…"

"Don't tell me happy birthday, Page, because you…"

He smiled like the sunshine that flowed between the weave of thick expensive drapes that hung before the redwood balcony. He held me in the stream of sunshine.

He looked better in the sunshine, better in the sunshine. I was wearing green. Someone on the radio recently said green is the secret color of Venus, the planet of love, color of ego, too. Green took on a special meaning. "You are a lover," he whispered. "Today is my birthday." He laughed. "Maybe I'll go in late—not much—I'll be there…but the world can wait today for Marshall Hart."

"Page," he kissed me hard, his mouth opening, back in the throat kind I'd come to know after the first tentative explorations.

Page Hart, I thought, and looked, daydreaming, unseeing, into the sunlight struggling to come in.

He rocked us. I heard the creak of heavy wood, clean, and thought of my children, in neatly spread beds, eating good conservative dinners at half past five.

I spread my fingers within his, kissed him on the jowly redside burned cheek, spread his fingers open and closed, closed and opened, feeling as if I had a kind of power—like sunbeams spurting through holes in drapes, like ants discovering honey and crumbs. They've searched a long, long way, their lives are in peril...how do they return the sample crumb down the long sacrificial distances and then survive themselves? No matter. They're only part of a chain of events. Whether you survive or not, the movement, the action, the feeding must take place. "Move with your spirit," Daisy had said— "Don't miss your action," Doug had added to that.

I reached my arms up through the sunbeams and stretched.

Honey crumb upon my head like a maiden bearing a basket to her liege on the Nile, I smiled and did not harden against the philosophical abstractions that had brought me here at last.

I drove the short stretch of freeway back to my place, oblivious to the dirty car, still enclosed in the good smell of new upholstery from Marshall's apartment. I sneaked in, hoping the landlord—who lived downstairs and next door to the angry lady beneath—wouldn't see. I felt like a whore slipping in bed beside Doug, I thought green, green, loving, egotistical thoughts. "You're a lover," rang scintillatingly through my body—lit up like the electric filament in a clear bulb by the thought. Special. I had been held in his big hands, held. My whole body held the thought beneath the once-was-an-electric-blanket on this bed, under the brown bedspread my dad had given us once. The spread had looked so like the stylish ones my sister bought with her charge cards; now it had a wide blotch of the baby's oil splashed over it, but it was all we had and had looked pretty to me. Lying there, seeing Doug's ashen complexion in his sleep—not a beard, really, but a dark cast against his white skin, I saw him move. Not now. Not yet. I stilled any motion, stilled my thoughts too for a minute, so he would not pick them up. What else do I have that's green? I remembered a soft, sea green sweater

I'd picked up from the give-away closet at the church. That would do. My eyes were green. I saw my green eyes looking out as if I were not me. Pretty eyes, maybe, after all?

I tried for a moment of sleep but was awakened by the inner whisper of a voice not of my own thoughts, nor that of Elizabeth's, but a fatherly voice that spoke in the cadences of a Cayce reading, with controlled mirth, admonishing me clearly and succinctly, "Just don't make a habit of it"—as if he had seen! I chuckled back, then wiped away this voice—so familiar and comforting somehow—out of my way with aplomb, rationalizing it away as I had Elizabeth's, denying again, the very phenomenon I had sought in all these long years of study in the mysteries.

That day we had a garage sale; it had been planned before this happened. I sat at the foot of the concrete stairs. The children played in the distance on the grass. In the new, nearly hot April sunshine I sat in my green sweater. A family of poor Mexican people climbed out of a dark, hot-colored car and walked down the driveway that separated us from the landlord's. I smiled at them. This garage sale was part of a feeling I'd had about getting rid of the old things, making my place more substantial. The falling-down blue couch would go but I'd save the print bedspread that had covered it—birds and flowers were eternal. Light caught Doug's hair as he swung the banister while coming down with a crummy lamp and water-marked end tables.

For a minute he looked like the boy I had married. He wore the lavender shirt I once got him—for what job was it? Oh yes, selling sewing machines at the air-conditioned shopping mall. That was nice. I was so pregnant that summer and I could go there and wait. He looked sunny, a little color now in his cheeks because of the heat, his light brown hair glinting copper. And he looked happy too, busy cleaning behind everything he removed. Cleaning was his happiness. Good thing he liked it, or the apartment would have been condemned some while ago. I could even joke to myself, inside my own head. *Is this me*, I wondered, *not Daisy's fumble-tongued flunky after all, not the humorless wretch who did everything wrong, or too late, or not at all?*

That day ushered in a new period. Nights of trying to work it out—once, that is, we got Doug's attention. I think he would have been happy to clean and to be left alone, but fearless honesty and dealing between yourself and God, were the hallmarks of my surrender to Spirit, and Marshall, wanting to do the manly thing, complimented Doug when he came immediately to see us after that first distracted day driving up and down the bay making the rounds of his accounts, to tell Doug, "You're a very lucky man." And, "I think I'm in love with your wife." So that Doug was forced to see...something, and became fearful in his foggy way although he tolerated Marshall's presence because he was, as always, as magnetized and admiring of Marshall's worldly proficiency as I had been of Daisy's spiritual gifts.

So began nights of withstanding the pressure of love. Then Marshall would ask if we wouldn't mind if he came for dinner, knowing full well Doug had choir practice. Oh sure, I'd say, as nervous as one of the birds from the India print spread that now hung on the wall. Oh sure.

One night I made liver and onions for him. "Yummm." But he thanked me, seemed touched. We sat with a candle looking out the wide, night-black, curtain less window, our chairs creaking (I couldn't sell those at the garage sale or we would have had nowhere to sit.)

"Fine dinner," he said.

Jokes. We were friends again, just friends. He brought up someone or other, someone he'd seen recently as a "friend." Why did he always do this to me? The bird, struck forever in a frieze on the thin cotton, inwardly pleaded as the cat inched forward, paws so soft, crown of golden hair so fine, so smooth and heavy to the touch.

"Ummm, I thought you said that...all you wanted to be is...friends with her." Shit. I'd revealed too much of myself.

"Oh yeah, you're right, that's all she and I have ever been— not like us...but we're just 'friends', aren't we?" he teased, lingering on the word "friends," warning me to retreat from my resolve.

He catalogued his old relationships, comparing them, then concluded quietly, "You and I are...romantic." He touched me again and clenched his glass. It was so dark in here now...the window open just a little let in a whiff of spring air.

"Wait here. I have something for you."

I brought back a carefully-tied-to-look-casual scroll made of two sheets of typing paper, on which I had written a poem overlaid with the sketch of a full-hipped spring crocus opening to bloom.

How many times had I tied and untied the ribbon, left over from the Christmas box of saved things, bits of paper and ribbon from other people's celebrations. When would I have anything new?

While he read it I looked at the gold and diamond ring he wore on his wedding finger, the one, he'd joked, that meant he was married to himself. Was it his protection against the women he'd seen since his divorce? I whirled over to the sink to look housewifey and clean up the liver. I felt too much to face him.

Those days passed so quickly. Daisy was alert that something was going on, and at the same time indifferent. "Where've you been, chicken?" she asked casually one Tuesday evening. She'd allowed me to attend a special class with Sam and Jade as my peers in that process now formally titled "Reassociation", composed of techniques derived from a metaphysical psychiatrist's lecture she'd attended recently, from the space beings she claimed were hovering ever nearer to repay the ancient debt they owed the group—and of course, from Spirit.

"I've been here," I assured her, because the deal was that I was to attend either Tuesday or Thursday evening and assist with one session in order to become fully trained, to become a "Reassociater".

"I **was** here Thursday, you weren't," I asserted.

"That's good," she murmured, off to something else.

Tonight's reassociation subject was Chad, a short man about thirty or so who wore glasses and had a caustic wit.

Daisy floated in about half-way through.

"How tall are you?" she asked Chad.

He told her. "Stand up then, will you?" she suggested. He hesitated, then sprang up and spun around.

At the break getting coffee in the kitchen, standing close in to Sam and Jade I could only partly hear her.

"I just wanted to see…if he could deal with his height…bring it out in the open, see?"

Reconvening, Chad told us about the vasectomy he'd had in his last marriage—a marriage with no children. He had some regrets. Tears emerged then more jokes.

He ended the session talking about reversing the vasectomy. Four years later he was one of the last to leave Daisy. In the meantime he'd married an older woman in the group and then left her for Daisy's sister Amy. He never did have a child. Did Daisy know so well, could she know in a half hour why a man might sterilize himself without his young wife knowing it, and then come to Daisy to be "Reassociated"? With brilliant flashes, Daisy swept in and out of the Reassociation sessions, finishing this, tying off that. There were moments that seemed brilliant indeed, moments when a smile broke over someone's face, splashed across their insides it seemed, so great was their relief.

Every Tuesday, or every Thursday, I made it to the reassociation sessions, love no exception to the rule, nor nervous discussions between Doug and me—and Marshall, who came around sometimes almost believing he was a counselor, helping us to face things, helping us put it all back together. All exigencies were eclipsed by faithfulness to the terms of this opportunity she was at last presenting me—to become trained as a reassociater, a counselor, to at last step closer to the ministry. Nothing stopped me. No crying child, nor fear of spending the last dollar of the day to fuel the long old pale blue Mercury station wagon to get there—not even the hope of flowers, or poetry (the white sheets flowed from me into the single formica drawer of the corner desk we'd gotten for free for moving the church babysitter from one messy house to another.) Marshall received the poems with delight—somehow as though they were his due. I thought they were too, so no matter.

Now I looked forward to his step more than anything in the world. The nights, when Doug and the babies went to ambivalent sleep, were ours. The torment, the trying not to, the listening for his step, suddenly seeing—what a beautiful man he was, sharp and crisp in pale blue suits, yellow and white striped shirts.

One night when Doug was at choir practice again, we sat on the brown vinyl couch someone through the church had given me— the universe I believed—emblematic of the hope of new life. And he leaned closer to me, as if he had come to collect me, I thought, on his way to somewhere else, as if in his hunger for beautiful experiences I was not to be denied to him. His face looked like a ram's to me, as if he were butting against my intellectual pretentiousness—a thin mask for fear.

He struggled nearer, removing his suit jacket. He smiled. He seemed so happy. Nervous, I did not move nearer. He struggled across the couch, disrupting the bird print drapery that hung on the wall behind it. "Caroline—Page—Ryder," he said, and touched my hand, dramatically recoiling as though burned, looking around slowly—out the darkened window, toward the bedroom where the children slept, then out the darkened window toward the doorway where Doug might suddenly enter; his step was not so audible on the stair.

He lunged, like the Aires ram, all head, against the next embattlement. At first his kiss was odd and dry, just like the first time, slyly followed by opening his mouth inside mine, advancing his tongue as if uncurling a fist. "Ummm," I tried to say with my mouth full of advancing ram. He wrapped his arm fast around my back. "Not here, by the window," I protested. I got up quickly, making virginal jokes; "I'm not getting up with that in mind, you know." He looked around again, carefully, then picked up his coat and leaned above me in the space behind the front door that no one could see from any direction.

"Page, Page," he said as though in pain, "I don't know what this thing is; when I get up I think of you, when I wake up…and I…I have to see this thing through." He cradled my face and kissed it— invaded it, pressed himself from above me against the wall. What a relief to have to stand on tiptoe to reach him. The ram's wet, warm lance invaded my mouth. He felt; he cradled; he pushed. I loved him. How dare I? "Within a year…" I dimly remembered the prophesy Doug's aunt had made when she visited me alone in this apartment the night she made her transition. "Within a year…"

He left because I told him to go. His stride on the stair shook the building. I watched the taillights, red and beaming, of his canary-yellow Camero, thought of his lust-ruddied cheek when we'd kissed, heard his thoughts as he rounded the corner by the Safeway store: See you later, Page—Page, when I wake…

Marshall Hart

Chapter Twenty One

I told her what I'd done, murmuring, "Well, I finally did it, Daisy." Daisy turned the car from Bollinger Road onto Rainbow Drive where she lived. She had the baby Anson in the back; otherwise we were alone. She drove for a while with that icy, in-between-worlds stare she could get. She didn't say anything. The cruel, self-deprecating thoughts began: You weren't supposed to tell someone something like this; it's supposed to be between yourself and God alone; my telling her meant that I hadn't really done it, that it had been phony or with the wrong person.

Inside her townhouse apartment in a complex that had a swimming pool—I envied that, didn't I—we took our clothes off in the little redwood-fenced patio. Hanging plants cascaded toward Daisy, caressing the air as if they were the palms bent to fan an ancient Nile queen. I felt hesitant…this was all wrong. My moment of triumph. I was always so slow. You had to pry me into action, it seemed. "Daisy?"

"Well," she tossed after a long, long time, "who was it?" She dispatched her words as if they didn't matter, as if this was just an exercise, like remembering colors and what they mean when seen in an aura. "It was Marshall."

No answer. The Nile queen, looking down the length of her barge, on a sultry sky-sullen day, thought she would like some entertainment. "Bring in the girls to dance," she cried, angry at the day. Were she on land she would throw a stone into the sullen sea of sky. Her nerves were brittle today with the great nothing boredom of subjects so submissive that it appeared she had castrated them of their souls, just as she had castrated the eunuchs of their unfortunate organs—tossed away like dead leaves, like so much ephemeral garbage.

"Marshall? Oh."

The displeasure was apparent. I probed, tried to liken this to her experience with Yvette. Now Daisy lightly referenced **another** encounter of her own, with a new man at class, one who liked Yvette (a surly, pushed-in face, thick-necked, prison-looking fellow, I thought.). "I thought he might have been 'sent' to me, the way Sam was," Daisy mentioned. I guessed she "followed it through" for an afternoon or for an hour. I wondered. For a delicious moment I saw the pair and stifled a laugh. But I was so nervous that I turned and rearranged a midair plant to point a little more authoritatively toward Daisy.

Unable to turn back the river of self-abasement that had settled anew, I talked on in the same old stupid way, in this too-warm-for-spring day, to this Nile queen, who merely basked, looking perfect, the way rulers or exceptionally good people do.

"Maybe," she finished off my boring sycophant's appeal succinctly, "you're just not ready yet chicken."

Maybe, I thought later, and turned rapidly from the left turn lane on Rainbow Drive back onto busy, not pretty Bollinger Road.

I drove hurriedly. After today must come tonight. This hour must displace the last. Signal lights wiggled in my vision. Why was I crying? I thought of the sun, of the summer, of the moments that never came with Daisy. Maidens ran across my mind's eye, flushing all the unworthy away from the only blue-eyed ruler the mid-Nile region had ever known. "Come with me," one day would say the ruler—one maiden dreamed. "Walk with me on the bow of the great strong vessel our fathers built—yours and mine. Yours with his sweat and mine with his mind. Walk with me." But I had waited, always with the passersby; though I was so loyal I cut my hair off once when hers fell out with the birth of the second royal heir, and I gave it to her for a thick, living wig.

What did she want from me? I cried into my lap. It was all too strange…all this time waiting to make my spirited jump into adultery for her—now that's what Doug said I committed. Lately Doug was looking pale and shaken. No more did he urge me toward Marshall in our mentor Daisy's voice. No more did he urge me to "take one step toward your growth…" And the brave, blank, Daisy-like smiles he threw up at Marshall when his friend had announced, "I think I'm in love with your wife, man," were fast fading from his sad little head.

And now I knew, now I felt each time Marshall touched me, knew as the rush of normal blood swept through me in response, unlocking the knowledge inherent in the cells of my body that Doug, like his little baby girl, was not **right** somehow. How had I missed it before? Better to think of the Nile lady than of this, it was too sad. And at the light before the Safeway store, the thought came as though pulled out of the dusk-darkening spring sky, blueing to dark azure or lapis—to the color of Daisy's eyes by night—that maybe she **knew** this, **knew** I would discover it. Was this her gift?

The queen was back in her summertime reign in the land of my faith. I could stand it a moment longer, could stand going back to the ketchup-covered drapes, and to the man I knew was not quite normal, to the baby I knew now might never because of him. Might never be? Tears spilled over my sunburn, little cooling the new, burning knowledge. Nothing would remain as it had been for me, but would become more of what it had just begun to be. Where was that thought coming from? Why had I let Daisy teach me to be psychic? Now the eyes of Daisy and the Nile-by-night blue, lapis lazuli, dark-eyed sky were one and the same, foaming with gathering clouds like the white waters of the Nile beneath the prow of her boat. *Stop crying, dummy,* I admonished myself, climbing out of the ratty old car and going upstairs to leave the poor babysitter free. It was almost nighttime now.

At one o'clock, riding with Marshall through the empty streets—he called me out of my bed to tell me he couldn't sleep, **impelled** to think of me—we returned to his apartment and didn't speak of our guilt. He led me to the bedroom where we lay though, sadly thinking of Doug, kissing without meaning to kiss, compelled, until our clothes were away from us and all there was in the dark were our arms and lips and the powerful intercourse of our bodies, surrendering over and over again to clutch of gonads imploding with desire.

I felt his teeth as his tongue swept over and over again in my mouth, his arms as they arranged my body—in that curious way of his—for each opening he would take, felt the brush of breast as I lingered over him while he reached for a cigarette after, then thought better of it and implored me to reenter his arms in an intent silence more intense than any moan. And I rocked against the guilt as if I were an animal, feeling the short withdrawals of his sex as if they were an athlete's challenge. With all my height and strength I met each thrust in, as if it were the last this body might know, as if this love would have to last until the end of my days. And as he drew me to him and we felt the come blaze from us like twin spirals drawing us deeper and deeper, I **saw** the "fires of lust" with my trained clairvoyant eye more vividly than anything spied in that moon dark psychic—Rebecca's—visions—saw his face there amid the fire that consumed the bed; and pouring from it I saw a look of glee, of love, of pride and the wild happiness a man feels who sees his lover's naked breasts inflamed, feels the rigid folds of her sex opened to him like an antediluvian flower erect in its satiny glory, calling to him from the fields of evil pleasure that brought the fall, with its crimson pistil trembling anew for the crashing satisfaction of his flesh.

And I saw myself as within the vision—a vixen in the dark, my gold-flecked, green gleaming cat's eyes radiant with the desire to be fucked, and my body pregnant and alight with his sperm that flowed in warm, wanton rivers down my thighs, my lips pulling at his, my tongue licking at his teeth and teasing up the phallus in the minutes after before he was renewed—so that I could come again—and ring out from the loins like a bell flaring into the dark interstices of the galaxy.

Oh we hid these visions from ourselves and covered them over each with solemn, distant thoughts of friend and husband— thoughts vaguely grasped in those refractory periods often no longer than one deep breath—but before I slipped back through the grey pre-dawn streets and into a bed I no longer inhabited, we each had known at last, a satisfaction of desire so great we were made afraid.

On Friday I rode with Jane, Marshall's ex-wife—at least she didn't know—and the babies to the park. She had no idea about Marshall and me. Jane punched her dash radio button set to the local country western station. "You've picked a fine time to leave me, Lucille," the radio rang out. I surrendered to the immense tableau of synchronicity that seemed to descend nearer-ever nearer. The car radio, as if it were the voice of the creative force itself, implored me to consider Doug's plight. In shy delight, too, I

Jane Hart

absorbed the words; why was it that every melody, breeze and springtime sight was alive in the drama—splaying out from Marshall's dark bed in the Live Oak Apartments?

Flowers sprang up everywhere I noticed, on scraps of lawns in the shabby houses past the apartments. So what if these were only soft, heady, unchokable dandelions? Their heads trembled in the breeze as if in desperate salutation as we passed. Oh, how I loved him. I stroked the soft green sweater I'd retrieved at Daisy's Fourth of July sale, from a time that seemed so placid and long ago. Jane swung her large, white, older car around the corner toward the store and I glanced up to see a little boy swinging from the metal railing of a stairway identical to the one in my building. Lately, it was as if I were dangerously suspended off the edge of our concrete stairway all of the time, and I thought Marshall was there to catch me, in his great arms swelling out of freshly laundered shirts. Even his car was a cocoon that bore me by night away from the shabby street, from its platoons of ugly apartments, with his stereo, too, blaring "You picked a fine time to leave me, Lucille," as if it were a portable conscience.

Jane scanned the peripheries of the valley as she drove, surveying the low outlying hills with the Sagittarian's lifelong longing to be on the road. We all had a different emblem for "going home" I realized. Home to me was to the mother consciousness, to the way station of the heart, to the point of reconciliation of all beginnings and of all endings, to the point of inception before the deception of self led us to wander—like Dorothy in Oz away from the simple secret that we, somehow, had brought with us and knew all along. Daisy had mentioned, "going home," more and more, but her journeys, and ours lately, were only leading us on stronger and stranger quests and away from some awareness I could only angrily strain to remember.

(It was Elizabeth who had taught that we came from the heavenly realm, and should choose selflessness over self-will to go home to Christ consciousness. Elizabeth—I pushed the thought of her Cayce wisdom out of my mind quickly. I could be making terrible karma doing this with Marshall, but I wouldn't think about it now, while spring burst into being everywhere around me.)

Jane had said after her latest aborted attempt to rid herself of this valley—after she returned from her latest trip to see her "people" in Valdosta, Georgia with her rebound-from-Marshall, alcoholic husband in tow—that we had no seasons in San Jose, that the amorphous, all-the-time fall/spring weather here made her uneasy.

But now I noticed birds perched on the shoulders of the statue of Saint Lucy in front of the Catholic church across from the Safeway store. Pansies in the border next to the walkway leading toward the church steps flittered vigorously in the new breeze. Fuchsias, like curly, fresh-washed hair, spilled out over the gate of the one old apricot ranch house that remained sandwiched between the adults-only apartments around the corner and the huge public park.

We parked by those apartments and crossed the street into the back end of the park, preparing to walk the long stretch to the modernistic play equipment at the other side. It didn't seem hard to shuffle the babies across that street busy with heedless suburban motorists, nor was there worry in turning them loose to toddle and tumble down the little manmade hills, nor was there tedium in the long, long walk to the tanbark play pits and wood and chain equipment. There Jane and I could sit, me digging in the moist sand forestalling the impulse to write a word sonata on that gritty slate, so encumbered was I by the memories of his bed.

Watching her sad, fogged-over blue green eyes—*the color of a lamed wanderer,* I thought, I stifled the hot desire to tell someone who knew him well, to glory out loud in the after waves of the bed. Jane had grown heavier since those days when she'd been married to Marshall. The strained, immature, "playing house" type of friendship we'd once had when we were mutual newlyweds, fresh out of our relationships with our mothers—the competition, and the unsure ness of that—had settled into the wood of mutual hardship, like varnish scrubbed away by a disenchanted young housewife. Bent on ferreting out food stains and baby scribbles, grape juice and scratches before she finally gives up, the varnish gives up and floats away or into the naked wood. Now our friendship had become a comforting commonplace in mutual weariness. She mentioned Marshall.

Why not? Only weeks before, she and Doug and I had been united in our efforts to bring the two of them back together. After certain machinations on my part, we'd managed to get them to sleep together one more time—this time at Marshall's apartment.

(We didn't take her new husband seriously.) And the other two or three times they'd slept together since the divorce had been at our places.

"He's the worst lay I've ever had," Jane laughed uneasily now, her jeans rolled up over large white calves.

I found this incredible, but some relief for my guilt where her feelings were concerned.

Jane had become indelicate since she'd left Marshall, and her new husband had not helped. She'd married him in Reno at the end of a drunk the hour after her divorce was final, after a blind blur of drunk months spent in the arms, she confessed to me once, of "two hundred men or more." These were moments without pleasure, she admitted to me after I asked—I asked her everything—and moments she couldn't remember clearly at all.

Sating a thirst for detail quickened by what I'd thought to be my dullard's life, I had, over these years, drawn from her vicarious memories of egoistic nights spent reveling beneath the feeble lights of the Cowtown bar or the similar Saddlerack while she shut out the secondary telepathic awareness of Marshall ambling through his mother's garden at dusk, of Marshall later putting out the light and slipping between line-fresh sheets in the room next to the "folks" he'd returned to, temporarily, after his divorce.

At Cowtown she was loved, once, by "a cowboy with his own plane," she boasted once, or by the bouncer of this or that place, by men who were often tall, as Marshall was; they had to be to fit with her, to match her six feet and increasing weight. But the last ones before this "husband" weren't even tall. Who cared anyway, staggering out of the Saddlerack at three a.m., swaying around skinny lovers in doorways or between cars on a sad Friday, or Tuesday, or Saturday or whatever. Who cared anyway?

Remembering this I didn't tell her anything, or even laugh, when she said he was the worst she'd had—and she'd had a lot.

At five Jane deposited me and the children back at the "bird's nest," as Marshall called the peculiar barren perch that was our apartment, and I listlessly completed the task of feeding the children something and readying them way too early for bed. Doug was sleeping.

I had tried to interest Marshall in these special children. On the first, madly-in-love-night or two, "visiting" us, he'd tucked them in tenderly and momentarily made them his own. "Aren't her sheets damp, Page?" he'd asked. "She can't sleep like this." Hope had swelled, but afterwards he appeared to screen out any concern for them and concentrated solely on me.

At eight thirty he stopped by. "There's something missing," he sniffed, regarding me in a sort of drugged, compulsive, leering happiness over the bare Formica table, while his aura snapped red and third-eye-searing violet, electric with unspoken desire. He looked tired too, and almost resentful, as though helplessly dragged away from the routine and conservative reality he so much believed in.

"Missing?" I inquired, also wearied, and feeling the interlock on another level of fire-blue, auric rays that must bring, no matter what we had forsworn, another round.

He sniffed at me carnally, more his ascendant bull than solar ram at this moment. He regarded my person. I couldn't imagine what could be missing, even beneath his conservative, though lust-filled gaze. I was actually wearing a bra, and real shoes instead of Birkenstalks. I was becoming as plastic as I could be, as plastic as he, or his mother could wish, I thought, bent by the collision with his will, just as if, I fantasized ruefully tonight, I were a giant galactic body out of orb impacted by, reshaped and reshaping another…

"Page," he spoke sharply, though low and out of Doug's earshot. My attention reverted to further fears of rearrangement and revision. In addition to buying a new green shirt at a discount fashion shop, I had new underwear on and even a smidgeon of lipstick makeup stealthily purchased from the T G & Y next to Safeway.

"It's perfume, that's what it is, that's what's missing," he said, confirming the unthinkable. Weren't the posies of flowers I gave him, enough? Wasn't it enough that I now wore real deodorant again, and not the organic, good-for-you stuff from the health food store that, he pointed out, didn't work, but that I knew could not decompose your underarms. We at Daisy's church were striving to birth a new consciousness. He was regressing me into the solemn fifties. His eyes flashed, a brilliant pale chartreuse, seeming to grow closer—his nose to grow more prominent, like the ram's. He stroked the thick bovine neck—of his ascendant, not so subordinate to the sun. Lightening quick the tumescence rained opalescent liquids on the moon-bright, perfect new under things.

He leaned back against the windowsill, right into the ketchup-splattered plastic drapes, so ugly that I never pulled them closed. How could he not hate the dismal fact that the condiment had been left to harden on the drapes in a wild streak after Veronica, in one of her miserable upsets, had landed it there. He didn't seem to see the vivid red streak at all. Grateful for that, I put out the light and lit the candle with the window wide open and the fresh spring night air streaming in.

"Isn't this nice? It's not smoggy yet," I suggested.

He agreed, with the weariness of the ram or bull, exhausted and acute in its escalating rut. "When we grew up," he added, "all you smelled, even in late August were 'cots ripening and even further out the smell of sulfur from the drying sheds. Those were good times," he said sadly, powder grey, pale blue, fading chartreuse eyes bleeding into mine as if he longed to empty out his soul into some safe chalice.

When we grew up. We were the same age; only he was six months older. When we grew up. Suddenly the whole valley seemed ours, the invading stream of shiny, compact cars rolling night and day, up the ribbon of highway between San Jose and Santa Cruz now were our mutual problem, were our mutual joy when we were with them, could "blast off" for a drive to the mountains in his canary yellow Camaro—and the smog the cars created was the harbinger, for us both, of the loss of the "old times" when the Indian summer skies hadn't mutated yet to the white, alert-level, tasteless danger that kept children indoors and "blasting off" to a minimum.

After Doug woke up and finished picking up the sleeping children's room, he wandered uncertainly toward us. Marshall suddenly stood, his light head haloed by the bare ceiling light obscured by his height. "C'mon man." He guided Doug back the short distance into the living room. We all sat around uncertainly, me with Doug but on the opposite end of the vinyl couch, Marshall in an uncomfortable chair he had brought in with him, suspending it lightly in one hand while he carried it from one room to the other.

Guilt, lust and unease settled close in around us like the distant odor of yet-to-be-washed diapers in the plastic pail unevenly sealed and shut into the cupboard at the end of the hall. This would not be easy.

After her initial indifference, Daisy had kept infusing me with hard-line advice. "Sit down together, Page, do it, and put out exactly what you're feeling, each of you, and listen for truth as you speak, as you each speak. Do it—and you'll know what to do then—it will take care of itself." I'd fumbled around and tried to convey to her what I felt for him, but she'd burned out those unformed words with her laser-bright stare, her arched eyebrow jumping in rhythm to the word "ego" she whispered when I almost, once, hinted at the magnitude of my feelings.

Would my resolve to have her discussion, tonight, then "take care of" things? Would the long lingering of my breasts bubbling over my heart against his chest and belly in the guilt-drenched, opaque dark, would the lovely sweep of frenetic legs and hands, would the rich ferment of green and brown eyes and light hair and loamy openings to home he felt when he broke in and began his red, wrenching, phallic dance against his will, end then, tonight?

During the nights we had held to our resolve and even believed that it was over, the vivid memories of those electric nights we'd given way to, sputtered and pinged like bursting bulbs, resonating behind our eyes when we looked passed each other "as just friends," shocking the tips of our fingertips when we touched, "accidentally."

And when the three of us had driven around sometimes, with Marshall at the wheel of Doug's and my station wagon, with the back seats down and the babies free to play in the disarray, I sat between them, heat dripping from my thigh to Marshall's, riveted demurely against his body, conscious only of the rocking of the car and the little new alternate presses of his flesh against mine; I strained to feel him through my jeans and his slacks, glancing only briefly and then sidelong at his ruddied face and bleary eyes—unchanging as if he were in Daisy's deepest trance.

Doug, although lost in a horror of his own, had soaked up this heady camaraderie, often seemed drugged himself, looking up into Marshall's eyes as he did in awe, or grappling with him on a lawn when we stopped to picnic or play, or to air the kids at the park.

For a long time we sat this night in silence beneath the bright living room light before diving into Daisy's polemics. We each looked about the room—at the tattered, corner less posters, up at my attempt at hanging plants—somehow woebegone and dark here—and out through the screen less living room window. Even in the blaring light we felt a softness, an unspoken and subliminal pact that no one seemed ready to disrupt. Somehow we three needed each other in a way that the light of ordinary words would expose but not truly illuminate.

But, true to truth and to my liege, I made them speak out and say each what it was he wanted; I did the same. Doug wanted his wife, he flatly stated. Marshall stumbled, fiddling with the edge of the bird print as though bored, and then said slowly that what he wanted was one time together—with me—just one time without guilt, without...and then he trailed off, adding that of course he knew we were finished, and that I was Doug's wife, of course. I echoed Marshall's sentiments, carefully, and then Doug and Marshall and I stared around the room beneath the bright light, and Doug, looking grim, vicious and uneasy—why should he just now, he was getting what he wanted—said that it was growing late, and then we all laughed and talked about nothing for at least an hour more, looking covertly at each other as if we were flirting, wanting to hang on to...something.

Then Marshall and I, who had been looking away from each other all night, began to look, and Doug was like a shadow in the room between us, a ghost, to whose presence we gave terrible homage. Was Elizabeth right, I suddenly wondered? She'd said a love triangle included an element of attraction between the same sexed individuals, that we were all sixty-forty—it was so confusing.

"It's late. I should go." Marshall sat unmoving in his uncomfortable chair, diddling with the bird drape, glowering at me occasionally as if it were my fault and as if I were the deliberate source of some awful discomfort. "Ok folks, I should go. Really, I don't have to work tomorrow but I'm sure you two want to hit the sack."

I looked at Doug. His face was ashen, mysterious. We were breaking his heart. I felt unreasonably angry at him.

"Yes, I guess so."

"We can't resolve this now, can we?" I rescinded our earlier agreements.

"Noooo," Marshall drawled, tapping his large, neat deck shoe impatiently on our uneven carpet. "We'll have to finish this later." He rose and tucked his shirt into the top of his faded jeans. "Maybe tomorrow," he added grimly.

"Or you could stay here—I mean it's late and we could continue this tomorrow—right away."

"I could," he laughed, and then turned away and picked up his light jacket from the couch.

Doug's head was downcast. Then he giggled. "No—no way!" But he looked up, happy and excited and flushed. I had moved closer to Marshall who was standing by the door.

"Well, wait a minute, let me think about this," Doug piped helplessly. "It is getting late," he rejoined as nervously as a bride, and began tidying round, turning off the overhead light at the switch. That seemed to be our signal to file under the only light in the hall toward the bed. "Oh, all right," Doug murmured feverishly, "it's all right if we all sleep here, until morning."

By the light of the one pink candle I lit on the dresser top, Doug's eyes wore a grim, haunted, secretive look, and a smile that seemed eerie. "Oh all right," I echoed. "Well, let's get to sleep," someone said.

Marshall already had his shirt off and stood over us in his white, white, underwear and T-shirt, looking silly, looking large. Then they stepped to the bureau to bend together over the candle, Doug carving at it with a little knife to brighten the wick. Marshall sat on the bed while Doug carefully brushed the candle shavings into his hand to place them in the wastebasket. Doug completed his task, Marshall took his socks off and laid his big gold Expandex watch with them near his shoes. Doug, finally finished, breathed audibly and disrobed in a manner imitating his best friend's.

At last we lay in and out of the sheet and the old brown bedspread while candlelight danced across these, blowing uncertain light across the surfaces of long lean legs with light hair, over faces folded into hands, and over our exposed backs.

"Goodnight," Marshall intoned, grasping my flesh for a moment to emphasize his greeting before parting formally into sleep. His hand pressed like a big paw; ever his first caress felt unfamiliar or distorted. He pulled away. I lay without breath.

The candle sputtered. Doug stretched cold, grey by the dim light, slinking his hand over my thigh. I felt the left side of my body recoil and lay, unmoving. Then Doug pushed his hand way across my lower back, brushing Marshall's body for a moment and then drawing, clammily back to rest his cold fingers against my spine. Marshall—turned toward me from the other side—began to nuzzle me a little. He seemed honestly unaware of what he was doing. But Doug imitated him somehow, and soon their bodies, so dissimilar, worked against mine. Marshall traced his fingertip down the curve of my throat, and I watched, mercifully detached and distant from the place where I lay on my back between them in the bed. I saw myself arch slightly and my entire right side move toward the heat where Marshall moved with stubborn control, imperceptivity against me.

Doug became active, abruptly kissing me with cold, unpleasant lips; his sparse moustache scratched the cleft above my lip. I acquiesced and supported his movements, encouraging him by mechanically stroking his back while he lay across me. He retreated. Marshall swooped up once and kissed me quickly, opening my mouth, circling its radius with his broad, insistent tongue. Then he drew back and lay as though asleep, rigidly quiet.

Doug repeated Marshall's kiss, as if he were a young bird being taught by an elder (or a counselor) how to fly, or to eat for the first time, and he kissed me quickly again with cold lips, leaving me covered with a moist drool. When Doug made a show of kissing me again, drawing it out longer than the last, Marshall played his hand stealthily across my lower belly and I felt the familiar wall of heat begin to rise—and as if outside of myself, allowed it to overcome the rasping irritation I had learned to feel at Doug's touch. Marshall toyed harder with my body, spearing my leg through crisp shorts stretched taut like a military tent, and already congealed, at the tip of the spear, with moisture.

"Doug, are you all right?" I asked, deeply concerned. "I'm fine," came the muffled, wild, unfamiliar voice as though from across the room. Marshall ran his hand up my belly to the underside of my breast. Doug possessively cupped the other breast with his hand that felt unevenly callused and butter soft at the same time. He gripped harder and I winced. Marshall responded supportively, gently sweeping his broad hand over my shoulder, down my arms and into a wide arc that ended with his hand confronting Doug's. Doug released my breast. Marshall caressed its soft slope languidly, with one finger, so that Doug could see.

"A woman's body," he said, with a catch in his throat, "is like silk. You touch her slowly, first, like this." Doug complied with the wishes of his mentor. Marshall led Doug doggedly from this caress, through some of the strangest sex I had known. I did not retain the memory of all of it after, but was fairly certain that Doug was above me and allowed to attempt the connubial act while my lips and mouth were being eaten by Marshall's tongue, while he pressed his ram's love into me from above, and that I surrendered to a state that defied usual memory.

There are fragments; being rotated and ridden in tandem with kisses from the hot and the awkward, with caresses that seemed somehow yellow and red, and of someone—me I think— whispering, unceasingly afraid for him, "Doug, are you all right," only to have a robot choke back again, "Nothing's wrong."

But I remember somehow too, when Doug had had his due— or tried to, after a long, frustrated chafing—that he left for the living room. Did Marshall make him? For it was Marshall with whom I mated in the blue white predawn, in a mutual mental state in which all terrible thinking was eclipsed and eradicated by the sharp sensory interplay, by the licking of rippling yonic lips and phallic tip, of boundary-less breast and chest, of fingers circling and angrily gripping light brown and pale blond Grecian hair, until, when Doug returned, there was some sleep and then clear recognition only when I stood somewhere near my tortured young husband in the bathroom in the morning. There he had taken me aside while Marshall dressed, and I bantered with him in that tone of gay insane abandon with which we had approached the bedroom, lest the final guilt that hung for me in abeyance, like a voluminous, weighted, medieval curtain, would heavily drop, and blot out the new light.

Doug Mitchel

Chapter Twenty Two

On Thursday night she was waiting there for me. I had driven down to the church through the old, windy, palm-lined streets near the Egyptian museum, racing between the shadows cast by the monolithic trees, ragged, bleary-eyed, tearful and ashamed—at the same time ignited and lilting beneath the moonlight dancing over the old pavement, spliced by the shadows into a luminous moving picture of hope. I was enamored of the moon, as of the sun, and I was sure that Marshall would be my eternal companion, that I was ready to storm the Bastille and enter. *That's all I've been missing,* I thought—*a mate!*

She met me at the door to the kitchen side of the church, its back but real focal point. She smoked, long, languid puffs—in, out, filling the dark sky. I looked up at her from the parking lot three long steps below. The sky dissolved into nothingness behind her—she was so bright.

"We—ell, so you want to speak to me."

I felt as if I had traveled hundreds of miles by flying "shoe ship" in Atlantis to confront a goddess, a priestess of the highest order.

And now tell me about love, oh great mentor.

I would be coy. I had all the cards, after all.

"So," she looked up into the sky over my head. She could never look interested in anything anymore until it was brought to her, like curious captives from foreign lands were brought to their liege for scrutiny.

"I haven't that much to tell," I murmured, for once really being smooth. Why not? Soon I would be in, the Bastille doors folded down for me to enter across.

"I hear you haven't been coming to the reassociation sessions."

"Haven't been coming? Who told you that?"

"Never mind," she said, in the whisper soft voice she sang in.

Amy, I read psychically through the syllable. Shit. Tears immediately filled my eyes.

"I have too," I kept myself from blubbering. There's no way I would go in now, not on the verge of tears. I felt guilty thinking that way. Honesty. Honesty is what she taught. Being all that you are unflinchingly at any given moment.

"You haven't been coming," she reiterated with a faint note of triumph. "Oh haven't I?" I said firmly, in defiance, at least a shadow of the fine princess I was in that long ago lifetime—in so many long ago lifetimes, when my powers rivaled or surpassed hers.

You're damned right I haven't been coming to some of the meetings—to the ones you assured me I didn't have to attend. You know what I've been doing at night, Daisy; you manipulated me into Marshall's bed, into someone's bed, I thought. Dealing with my attractions was the last act that meant the ministry for me. That, and these stupid reassociation sessions.

You're not going to pull that on me again, I worried. *That— here's the carrot, Page; now you see it, now you don't shit—no, not...please,* I pleaded with her in my thoughts.

"You told me to come to one of the meetings per week— that's all." She wasn't even humble enough to ask—Oh, did I?— the way some people do who forget things and are proud.

Her lack of response and the further curling of the silvery smoke told me, however, that I was on firm ground, that I was right at least—she had said that I had only to come one night of the two. But I knew that. Why was I wondering? Her presence confused me utterly.

Still she wouldn't unblock the doorway, and I had to look at her for three more minutes before she deigned to whirl around and leave at last—I had to stand there before her looking fully like a numbskull before she would let me pass.

Inside, she softened, suddenly brimming with ease and good cheer. "I would say that we're a special group, don't you think?" she tossed over her shoulder from the storage closet at the end of the long room that led to the passageway into the church.

"Oh sure," I answered, caught up despite myself in her flouncy tailwind as if in a stream of sparklers.

She brought a new white pot set and a bag of Miracle Grow potting mix from the cupboard. "Why don't we repot that poor baby by the window," she suggested.

"Sure." For seven years, anything done for Daisy had been a privilege, like painting Tom Sawyer's fence.

While we cracked the pot and slipped out the squeezed bulbous clump of roots inside, Daisy chatted.

"Ohhh"—she flipped her fingers away from the muddy ball—" It's mad at me for leaving it here so long," she said in baby talk, sucking the tip of her thumb.

I anchored the fat ball of dirt and jellylike roots for her. She strained, then freed one side of the mass from the other by running her fingers through the tangles the way she must through Sam's ultra wavy hair, I thought. We all had the unisex, layered haircuts now. They looked best on Daisy and Rebecca and Sam—on people who had curly hair. I admired Daisy's golden waves and her gold glasses that picked up the light from the overhead fixture and flashed it back to me.

"How're things going with you, sweetheart? This business can be pretty rough, I know."

"Oh, ok." Then words poured out. "At first I felt like a lady of the evening, you know, running from bed to bed before dawn. And now…" .A great white shadow, moon dark and deep, rose upward into the cache at the base of my throat and choked me. "…Oh, Daisy…But I'm not suffering from lack of sleep," I tried to joke. Was it out of place?

"Marshall," I ventured shyly, "is different than when you knew him, Daisy. He's able to nail me, lots of times." That was one of her all time favorite concepts—that one person could ignite another to self-confrontation through the power of the word—that truth, once spoken, must live.

"Oh." She was making two new plants of the one that had become root bound, trying one pot and then another.

She didn't seem to hear. There was so much I needed to tell her. Two faint lines creased either side of her mouth. Her shoulders were bare except for thin dress straps and her tan was reddish and golden already. Lines made a lazy pattern down her neck. She looked up through glasses that, since she wore them for nearsightedness, enlarged her already dominant blue eyes even more.

"Did you do what I told you to do? Did you all three, together, punch out with what is really happening for you in this?"

"Yes, Daisy, we did."

"Well? What happened?" A direct, if glassy look.

"Well, we ummm…ended up—but that was not what we said at the beginning—we all ended up staying there together."

Seeing the wry, knowing look I went on, mustering up a giggle and a nonchalant air.

"We…all stayed there, and we tried…oh it didn't really work out like that or anything…I guess a sort of stupid orgy or something."

"So it's just physical?" She got up and went to the cupboard for more dirt. Doubt, like mutant moonbeams, lurched up. *Just physical?* The turmoil of that…the disappointment…the dirtiness, unraveled the order of my thoughts—what order could there be around Daisy—and I forgot to tell her what we had said before Marshall and I forgot ourselves.

"All I want," Marshall had pleaded, "is one time with you without guilt, one time without the turmoil, one time," he had implored, sitting across from me in the little boxlike apartment living room, "one time alone with you, one time for us."

Maybe that was why we eventually decided to lie, but not until I tried to: "act from the spirit of my being" a while longer. I would live the truth or die. After Daisy separated the daughter from the mother plant, I left.

Elizabeth scheduled a conference for Santa Maria again, this time at the Madonna Inn. Doug and I interested Marshall in coming. Marshall remembered the trip all of us had taken to the Santa Maria Inn in 1972. For this venture, we used our station wagon, threw our clothes together. I acted charming, wearing perfume too and despising myself for that far more than for any strange interlude I'd experienced lately in the interest of truth. Marshall had to make a weekend service call at a restaurant that was out of our way. The owner treated us to lunch. The children threw things across the table and cried in the car when we started out again.

"No," Marshall said, driving, when we were almost to the freeway. "What these kids need first is a nap." Veronica writhed next to me in the back seat. I tried to stifle her, calling to her to stop. But it was all going wrong. Molly sat in front with Marshall and Doug instead of me—a concession to Doug, who was still at the stage of wanting to share his wife, although of course we had agreed not to. It was as though Marshall was married to both of us, also as if we were the three musketeers living out a freedom no one of us had known.

Marshall carried Veronica up the concrete stairs and into her room to rest with Molly. When she couldn't sleep, he brought her into "our" bed and rubbed her thin little back and patted her head. Then he "painted her face," as his folks had done when he was a little boy, tracing an imaginary clown's face onto hers—with special attention to the reddened little forehead, banged and bruised so many times from what the neurologist had called "ataxia". She finally curled into sleep around his big hand. Doug watched this, a little boy himself in so many respects, and so impervious to what we both were witnessing.

But I felt as if God's good grace were walking in our apartment in shoes from the Big and Tall. "That poor little gal was tired," Marshall murmured. "You know," he said, even more quietly to me when Doug went into the kitchen for something, "when she was screaming like that I thought she might belong in an institution or something; and she looks like a little rug rat...but now...."

"Oh Marshall." I felt the guilt harden about me like the ketchup on the infamous curtains—but I felt as if I were his woman now, guilty...but his, struggling towards the hope of him like a drowning woman toward the dry land, or one of the unsinkable ships in his lithographs. "Oh, Marshall, it's true—I'm glad you can see—she's so sweet, and sad." My eyes asked him further to help, to take us up onto his ship. He would think about it. I **knew** he was thinking about it, but had not decided, was ringed all about by a bright crystaline new feeling for me, more intense than he had ever felt, and that he was determined to taste the feeling, in his natural Arien selfishness, no matter what; but I felt that there was something else, a possibility...

We scrapped the trip.

The days wore on, long and spring balmy. Beautiful, beautiful days when I was up long and arose early, greeting the dawn in my green sweater—just Marshall and I—off somewhere in the early early morning. How I wished it would be a permanent thing. I dreamed, but I feared more than I dared dream. Things were too good to be true. I felt that I had come up for air after drowning, or been given the sun, like a little plant in a dark room, grown yellowed and beginning to die. With him, life was different, and beautiful. We lay out in deck chairs in front of his place or played tennis in the late springtime, our faces ruddied. Panting, we ambled up the long sloping pathway back up to his plush apartment on the hillside.

Did everything have a season, I wondered? Did time, in turns, rain happiness like this on everyone? I wasn't sleeping with him, that wasn't the issue—I still believed in perfect honesty, in struggling for truth, and that truth was magic, like Daisy, and would solve everything. I knew that I cared for him, was that emotion as primitive and fumbling as Daisy thought?

At the Sunday morning minister's training meeting—I kept trying—held earlier this day, we had defined abstract concepts esoterically.

"What is 'being in love,' Daisy?"

Disdain. Daisy put me off, answered the next person's question, not mine.

"Daisy." I was full of sunshine anticipating the day and wouldn't be stopped, though the dark feeling of shame and inferiority lurked on. "What is 'being in love'?"

"Leave it to you to ask that, sweetheart."

What a primitive, over-feeling cow I must be, I thought, as Daisy (obviously disgusted) embarked on a reasonably clever definition. A sudden speculation, though, like sunlight, broke through the freeze of self-consciousness. Oh, I could see Rebecca rap her pencil on her chair arm, and examine one silver-sandaled foot that tapped the donated rug in utter boredom; I could see Amy's hands, angelically clasped, patting straight blonde wisps of hair into place, mercifully suppressing chimes of agreement with her sister, until that sister had at least spoken. But I was away and wondering, *didn't Daisy look nervous—could she be? Could it be she doesn't know what love is?* In awe of Daisy—and in this room with these people—it was as if I were looking at a towering, living monolith 58 stories tall at least, asking these questions. But the question stubbornly remained: Did she know what it's like to be in love with **someone**—not just with truth?

"And it's the sustaining of these energies," Daisy finished her definition. I could give a damn. As the monolith towered over me, I hid my ungainly, smitten self in the thought of the frothy white fizzes we would drink on Marshall's redwood balcony this afternoon.

Now, resting after tennis on that balcony, he touched me with his toe. "Woops—I can't do that anymore, can I?" We were in remission again. We had promised Doug and ourselves, hadn't we?

I went home, crisp and polite, didn't touch him. That seemed to appease Doug, although he was still strangely gracious about my being alone with the blond giant.

"He's just a whale," Doug reassured himself. "He's hollow inside." We laughed, became a unit again, fused together by Marshall. In the bed where we all agreed to sleep the second time, there was some experimental touching and the carnal burning of Marshall next to me and then it happened all over again.

Sure, when I touched Marshall, the horns of the ram tangled up in live wire bored and riveted me like the hapless victim of a great shock. But if it had been "just physical" as Daisy had said, then I would have gotten out of the bed the three of us had slept in disgust—out of the bed in which Marshall functioned like a sex-therapist, to ease his guilt I guessed? If it weren't happening to me, I might have laughed.

On Thursday I showed up at the dark church early. Amy arrived with the key and let me in. I was *allowed* to help her make coffee. Last Thursday night I'd been alone with Amy and the reassociatee also. Where were Sam and Jade? And why was Daisy giving Amy the authority to conduct sessions without her? What had changed?

Amy recounted smugly how there'd been this important session on Tuesday night of last week. "A lot of policies got set; Sam and I and Jade were here—in the energy of that—you know?" I submitted for now, because I thought I was going to become a part of the group of couples who got together at Daisy and Sam's for dinner and games, who might be just people together twice a week. Conversely, I submitted because I believed I was going to "fly," as Daisy demanded when I'd come to her again, miserable

and confused after the last time with Doug and Marshall—
submerged in the feeling of being dirty.

"Instead of worrying about either of these two men," she had
admonished, "why don't you fly, go for Spirit?" Only now where
were my wings? To be a reassociator was a beginning, a tap into
the intense enthusiasm I'd had as a nineteen-year-old—who wanted
to teach the world.

Tonight Daisy walked in, dropped her keys and asked Amy if
there was coffee yet.

"Sure darlin'," drawled Amy for some reason. No matter, I
could take it awhile longer.

During the weekdays when the children where napping, I'd
walk around the apartment. Its uneven floors creaked. I'd look out
the big picture window with plastic drapes sagging to one side on
the rod not even Doug, ingenious and industrious as he was, could
brace until the landlord gave us new materials to replace the old.
On those afternoons I'd pace and look out—the sky seemed so
white, creamy. It seemed to want to sweep me out into it where I
could read the future of the stars and of the people who played out
the dramas on earth linking them to those celestial stars.

I knew I had come from one of them, knew that I was one of
the host of angelic beings that fell from the morning, or from the
time, as Cayce put it, when the morning stars sang together in the
beginning when we were angelic beings not separated, as from the
loving Father/Mother God—in the way kindergartners at a school
where Elizabeth once taught, had dreamed. (We were all Elizabeth's
children, weren't we, kindergartners alike telling her our dreams?)
One child had dreamed she was in a great boat in the heavens,
comfortable and joyous, but that the boat tipped over and that they
plunged into the earth. The child didn't say "into," she said "onto,"
but I knew what she meant, because Elizabeth had told it to me,
told me the true story. Elizabeth had always told me the true story.
Suddenly I remembered Elizabeth trying to tell me about Daisy at
the last Asilomar conference: "Daisy won't let anybody lead or
teach who could outshine her."

Daisy had said—ironically, since she was the one who had
suggested sex with another man in the first place—why don't you
forget about both of these men and FLY! It sounded great but I
could only dimly understand what she meant. Fly, where? Where

could I fly? I could plunge deeply into the affairs of the church and still not fly, because I lacked the courage to tell Daisy that I wanted even a class of my own. Where could I fly? I watched a moth slowly buffet the plate glass window. Where could it fly? Where could I fly?

In May, Ambrose Wales would be coming up again from Los Angeles—this time without Elizabeth—to conduct an Atlantis seminar. Driving alone on the way to the church the next day, I determined to take a greater part in things. Ambrose had always wanted to stay with Doug and me. Now he'd written that he wanted us to drive him to San Francisco so he could take slides of the Palace of Fine Arts, whose architecture, he said, reflected the styles of the late Atlantean Island of Poseidia. Swinging from 17 onto 280, looking up into the bright blear of the early morning, yet overcast sky, I called out to the most high, to the Creative Forces, for help—I would fly!

There, carved in the wide, spacious clouds blown from Santa Cruz sea breezes, I saw the faces of the three of them—no four— Rebecca and Amy about a greater Daisy, and in the background, Jade. This tableau, this frieze, floated above all those who journeyed beneath the heavens like a Goddess Mt. Rushmore. Elevated and enormous and serious they were watching me now, overshadowing me, as if they were the most high. "How long, how long are you going to let us do this to you?" they cried kindly down the fierce rushing wind corridors of mind, as if they loved me, angrily, as if they rued their earthly actions, woefully, as if I would not listen— "HOW LONG?"

When I entered through the back kitchen door of the church, they all were talking about Ambrose Wales, where he would stay. "I'll put him up," I offered abruptly. Gathered about the table at the morning business meeting at the church they all looked at me quite dubiously: Daisy, Rebecca, Amy and Jade sat grouped together at the end of the long table flanked by Sam, Peter, Connie, Stephen, Patsy, Mary Grace, Yvette, Chad, Kendra, Russell and a man I didn't know, who made jewelry in Santa Cruz and was lately "in" with Daisy and Sam. Now they all looked at me as though I wouldn't do it right. I stared back, resolute.

Ambrose B. Wales

Ambrose Wales was my friend. Now I couldn't have any doubts about my ability to undertake this simple responsibility or any other. Sure, there was a time when I might have spoken out before thinking things through, but times had changed. Throughout the spring I had kept the bundles of Daisy missives flowing to the Meridian Post Office like skaters sailing across a glassy lake, and the flyers reached their destinations: Area B or C without a hitch. I knew the zip codes by heart: Los Angeles proper, 90065, Los Gatos, 95030, and so on. It didn't seem fair. Still the looks in their eyes brought self-hate. How could one be distorted in so many mirrors? I would talk to Daisy about it.

It took me three days. The words like the gravel stuck with the gum that the kids dropped outside in the nursery parking lot, pained me and came up and down in my throat like poison I knew I had swallowed, but that it was too late to regurgitate. I felt as if I were a leper, a hideous cancer patient, pathetic and that no one should see.

Acacia, the Mexican girl who now acted as receptionist and never did a dish, as I would be expected to do during the Atlantis seminar in May, had burnished the door to Daisy's office once a week with Liquid Gold, and it could have been the entrance to the boy ruler Tutankhaton's tomb. Perhaps Acacia thought of this as she rubbed. Posters of Egypt were everywhere inside the temple room, flanking the altar. Daisy was "clicked into" Egypt again.

But did Acacia know, did Daisy, what I knew—and **some** things, I knew that I knew. Elizabeth had speculated that the little king Tutankhaton—the boy king—might have been a former incarnation of Jesus. So that after the opening of "King Tut's" tomb, people had reacted on a soul memory level to the mystery surrounding this elder brother, whose life—whose lifetimes—had created a pattern for us to follow.

When Daisy did not answer my knock, I pushed the glowing, golden door open. She sat—unusual in itself—at the desk chair. Usually she perched, lightly, on the edge of the desk, dragging her cigarette in the most Californian manner, and I admired her no end. This time she sat, as impassive as the great face of Isis in Daisy's favorite, huge, poster.

Did she expect me?

"What do you want, Page?" Total disgust, I could hear it. So the gravel stuck, eclipsed reason.

"What I want to know," I eked out the hideous request around the mound of gravel and bilge inside me. "What I want to know is why there are people around here who do less for you than I, people whom you haven't known as long—it's been seven years, hasn't it, Daisy?" *Whom you let rub your door,* I wanted to say but couldn't. "Who are becoming the counselors, the readers, the teachers."

I felt shame and self-disgust. I criticized myself roundly before she could. How jealous, to compare myself with others, but I couldn't stop: "**They** are teachers."

"They are teachers," she repeated with different emphasis. Daisy stood up and looked through the little green-curtained window that gave her a view from her office into the back of the sanctuary, into the temple room.

"Look, you're talking about teachers. Is that all you want to be? There is something better in store for you," she murmured. "To teach is merely to impart knowledge on a mental level; to be a minister is to Be the Living Life. Which do you want? No, something inside you compels you to go the distance. And your desire to lead—your ego—keeps you learning the humility of being in the background. That's it, isn't it, Page, isn't it really? Look at me."

She looked at me and the supportive technique to naming truth—the "psychic grin"—worked, to my dismay. Her eyes provoked a ripply grin that we all had believed to be as she had explained it: a thought form bubble created in the lower self's desires only and not matching the true purposes of the soul and its expression, had burst and released the energies of Spirit, unblocking the whole Being. I sat grinning, nervous and crying behind my eyes. I recognized enough truth in the technique to walk away—Daisy never said goodbye to anybody—through the golden doorway of her office, and out into the sunlight where I sat on the wide outside steps that led into the church.

Only then did I realize that I hadn't really talked to her in dishes and doubts specifics about the seminar. I'd only committed, somehow, to go on like this, and there was no going back at the moment. I would have Ambrose B. up, of course, and I would have to do it under the great grey pall of submissive self-doubt that I had allowed Daisy to throw around me through the doubting eyes of her followers. I felt as heavy as the cement I sat on, and as cold as the ground beneath it.

Chapter Twenty Three

"Wake up. You were dreaming."

Marshall sat across from me in his big, bent wood rocker on its swivel base. "Want another drink?" It was good Doug still wanted me to see Marshall, now that he believed we weren't having sex.

"Sure." (Me? Say that?)

"Were you listening to me, Page? I was telling you that the way they're doing things down there is just politics." I guessed that "politics," was an "in", popular expression now in the earth—once in a blue moon I watched the news. But like a drowning person emerging onto rough sands, I didn't know what to grab onto. The water was what I knew.

"Politics, Marshall? How can that really be true? Wait a minute, maybe I haven't explained about the church clearly enough. Daisy always asks to be guided to truth. She follows her intuition always. She would give up anything for truth. I've seen it, I know it."

Marshall smiled at me. "Then why have you been there for seven years, studying to be a teacher, right, and you've never once taught anything—except you've taught me more in these few weeks than anybody. I've been in a hole since my divorce."

"Because I couldn't take responsibility," I cut in. "It's true, Marshall. I have to admit that when they gave me little jobs to do, when they first started things, I never followed through. I had two babies then, but still…"

"That was seven years ago. You were a nineteen-year-old kid when you met them. Page, you're a beautiful person, and who knows, who knows what could happen if you left, the way you told me five minutes ago you might. It came out of your mouth. And I think it's the only breath of fresh air that's come out of that place for a month of Sundays. They have you leaving your own kids to go down there three times a week to put out her lousy mailer so she can lariat in a few more suckers."

"Marshall!"

He crashed his way on. "And you've done a damn good job. Sure, she's patted you on the back a few times, just to keep you going—that gal is something else. But you...you're a twenty-seven-year-old woman, baby. And on that subject..." He held up his glass to the light of the Tiffany shade he'd procured with some sharp trading not too long ago. He looked into the wine glass as if he were hunting down the flecks, the motes that drifted and fell through the amber wine.

"**You are a lover**." He seemed so sure of himself now. "Come here," he said. Was this the hulking, nervous humorist who had paced their apartment on an ocean of Fridays and worried why things weren't working out with Gina, or DeeDee, or whomever. Maybe I had helped him, taught him. On his lap in the chair, I didn't have to worry about being too tall, too big for him. I felt like a crumb of bread on an oversized saucer plucked up by a fleshy, gold-ringed hand and popped into the mouth of a red-side-burned, yellow-haired Gulliver with good taste, with superlative taste in Tiffanies, in oak, and in other things.

The way I enjoyed him alarmed me anew.

"Let it be," the Beatles sang through the crystal clear stereo radio. "Listen, Marshall."

I tried to distract his attention back to the real meaning of things. He traced my high-boned cheek with his big hard finger, hugging me to him and then, like a wine glass, tipped me back away from him and opened my mouth very gently. The rocker almost toppled as he kissed into me. *Like an overripe fruit* I thought, *slit by an antique, marble-handled knife.* I could see his gun case behind him when I opened my eyes to try to breathe again. Oak, too, its glass face stared out proudly up at me, two or three perfectly chosen pieces facing from the display. There would be more, I knew, picked up here or there, swirled into his atmosphere like psychic knives drawn back to the wizard of morning. To the red wizard of the dawn.

Daisy talked of wizards. Not this man. But wasn't he one? Transforming me into a partner in this crime of waking me up to morning. A sadness was forming in my reddened forehead; a crisp tight guilt raided the liquid flesh—mine—that he was pouring into himself.

"Marshall. What about Doug?" Like a light flipped on he stopped, the ravaging giant scaled down to a handsome young man in a business suit in a king-sized rocker on the top floor of a condominium-style apartment; just waiting to be told what he could do next, just waiting to upsurge against this woman, his pretty, carefully wrought piece, the satisfying acquisition of this moment.

He would be proud of me today: my own stained glass lamp hangs illumined above my antique, round oak table. Suspended in time, he lives in memory like a giant oak arm that lifted me into another time away from that captivating witch. It took a wizard to stop the roots embedded in my soul's experience from sprouting out new runners in Daisy's direction.

Daisy was like a gossamer kite tail to which I was attached. I was growing up and I needed to fly. I became increasingly aware that this was no way to live whenever I spent time with Marshall.

As I was about to leave that night, when we stood together lingering on the landing, his wan blue eyes emanating a weak resolve that I saw he could keep, I knew, suddenly, that the truest move I could make was to lie. Despite what Daisy said it would be kinder to Doug. And in his eyes there was the relief when we decided—there in the doorway—we weren't finished, but the ragged ruining of the man we both cared about must end.

Beside Marshall that night after making love again I heard the clock bong, a good, strong, peaceful bong. I could smell the clean leathery scent of the living room furniture. I felt the impression of his heavy body in the bed, longed anew for something solid and believed anew that the exuberant happiness of a strong companion could be mine too, and not Daisy's and Amy's or Rebecca's alone. They appeared to have joy, always smiling solicitously at their man-mates who catered to them, and yet were the strong council, the backbone, of their decisions. The Tuesday morning business meetings were still conspicuously void of active male participants, but the men were in and out from the printers and some, Jade's new man Russell mainly, tried to shake the present order. Russell foiled himself, however, because—I could see it—he was as eager as a child—as I—for her wonderful acceptance. He was tall, thin with a dramatic mouth and upside-down eyes. He leaned close to her and made jokes too fast—one after another in a row—and brushed the medium brown hair just going to grey, away from his face.

"But why, why, Daisy, does it have to be that way? I can't see why I can't be a minister when I want to? You claim that Sam is a minister now because you are 'one energy' and whatever you have manifested, has manifested in him. Some people minded when Sam became a minister"—Russell swept the gaze from his gleaming, white-showing-beneath-the-copper irised eyes over me once, and forgot me. The point was made.

But Daisy just laughed. I could see Russell flush. He had been a school teacher and now was talking about a school for the church children—well, for Anson anyway—so that he would never have to tred the dangerous concrete hallways of the schools "out there" in "the world."

"Oh Christ, Daisy, can't you see? I've paid my dues too. Just because I'm a man…"

Sam passed the table with a stack of fresh flyers laced with his latest, intricate art nouveau border designs. He smiled happily at Daisy. "We'll have to give Russell something to do too, won't we Rebecca? All that Leo energy needs some kind of outlet, don't you think?"

That might have sounded patronizing to Russell but I knew that the women were the guardians, the keepers of the flame and they believed, as taught by Daisy, that you had to earn and demonstrate your ability and readiness for that trust. They had a healthy fear of the strong-armed shove of the men who had crushed their spirits in other lifetimes, if not in this one. They were careful about who did what and what he did.

"Just because you can shove and because you're a man is not a guarantee here, Russell; you have to be ready." I had muttered this to him after the meeting when we met accidentally alone in the red-carpeted, day-cool temple room.

Now Marshall stirred, the indentation in the mattress broadened even more. He smiled in his sleep. I touched his back and stroked the flesh that felt like anything of Marshall's you could feel with your hands, or even with your mind, large and eager, new young man and comfortable. He strained for something in his sleep, strained to speak then dove deep into sleep again, like a stone settling under the swollen waters of a river. The restless virility of his youth drew him to a turbulence of emotion in me that I think he would have shunned in stodgier maturity.

When I saw him once since then he was fatter, dim somehow in that restaurant. He waved me away as fast as he could so that I could not alarm his short, dark-haired, plump, curious, older wife. I thought of the eager, prancing boy, realized that something had been lost.

The choir in white tops swayed in front of the real and artificial shrubbery behind the altar. Daisy rose into the room from the back door like the scent of an outdoor rose coming in, so sweet. I had scurried in late, face lightly tanned, wearing a new, bright green, short-sleeved blouse and slid down into the middle of one of the pews. Now the beat rose and presaged something great.

"Rejoice in the Lo-ord ah-al-ways, and again I say, rejoice," sang the choir. After that Sam swung into "Brother Love's Traveling Salvation Show." To "Ho-ot August night," Daisy thumped her dainty feet on the plush ribbon of red that overlaid the wall-to-wall, deep red carpet.

She swung into motion, like somebody long experienced, secure in her popularity. The jubilant, self-consciously humble faces of the newer choir members (new since I had bowed out) swung toward her and cast their eyes down, very aware, as I had once been, that they were being watched. Outside a spring bird trilled a magnificent harmony to the muted "ooohs" and "ahhs" Sam synchronisticly brought up with a wave of his broad, tanned hand under the perfect white of his new choirmaster-minister's robe.

When the choir subsided, Daisy breathed deeply, *like a showman,* I thought. *I would never never dare to do that.* Her words, as though drawn from somewhere else, much higher, rained on the group, and especially on me, with hypnotic clarity. I could not stop listening, could not stop thinking that she was speaking to me, to the prodigal daughter.

Her smile, understated and fleeting, conveyed great wisdom and restraint. Oh, I could not be sure of anything now. Maybe today would be the day. I had done everything required, everything she required of me. With the sweat of my other palm I polished my blue lapis, special stone ring. The women's voices, now, alone wove a high unobtainable trill and a mellow alto honey into the brash burnished gold of the hardworking amateur tenors, baritones, and the one lonely bass, Wayne, still singing, still working Ford's midnight shift and giving all of his money to Daisy.

After, I passed through the adoring throngs in this unfamiliar and uneasy-smelling glory hall. People crowded the kitchen, the gravel parking lot. Amy called to me to check to see that no children played about the railroad tracks. "You be in charge of shifts—some mother should be there—you'll do it won't you?" The sneer she didn't know she had, followed. Oh how stupid she was. *I am undercover,* I thought. Somewhere outside my burning embryonic longing "to fly", life continued on as usual, and Amy probably thought she was doing me a favor, to throw me that crumb.

In the sunlight I stood near enough to Sam for him not to notice, but to derive some comfort from his presence. It had been a long time since we'd talked. I insinuated myself so that he and I were nearly back to back, separated by two or three feet of space. Then two little kids came between us and huddled together there over something interesting they'd brought from the basement nursery. I walked toward Wayne, ahead of me turned away, talking to Vince who, jilted by Jade for Russell, made a habit lately of listening to anyone's bitter complaints about anything the church hierarchy was doing. Jade was definitely part of the hierarchy now. I'd walked into the church one day to see her face the altar while Daisy murmured over her, "And the last shall be first," just as she had implied to me at Rebecca's house three years earlier.

I halted, toed at the gravel and eaves dropped.

"...an $850.00 merry-go-round—not one that you'd ride on or anything, man—" Wayne drawled, troubled, "but just a pretty little thing you'd hold in your hand—a music box or somethin'. I saw it... When I went over't their place to weld a pipe for Sam in the big old house the church bought them...that thing wasn't any bigger than my hand. She-it, man. I've worked for more than merry-go-rounds, haven't I?"

Wayne squinted at the sun. Wayne didn't get time or many "invites," as he put it, to go and sunbathe with those who made a practice of that stuff, though he had a well-formed, manly body beneath his spare-haired head. And without his glasses, with a good tan, he could have been comparable to some of the others. Did Daisy like the sun because it turned her golden and made her look better? How banal of me to wonder, but the fact was that Daisy turned herself golden and it enriched her looks. And she wore gold now—

lots of it—more and more. Yes, she still wore significant stones to accomplish significant purposes, but all hung from or were cast in gold.

"It was a purdy little thing," pleaded Wayne, "and she said that we sustain her, the Overall Body does, man." (Now he sounded as if he were arguing with his doubts, fighting his shadow, too.) "I guess the idea is that she attracts to herself that stuff that belongs to her 'to lift up her spirit'—I guess that's what she says—the stuff 'belongs' to her, 'in her energy', for 'the upliftment', she says, and because she's our minister, it's for our upliftment too. But $850.00, man. That's a lot of bread." Bread. Wayne tried to use Californiaisms in his speech.

Vince just squinted, lost in being bitter at Jade.

I broke in. "Wayne, what are you saying?" He must have thought I was really "in with Daisy," was a spy.

"Nothing. I wasn't saying nothing important, just bellyaching."

"Oh." It was hopeless. Now I was alienated not only from the hierarchy but even from the most humble cells in the body. Clearly Wayne and Vince weren't going to talk until I left. I stretched up high, wandering back by the tracks, found two women chatting who seemed alert to the children. *I can go home,* I thought; *get out of here.* Daisy emerged white in the low doorway, a momentary giant shepherdess above the flock. "Can I see you a minute, Page?" she asked.

I felt the threads, the delicate bondage; ensnare my beating heart. I smiled. She had full view of my green eyes with the dancing brown specks. (They seemed to me a mélange of dumb, down-to-earth colors when I was nervous—not like hers.) Glitter ice blue, her eyes broke through the crowd and located Sam who responded instantly to Daisy's telepathic tug. He turned all the way around on his toes, laughing up at her, proud that they could do this effortlessly and accept the telepathy without wonder. That was a step further through the mind: I knew that was his philosophy.

"Come." She took my hand. Oh boy. This was it.

She guided me toward her office past the anteroom where amber light filtered over her through the tall, rectangular window made up of small, perfect squares of opaque glass.

The warmth of her office wrapped itself around me. We talked. Serious and adult. I dropped the child mask. She waved her gold-encircled wrist slowly, carefully when she brought up the subject of Doug—and my guilt. It was as if she had thought better of dismissing before.

"The whole is always greater than the sum of its parts, Page, sweetheart. We see with limitations, an event, an action, but we do not really see. Like you and me," she said. "We are defined within the limits of this room, but we have our Being in the universe, and it is our sustenance." Did she know I knew about the merry-go-round? Could I be wrong about her? I wanted to be wrong about all the doubts I was having lately, wanted to bury my head in her lap—like her child, her sweetheart, her friend—like John the Beloved resting against the breast of Jesus. I wanted to come closer into the amber room, hear the heartbeat of the universe. But as usual I couldn't say anything.

I told Marshall about all this the next time we were together, about my visit with Daisy and of the guilt I felt in her presence, now that I was lying just to make love to him.

"Oh quit it, babe. That chick can take care of herself. She's aggressive and I heard that that little gal's got quite a sex drive."

"Who told you that?"

"Brother Bill. Oh, that was years ago, back when Jane would let him stay with us when he came down from Oroville. But what you've told me since reinforced it. Don't feel you're letting her down or something."

"Shouldn't I?"

"She's had two men after her. She's got you, and me too, if I listen to anymore of this shit."

"Marshall. Don't you see? She's the most courageous…She's got guts—and she's devoted to the truth."

"You have guts."

"Me?"

"You because you're finally doing what you should have done all along—finally becoming your own person."

I bit my nails.

That I could not handle her was becoming more apparent. She was both my nemesis and my goddess and I was chained to her with the bitterness of one oppressed. I would find a way.

One morning I awoke from a dream sure that I had found that way. I stumbled out of bed, anxious to go to her. I felt love, the love of the heart, but more. I dreamed that I—and it was like riding hiatus of that semi-sexual feeling—to go there after her, to ask her, as I had in the dream, to come out with me. I knew that's what she had done with some of the other women.

It was 10:30 when I got there. All the other women were hanging about outside in the front or in the foyer by the sink in the kitchen smoking. She was inside I thought, so I walked past the velvety pews, down the soft red throat of the center aisle, but still I could not see her. Then, austere sunlight through a window on my right beckoned—it felt good, when we touched in the dream. I was in love with her too, wasn't I? Like Amy had been, like they all had been. For a minute this eclipsed even Marshall. I had to find her— perhaps even now she would accept me now that I was fully a lesbian—that must be what the dream meant. Outside the open street side doorway she sat, blonde, attractive, legs showing; I saw the back of her rejecting, unforgiving head.

Daisy. Ummm. I could see there was somebody with her. Bending away I couldn't see who—oh—the pansy-planter, the gay apostle. Nuts. They talked awhile; he bent toward her—in love too, probably. Then I approached her. Is this what charisma is—that sense of a private unspoken love affair with each one? I thought of Rebecca. Once we talked about men, how frustrating they were. "Too bad you couldn't feel that way about a woman," I joked.

"I don't know," Rebecca had answered, with a clear, deep true look of pain—about Daisy I somehow knew—I just knew it was.

Then the man left, walking the length of hedged walkway and around the corner—to check on the flowers he'd planted that flourished at the feet of the statue of Jesus.

"Daisy, Hi there." She said nothing. I was quiet at first respecting her silence, her space. Ho hum. Nothing much to say here…except "Will you go to bed with me so I can pop my thought form bubble about women—do I really have one—and see what is me."

Instead of asking her…"Will you go out…to a bar or something," as I had done in the dream, I just did numb nothing and then finally after her friendly, flirty, "Yeees?" I said:

"I had this dream and it had this part in it…Well it was mostly symbolic about me and…various attraction 'thingies' (I used Amy's word—would that help?) And ummm well…I guess I thought it was telling me to ask you…out somewhere…but that was only one part of it…pretty weird anyway, huh?"

She looked away, cold and impervious…or—what? There was something else, but I couldn't make it out.

Now I couldn't feel the least attracted to her, not in the day anyway…ohmygod, no… All that I felt was supremely stupid.

After a long while she asked, "What do you think about the choir singing again for Pixy Talbott's 'Your Psychic Hour,' on Cable 2B?"

"Oh I don't know," I laughed, as jovial and efficacious as the grim reaper would be, dancing down the middle aisle of the church on Sunday singing "Aquarius." Daisy hated deadpan services. "Rejoice," she would often say with a droll, turned down mouth, imitating what happened so commonly in churches. "Rejoice, re joice," she would drone slowly, in a deeper bass than Wayne's, sounding like a fog horn on 33-1/3 rpm's. And now I was being the same kind of dismal bummer as those down-hearted asinine preachers who slammed out the deadening "re juices" at their sleeping congregations. I couldn't even be a lesbian right. I guessed propositioning your minister, was supposed to be fun, light-hearted—gay.

"Oh, ah sure. That would be fine for the choir to sing on Pixy Talbott's show. Just fine. I've got to go now Daisy," I said like a leaden jester after popping up with a joke so bad it would cost him his head. "I've got to go now."

"O.K.," she tossed off, quite absorbed, it seemed, in mentally scheduling Pixy Talbott's, and in gardening maybe too, because she had her fingers around a pansy, lovingly, but she pinched off the red, soft-lipped bud as though she would yank it up, squeeze it onto itself and dissolve it into a powder.

"Pixy Talbott's—oh we'll see," she was still murmuring when I left. "Well, I handled that," I grimaced. What's next? I thunked out through the church toward the car, feeling full of sexual daring indeed.

Later that day, Marshall and I let the door at the bottom of the stairs to his apartment shut itself. Marshall was attired in tennis whites. Was I dressed right? We stepped out into the sunlight.

He laughed at himself. "The winter whale floats up to the surface." He could be self-deprecating, too.

"You don't look like a whale, dummy. You look like a mustached walrus," I rushed to joke. (He was trying to grow one and the red stubble glinted in the late May sun.)

I didn't look too "tennis-y" in my church scrounged cut-offs, but no matter; Daisy had taught me iron resistance to the opinions of "the world." We found the path down to the courts behind the back cluster of quiet apartments. Where I lived, the Vietnamese family would be out, neatly dressed, playing ball behind the laundry room. And the cars of the teenaged boyfriends of my sometimes babysitters would be lined up with their radios left on, while their owners were fighting with the girls' mother about taking them out—noise everywhere.

We reached the top of the long narrow path down to the tennis courts. Only then could I hear the subdued rushing from the ribbon of freeway that spliced San Jose to Santa Cruz. Marshall looked well-heeled, trying out all the pleasures prescribed for him by his age and affluence. We wove down the path, tumbling, running too quickly, then trying to catch ourselves.

Marshall, I think now, wanted to "live," to get, to have what the cream of conservative young bucks could take in 1977—and what he felt he'd been too long denied. He'd married a girl from the wrong side of the tracks his mother said when he'd returned home to clean up the debts Jane had incurred in the last unhappy bit of their marriage. He been denied his due and he was determined to get it now. Get everything out of life he could get.

I never thought that my cut-off jeans didn't make it; that I should have worn white on white. I just breathed in the sunshine and the acacia and the fresh, freeway-windy air and vaulted over the net once to show off. Probably young women in white on white didn't vault nets either, just because it was spring. They waited until they won or something and then probably the man did. But to hell with it.

"Oh Marshall, there's a peach tree. Remember, I used to draw in the apricot orchard behind the apartment we lived in when we were all first married. Come back with paper later and I'll teach you to sketch."

"Oh." He was rubbing his hand on the grip of the racket, as though trying for some correct posture.

"Ready?" I ran back to my own side and served him one hard. It hit outside the lines squaring the court.

"I haven't played in a long time," I apologized.

"You don't have to worry about that, Page." His eyes under the heavy blond brows glinted admiration. Was I his ticket into an unlived hippie youth? Maybe he didn't want to be Brooks Brothers, or the Big and Tall Men's equivalent of that cliché.

"Serve another one." We were finding out about each other too. It mattered, I guess, to some faint remnant of normal upbringing, that a man could handle his body, was comfortable in it. Doug was completely uncoordinated—got angry if you tried to play an outdoor game with him. Marshall returned the ball—over the line but within reach.

"All right," I said. "Pretty good."

We rallied. He turned red. In our overkill fashion we pinged and swacked back and forth for an hour. He got better. The returns were angled in. One of mine was deadly. After he touched the ball it cleared the huge cyclone fence behind him.

"I'll go get it."

"Forget it. Let's rest. This boy needs a breather."

I lay down on the bare ground beneath the peach tree, over twigs and soft tendrils of stray grass. He hesitated, in white on white, but lowered himself to the ground. I lay on my back. Ruffly cream puff clouds departed for Santa Cruz one by one.

"This is fun, Page. We should do it again."

Encouraged, I countered, "Let's write a poem together. I'll say the first lines, you fill in when I tell you to.

> The day
> Is a blessing
> The peach tree
> presides…
> Over my feelings for you—
>
> (Your turn.)"

"And I…uh…
Feel free to kiss you."

He loomed over me and kissed me on the neck, under the chin. I felt like a fruit with a golden skin, all skin, and a molten middle.

From my scalp to my toes in green tennis shoes, I didn't care about anything but the feeling of molten gold forming itself into a freeform band struggling to cleave to his body. He lay across me to kiss me, raised my knees on one side of him, and my upper body like a cobra rose to meet his kisses. His white legs, reddening in the sun, pointed toward the peach tree. No one was around. He looked me over and over again through raw, reddened eyes.

"It's been a long time since I've felt like this. And you and I...you and I..."

I looked long into the lust-reddened blue eyes, drawing from them a glimmer of new self esteem. He patted my knee. "Let's go up."

"You'll not have me so easy, sir," I mimicked an Irish maiden, just because I felt like it, on this fine green spring afternoon.

"Not lay with me then, wench," he returned, "not lay with me will ya—then ya've got another thing comin' to ye."

I looked up at him. He stood, his head ending six feet five inches into the glimmering, magnificent sun.

"Please," he asked, in a tone as if he were asking his mother to pass the salt or the cream in the sterling service at home.

My eyes widened. I could feel them.

"If you're wanting me, sir, then I should feel gladdened for your attenshun."

We laughed at the mincemeat brogue, each secretly pleased. I knew that we had the makings of mental companionship. This kind of frivolity and parrying could weather.

In the apartment he seemed to contain himself, to keep the spirit of a date. He carefully made lemonade. We sat on the stylish, enclosed redwood flap that the Live Oak apartments called a balcony.

He pointed out the stained glass window hanging now in someone's upstairs window that faced the courtyard. He boasted, "Somebody's caught the spirit." He was proud of his new stained glass window that hung over his kitchen window, the red and green colored glass casting a rainbow shadow over his refinished rectangular oak table, darkening and cooling the dinette area.

These rituals almost made me forget Daisy and Doug; I would enter Marshall's conservative world. Marshall broke into my thoughts. He looked down his reddened ram's nose at me. "I don't think it's half bad that Doug's sending you here again to 'visit.' I wouldn't, but I'm grateful." He shifted in his deck chair. "No, I wouldn't if you were my wife, if you were my lady."

His wife? Sunny hope, excitement, welled up…If I were his lady, if…Remembering Doug, the thought was quelled as if by a Santa Cruz breeze tumbling down through the mountain pass and dumping rain on San Jose in May.

He drew closer. "Come here." Quickly he pushed me inside past the heavy drapes toward the couch as though angry. He tried to unbutton the green blouse, but it would not give. He stripped it off me. The swollen tongue of the young ram swept through my mouth again. The stereo left on low was playing Brother Love's Traveling Salvation Show: "Ho- o-o-ot August night…" rang through me.

Afterwards, Marshall picked me up and carried me to the opening between the drapes.

"See that," he asked, laughing at what we had done as if he were a free spirit; or a ram after thrusting through a buttress; or a bull lost in May flowers.

"How can they see us? They're too busy making love, Marshall. The whole world must be making love today, right?"

"Yes," he said, "behind his stained glass window that guy's looking out, lusting for my lady."

My lady. He must be impressed with what just happened. "You **are** a lover, lady." Now he sounded just like other white collar, sleek Lotharios must—now he was confident. The molten gold that ran through my weak-for-him peach skin body had transmuted him, as if through alchemy, from silver to gold. His hair in the amber May twilight didn't look as silvery or as much like his mother's as it usually did. Now it looked golden, like Daisy's bracelets. I was still silver. I looked at my blue lapis round stone set in the five-pointed silver star—the one Daisy coveted, and wondered if it had brought me this.

I felt as if there were miracles, that anything was possible. The wine nectar scent of acacias and the faint, faint taste of salt from the sea thirty miles away, came in with the breeze through the open doorway. Elizabeth had said that at moments we all stepped completely into the emotions of past lifetimes. Now I was a courtesan whose wine merchant master seaman had come home across the wine-streaked Aegean to her "house." I was his. I knew no other woman could please him.

The image flicked to that of the giant, late Atlantean, earliest Grecian god-man I'd seen that first night in bed with him. I told him the fantasies—why did I express it like this—didn't he believe in past lives? But he picked it right up—as though thirsty, I hoped, for that was my secret dream, that he was my spiritual mate, the one with whom I would storm the door to the amber room; I hoped he could be my white-robed co-minister.

He lapped up the "fantasies" like a great cat, particularly the first one. He loved ships; the hallway to the vanity and the walls of the vanity and the shower room were lined with the old expensive lithographs of sailing ships.

"And I came home to you...you little whore...after a good long sail, and then..."

Before the great mirror in the vanity he dressed for dinner. "Doug wants you to have dinner here? What's his problem?" Marshall muttered, seeming amused. Watching him I could see how quickly he picked up from my imaginative ramblings, from my touch, that he was really beautiful. His mother had helped this along, years ago, of course. I sensed she thought this last child she dreaded to have, this second, male child, the most beautiful from the cradle onward—where he would touch himself, fat and perfectly blond with the little broad shoulders and swaying plump behind. And he was a good boy too, neat and obedient—usually, though more daring than his brother, Frederick, more forceful, oddly enough, than her husband. This story I read from her looks at him, from the embarrassing, resentful stories Jane had told me about Marshall's and his mother's relationship, and from my own tongue which could ferret out the truth from people sometimes without their full awareness. His mother was so correct—perhaps my erotic cradle image was too extreme, but still he soaked it up, the renewed confidence in himself, as if he'd been born to it. He patted his white gold hair with the air of a sea-wandering merchant who was growing richer and richer—who could have **anything** he might desire—and then more!

Daisy at Asilomar

Chapter Twenty Four

"Come down," Daisy said, "come on down here." Gee, invited. I walked downstairs to the basement of the church. A great strip of rainbow ran down the stairway, and in the nursery, where the students of the new reassociation class—led by Sam and Jade and Amy—clustered, Pegeen had also painted a unicorn. In this magical realm I felt like shit. A student again. I cried inside.

We paired up to learn "channeling." I was coupled with that guy who looked (and sounded) like Professor Irwin Corey. Elizabeth said that one who was a psychic and persisted without the spiritual motive, for material or selfish gain, became a Frankenstein. I thought of this when it was my turn to "read" for the professor. When I began without censure to catch the thread and spill out my reading for him, I called him Frank by mistake, but he didn't get the joke.

When it was Frank's turn, he hap-haphazardly spewed verbiage projected from his unconscious for my "reading," persisting in this boring monologue by imitating Daisy's "in spirit" voice. I was the only one here who knew that Daisy had originally borrowed the voice from Elizabeth—the only true psychic around. Hadn't Daisy practiced as a psychic, though, for more than material gain—gosh, for the gain of all of us, for our lives, our souls? And didn't I love her—more than ever—love her so much my heart ached. I knew now it wasn't at all a physical thing with me as with some—but a love of spirit as she called it—now I knew what that word meant.

She stuck her head in after awhile into the basement alcove where Frank and I labored together after the others had taken a break. She liked to float about, overseeing Amy, Jade and Sam's new leadership, but in my case, no doubt, she came to shepherd me back to rejoin the flock of students—perennial student, Page. She looked at me, right at me.

"Are you still here?" she asked in her whisper voice, loud somehow, reaming me with her blue eyes. Attuned at that moment to the higher energies invoked by channeling, I cut immediately above the powder dust of her charm (she was looking at me) and I heard her, loud and clear, on another level. "Are you still here?" I felt guilt that I was still here, for I sensed somehow that it was time to go on. She didn't know it, not consciously, but **I** knew it, and the "I" that loved me, loved her too. It was as if her soul was trying to urge me to do what her personality could not.

Tears almost filled the back of my eyes, threatening to spill before Frank, but this was too serious, too important, even for my real love for her. For she had taught me to be myself. Especially lately: "Follow your spirit," she'd said. And I'd taught myself, after the long nights of terror, the singing fear that I'd go mad. In that time, under that time, I'd found the Christ within, neither male nor female, and not just as lived by the elder brother, by Jesus the son, but by myself. Then, as the months had progressed and that inner, quiet, still small voice had become stronger, as I learned it told me the Truth, I had to trust it because I couldn't hold onto anything else. I was drowning inside—albeit because of Veronica's misery, because of my retarded husband, because of the denials and suppressions of Daisy herself—still, I found It. The It I had been looking for all of my life, the It I'd had glimpses of and never really lost, the It I might lose sight of and fade from but that would live, because, as Daisy so often said, "Truth lives."

As the months had progressed and the seas of fears began to subside, I walked about with it, more peaceful on the inside. Daisy noticed this one day, and said—always the two-edged compliment— "This is the first time I've seen you get a grip on life." She was right. I'd call her sometimes, and she'd sense it again and say, "Now you must test it, try it out, share it with others—begin to deal from your center and not the outer ring, to express what you really feel." And I'd dared to do that, until it had become like the sensation of a cord pulling from my solar plexus, or like a river, a strong river. I fell on my face a few times, because like any other exercise for living, it was an exercise and artificial, but I acted as she had advised, pushing through the crust of reserve I'd built up, through the damages and the traumas, to feeling myself, feeling stronger for the first time in years.

I knew when she popped her head in the door she was begging me to graduate, to go on, to stop what she would do, must do, to keep me back. I must leave her. "You are my soul," she once told me, during a phase when she taught that each person close to you is in "relativity"—is relative to and representative of a certain aspect of yourself. "And Art," she had continued, "is the part of me that blames others for things. You know how he blames me for the divorce." How complicated and true her words had sounded at the time. Now I wondered if Art hadn't blamed her with "righteous anger," another of her expressions that meant she was right and divinely ordered to be pissed, or that (her) truth, too long pushed down, exploded forth—in righteous anger. So how could I make that out? How could I make out any of it? Now our exercise was nearly finished. I was coming down from the higher consciousness invoked in the effort to channel, sinking back down into the ordinary muddle.

I started up the stairs before the class was over, the class in which I shouldn't be, racked with uncertainty and turmoil, and made my way up the passageway, past a magic dragon and a wizard, past little pink toads and stars, through the kitchen where a bunch of strangers sat, down the back stairs to the gravel parking lot and away, headed somewhere, with a crawful of sadnesses and unnamed thoughts that seemed to peep in from the future. I had neither the framework nor the willingness to retain them, so they slogged around like sodden waves, waiting for a future that would spill them out free, white and lacey—frothy clean—upon the sands of my life in tomorrow.

Leaving my car somewhere on the street, I ran, face full and eyes bleary toward the ragged open spaces of an inner city park somewhere near the church. I fell among the litter strewn by the children I saw in the distance, whose faces bore the imprint of each of the five races of humankind described by Edgar Cayce. These were the reasons, I blubbered; these were the ones who would be freed by the truth. I let my soul cry, praying into the uneven, rooty ground, out into the old palm-lined streets of this new Egypt, at the sky, to the Creator, the Creatress, to the wind, to the May sun's eye obscured by a ribbon of smoggy cloud. Lord, Knowing One, Mother/Father of All, show me!

Some kid paused in her play and sidled over to me where I sat, wrecked, on the grass. I dragged myself up, a spectacle, and resolved to try to speak to Daisy one more time. How could I be a student with Mr. Frankenstein again, how could I listen to him again in the bowels of that basement, or face another business meeting like the last where I was chastised for letting Ambrose Wales go to San Francisco during his stay to take slides—when they wanted him in church because they were sure that was the day he would have broken his thought form bubble. "Everyone's promoted," Daisy had commended the members of the core group for their conduct during the seminar, "except Page— she's in limbo." How could I let Rebecca blame me because I hadn't received her telepathic message reminding me to serve the Overall Body and bring Ambrose back to their clutches. Even if I **had** missed a clue, where was compassion for the fact that I was tired, drained by the romantic merry-go-round prescribed for me by Daisy's insistence that I "take one step into my desires." I'd stepped—and created a landslide. Most importantly, how could I listen to Daisy whispering the promises she had held in trust for me, to Jade and others, and before the sacred altar?

Daisy was emerging from a meeting in Rebecca's office when I cornered her. "I want to talk to you again, do you mind?" I blurted to her back. She turned as if to leave the room and pass me. As an afterthought she added, "All right, not here." She glanced sideways at me, raising one eyebrow, a tinge of amusement in the glance, the voice. Before Rebecca, left they exchanged looks. I stared at Daisy, pleading. She ignored me for a while, turned back to Rebecca's desk and seemed to sort through a stack on the desk for a paper of some kind. Finally I clambered after her through the pews across the cool, soft, red carpet.

We sat outside on the brick buttress that formed the flowerbed facing the side street that ran by the church. It was almost rain, but Daisy absorbed the sun, reddish-orange legs freshly shaved, glistening. She pulled at her cigarette and looked vacant. "All right, tell me what it is you've been sitting on." She planted her hands out from her body on either side of the flowerbed, fingers curled under the little brick ledge. A flock of gulls cooed above us and fluttered from the church rooftop across the street to another rooftop, and then one of them, with a silvery gleam dancing on the sheen of its wings, floated up into the opaque sky. Daisy's eyes, following the gull's flight, were as impervious and cloudy as the sky she continued to gaze into, after the gull was gone. I thought she was mad, sensed it, but her voice was as delicate as whipped butter, frothy, filtered through with air: What was in the hidden spaces?

"I've been changing, Daisy."

"You have."

She stared out at the overcast sky, crossed and uncrossed her bronze legs, slippery from baby oil. It looked as if she had a lot of stuff, much more important than me, on her mind. She looked vaguely disgusted. I felt disgusted. I choked over the ugly words I had to say.

"It's just that I talked to Elizabeth at Asilomar and she... she...said you feel like a jealous sibling towards me, and that it might be these feelings of rivalry that—you remember I dreamed once that we had been sisters in Egypt. You were adopted by Elizabeth first, and then she had a natural child—me. She favored me. She shouldn't have, but that's how...it might have happened. And remember the lifetime I discovered in the last century—we both loved the same man and he went with me—?"

"I don't remember anything like that," Daisy interrupted me, looking at me deeply once, yawning, then peering back into the sky and drumming her pearl and bronze fingers against the brick, impatiently. Unfortunately I felt as if I were falling into her eyes, dropping like a stone into her irrepressible beauty.

Sam stepped through the open doorway, saw us and retreated. He wouldn't appreciate this at all, would he? He hung about Daisy lately as if she were the sacrificial lamb she often talked about in services, as if she were being offered for us, for the people, for a higher purpose. He always screened her phone calls now and protected her.

But I had to press on. Daisy had taught me to speak something out as if it were true and then listen to its ring, its energy. I pressed on because in a confused way I wanted to test out Elizabeth's words. I blurted out everything Elizabeth had told me. There. Silence. I watched Daisy's eyes. She seemed to concede. My wonderful Daisy. The truth would be out—we would be right again.

"I've always felt like more of a sibling toward you."

She knows it? Amazed, I said, "You agree then with what she said?"

"No I don't agree at all; I didn't mean to say that. I meant I felt like a mother toward you, sweetheart."

I stared at her, that was all.

"Let's go in. Shall we?" She patted my hand. Her warm dry palm graced mine. I stumbled getting off the brick ledge, and dug each foot hard into the white concrete like a horse stamping to get out of a corral that is too small for it. I dug my hands deep into the pockets of the green sweater in shame. During the rest of the afternoon and throughout the evening she treated me warmly. I was under her wing, could feel the warm nimbus reach out three feet or more and keep me close wherever I followed her. What I'd thought could not be true. It was over anyway.

"Page, would you get me another cup of coffee?" she asked after awhile.

"Sure." Honored, I fluttered away from her into the kitchen and back out again. "Here it is," I cooed.

"Never mind. I've already gotten her one," laughed Jade.

"Well then, she'll have two," I said, buoyed by a new confidence and the echo of my old role. Her poolside promise, 'One day all this will be yours,' didn't seem impossible in the way she was treating me now, didn't seem as far removed this night.

"Page has a wonderful vocabulary, doesn't she, Jade? I said 'sibling' when Page and I were talking earlier this afternoon, but I meant 'mother.' Sometimes I lose the word in the energy. You know that, Jade." Jade smiled at me then touched Daisy's right hand possessively. I knit my brows for a moment and then looked into Jade's eyes across Daisy's shoulders, and laughed. I made Jade laugh too.

"Children, children," Daisy murmured. "I feel like I've got two kids behind my back, pulling on my skirts."

"Then you're twice blessed," I joked.

We all laughed. An amber river ran over us. I could forget Jade tonight, even love her.

When it was time to leave, I ran out to the car over the gravel parking lot Sam had laid. I wanted to get away from myself, from the self that I was around them, and breathe.

The next night I lay in Marshall's arms, cradled by the strong Germanic limbs entwined about me like an oak's, thinking about Daisy and me. "I'll never be your beast of burden," sang Mick Jagger from the left-on-all-night-radio. The white light of morning reached into my puffy eyes. Staying up all night through the dark had washed some of the fear out of me. Marshall got up after awhile, looked so strange. The faces I'd seen again during the night, the faces I knew to be past lives—the fat, lumpy-trunked Grecian I'd accepted, the red Atlantean giant—all swirled around like funhouse mirror images, and then sprang back into the man before me.

"I'll never be your beast of burden.

Never
Never
Never
Never
Never
Be…"

The touch of a man, the salt, the sweet look, the white-yellow hair, the faraway, yet close touch of the new blue eyes, the foreignness and the warm touch, like forgiveness; these awakened me as if from a sleep.

He looked down at me, standing beside the bed when he returned with coffee. I drank some tentatively, afraid to be too much stimulated. He laughed, delighted and amused. The clock chimed. He looked into my eyes that he had often described as green moss woodsy, and at my light brown hair he'd said radiated like reddish Madrone bark. His eyes that usually looked shallow blue and milky, seemed alight with the possibility that real love would flush them clear and clean like a deep well. Our interludes had stamped approval on each other's budding, held-back adult self-esteem.

He reached out one long arm to me, as sturdy as the oak's core white artery. He touched my shoulder, brushed my Daisy-tanned Madrone skin with a fleshy fingertip. I looked back, a woman, my breasts free above the sheet, at this freshly minted man. It was quiet in the bedroom. Pearly and clean like white wine in a crystal glass. Looking away from him I heard what the stereo sang:
"Time washes clean
Love's wounds unseen."

"I'm gonna fly like an eagle," a new song began.

"She hasn't hurt me purposely, Marshall." I tried to pick up the threads of last night's conversation about Daisy.

"If you say so." He looked at my breasts, a rapturous look, then away, pulling at his cigarette, then stubbing it in the ashtray.

"I think things will straighten out at the church—I will be a minister one day."

He smiled and looked at the clock, stood, and opened the king sized closet. Pale, extra long shirts, white with blue shirts, striped yellow on white shirts, powder blue and cream shirts, smelling of starch, blossomed out, unfurled like flags from the copper hangers. He selected a shirt to cover his huge back. He laid a tie over the knotted brown bedspread and pulled navy socks, a pair of rose, folded shorts, a white tee shirt and a pressed handkerchief out of the oak highboy.

In a few moments he stood with his back to me, stuffing tails of a canary and powder, pinstriped shirt into hard-pressed slacks. Suddenly I felt a pang, a longing for him so profound as to bring tears to my eyes, tears which I slowly rubbed out as he turned to face me. He lifted me from the corner of the bed where I sat naked and said, "Baby. It's time to get up now. We have to go." I wrapped my arms around his big body—he seemed to stand more than six feet five inches tall—and kissed his throat. "You know," was all I could say. Now he seemed to have beautiful eyes that looked into mine with the patience of a wizard who knows how slowly magic sometimes burns.

I got up, back into old underwear—no choice—into my crumpled pants, green shirt and fuzz-balled, sea foam sweater and looked up at him. "I love you, baby," he said. "Someday there will be a time for us. You know it too…don't you?"

I do and I don't, I said to nobody but myself. "I wish I could go with you, Marshall." My apartment, steamy and dark, cold and hard; Daisy's church to clean today, didn't appeal.

"Be real, baby, I've got to work."

It didn't matter. I knew what I had to do.

I drove to the church to clean the bathrooms for Daisy's latest Magic Meditation Seminar. Slavery…of one kind or another seems to be our lot, *shouldn't it be the slavery of love,* I thought. *Shouldn't it after all?*

Tears rolled down my face; I tried to hold back my feet but they walked to her office. I didn't care what Marshall would say, this was between her and me. I've thought about what you said, my crowned queen, I didn't say, thought about you all night, thought about what things would be like if I left you. Your eyes are the sky for me, your slender fingers ringed with lapis, touch my heart and open the world, Daisy, but I have to leave. I choked with the thought. I have to breathe this sweet spring air that's lent to me this new confidence. "When joy and beauty/Once have lived/In the human heart then /How/Can that one/Accept any less/When he has known the sun—" was a poem I'd given to Marshall recently—was it really…to you?

In the human heart I squared myself, shuffled the clutter of thoughts away like untidy papers in my desk drawer. I shuffled like a dog, I thought, like a little Pekingese, like a nothing toilet-bowl-sweeper-outer. Was I that, just the toilet bowl cleaner, a solvent to break up the shit of her dream and absorb it into the waters of my emotions, into the spiritual river of my soul? I didn't stop the tears. They ran like foolish water, like an ages old solvent across my cheeks like a fool's. I washer fool, her prime fool and I was going to leave her. They were the tears of love.

Inside the office she sat alone and looked up, bored.

"Daisy I've thought, sure I've thought of what you've been telling me…of how I have to be a student a little while longer, of how it's only my ego that's holding me back…but something's wrong, very wrong, Daisy—I don't feel right about it." I leaned forward in the chair, strong, all sinewy muscles about to strike because of the terrible pressure of the truth welling up inside of me, impelling me like a blind unforgiving force. The tears coursed, ran, streamed, coursed in sheets down the angular planes of my cheeks. Still I could not stop.

"You…have a thing about me, Daisy," I exclaimed, reaching for Elizabeth's words. "You're jealous, you're bad jealous of your throne, of your lair." I was nailing her, just the way Daisy had taught us to do. "I don't want to enter it, climb onto it—I just want—I want—Daisy, I just want myself—what is mine. What I worked to earn these seven years and over all of these ages. All I want is to teach, to comfort and to teach, to give hope. Daisy, can you hear that? Can you hear me?" I looked full square into her eyes like a blaring radio, like a trumpet, like—

I glinted green across the room into her face. I heard Daisy say a word I could not understand. Amy entered the room dressed in phony little white ruffles. "Listen to this, Amy," Daisy grabbed her arm, pulling Amy in her white confetti dress in between us like a shield.

I said it again, quiet, hard, hot…like meat burning in a brazier—human meat—or my soul—I said it again, double fool before Amy, the tears lugubrious and shameless but quiet.

"You have a thing about me Daisy. I know you do. I feel it, right now in this room. A thing that has stopped me, will always stop me; it is a poison chemical between us. It's…I don't know… jealousy …or a thing on me, Daisy, just as Elizabeth said, as I said, and I know—you know it too." Her eyes hiding over Amy's shoulder gave themselves up to me, two traitors, two little crystal balls that gave the medium's fortune to me instead of mine to the gazer.

"Tell me the TRUTH! If you don't, if you deny it, you murder all that's truth—all I've bared to you all these years." (Not to mention all Elizabeth ever taught us of Cayce—have you forgotten, Daisy?) My eyes ran like the blood from red meat—but I could meet her eyes. She looked down.

Amy stared for a minute, then said as though on cue, "It must be an awful big piece for you, Page, to have so much energy."

For me? For a minute I thought they had weighed it, heard it, turned it over in their minds as we had been taught to do over the years.

For me—for me! Daisy had dragged Amy's ruffly hated clone body in here so she could tell me that I had yet again something to learn—that I had made another mistake.

Amy retreated, a blur to my eyes. Prisms of water colored the space between Daisy and me like cathedral stained glass. Who was the confessor? I stood ready should she try to confess her soul. My love would take it, bury the mistake—however great—in my aching heart.

She stared away, said nothing. The door closed by Amy made the room a little box. I hung over Daisy like a lance, looking deep, deep into her eyes, unafraid, and waited, spent and poised, heart roaring, face feeling like a stone with a great pent waterfall seven years, seven hundred years, seven hundred thousand years old streaming, spinning by me like rain. I fixed on Daisy like ice on glass.

She returned from her distance and brushed my face with her dry, air sign, papery-touch eyes, hard and shallow and set in a squint; yet just for an instant, molten with liquid at the very, soft, center. Water to water we looked.

Then she turned, as so many times before, to leave, turned towards the window in her Saint Catrina—or Catherine—or whoever she really was stance, looked up like a martyr in pain, as if thinking.

But she turned on me and stared at me with hard eyes now only barely crying and said, "And if I did, I'd only have to admit it to God."

The next day on the phone I told her I wouldn't be there for her seminar. "Have a nice little vacation, sweetheart," she said, her voice trying to warm.

But then I left, and never came back.

Jessica Madigan as a young woman in Jackson, Mississippi.
Put in an orphanage, she was adopted by the intuitive James Moore
who owned a mattress factory; he named her Jesse Lorene Moore.
Growing up in the south, she had much sympathy for "colored"
friends which led to a lifelong dedication to those society cast out.

Afterward

In memory of Jessica Madigan (1911-1986)
(the inspiration for Elizabeth C. Barnett);
all photographs courtesy Jery Vincent Stier.

Once upon a time in the latter part of the last century there lived a great lady who loved the Edgar Cayce philosophy with all her heart. She understood the mystical essence of that great work—that human beings live more than one life in the journey toward Heaven. That life is purposeful, continuous, that you "meet yourself" in karma until learning that the Christ attitude of love and compassion turns karmic stumbling blocks into stepping stones.

Jessica Madigan set the stage for a group of young seekers (upon which the preceding fiction was based) to play out their past life parts and bring eternal principles to life. Introduced to Jessica by their charismatic leader, Marsha Hunter Mossman, they awakened to the truth. When Jessica and her "golden girl", Marsha, presented past life plays at lovely Asilomar above the western sea, it became a shining spot—a timeless Camelot.

The following images courtesy of Jessica's
faithful friend, Jery Vincent Stier
(the inspiration for Ambrose B. Wales).

Edgar Cayce's eldest son Hugh Lynn; Jessica sensed he was her twin soul based on researching many lifetimes together including that of the English poets, Elizabeth and Robert Browning.

View of the main lodge at Asilomar in Pacific Grove, California. Jessica helped Hugh Lynn Cayce develop the early mailing lists for the first Association For Research And Enlightenment conferences there. She and Hugh Lynn once enjoyed a close spiritual friendship.

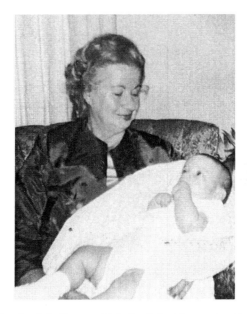

Jessica Madigan with baby John Cayce Austin.

Jery V. Stier, Elizabeth Crisman, Jessica Madigan and Larry George. He was the young man she rescued from an institution. He bore a past life resemblance to Lord Byron who kept his daughter Allegra from her mother and let her die in a convent at age five. Jessica encouraged him and he became a chemist for the F.D.A.—writing poetry in his spare time. Though she never had children, many came back to her from past lifetimes and were closer to her than many natural children.

Upper left: Jessica's pink little home on Camino Real in the Mt. Washington district of Los Angeles. Upper middle: she walks down the hill by Yogananda's place. Upper right: her beloved dogs Richard, Taffy and Danny, among many pets she saved from laboratory experimentation or found wandering along the freeways. Her pets sometimes stained her house and chewed up her manuscripts. But she was all heart and dedicated her life to the Christ message contained in the Edgar Cayce readings. Lower picture: Jessica at her Santa Maria conference of The Philosophical Roundtable. Behind her are posters Jery Vincent Stier would hang with images of the twelve signs of the Zodiac.

Jessica's past life parties at her conferences were magical. To be in a room full of intricately garbed personalities from far off times including Palestine, Greece, Egypt, King Arthur's Court and beyond was an unforgettable experience for participants. The woman on the right is Kricket Clark, (the inspiration for Vicky).

Bottom left: Jessica said she became a different person when she lectured, as if a past life self took over. Right: Jessica's past life as Nell Gwyn, mistress of Charles the Second. Nell was a charismatic actress who was careless about her clothing that sometimes bore slight stains. Our strengths and our weaknesses carry over from life to life.

Jessica Madigan lecturing to the young seekers of the Family of Man Inc. at their Aquarian Hall on Hamilton Avenue in San Jose, the inspiration for Sunshine Hall. She talked of dreams and twin souls and past lives and karma. Marsha Hunter Mossman brought her to young people torn by the turmoil of the sixties. The knowledge and wisdom they received was living water healing their hearts and helping them setting lifetime ideals. Jessica Madigan brought the best of the Edgar Cayce philosophy to them—even though her close relationship with Cayce's son had been put asunder by those jealous of her natural gifts. She never sought an affair with him (both she and Hugh Lynn were married to others), but she basked in his tutelage. He told Gladys Davis Turner, Edgar Cayce's secretary and twin soul that "Outside of my father, Jessica Madigan was the most psychic individual I have ever met."

Left of Aquarian Hall a life size statue of Jesus stands beneath a tree. Made of concrete it was given to Marsha Hunter in Billings, Montana and carried by Ron Hunter to the sites where the Family of Man held services. A voice had predicted the gift of the statue moulded from a French cathedral statue design.

The lovely Marsha Hunter Mossman, lecturing at Jessica Madigan's conference at Asilomar, California. She made universal laws and arcane principles, accessible to many, including the Egyptian concept of Eternal Life represented by the ankh below.

A few of the many of young seekers in the Family of Man who were
led by Marsha Hunter Mossman to meet Jessica Madigan.

Corry Farrel

David Farrel

John Mossman

Lynn Rogers

Gloria Sherry

Donna Araman

Jessica Madigan at Asilomar recalling her past life as Hatshepsut.

September, 1973 at The Philosophical Roundtable conference at Asilomar. Jessica's play, the Shadow of the Sun Disc, is enacted with Marsha Hunter as Nefertiti, Donna Araman as Nezmut, with Corry Farrel as their attending maid.

Front, left to right: Lynn Rogers (Flautt), Ronald Arthur Hunter 11, Mike Flautt; Back, left to right: Ron Hunter, Jessica Madigan, Donna Shadowsky, Virginia Diamond.

Back row, left to right: Donna Shadowsky, Jessica Madigan, Ron Hunter, Sandy Sullivan, Wally Thompson, Marsha Hunter Mossman John Mossman, Corry Farrel (with black wig), unknown, unknown; Front row left to right: Mike Flautt, Ronni Hunter, Lynn Rogers (Flautt), George Fairchild, Tim O'Neil, Loren Green, Jo O'Neil, Jim Shadowsky.

Left: Corry Farrel, Marsha Hunter and Ronni Hunter; Right: Ronni
Hunter, Jim Shadowsky, Terry Araman, Mike Flautt

Left: Marsha Hunter, George Fairchild; Right: Marsha Hunter, Corry
Farrel and Donna Shadowsky.

Marsha Hunter Mossman and John Mossman (extending his belly to portray Akhnahton) in Jessica's play, The Shadow of the Sun Disc.

Donna Shadowsky (Araman)

Marsha Hunter Mossman speaking about universal laws at Asilomar.

Marsha Hunter began her group as The Temple of Living Water; it became the Family of Man Inc.

Jessica Madigan shared Edgar Cayce's birthday (March 18th): his in 1877, hers in 1911. Many believe she was his intuitive interpreter and that her plays and gatherings brought the philosophy expressed in the readings, to life. He was a feeling mystic, so was she; no scientific analyses have ever captured the essence of his Work so well. When Jessica wrote to Edgar Cayce in Virginia Beach for a reading at Christmas of 1944, she "saw" a shadow fall over her letter and knew, somehow, he wouldn't be able to fulfill her request. He died in January of 1945, after giving more readings for service people overseas than his health could sustain. She came to Virginia Beach in 1949 and met his son Hugh Lynn Cayce who recognized her abilities and made her an early A.R.E. lecturer. She wrote articles like "Karma is Your Opportunity" for their Los Angeles Lecture Series in 1952. She wrote: "We are like actors upon a stage. We play many parts. We have many roles to perform. But the ultimate is simply that we become humble in self, that we forget self, in order to become one with God."

Memorial display for Jessica Madigan at Palos Verde, California. Reel-to-reel tapes of her Akashic readings, along with booklets she wrote and circulated around the world through Fate Magazine, surround her portrait. The dove of peace lights on her image; symbolic of grace balancing karma through compassion and forgiveness.

In this afterlife montage by Jery V. Stier, Nefertiti and her father Aye meet again. Jessica identified herself and Edgar Cayce with the patterns of Nefertiti and Aye. Perhaps, out of the body now in the realm beyond time and space, Jessica unites with Cayce in spirit form, guiding souls on earth to express the love of the Father/Mother Creator.

THE JESSICA MADIGAN LEGACY

Jessica Madigan's works (including her dream interpretation series) can be ordered very affordably through Mei Ling's Bookshelf Classics, by contacting (408) 559-5995 or emailing lynnrogersma@yahoo.com.

Sonshine Freedom's book, *The Mystical Life*, traces her awakening to life as an esoteric leader and describes Jessica's inspiring influence. Her book and art can be obtained at sunshinefreedom@aol.com.

At Jessica Madigan's encouragement, Lynn Rogers wrote articles, short stories and books. The Caroline Ryder's series traces the awakening to Spirit and the secrets of soul mates; it spans the 60's to the millennium.

The first volume, "*Born In Berkeley*—part memoir, part fiction—is set mainly in that small cavity of time between the Beat era and the emergence of the hippies, roughly 1965–1968." Los Gatos Weekly. "Lynn Rogers was 16 when she met Cassady and Kesey in Manzanillo, Mexico." San Jose Mercury News, "A Beat Generation Scrapbook."

(The second volume in the Ryder series is The Rainbow's Daughter.)

The third volume, "*Where The Flowers Have Gone* is a romance told from two different viewpoints, set in two different time periods—the '60s and its cultural opposite, the '80s. It's a steamy look back, says the author." Los Gatos Weekly.

Additional books in the Caroline Ryder series and the new fiction title, *A Valley of Ashes*—a mystery set after 9–11 on the underside of Silicon Valley—can be obtained through the author or from inklingpress.com where web pages "about the author" can also be viewed.

Collector's copies of her nonfiction work: *Edgar Cayce and the Eternal Feminine*; the Past Life Scrapbook; and the new Arcadia's *Images of America: Alviso, San Jose* (with Robert Burrill) are now available:

"Alviso provides a whirlwind photo history of the port community—a romantic haunt for the free spirit in all of us." Metro/Arts.
"*Edgar Cayce and the Eternal Feminine* explores the links between the Eternal Feminine and the Work and thought of Edgar Cayce…In a world that desperately needs women's gifts and the Eternal Feminine, this book is a shining star." Dr. Pamela Bro, Yale.

Since Jessica Madigan's passing, Lynn Rogers took her masters at Cayce's Atlantic University in Virginia and published the books shown here (with work by Jessica Madigan/Jery Stier and Sonshine Freedom):

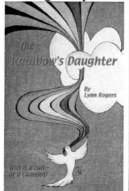

Books by Lynn Rogers include: *Born In Berkeley* (2002); *The Rainbow's Daughter* (2007); *Where The Flowers Have Gone* (2006);

Edgar Cayce and the Eternal Feminine (2004); *Alviso, San Jose* (2006; and *A Valley of Ashes* (scheduled for 2007) and a *Past Life Scrapbook*.

For further information on how to obtain books, attend Creative Writing and Wise Women's Circle classes, schedule lectures or private intuitive counsel with Lynn Rogers, contact the author at: lynnrogersma@yahoo.com or call (408) 559-5995.

Until they meet Jessica again in eternity, many of her "children" remember their time with her as a glimpse of peace at The Rainbow's End.